No Quarter!

by

Captain Mayne Reid

No Quarter!

by Captain Mayne Reid

ISBN: 978-93-67140-60-4

Published by

DOUBLE 9 BOOKS

2/13-B, Ansari Road
Daryaganj, New Delhi – 110002
info@double9books.com
www.double9books.com
Tel. 011-40042856

ABOUT THE AUTHOR

Captain Mayne Reid was a celebrated 19th-century author known for his adventurous tales, particularly in the genre of boys' literature. He developed a passion for outdoor exploration and adventure. Reid's writing often drew from his experiences as a soldier, explorer, and naturalist, capturing the excitement of wilderness and frontier life. His most notable works include "The Rifle Rangers," "The Scalp Hunters," and "No Quarter," which combine vivid storytelling with themes of bravery, survival, and camaraderie. His engaging narratives and rich descriptions made his books immensely popular in their time, influencing generations of adventure writers.

Reid's engaging style and vivid descriptions made him a pioneer in adventure fiction, earning him a dedicated following during the Victorian era. Reid's legacy endures as a pioneer of adventure fiction, particularly in the portrayal of the American West and the rugged individualism of its characters. He passed away in 1883, but his stories continue to inspire readers seeking thrilling escapades.

CONTENTS

Prologue

There is no page in England's history so bright, nor of which Englishmen have such reason to be proud, as that covering the period between 1640 and 1650. This glorious decade was ushered in by the election of the "Long Parliament," and I challenge the annals of all nations, ancient or modern, to show an assembly in which sat a greater number of statesmen and patriots. Brave as pure, fearless in the discharge of their difficult and dangerous duties, they faltered not in the performance of them—shrank not from impeaching a traitor to his country, and bringing his head to the block, even when it carried a crown. True to their consciences, as to their constituencies, they left England a heritage of honour that for long haloed her escutcheon, and even to this hour throws its covering screen over many a deed of shame.

"Be a King?"

"Am I not one?"

"In name—nothing more. Ah! were I a man and in your place?"

"What would you do?"

"Give your island churls a taste of kingship, as we know it in France. My brother wouldn't let his subjects so beard him. Oh, it's abominable!"

"Ah, *chère*; for subjects your brother has a very different sort of people to deal with. In France they're not yet come to clamouring for what they call their rights and liberties. Here in England they've got Magna Charta into their heads—to a craze."

"I'd have it out of their heads, or have their heads off. *Ciel!* I'd reign King as King should, or resign. No! not resign. Sooner than that I'd waste the country with fire and sword—make it a wilderness."

It was Henrietta, wife of Charles the First, who thus expressed herself to her husband. They were alone in the gardens of Whitehall Palace, sauntering side by side on a terrace overlooking the Thames, the afternoon being an unusually fine one. As they made a turn which brought Westminster Hall before their eyes, the angry fire in those of the Queen flashed up again, and she added—

"Anything but be dictated to by that *canaille* of a Parliament! Anything but let them go on as now?"

"How am I to hinder it, Henriette?" the King timidly interrogated.

"Dismiss—send them packing back to their constituencies, and let them prate away there as much as they please. Dissolve and do without them, as you've done before."

"That would be to do without the money we so much need. My subjects are determined to resist every tax levied under Privy Seal or otherwise. I can no longer raise loan or sell monopoly. Your own secretary, Sir John Wintour, has just been telling me how the people of Dean Forest have been harassing him about the grant we gave him of its timber and mines. Impossible now to obtain the most insignificant supplies without their being sanctioned by this *cabal* called Parliament."

"Then make the *cabal* sanction them."

"But how, *chère*?"

"Have a score or two of them arrested—lodged in the Tower; and let Monsieur Tom Lunsford take care of them. He'll soon cure them of their seditious inclinings."

"To do that were as much as my crown's worth."

"If't be worth no more, you may as well cease wearing it. Fling it into the Thames, or melt it down and sell it to the Ludgate Street goldsmiths for old metal. Shame of you, Charles! You talk of kingly rights, yet fail to exercise them—fear it?"

"My subjects talk of rights, too."

"Yes, and you encourage them—by your timidity. Ever on your knees begging this and begging that, when a true king would command. Subjects, indeed! more like our masters. But I'd teach them obedience. What would they be without a king? What were they born for but to administer to our wants and our pleasures?"

Words worthy of a Medici; the sentiments of a queen two centuries and a half ago. Yet not so very different from those entertained by most Royal personages at the present day and hour. But few of them who would not sit placidly upon their thrones, see subjects slain, and realms reduced to desolation, rather than resign crown or yield up one iota of what they are pleased to call their prerogative. How could it be otherwise? Environed by sycophantic flatterers, heads bowing, knees bending, tongues eternally bepraising; things in human shape giving them adoration as to God Himself—ay, greater than to God—how could it be otherwise? Not so strange that this proud, pampered woman, from her cradle accustomed to such slavish obedience, should verily believe it but her due.

"*Their* rights?" she continued, with a satirical laugh. "An absurd notion they've got into their Saxon skulls. Ah! *mon mari*, were I you for a month—for a week—I'd have it out—stamp it out—I would."

And to give emphasis to her speech, she stamped her foot upon the ground.

A pretty foot it was, and still a handsome woman she, this daughter of the Medicis, notwithstanding her being now somewhat *passé*. Ambitious as Catherine herself—"that mother of a race of kings"—intriguing, notoriously dissolute, not the less did Charles love her. Perhaps the more, for the cuckoo's cry is a wonderful incentive to passion, as to jealousy. He doted upon her with foolish fondness—would have done anything she commanded, even murder. And to more than this was she now instigating him; for it was to stifle, trample out the liberties of a nation, no matter at what cost in life or blood.

Wicked as were her counsels, he would have followed them and willingly, could he have seen his way clear to success. Men still talk of his kindly nature—in face of the fact, proved by irresistible evidence, that he rejoiced at the massacre of the Protestants in Ireland, to say naught of many other instances of inhumanity brought home to this so-called "Martyr King." He may not have been—was not—either a Nero or a Theebaw; and with his favourites and familiars no doubt behaved amicably enough; at the same time readily sacrificing them when danger threatened himself. To his wife his fidelity and devotion were such as to have earned for him the epithet "uxorious," a title which can be more readily conceded. But in his affection for her—whether upheld by respect or not—there was a spice of fear. He knew all about the scandals relating to her mother, Marie of France, with Richelieu, and his own and father's favourite, the assassinated Buckingham, now sleeping in his grave. Charles more than suspected, as did all the world besides, that this same Queen-mother had sent her husband—king as himself—to an untimely tomb by a "cup of cold poison." And oft as the dark Italian eyes of her daughter flashed upon him in anger, he felt secret fear she might some day serve him as had her mother the ill-fated monarch of France. She was of a race and a land whence such danger might be reasonably expected and dreaded. Lucrezia Borgia and Tophana were not the only great female poisoners Italy has produced.

"If you've no care for yourself, then," she went on with untiring persistence, "think of our children. Think of him," and she nodded towards a gaudily-dressed stripling of some ten or twelve, seen coming towards them. It was he who, twenty years after, under the seemingly innocent soubriquet of "Merry Monarch," made sadness in many a family circle, smouching England's escutcheon all over with shame, scarce equalled in the annals of France.

"*Pauvre enfant!*" she exclaimed, as he came up, passing her jewelled fingers through the curls of his hair; "your father would leave you bereft of your birthright; some day to be a king with a worthless crown."

The "pauvre enfant," a sly young wretch, smiled in return for her caresses, looking dark at his father. Young as he was, he knew what was meant, and took sides with his mother. She had already well indoctrinated him with the ideas of Divine Right, as understood by a Medici.

"*Peste!*" exclaimed the King, looking vexed, possibly at the allusion to a successor; "were I to follow your counsels, Madam, it might result in my leaving him no crown at all."

"Then leave him none!" she said in quick return, and with an air of jaunty indifference. "Perhaps better so. I, his mother, would rather see him a peasant than prince, with such a future as you are laying out for him."

"Sire, the Earl of Strafford craves audience of your Majesty."

This was said by a youth in the official costume of the Court, who had approached from the Palace, and stood with head bent before the King.

A remarkably handsome young fellow he was, and the Queen, as she turned her eyes on him, seemed to recover sweetness of temper.

"I suppose my company will be *de trop* now," she said. Then facing towards the youth, and bestowing upon him one of her syren smiles—slyly though—she added, "Here, Eustace; bring this to my boudoir," and she handed him a large book, a *portfeuille* of pictures, she had been all the while carrying.

Whether the King caught sight of that smile, and read something wrong in it, or not, he certainly seemed irritated, hastily interposing—

"No, Henriette, I'd rather have you stay."

"*Con tout plaisir.*" A slight cloud upon her brow told the contrary. "Charles, too?"

"No; he can go. Yes, Trevor. Conduct the Lord Strafford hither."

Eustace Trevor, as the handsome youth was called, bowing, turned and went off, the Prince with him. Then said the King—

"I wish you to hear what Strafford has to say on the subject we've been talking of."

"Just what I wish myself," she rejoined, resuming her air of *braverie.* "If you won't listen to me, a weak woman, perhaps you will to him, a man—*one of courage.*"

Charles writhed under her speech, the last words of it. Even without the emphasis on them, they were more than an insinuation that he himself lacked that quality men are so proud of, and women so much admire. Almost a direct imputation, as if she had called him "coward!" But there was no time for him to make retort, angry or otherwise, even had he dared. The man seeking audience was already in the garden, and within earshot. So, swallowing his chagrin as he best could, and putting on the semblance of placidity, the King in silence awaited his coming up.

With an air of confident familiarity, and as much nonchalance as though they had been but ordinary people, Strafford approached the royal pair. The Queen had bestowed smiles on him too; he knew he had her friendship—moreover that she was the King's master. He had poured flattery into her ears, as another Minister courtier of later time into those of another queen—perhaps the only point of resemblance between the two men, otherwise unlike as Hyperion to the Satyr. With all his sins, Wentworth had redeeming qualities; he was at least a brave man and somewhat of a gentleman.

"What do you say to this, my lord?" asked the Queen, as he came up. "I've been giving the King some counsel; advising him to dissolve the Parliament, or at least do something to stop them in their wicked courses. Favour us with your opinion, my lord."

"My opinion," answered the Minister, making his bow, "corresponds with that of your Majesty. *Certes*, half-hand measures will no longer avail in dealing with these seditious gabblers. There's a dozen of them deserve having their heads chopped off."

"Just what I've been saying!" triumphantly exclaimed the Queen. "You hear that, *mon mari?*"

Charles but nodded assent, waiting for his Minister to speak further.

"At the pace they're going now, Sire," the latter continued, "they'll soon strip you of all prerogative—leave you of Royalty but the rags."

"*Ciel,* yes!" interposed the Queen. "And our poor children! What's to become of them?"

"I've just been over to the House," proceeded Strafford; "and to hear them is enough to make one tear his hair. There's that Hampden, with Heselrig, Vane, and Harry Martin—Sir Robert Harley too—talking as if England had no longer a king, and they themselves were its rulers."

"Do you tell me that, Strafford?"

It was Charles himself who interrogated, now showing great excitement, which the Queen's "I told you so" strengthened, as she intended it.

"With your Majesty's permission, I do," responded the Minister.

"By God's splendour!" exclaimed the indignant monarch, "I'll read them a different lesson—show them that England *has* a king—one who will hereafter reign as king should—absolute—absolute!"

"Thank you, *mon ami*," said the Queen, in a side whisper to Strafford, as she favoured him with one of her most witching smiles, "He'll surely do something now."

The little bit of by-play was unobserved by Charles, the gentleman-usher having again come up to announce another applicant for admission to the presence: an historical character, too—historically infamous—for it was Archbishop Laud.

Soon after the oily ecclesiastic was seen coming along in a gliding, stealthy gait, as though he feared giving offence by approaching royalty too brusquely. His air of servile obsequiousness was in striking contrast with the bold bearing of the visitor who had preceded him. As he drew near, his features, that bore the stamp of his low birth and base nature, were relaxed to their meekest and mildest; a placid smile playing on his lips, as though they had never told a lie, or himself done murder!

Au fait to all that concerned the other three—every secret of Court and Crown—for he was as much the King's Minister as Strafford, he was at once admitted to their council, and invited to take part in their conspirings. Appealed to, as the other had been, he gave a similar response. Strong measures should be taken. He knew the Queen wished it so, for it was not his first conference with her on that same subject.

Strafford was not permitted time to impart to his *trio* of listeners the full particulars of the cruel scheme, which some say, and with much probability, had its origin in Rome. For the guests of the gay Queen, expected every afternoon at Whitehall, began to arrive, interrupting the conference.

Soon the palace garden became lustrous with people in splendid apparel, the *elite* of the land still adhering to the King's cause—plumed cavaliers, with dames old and young, though youth predominated, but not all of high degree, either in the male or female element. As in modern garden parties given by royalty, there was a mixture, both socially and morally, strange even to grotesqueness. The Franco-Italian Queen, with all her grand ideas of Divine Right and high Prerogative, was not loth to lay them down and aside when they stood in the way of her pleasures. She could be a very leveller where self-interest required it; and this called for it now. The King's failing popularity needed support from all sides, classes, and parties, bad or good, humble or gentle; and in the assemblage she saw around her—there by her own invitation—such high bloods as Harry Jermyn, Hertford, Digby, Coningsby, Scudamore, and the like, touched sleeves with men of low birth and lower character—very reprobates, as Lunsford, afterwards designated "the bloody," and the notorious desperado, David Hide! The feminine element was equally paralleled by what may be seen in many "society" gatherings of the present day—virtuous ladies brushing skirts with stage courtesans, and others who figure under the name of "professional beauties," many of them bearing high titles of nobility, but now debasing them.

Henrietta, in her usual way, had a pleasant word and smile for all; more for the men than the women, and sweeter for the younger ones than the old ones. But even to the gilded youth they were not distributed impartially. Handsome Harry Jermyn, hitherto reigning favourite, and having the larger share of them, had reason to suspect that his star was upon the wane, when he saw the Queen's eyes ever and anon turned towards another courtier handsome as himself, with more of youth on his side—Eustace Trevor. The latter, relieved from his duty as gentleman-usher, had joined the party in the garden. Socially, he had all right to be there. Son of a Welsh knight, he could boast of ancestry old as Caractacus, some of his forbears having served under Harry of Monmouth, and borne victorious banners at Agincourt. But boasting was not in Eustace Trevor's line, nor conceit of any sort—least of all vanity about his personal appearance. However handsome others thought him, he himself was quite unconscious of it. Equally so of the Queen's admiration; callous to the approaches she had commenced making, to the chagrin of older favourites. Not that he was of a cold or passionless nature; simply because Henriette de Medici, though a Queen, a beautiful woman as well, was not the one destined to inspire his first passion. For as yet he knew not love. But recently having become attached to the Court in an official capacity, he thought only of how he might best perform the duties that had been assigned him.

Though there might be many envies, jealousies, even bitter heartburnings among the people who composed that glittering throng, they were on the whole joyous and jubilant. A whisper had gone round of the King's determination to return to his old ways, and once more boldly confront what they called the aggressions of the Parliament. These concerned them all, for they were all of the class and kind who preyed upon the people. Groups gathered here and there were merry in mutual congratulations on their fine prospects for the future; hoping that, like the past, it would afford them free plunder of the nation's purse and resources—ship tax, coal and conduit money once more, loans by Privy Seal, and sale of monopolies—all jobberies and robberies restored!

But just at that moment of general rejoicing, as a bombshell bursting in the midst of a military camp or regiment of soldiers in close column, came a thing that, first setting them in a flutter, soon seriously alarmed them. A thing of human shape withal; a man in official robes, the uniform of a Parliamentary usher from the Lords. He was announced as waiting outside, rather claiming than craving an interview, which the King dared not deny him.

Summoned into the Audience Chamber, where Charles had gone to receive him, he presented the latter with a document, the reading of which caused him to tremble and turn pale. For it was a Bill of Attainder that had been agreed to by both Houses against Thomas Wentworth, Earl of Strafford. The fluttering among the courtiers became fright, when the King, returning to the garden, made known the usher's errand. To his familiars at first, but it soon passed from lip to lip and ear to ear. None seemed so little affected as Strafford himself. Sin-hardened, he was also endowed with indomitable courage, and maintained a bold, high bearing to the last of his life, even to the laying his head upon the block—an episode which soon after succeeded,—the craven monarch signing his death warrant as if it had been a receipt for one of his loans by Privy Seal.

Far more frightened by the Parliamentary message was Archbishop Laud. For him no more pleasure that day in the gardens of Whitehall. His smiles and simpering all gone, with pallid cheek and clouded brow, the wretched ecclesiastic wandered around among the courtiers, seeming distraught. And so was he. For in that Bill of Attainder he read his own doom—read it aright.

Grand, glorious Parliament, that knew not only how to impeach, but punish the betrayers of the people! Knew also how to maintain its own dignity and honour; as on a later occasion, when the King, once more maddened by the stinging taunts of his wicked wife, entered the august assembly with an escort of bullies and bravoes—Lunsford and Hide among them—to arrest six of England's most illustrious patriots: an attempt eminently unsuccessful—an intrusion handsomely resented. As the disappointed monarch and his disreputable following turned to go out again, it was with a wonderful come-down in their swagger. For along the line of seats, on both sides of the House, they saw men with scowling faces and hats on their heads; heard, too, in chorus clearly, loudly repeated, the significant cry—"Privilege!"

Chapter One
A Sword Duel in the Saddle

"He who is not a Republican must either have a bad head or a bad heart."

The speaker was a man of military mien, cavalry arm, as could be told by his seat in the saddle—for he was on horseback. Not in military uniform, however, but dressed in a plain doublet of dark grey cloth, with a broad Vandyke collar, high-crowned hat, buff boots reaching above the knees, and turned over at the tips. Nor did his wearing a sword certify to his being a soldier. In those days no one went without such weapon, especially when on a journey, as he was. Thirty, or thereabouts, he looked a little older through his complexion being sun-browned, as from foreign service or travel; which had also left its traces in his hair, a strand or two of silver beginning to show in a *chevelure* otherwise coal-black. His fine sweeping moustaches, however, were still free from this betrayer of middle age; while his well-balanced figure, lithe and tersely set, bespoke the activity of a yet youthful manhood. His features, oval and regular, were of a type denoting firmness; handsome, too, with their tint of bronze, which lent interest to them, lit up as they were by the flashing of eagle eyes. For flash these did excitedly, almost angrily, as he so declared himself. By his speech he should be a Puritan, of extremest views; for that he meant what he said was as evident from the emphasis given to his words as from the expression on his face. Still, his hair showed not the close crop of the "Roundhead;" instead, fell down in curling luxuriance as affected by the "Cavalier;" while a plume of cock's feathers set jauntily on the side of his hat gave him more the air of the latter than the former, in contradiction to the sentiment expressed.

There could be no mistaking to which belonged the personage to whom he addressed his speech. Of the Cavalier class sure, as the effect it produced upon him would have told of itself. But the style of his dress, air, bearing, everything proclaimed him one. A youth not yet turned twenty, in garb of silken sheen; coat and trunks of rich yellow satin, Cordovan leather boots, with a wide fringe of lace around the tops; spurs gilt or of gold, and a beaver over which waved a *panache* of ostrich feathers, upheld in a jewelled clasp. His sword belt of silk velvet was elaborately embroidered, the needlework looking as though it came from the fingers of a lady who had worked with a will and *con amore*; the gauntlets of his white gloves ornamented in a similar fashion by the same. Handsome he, too, but of manly beauty, quite differing from that of the other, even to contrast. With a bright, radiant complexion, and blonde hair falling in curls over his cheeks, yet unbearded, his features were of the type termed aristocratic; such as Endymion possessed, and Phidias would have been delighted to secure for a model. Habitually and openly wearing a gentle expression, there was, at the same time, one more latent, which bespoke intellectual strength and courage of no common kind. Passionate anger, too, when occasion called for it, seeming to say, "Don't put upon me too much, or you'll find your mistake."

Just such a cast came over them as he listened to what the other said; a declaration like defiance, flung in his teeth. Although meant as the clincher of a political argument which had been for some time going on between them, the young Cavalier, taken aback by its boldness, and doubtful of having heard aright, turned sharply upon the other, asking,—

"What's that you said, sir?"

"That the man who is not a Republican must either have a bad head or a bad heart."

This time more emphatically, as though nettled by the tone of the other's interrogative.

"Indeed!" exclaimed the youth reining up, for they were riding along a road.

"Indeed, yes," returned the older man, also drawing bridle. "Or if you prefer it in another form, he who is not a Republican must be either a knave or a fool."

"You're a knave to say so!" cried the silken youth, whose rising wrath had now gathered to a head, his hand as he spoke crossing to the hilt of his sword.

"Well, youngster," rejoined the other, seeming, on the contrary, to become calmer, and speaking with a composure strange under the circumstances, "that's speech plain enough, and rude enough. It almost tempts me to retort by calling you a fool. But I won't; only, if you value your life you must withdraw your words."

"Not one of them! Never, so long as I wear a sword. You shall eat yours first?" and he whipped out his rapier.

Though journeying side by side, they were quite strangers to one another, an accident having brought them together upon the road, both going in the same direction. It was up the steep declivity leading from the town of Mitcheldean into the Forest, near the point where now stands a mansion called "The Wilderness." Nor were they altogether alone, two other horsemen, their respective body servants, riding at a little distance behind. It was after surmounting the slope, and having got upon level ground, that their conflict of words reached the climax described, likely to end in one of blows. For to this the fiery youth seemed determined on pushing it.

Not so the other. On the contrary, he still sat composedly in his saddle, no sign of drawing sword, exhibiting a *sang froid* curiously in contrast with the warmth he had shown in the wordy disputation. It surely could not be cowardice? If so, it must be of the most craven kind, after that demand for withdrawal of the insulting words.

And as such the Cavalier conceived, or misconceived, it, crying out,—

"Draw, caitiff! Defend yourself, if you don't want me to kill you in cold blood!"

"Ha-ha-ha!" laughed the other, lightly and satirically. "It's just because I don't want to kill *you* in cold blood that I hesitate baring my blade."

"A subterfuge—a lie!" shouted the youth, stung to madness by the implied taunt of his inferiority. "Do your best and worst. Draw, sirrah, or I'll run you through. Draw, I say!"

"Oh, don't be in such a hurry. If I must I must, and, to oblige you, will, though it dislikes me to do murder—all the more that you've a spark of spirit. But—"

"Do it if you can," interrupted the Cavalier, unheeding the compliment. "I've no fear of your murdering *me*. Maybe the boot will be on the other leg."

Again that strange expression came over the face of the older man, half-admiration, half-compassion, with a scarce discernible element of anger in it. Even yet he appeared reluctant to draw his sword, and only did so when the opprobrious epithet *Lâche*—for the Cavaliers spoke a smattering of French—was flung into his teeth by his now furious antagonist. At this, unsheathing, he called out,—

"Your blood be on your own head. To guard!"

"For God and the King!" cried the challenger, as he tightened grasp on hilt and rein, setting himself firmly in the saddle.

"For God and the People!" followed the response antagonistic.

A prick of the spur by both, a bound forward, and their blades crossed with a clash, their horses shoulder to shoulder. But on the instant of engaging, that of the Cavalier, frayed by the clink of the steel and its flash in the dazzling sunlight, reared up, pivoting round to the right. This brought his rider left side to his antagonist, giving the latter an advantage: and so decided, it seemed as though he could bring the affair to an end at the moment of commencement. For his own better-trained steed had stood ground, and wanted only another touch of the spur to carry him close enough for commanding the bridle arm of his adversary, and all under it, when with a lunge he might thrust him through. Surely he could have done this! Yet neither spur nor sword were so exerted. Instead, he sat quietly in his saddle, as if waiting for his adversary to recover himself! Which the latter soon did, wheeling short round, and again furiously engaging; by a second misconception, unaware of the mercy shown him. This time as they came to the "engage" the Cavalier's horse behaved better, standing ground till several thrusts and parades were exchanged between them. Clearly the silk-clad youth was no novice at fencing, but as clearly the other was a master of it, and equally accomplished as a horseman; his horse, too, so disciplined as to give him little bother with the bridle. A spectator, if a connoisseur in the *art d'escrime*, could have told how the combat would end—must end—unless some accident favoured the younger combatant. As it was, even the Fates seemed against him, his horse again rearing *en pirouette*, and to the wrong side, placing him once more at the mercy of his antagonist. And again the latter scorned, or declined, taking advantage of it!

When the angry youth for the third time confronted him, it was with less fury in his look, and a lowered confidence in his skill. For now he not only knew his own inferiority as a swordsman, but was troubled with an indistinct perception of the other's generosity. Not clear enough, however, to restrain him from another trial; and their swords came together in a third crossing.

This time the play was short, almost as at the first. Having engaged the Cavalier's blade in *carte*, and bound it, the self-proclaimed Republican with a quick *flanconnade* plunged the point of his own straight for his adversary's wrist. Like the protruded tongue of a serpent, it went glistening into the white gauntlet, which instantly showed a spot of red, with blood spurting out; while the rapier of the Cavalier, struck from his grasp, flew off, and fell with a ring upon the road.

Chapter Two
Foes Become Friends

The young Cavalier was now altogether at the mercy of his older, and as proved, abler antagonist; knew the latter could take his life, and had the right, as well as good reason, from the great provocation given him in that shower of insulting epithets—the latest of them "*Lâche!*" For all, he quailed not, neither made attempt to elude the next thrust of the victorious sword. Instead, stood his ground, crying out,—

"You have conquered! You can kill me!"

"Kill you?" rejoined the victor, with the same light laugh as before. "That's just what I've been endeavouring *not* to do. But it has cost me an effort—all my skill. Had you been an ordinary swordsman I'd have disarmed you at the first pass after engaging. I've done it with others, half a dozen or more. With you, 'twas just as much as I was able, without absolutely taking your life—a thing far from my thoughts, and as far from my wishes. And now that all's over, and we've neither of us *murdered* the other, am I to say 'Surrender'?"

He still spoke laughingly, but without the slightest tone of satire, or show of exultation.

"You can command it," promptly responded the vanquished youth, now doubly vanquished. "I cry 'Quarter'—crave it, if you like."

It was no fear of death made him thus humbly submit, but a sudden revulsion, an outburst of gratitude, to a conqueror alike merciful and generous.

Ere this their attendants had got upon the ground, seeming undecided whether to pitch in with their masters, or cross swords on their own account. Both had drawn them, and waited but word or sign, scowling savagely at each other. Had it come to blows between the men, the result, in all probability, would have been as with their masters; the Cavalier's lightweight varlet looking anything but a match for the stout-bodied, veteranlike individual who was henchman to his antagonist. As it was, they had not resolved themselves till the combat came to an end. Then hearing the word "quarter," and seeing signs of amity restored, they slipped their blades back into the scabbards, and sate awaiting orders.

Only one of them received any just then—he the heavy one.

"Dismount, Hubert," commanded his master, "and return his weapon to this young gentleman, who, as you can testify, well deserves to wear it. And now, sir," he continued to the young gentleman himself, "along with your sword let me offer you some apologies, which are owing. I admit my words were rather rough, and call for qualification, or, to speak more correctly, explanation. When I said, that the man who is not a Republican must be deficient either in head or heart, I meant one who has reached the years of discretion, and seen something of the world—as, for instance, myself. At your age I too was a believer in kings—even the doctrine of Divine Right— brought up to it. Possibly, when you hear my name you'll admit that."

"You will give me your name?" asked the other, eagerly. "I wish it, that I may know to whom I am beholden for so much generosity."

"Very generous on your part to say say I am Sir Richard Walwyn."

"Ah! A relative of the Scudamores, are you not?"

"A distant relative. But I've not seen any of them lately, having just come back from the Low Countries, where I've been fighting a bit. In better practice from that, with my hand still in, which may account for my having got the better of you," and he again laughed lightly.

The young Cavalier protested against the generous admission, and then went on to say he knew the Scudamores well—especially Lord Scudamore, of Holme Lacey.

"I've often met his lordship at the Palace," was the concluding remark.

"At what palace, pray?" inquired Sir Richard.

"Oh! Whitehall. I did not think of specifying."

"Which proves that you yourself come from it? One of the King's people, I take it; or in the Queen's service, more like?"

"I was, but not now. I've been at Court for the last few months in the capacity of gentleman-usher."

"And now? But I crave pardon. It is rude of me to cross-question you thus."

"Not at all, Sir Richard. You have every right. After being so frank with me, I owe you equal frankness. I've given up the appointment I held at Court, and am now on my way home—to my father's house in Monmouthshire."

"Your father is—?"

"Sir William Trevor."

"Ah! now I can understand why your blood boiled up at my strenuous defence of the Parliament—the son of Sir William Trevor. But we won't enter upon politics again. After blows, words are inadmissible, as ungracious. Your father's house is near Abergavenny, if I remember rightly?"

"It is."

"That's good twenty-seven miles from here. You don't purpose going on there to-night?"

"No; I intend putting up for the night at Monmouth."

"Well, that's within the possibilities; but not with daylight, unless you press your horse hard—and he looks rather jaded."

"No wonder. I've ridden him all the way from Witney, in Oxfordshire, since six this morning."

"He must be good stuff to stand it, and show the spirit he did just now. But for all he seems rather badly done up—another reason for my having got the better of you."

At this both smiled, the young Cavalier, as before, refusing to accept the complimentary acknowledgment.

"A pity," ran on Sir Richard, "to press the poor animal farther to night— that is, so far as Monmouth. It's all of ten miles yet, and the road difficult— pitches up and down. You should rest him nearer, by way of reward for his noble performance of the day."

"Indeed, I was thinking of it; had half made up my mind to sleep at Coleford."

"Ah! you mus'n't stop at Coleford, much less sleep there."

"And why not?"

"The Coleford people are mad angry with the King, as are most others in the Forest. No wonder, from the way Sir John Wintour has been behaving to them since he got the monopoly grant of what his Majesty had no right to give—rights that are theirs. Their blood's up about it, and just now to appear in the streets of Coleford dressed as you are, cavalier and courtier fashion, might be attended with danger."

"I'll risk—defy it!"

"Bravely spoken, and I've no doubt you'd bravely do both. But there's no need for your doing one or the other."

"If you describe these Coleford fellows aright, how can I help it, Sir Richard? My road passes through their town."

"True, but there's a way you may avoid it."

"Oh! I'm not going to skulk round, taking bypaths, like a thief or deer-stealer. I'll give them a fight first."

"And that fight might be your last—likely would, Master Trevor. But no. You've fought your way *into* the Forest so gallantly, it behoves him you all but conquered to see you safe out of it. To do which, however, I must ask you to give up all thoughts of sleeping either at Monmouth or Coleford, and be my guest for the night."

"But where, Sir Richard? I did not know that you had a house in the Forest."

"Nor have I. But one of my friends has; and I think I can promise you fair hospitality in it—by proxy. Besides, that little hole I've made in your hand—sorry at having made it—needs looking to without delay, and my friend has some skill as a surgeon. I could offer some other inducements that might help in deciding you—as, for instance, a pair of pretty faces to see. But coming from the Court of Queen Henriette, with her galaxy of grand dames, perhaps you've had a surfeit of that sort of thing."

The young courtier shifted uneasily in his saddle, a slight blush coming over his cheeks, as though the words rather gave him pain.

"If not," continued Sir Richard, without heeding these indices of emotion, "I can promise to show you something rare in the way of feminine beauty. For that I'll back Sabrina and Vaga against all your maids of honour and court ladies—the Queen included—and win with either."

"*Sabrina! Vaga!* Singular names! May I ask who the ladies are?"

"You may do more—make their acquaintance, if you consent to my proposal. You will?"

"Sir Richard, your kindness overpowers me. I am at your service every way."

"Thanks! Let us on, then, without delay. We've yet full five miles of road before us, ere we can reach the cage that holds this pair of pretty birds. *Allons!*"

At which he gave his horse the spur, Trevor doing the same; and once more the two rode side by side; but friendly now—even to affection.

Chapter Three
Beautiful Forest Birds

In all England's territory there is no district more interesting than the Forest of Dean. Historically it figures in our earliest annals, as borderland and bulwark of the ancient Silures, who, with Caractacus at their head, held the country around, defending it on many a hard-fought field against the legionaries of Ostorius Scapula. Centuries after, it again became the scene of sanguinary strife between the descendants of these same Silures—then better known as Britons—and the Saxon invaders; and still farther down the stream of time another invasion wasted it—Norman and Saxon arrayed on the same side against Welsh—still the same warlike stock, the sons of Siluria. This conflict against odds—commencing with the Norman William, and continued, or renewed, down through the days made illustrious by the gallant Llewellyn—only came to an end with those of the equally gallant Glendower, when the fires of Welsh independence, now and then blazing up intermittently, were finally and for ever trodden out.

Many a grand historic name is associated with this same Forest of Dean—famed warriors and famous or infamous kings. The Conqueror himself was hunting in it when the news reached him of the rising in Northumberland, and he swore "By the splendour of God, he would lay that land waste by fire and sword!"—a cruel oath, as cruelly kept. In its dark recesses the wretched Edward the Second endeavoured to conceal himself, but in vain—dragged thence to imprisonment in the dungeons of Berkeley Castle, there to die. And within its boundaries was born that monarch of most romantic fame, Harry of Monmouth, hero of Agincourt.

And the day was approaching—had, in fact, come—when other names that brighten the page of England's history were to fling their halo of illumination over the Forest of Dean—those of the chivalrous Waller, the brave but modest Massey, Essex, Fairfax, and greatest, most glorious of all, that of Cromwell himself. It was to be darkened too, as by the shadow of death—ay, death itself—through many a raid of marauding Cavaliers, with the ruffian Rupert at their head.

Dropping history, and returning to its interest otherwise, the Forest of Dean claims attention from peculiarities of many kinds. Geologically regarded, it is an outlier of the carboniferous system of South Wales, from which it is separated by a breadth of the Devonian that has been denuded between—so widely separated as to have similitude to an island in the far-off ocean. An elevated island, too, rising above the "Old Red," through successive strata of shales, mountain limestone, and millstone grit, to nearly a thousand feet higher than the general level of the surrounding *terrain*. Towards this, on every side, and all round for miles and tens of miles, it presents a *façade* not actually precipitous, but so steep and difficult of ascent as to make horses breathe hard climbing it; while in loaded cart or wagon, teams have to be doubled. Just such a "pitch" was that on whose top the bitter war of words between Eustace Trevor and Sir Richard Walwyn had come to blows.

But, though thus high in air, the Forest of Dean does not possess the usual characteristics of what are termed *plateaux*, or elevated tablelands. As a rule these show a level surface, or with but gentle undulations, while that of the Forest is everywhere intersected by deep valleys and ravines.

A very interesting geological fact is offered in the surface formation of this singular tract of country, its interior area being in most places much lower than the rim around it. The peculiarity is due to the hard carboniferous limestone, which forms its periphery, having better resisted denudation than the softer matrix of the coal measures embraced by it. The disintegrating rains, and the streams, often torrents, their resulting sequence, have here and there cut channels of escape outward—some running west into the Wye, some eastward to espouse the Severn.

Very different is the Forest of Dean now from what it was in those days of which this tale treats—territorially more restricted, both in its boundaries and the area once bearing its name. Then it extended over the whole triangular space between the two great rivers, from the towns of Ross and Gloucester down to their union in the wide sea-like estuary of the Severn. Changed, too, in the character of its scenery. Now, here and there, a tall chimney may be seen soaring up out of its greenery of trees, and vomiting forth volumes of murky smoke, in striking disagreeable contrast with their verdure. Then there was nothing of this kind;—at least nothing to jar upon the mind, or mar the harmony of nature. Then, too, it was a real forest of grand old trees, with a thick tangle of underwood, luxuriant and shady. For the Court favourite, Sir John Wintour, had not yet wasted it with his five hundred woodcutters, all chopping and hacking away at the same time. It was only after the Restoration he did that; the robber's monopoly granted him by the "Martyr King" having been re-bestowed by the "Merry Monarch."

There were towns in the Forest then, notwithstanding—some of them busy centres as now; but the majority peaceful villages or hamlets; country houses, too, some of pretentious style—mansions, and castles. A few of these yet exist, if in ruins; others known only by record; and still others totally gone out of history—lost even to legend.

The Forest roads were then but bridle paths, or trackways for the pack-horse; no fencing on either side; the narrow list of trodden ground running centrally between wide borderings of grass-grown sward; so that the traveller, if a horseman, had the choice of soft turf for the hoofs of his roadster. Only on the main routes between the larger towns, and those going outward, was there much traffic. The bye-roads had all the character of green lanes, narrow, but now and then debouching into glades, and openings of larger area, where the small Forest sheep—progeny of the Welsh mountaineers—browsed upon pasture, spare and close-cropped, in the companionship of donkeys, and perchance a deer, or it might be a dozen, moving among them in amiable association. The sheep and the donkeys are there still, but the deer, alas! are gone. Many birds that built their nests in the Forest trees, or soared above, are there no more. The eagle makes not now its eyrie in the Coldwell Rocks or soars over Symonds' Yat; even the osprey is but rarely seen pursuing its finny prey in the lower waters of either Wye or Severn. Still, the *falconidae* are to this day represented in the Forest district by numerous species, by the kite and kestrel; the buzzard, Common, Rough-legged, and Honey; by the goshawk and sparrow-hawk; the hobby and harriers; and if last, not least, in estimation, the graceful diminutive merlin.

Birds of bright feathers, too, still flit through the Forest's trees; the noisy jay, the gaudy, green woodpecker, and the two spotted species; with the kingfisher of cerulean hue; while its glades are gladdened by the sweet song of the thrush, the bolder lay of the blackbird; in springtide, the matchless melody of the nightingale—the joyous twittering of linnets and finches, mingling with the softer notes of the cushat and turtle-dove.

On that calm summer evening, when the clinking of swords on Mitcheldean-hill frightened the Forest birds, for a time stilling their voices, on another hill, some three miles distant from the scene of strife, the sweet songsters were being disturbed by intrusion upon their wild-wood domain. Not much disturbed, however, nor could the disturbers be justly characterised as intruders. Even the birds themselves might have been glad to see, and welcome among them, things of brightness and beauty far beyond their own. Women they were, or rather girls, both being under age—for there were but two of them. Sisters, moreover, though there was scarce a trait of resemblance to betray the relationship, either in features or complexion. She who seemed the elder was dark as a gipsy, the other a clear *blonde*, with hair showering over her shoulders, of hue as the beams of the sinking sun that shimmered upon it. For all, both were alike beautiful; in a different way, but unquestionably beautiful. And that they were sisters could be learnt by listening to their conversation: their names, also, as they addressed one another—that of the older, *Sabrina*; the younger, *Vaga*.

They could not be other than the pair of pretty birds spoken of by Sir Richard Walwyn; and, verily, he had not overrated them.

Chapter Four
Out for a Walk

Unlike in other respects, the sisters were unequal in height—the elder being the taller. With some difference in their dress, too, though both wore the ordinary outdoor costume of the day. It was rather graceful than splendid, for the hideous farthingale of the Elizabethan era was then going out of fashion, and their gowns, close-fitting in body and sleeves, displayed the outlines of figures that were perfection. Theirs were not charms that needed heightening by any adornment of dress. However plainly attired, there was in their air and carriage that grace which distinguishes the gentlewoman. Still, the younger was not without affectation of ornament. Her French hood of bright-coloured silk, looped under the chin, was so coifed as to show in a coquettish way her wealth of radiant hair, and beneath the gorget ruff gleamed a necklet of gold, with rings in her ears. There was embroidery, also, on the bodice and sleeves of her gown—doubtless the work of her own fair fingers. In those days ladies, even the grandest dames, were not above using the needle.

Sabrina's hood, of a more sombre hue, was quite as becoming, and more suitable to her darker complexion. Her general attire, too, was appropriate to her character, which was of the staid, sober kind. Both wore strong, thick-soled shoes—being out for a walk—but neither these nor home-knitted stockings, which their short skirts permitted view of, could hinder the eye from beholding feet small and finely-shaped, with high instep and elegant *tournure* of ankles.

Good walkers they were, as could be told by the way they stepped along the Forest road; for they were on one. It was that which ran from Ruardean to Drybrook, and their faces were set in the direction of the latter. Between the two towns a high ridge is interposed, and this they were ascending from the Ruardean side. Before they had reached its summit, Vaga, coming abruptly to a stop, said:—

"Don't you think we've walked far enough?"

"Why? Are you tired?"

"No—not that. But it occurs to me we may be wandering too far from home."

That Sabrina was not wandering might have been told by her step, straightforward, as also her earnest glances, interrogating the road ahead at every turning. As these had been somewhat surreptitiously, though not timidly, given, the other had hitherto failed to notice them. Indeed, Vaga was not all the while by her side, nor keeping step with her. A huge dog of the Old English mastiff breed more occupied her attention; the animal every now and then making a rush at the browsing sheep, and sending them helter-skelter among the trees, his young mistress—for the dog was hers—clapping her hands with delight, and crying him on regardless of the mischief. It was only when no more of the little Welsh muttons were to be seen along the road that she joined her sister, and put in that plea for turning back.

"So far from home!" repeated Sabrina, with feigned surprise. "Why, we haven't come quite two miles—not much over one."

"True; but—"

"But what? Are you afraid?"

"A little—I confess."

"And the cause of your fear? Not wolves? If so, I can release you from it. It's now quite half a century since there was a wolf seen in this Forest; and he—poor, lonely creature, the last of his race—was most unmercifully slain. The Foresters, being mostly of Welsh ancestry, have an hereditary hatred of the lupine species, I suppose from that mischance which befel the infant Llewellyn." Vaga laughed, as she rejoined:—"Instead of having a fear of wolves, I'd like to see one just now. Hector, I'm sure, would show fight; ay, and conquer it, too, as did the famed Beth-Gelert his. Wouldn't you, old Hec? Ay! that you would."

At which the mastiff, rearing up, set his paws against her breast to receive the caressess extended; and, after these being given him, scampered off again in search of more sheep.

"Then what are you afraid of?" asked Sabrina, "Ghosts? There are none of them in the Forest either. If there were, no danger of their showing themselves by daylight, and we'll be back home long before the sun goes down. Ha, ha, ha!"

It was as unusual for the older of the sisters to talk in such a light strain as it was for the younger to speak otherwise. Just then each had a reason for this reversion of their *rôles*.

Further questioned as to the cause of her fear, Vaga made answer, saying, —

"You're merry, sister Sab, and I'm right glad to see you so. But what I meant isn't a matter for jest; instead, something to be really alarmed about."

"When you've told me what it is, I'll give my opinion upon it. If neither wolves nor ghosts, what can it be? Bipeds or quadrupeds?"

"Bipeds, and of the sort most to be dreaded — brutal men."

"Oh! that's it. But what men are there about here deserving to be so characterised?"

"None about here, I hope and believe. But you know, sister, what's going on all around the Forest: those mobs of lawless fellows down at Monmouth and Lydney. Suppose some of them to be coming this way and meet us?"

"I don't suppose it, and needn't. The malignants of Monmouth and Lydney are not likely to be upon this road. If they did, 'twould be at their peril. The men of Ruardean and Drybrook are of a different sort — the right sort. Should we meet any of them, though they may be a little rough in appearance, they won't be rude. No true Forester ever is to a woman, whether lady or not. That they leave to the foreign elements Sir John Wintour has brought to Lydney, and the so-called Cavaliers on the Monmouth side — those braggarts of their blood and gallant bearing, most of them the veriest scum of the country, its gamesters and tapsters, the sweepings of the alehouse and stable! Cavaliers, indeed! who know not politeness to man nor respect for woman; care neither for national honour nor social decency!"

The enlightened young lady spoke with a warmth bordering upon indignation. With truth, too, as might one of her sort now about Tories and Jingoes. But, alas! now there are but few of her sort, youthful and enthusiastic in the cause of liberty; instead, ancient maidens of wealth and title, some of whose ancestors trod the stage playing at charity for the sake of popularity; patronising play-actors and endowing homes for strayed dogs! showing a shameless sympathy with the foul murdering Turk and his red-handed atrocities; last and latest of all, having the effrontery — impertinent as unfeminine — to counsel, ay, dictate, political action to England's people, telling them how they should cast their votes!

What a contrast between their doings and the sayings and sentiments of that young Forest girl—all that lies between the mean and the noble!

"But," she went on, in reference to the *gentlemen* of the gaming-house and hostelry tap-room, "we needn't fear meeting them here, nor anywhere through the Forest. The Foresters—brave fellows—are for the Parliament almost to a man. Should we encounter any of them on our walk, I'll answer for their good behaviour and kind-heartedness—something more, if knowing who we are. Father is a favourite with them for having taken their side against the usurpations of Wintour; though they liked him before that, and I'm proud of their doing so."

"Oh! so am I, Sabrina. I'm as fond of our dear Foresters as you. It isn't of them I had any fear. But, apart from all that, I think it's time we turn our steps homeward. We're surely now two miles from Hollymead; and see! the sun's hastening to go down behind the Welsh hills."

While so delivering herself, she faced round, the Welsh hills being behind their backs as they walked towards Drybrook.

"Hasten as it likes," rejoined Sabrina, "it can't get down for at least another hour. That will give us ample time to go on to the top of the hill and back to Hollymead before supper; which last, if I mistake not, is the chief cause of your anxiety to be at home."

"For shame, Sabrina! You know it isn't—the last thing in my thoughts."

Sabrina did know that; knew, also, she was not speaking her own thoughts, but using subterfuge to conceal them. It was herself had proposed the stroll she seemed so desirous of continuing. To her its termination would not be satisfactory without attaining the summit of the ridge whose slope they were ascending.

Thrown back by what her younger sister had said, but still determined to proceed, without giving the true reason, she bethought herself of one, false though plausible.

"Well, Vag," she laughingly pursued, "I was only jesting, as you know. But there's one thing I hate to do—never could do, that's to half climb a hill without going on to its top. It seems like breaking down or backing out, and crying 'surrender,'—which our dear father has taught us never to do. Up to the summit yonder is but a step now. It won't take us ten minutes more to reach it; besides, I want to see something I haven't set eyes on for a long while—that grand valley through which meanders my namesake, Sabrina. And looking back from there, you can also feast your eyes on that in which wanders yours, Vaga, capricious like yourself. In addition," she added, not heeding her sister's shrug of the shoulders, "we'll there get a better view of a glorious sunset that's soon to be over the Hatteral Hills; and the twilight after will give us ample time to get home before the supper table be set. So, why should you hinder me—to say nothing of yourself—from indulging in a little bit of aesthetics?"

"Hinder you!" exclaimed Vaga, protestingly. "I hinder! You shan't say that."

And at the words she went bounding on upward, like a mountain antelope; not stopping again till she stood on the summit of the hill.

Chapter Five
Waiting and Watching

Following with alacrity, Sabrina was soon again by the side of her sister. But just then no further speech passed between them. Not that both were silent. On the crest of the ridge, treeless and overgrown with gorse, Hector had run foul of a donkey, and after a short chase was holding it at bay. With his barks were mingled cries of encouragement from his mistress, laughter, and patting of her hands, as she hounded him on. Possibly had the Forester, Neddy's owner, come up at that moment, he might not have shown the politeness for which Sabrina had given his fellows credit. But the young lady meant no harm; nor much the mastiff. If he had, there was little danger of his doing it; the creature whose ancestry came from Mesopotamia being able to take care of itself. The demonstrations of the dog—an overfed, good-natured brute—looked as if being made either for his own amusement or that of his young mistress; while the donkey, on the defence, with teeth, and heels, seemed equally to enjoy the fun.

The elder sister, standing apart, had neither eyes nor ears for this bit of hoydenish play. If a thought, it was the fear of giving offence to the ass's owner, should that individual unluckily come along. As no one came, however, she left Vaga to her vagaries, and stood intently gazing upon the landscape spread before her.

A far and varied view she commanded from that elevated spot. First, a deep, wide valley below, trending away to the right, with a tiny stream trickling adown it, and a straggling village, the houses standing apart along its banks—Drybrook. But not as the Drybrook of to-day, showing tall brick chimneys—the monoliths of our own modern time—with their plumes of grey black smoke; cinder-strewn roads running from one to the other, and patches of bare pasture between. Then it was embowered, almost buried, in trees; here and there only a spot of whitewashed walls or a quaint lead window, seen through the thick foliage. Beyond village and stream rose another ridge, with a gradual ascent up to the "Wilderness"; and still farther off—so far as to be just visible—stretched a wide expanse of low-lying champaign country, the valley of the Severn, once the sound of a sea. As the young girl gazed upon it, the sinking sun behind her back, with the Forest highlands beginning to fling the shadows of twilight across the Severn's plain, and the white mist that overhung it, she might well have imagined the waters of ocean once more o'erflowing their ancient bed.

She neither imagined this nor thought of it; in fact saw not the fog, nor gave so much as a second glance to that valley she had professed herself so desirous of viewing. Instead, her eyes were fixedly bent upon the face of the acclivity opposite—more particularly on a riband of road that went winding up through woods from Drybrook to the "Wilderness." And still with the same look of earnest interrogation. What could it mean?

Vaga coming up, after having finished her affair with the donkey, observed the look, and it called forth a fresh display of that persiflage she so delighted in. Hitherto Sabrina had the best of it. Her turn now, and she took advantage of it, saying,—

"Why, sister Sab, you seem to have forgotten all about what you came here for! You're not looking at the Severn at all! Your glances are directed too low for it. And as to the glorious sunset you spoke of, that's going on behind you! Something on the road over yonder seems to be the attraction; though I can see nothing but the road itself."

"Nor I," said Sabrina, a little confused, with just the slightest spot of red again showing on her cheeks. Enough, though, to catch the eye of her suspicious sister, who archly observed,—

"Rather strange, your gazing so earnestly at it, then?"

"Well, yes; I suppose it is."

"But not if you're expecting to see some one upon it."

Sabrina started, the red on her cheeks becoming more pronounced; but she said nothing, since now her secret was discovered, or on the eve of discovery. Vaga's next words left her no longer in doubt.

"Who is he, sister?" she asked with a sly look, and a laugh.

"Who is who?"

"He you expect to see come riding down yonder road. I take it he'll be on horseback?"

"Vaga! you're a very inquisitive creature."

"Have I not some right, after being dragged all the way hither, when I wanted to go home? If you called me a *hungry* creature 'twould be nearer the truth. Jesting apart, I am that—quite famished; so weak I must seek support from a tree."

And with a mock stagger, she brought up against the trunk of a hawthorn that grew near.

Sabrina could not resist laughing too, though still keeping her eyes on the uphill road. It seemed as though she could not take her eyes off it. But the other quickly recovering strength, and more naturally than she had affected feebleness, once more returned to the attack, saying,—

"Sister mine; it's no use you're trying to hoodwink me. You forget that by accident I saw a letter that lately came to Hollymead—at least its superscription. Equally oblivious you appear to be, that the handwriting of a certain gentleman is quite familiar to me, having seen many other letters from the same to father. So, putting that and that together, I've not the slightest doubt that the one of last week, addressed to your sweet self, informed you that on a certain day, hour, afternoon, Sir Richard Walwyn would enter the Forest of Dean by the Drybrook Road on his way to—"

"Vaga, you're a very demon!"

"Which means I've read your secret aright. So you may as well make confession of it."

"I won't; and just to punish you for prying. Curiosity ungratified will be to you very torture, as I know."

"Oh, well! keep it close; it don't signify a bit. One has little care to be told what one knows without telling. If Sir Richard should come to Hollymead, why then six and six make a dozen, don't they?"

Sabrina turned a half-reproachful look on her tormentor, but without making reply.

"You needn't answer," the other went on. "*My* arithmetic's right, and the problem's solved, or will be, by the gentleman spoken of making his appearance any time this day, or—Why, bless me! Yonder he is now, I do believe."

The exclamatory phrase had reference to a horseman seen riding down the road so narrowly watched; though the speaker was not the first to see him. He had been already sighted by Sabrina, and it was the flash of excitement in her eyes that guided those of her sister.

The horseman had not all the road to himself; another coming on behind, but at such short distance as to tell of companionship—that of master and servant. He ahead was undoubtedly a gentleman, as evinced by the bright colour of his dress, with its silken gloss under the sunlight, and the glitter of arms and accoutrements; while the more soberly-attired rider in the rear was evidently a groom or body servant.

As the girls stood regarding, the look in the eyes of the elder, at first satisfied and joyous, began gradually to change. The distance was too great for the identification of either face or figure. All that could be distinguished was that they were men on horseback, with the general hue of their habiliments, and the sparkle of arms and ornaments.

It was just these—their brightness and splendour—as affected the foremost of the two, which had brought the change over Sabrina's countenance. Sir Richard Walwyn was not wont to dress gaudily, but rather the reverse. Still, time had elapsed since she last saw him. He had been abroad, in the Low Countries, and with Gustavus of Sweden, battling for the good cause. The foreign fashions may have changed his ideas about dress and its adornments. But little cared she for that so long as his heart was unchanged; and that it was so she knew by the letter which had betrayed her own heart's secret to her sister.

Almost simultaneously upon Vaga's features appeared a change too—almost expressing doubt. It became certainty on the instant after, still another replacing it, as she again exclaimed, contradicting herself—

"Bless me, no! That's Reginald Trevor."

Chapter Six
A Cavalier in Love

Reginald Trevor it was, for Vaga was not guessing. Something she saw about the horseman, or his horse, had enabled her to identify him; as she did so, that third and latest change coming over her countenance, giving it also a serious cast.

But nothing compared with that which now showed on the face of her sister. The varied expressions of hopeful anticipation, surprise, delight, then doubt, rapidly succeeding one another, were all past, and in their place a dark shadow sat cloud-like on her brow. In her eyes, too, still scanning the distant horseman, was a look that betokened pain, or at least uneasiness, with something of fear and anger. In truth, the expression on their face, though differing from each other, would have been unreadable to any one who was a stranger to them and Reginald Trevor.

Some knowledge of this gentleman and his antecedents will throw light upon the grave impression seemingly produced upon the two girls by the sight of him.

As the name might indicate, he was kin to the young courtier, late gentleman-usher at Whitehall—his cousin. Different, however, had been their lots in the lottery of life; those of Eustace so far having all come out prizes, while Reginald had been drawing blanks. A dissolute, dissipated father had left the latter nought but a bad name, and the son had little bettered it. Still was he a gallant Cavalier, as the word went, and at least possessed the redeeming quality of courage. He had given proofs of it as an officer in that army sent northward against the Scots, where he had served as a lieutenant under Lunsford. *Per contra*, as the father who begot him, he was given to dissipation, a drinker, dicer, wencher, everything socially disreputable and distasteful to the Parliamentarians,—far more the Puritans,—though neither disgracing or lowering himself in the eyes of his own party—the Cavaliers. If latitudinarianism in morals could be accounted Christian charity, none were endowed with this virtue in a higher degree than they.

Reginald Trevor had the full benefit of their tolerance in that respect: passed among them as a rare good fellow; no harm in him, save what affected himself. To use a common phrase, he was his own worst enemy. Beginning life penniless, he was no better off at the commencement of his military career; and his spendthrift habits had kept him the same ever since. At that hour, when seen coming down the road—save his sword, horse, clothing; and equipments—he could not call anything his own. These, however, were all of the best; for he was a military dandy, and, despite poverty, always contrived to rig himself out in grand array. Just now he was well up in everything, though possibly nothing had been paid for—horse, clothing, nor accoutrements. But he had got a good post, which enabled him to get good credit, and that satisfied him all the same. Thrown out of commission—as Lunsford and others after their return from the North—he had lived for some months in London as best he could; often at his wits' end. But swords were now once more in demand, with men who could wield them; and Sir John Wintour, who had commenced fortifying his mansion at Lydney to hold it for the King, casting about for the right sort to defend it, chose Reginald Trevor as one of them.

For some weeks antecedent to the time of his introduction to the reader, he had been in Sir John's service; acting in a mixed capacity, military and political, with some duties appertaining to the civil branch of administration. These had taken him all over the Forest of Dean, introducing him into many a house where he had hitherto been a stranger. But of all honoured by his visit, there was only one he cared ever returning to. It he could revisit again and again; had done so; and would have been glad to stay by it for the rest of his life. A lone house, too, though a mansion, standing remote from anything that could be called city, or even town; remote from other houses of its class. It may seem strange such a solitary habitation should have attractions for a man of his character; but not when its name is given—for it was Hollymead. This known, it needs no telling why Reginald Trevor was attracted thither; only to specify which of the two girls was the loadstone that drew him. Even this may be guessed—not likely Sabrina, but very likely Vaga. And Vaga it was. He had fallen in love with her, passionately, madly; and, stranger still, purely; for, in all likelihood, it was the first honest love of his life. Honest it was, however; and honestly he had been acting so far; his courtship respectful, and free from the bold rude advances which, as a rule, marked the conduct of the Cavaliers. For, despite all said to the contrary, their behaviour to women was more "gallantry" than gallant, and anything but chivalrous.

But, although behaving his best, Reginald Trevor had not prospered in his suit; on the contrary received a check which brought it to an abrupt ending for the time, and it might be for ever. This in the shape of a hint that his visits to Hollymead House were neither welcome nor desirable, rather the reverse. Not given him by the girl herself—she did not even know of it,—but conveyed by her father privately and quietly, yet firmly. Of course it was taken, and the visits discontinued.

That was but a fortnight ago, and yet Reginald Trevor was once more on his way to Hollymead! But very different the cause carrying him thither now to that which had oft taken him before; different his feelings, too, though not as regarded the young lady. For her they were the same—his passion hot as ever. And yet was it a flame burning blindly, without a word of encouragement to fan or keep it alive. Never once had she spoken to tell him his love was reciprocated; never given him smile or look that could be interpreted in that sense. For all this, he so interpreted some she had bestowed on him. Successes, conquests many, had made him vain, and he deemed himself irresistible—fancied he would conquer her, too.

Nevertheless, he felt less confident now. That rupture of relations had become a grievous obstacle. Nor was he on the way to Hollymead with any hope of being able to bind up the broken threads; instead, his errand thither had for object that which was sure further to sever them. It was not of his own seeking, and he had entered upon it with reluctance.

Dark and gloomy was the shadow on his face as he rode under that of the trees. At intervals it became a scowl, with resentment blazing up in his eyes, as he thought of that dismissal, so wounding to his self-esteem, so insulting. But he was armed with that which would give him a *revanche*; make the master of Hollymead humble if not hospitable—a document such as has humbled the master of many another house, angering them at the same time. For it was a letter of request for a loan, signed and stamped with the King's seal.

Chapter Seven
A Young Lady not in Love

"I do believe it's Reginald Trevor."

Sabrina said this in rejoinder, now certain it was not the man she had climbed that hill in hopes of meeting.

"I'm sure of it," affirmed Vaga, in confident tone as before. "If I couldn't tell him, I can the horse—the light grey he always rides. And that's his dress—the colour at least. I don't think he has many changes, exquisite as he is, or we'd have seen some of them at Hollymead."

She made this remark with a smile of peculiar significance.

"Oh! yes; 'tis he," assented the sister, her eyes still upon him. "I'm sure now, myself. The horse—yes, the dress too. And, see! a red plume in his hat— that's enough. I wonder where he's bound for—surely not Hollymead!"

It was then the grave look already alluded to showed itself in her eyes. "Perhaps you can tell, sister?" she added, interrogatively.

"Sabrina! why do you say that? How should I be acquainted with Mr Trevor's movements or intentions—any more than yourself?"

"Ha—ha! What an artful little minx you are, Vag! A very mistress of deception!"

"You'll make me angry, Sab—I'm half that already."

"Without cause, then, or reason."

"Every reason."

"Name one."

"That you should suspect me of having a secret and keeping it from you."

"Goodness gracious! How just you are in your reproaches—you, who but this very moment have been accusing me of that selfsame thing! I, all candour, all frankness!"

Vaga was now flung back, as a sailor would say, on her "beam ends." For, in truth, she had made herself amenable to the charge.

"Oh! you innocent!" cried Sabrina, pressing her triumph. "Though you are three years younger than I, you're quite as old about some things, and this is *one* of them."

"This what?"

"This that; the thing, or man, if he may be so called, we see riding down yonder road."

"You wrong me, sister; I've no secret concerning him. I never cared for Rej Trevor in the way you appear to be hinting at—not three straws."

"Are you serious in what you say, Vag? Tell me the truth!"

There was an earnestness in the way the question was put—tone, air, everything—that bespoke more than a common interest about the answer.

It came, causing disappointment, with some slight vexation. For Vaga, thinking she had been badgered long enough, and, remembering, moreover, how very reticent the other had just shown herself, determined on having a *revanche*. It was altogether in consonance with her nature; though she had no idea of advantage beyond that of mere fun.

"Curiosity on the rack!" she triumphantly retorted. "What you've just been dooming me to! How does it feel, sister Sab!"

"Sister Sab" made no response; in turn being fairly conquered and cornered. But her silence and submissive look were more eloquent than any appeal she could have made. And, responding to them, her conqueror relentingly asked:

"Are you very, *very* desirous of knowing how the case stands between myself and Master Reginald Trevor?"

"I am, indeed. And when you've told me, I'll give you the reason."

"On that condition I'll tell you. He is nothing to me more than any other man. And when I add that no other man is anything either, you'll understand me."

"But, sister dear, do you mean to say you *love* no one?"

"I mean to say that—flat."

"And never have?"

"That's a queer question to be asked; above all by you, you who so often preach the virtue of constancy, crying it into my ears! If I ever had loved man, I think I should love him still. But as it chances, I don't quite comprehend what the sensation is; never having experienced it. And more, I don't wish to; that is, if it were to affect me as it seems to do you."

"What do you mean, Vaga?" asked the more sage sister, bristling up at the innuendo. "Love affect me! You're only fancying! Nothing of the sort, I assure you."

"Oh! yes; much of the sort; though you might not yourself perceive it. Everybody else does, at least I do—have for a very long time—ever since he went off to the wars."

"What he?"

"Again counterfeiting. And vainly. Well, I won't gratify you by giving his name this time. Enough to say that ever since you last saw him you haven't been like you used to be. Why, Sab, I can remember when you were as full of frolic as myself, or Hector here. Yet, for the last two years you've been as melancholy as a love-sick monkey. True, there's been a little brightening up in you of late—no doubt due to that letter. Ha—ha—ha!"

Sabrina laughed too, despite the unmerciful way she was being bantered. The allusion to "that letter" was not unpleasant. Its contents, very gratifying, had restored her heart's gladness and confidence. Not that she had ever doubted her lover's fealty, but only had fears for his life. She said nothing, however, leaving the other to rattle on.

"And now, Miss Prim-and-Prudery, I want your reason for prying into my secrets, after being so chary of your own; I demand it."

"Dear Vaga! you shall have it and welcome. After what you say, there need be no shyness in my telling you now. I was anxious about you on father's account, and my own, too, as your sister."

"Anxious about me! For what?"

"Your relations with yonder individual."

She nodded towards the horseman with the red feather in his hat.

"Very good of father and you to be so concerned about me; but don't you think I can take care of myself? I'm getting old enough to do that."

She was only a little over seventeen, but believed herself quite as much a woman as Sabrina, who was three years her senior. She had the proud, independent spirit of one, and brooked no control by her older sister; on the contrary, rather exercised it herself. She was her father's favourite; a circumstance that would appear strange to those acquainted with his character. Hence, in part, her assumption of superiority.

"Of course you can," returned Sabrina, assentingly. "And I'm glad of it."

"I suppose, then, it's owing to your and father's united solicitude on my behalf that Master Rej Trevor hasn't shown his face at Hollymead for the last couple of weeks."

"I've had nothing to do with it, Vaga."

"Which seems to say that somebody has, then. I suspected as much, by your having said nothing about it. As you seem to know something, Sab, you may as well tell it me."

"I will—all I know. Which is, that father has forbidden his visits to Hollymead. I only learnt it from our maid Gwenthian. It appears, that the last time Mr Trevor was at the house, she overheard a conversation between father and him; father telling him as much as that he would be no more welcome there."

"And what answer did the fine gentleman make? I suppose the eavesdropping Gwenthian heard that, too."

There was such evident absence of all emotion on the part of her who interrogated, she could not well be making believe. The other, seeing she was not, responded with confidence,—

"Nothing, or nothing much, except in mutterings, which the girl failed to catch the meaning of. But the nature may be imagined from the way he went off—all scowling and angry, she says."

"Gwenthian has never mentioned the circumstance to me; which I take it is a little strange on her part."

She thought it so, for of the two she was more a favourite with the waiting maid than her sister, and knew it. Between her and Gwenthian—a Forest girl of quick wit and subtle intelligence—many confidences had been exchanged. Therefore her wonder at this having been withheld.

"Not at all," rejoined Sabrina, entering upon a defence of Gwenthian's reticence. "There was nothing strange in her keeping it from you. She supposed it might vex you—told me so."

"Ha—ha—ha! How thoughtful of her! But it don't vex me—luckily, no—not the least bit; and Gwenthian should have known that, as you know now, Sab. Don't you?"

"I do," answered Sabrina, in full conviction. For Vaga's laugh was so utterly devoid of all regret at what had been revealed to her, no one could suppose or suspect there was within her breast a thought of Reginald

Trevor, beyond looking on him in the light of a mere acquaintance. To prove this it needed neither her rejoinder, nor the emphasis she gave it, saying,—

"*I don't care that for him!*" the *that* being a snap of her fingers.

"I wish father had but known you didn't."

"Why?"

"Well, it might have saved him the scene Gwenthian was witness to; and which must have been rather painful to both. After all, it may have been for the best. But, worst or best, I wonder where Master Trevor is making for now? It can't be Hollymead."

"Not likely, after what you've told me. But we shall soon see—at least whether he be coming up this way."

Both were familiar with the Forest roads—had ridden if not walked them all—knew their every turning and crossing. Where that from Mitcheldean descended into the Drybrook valley it forked right and left at the ford of the little stream where now there is a bridge known as the "Nail." Left lay the road to Coleford, right, another leading back out of the Forest by the Lea Bailey. And between these two branchings a third serpentined up the slope for Ruardean, over the ridge on which they stood.

While they were still regarding the horseman on the grey, and his groom behind, two other horsemen came in sight, riding side by side on the same slope, just commencing its descent. Again Sabrina's eyes flashed up with delight—that must be her expected one—riding alongside his servant.

While indulging in this pleasant conjecture, she was surprised at seeing still another pair of mounted men, filing out from under the trees, side by side also, and following the first two at that distance and with the air which seemed to proclaim them servitors.

"It may not be he, after all!" she reflected within herself, her brow again shadowing over. "He said he would be alone with only Hubert, and—"

Her reflections were brought to an abrupt termination by seeing the grey horse, after plunging across the stream, turn head uphill in the direction of Ruardean.

There was no time to make further scrutiny of the *quartette* descending the opposite slope. In twenty minutes, or less if he meant speed, he on the grey would be up to them; and if Reginald Trevor, that would be awkward, whether on his way to Hollymead or not.

It was Sabrina who now counselled hastening home; which they did with a quick free step their country training and Forest practice had made easy, as familiar, to them.

Chapter Eight
A House in Tudor Style

It would be difficult to imagine a more enchanting spot for a dwelling-place than that where stood Hollymead House. Near the north-western angle of the Forest of Dean, it commanded a view of the Wye where this beautiful stream, after meandering through the verdant meads of Herefordshire, over old red sandstone, assaults the carboniferous rocks of Monmouth, whose bold, high ridges, lying transversely to its course, look as if no power of water could ever have cut through them. But the Wye has, in its flow of countless ages, carved out—in Spanish-American phrase *cañoned*—a channel with banks here and there rising nigh a thousand feet above the level of its bed. Between these it glides with swift current; not direct, but in snake-like contortions, fantastically doubling back upon itself, almost to touching. Here and there cliffs rise sheer up from the water's edge, grand mural escarpments of the mountain limestone, such as show the "tors" and dales of Derbyshire. The Codwell rocks below Lydbrook, forming the base of the famed "Symonds' Yat," are of this character, their grim façades seamed and broken into separate battlements, giving them resemblance to ruined castles, but such as could have been inhabited only "in those days when there were giants on the earth."

The view from Hollymead House—better still from a high hill or "tump" above it—took in the valley of the river where it enters the carboniferous *strata* near Kerne bridge. There was no Kerne bridge then; the stream being crossed by ford and ferry, a mile further up. Looking is that direction, in the foreground was Coppetwood Hill, an oblong eminence embraced by one of the great sinuosities of the river, more than six miles in the round and less than one across the neck or isthmus. At this neck, perched on a spur of the hill o'erhanging the stream, stood a vast pile of building, the castle of Goodrich, on whose donjon floated a flag long ere Norman baron set foot on the soil of England. For there the Saxon Duke Godric lorded it over his churls and swineherds; his iron rule at the Conquest replaced by that of the Marshalls, and later the Talbots, alike stern and severe.

Looking beyond, and north-westward, a wide stretch of country came under the eye, thickly wooded and undulating, the ancient kingdom of

Erchyn—now called Archenfield—backed in the far distance by a horizon of hills, many with a mountain aspect, and some real mountains, as the curious Saddlebow, with a depression or "col" between its twin summits; Garway, the Cerriggalch, and the long dark range of the Hatterals.

To the west was a very conglomeration of mountains, seemingly crowded against one another, yet all apart, each distinguishable by an outline and aspect of its own. Most conspicuous of these, the conical Sugarloaf, the two Skyrrids—one of them named Holy Mountain—and the Blorenge, all towering above the town of Abergavenny, which is surrounded and embraced by them as the arena of an amphitheatre by its outer and more elevated circle.

Sweeping round the sky line, north and north-east the eye was met by many a bold projection, as the Longmynds and Clee hills, with their blue basalt, and the Haugh wood, summit of the famed Silurian upcast of Woolhope. Farther on to the east the Malvern Beacons of true mountain aspect, remarkable from their isolation, but still more in that there the geologist can see rocks the earliest stratified on earth, some metamorphosed, and all trace of stratification destroyed; while there, too, are visible the rocks of igneous agency, upheaved both by plutonic and volcanic forces—the gneisses, basalts, syenites, and granites.

Eastward over the Forest edge could be seen, extending far as vision's verge, the wide plains of Worcester and Gloucester—as said, an ancient sea bed—through which now flows the yellow Severn; and on a clear day bends and reaches of this grand river might be distinguished glistening, gold-like, in the sun; the level expanse of its valley diversified by several isolated and curious eminences—hills and ridges—as May and Breddon due east, and, more to the south, the Mendips and Cotswolds.

Alone looking southward from Hollymead no mountains met the eye; in that direction only the undulations of the Forest itself, clad in its livery of green—all trees. But immediately in front of the house, and sloping gently away from it, was a wide and long stretch of park-like pasture land, where the trees stood solitary or in clumps, a double row of grand oaks bisecting it centrally, guarding and shading the avenue which led to the public road outside. This passed from Ruardean out of the forest by a steep descent down to Walford, thence on to Ross.

Architecturally, Hollymead House was a singular structure. For it was in the early Tudor style, built when bricks were a scarce and dear commodity, and timber, in the inverse ratio, plentiful and cheap. The walls were a framework of hewn oak—uprights, cross-beams, and diagonal ties—due to the handiwork of the carpenter, only the spaces between showing the skill of the mason. And, as if to keep ever in record the fact of this double yet distinct workmanship, the painter and whitewasher had been now and then called upon to perpetuate it by giving separate and severely contrasting colours to what was timber and the interspacing material of mortar and brick. The result a striped and chequered aspect of the oddest and quaintest kind. Sir Richard might have had it in his mind when he made the figurative allusion to a cage and pair of pretty birds. Still it was not exactly cage-shaped, but more like several set together, some smaller ones stuck against or hanging from a large one that stood central; the congeries due to a variety of wings, projecting windows, dormers, and other outworks.

Equally odd and irregular the arrangement inside. An entrance-hall with a wide stairway carried up around it, the oak balusters very beams, with a profusion of carving on them; on each landing, corridors dimly lighted leading off to rooms no two on the same level; some of them bed-chambers, only to be got at by passing through other sleeping apartments interposed between. And, turn which way one would, along passages, or from room to room, short flights of stairs, or it might be but a step or two, were encountered everywhere, to the imminent risk of leg or neck-breaking.

Though such a structure may appear strange to the modern eye, it did not so then, for there was nothing uncommon in it Hollymead House was but one of many like mansions of the day, though one of the largest and most imposing. Nor are they all gone yet. Scores of such still stand throughout the shires of the marches, and in perfect repair, to commemorate the architectural skill, or rather the absence of it, which distinguished our ancestry in the Tudor times.

The owner of Hollymead, Ambrose Powell, was a man of peculiar tastes and idiosyncrasies, some evidence of which appears in the baptismal names he had bestowed upon his daughters. A fancy, having its origin in the fact that from a hill above the house could be seen the two great western rivers, Wye and Severn—poetically, *Vaga* and *Sabrina*—themselves in a sense sisters, nurslings from the same breast of far Plinlimmon. From the summit of that "tump" his elder daughter had looked on her name-mother at a later date than she made pretence of when urging the younger up the ridge between Ruardean and Drybrook. It was a wild, witching spot, the grey rocks of mountain limestone here and there peeping out from a low growth of hazel, hawthorn, yew, and holly. But the summit itself was bare, affording on all sides a varied and matchless panorama of landscape. Being within the boundaries of their own domain, Sabrina oft climbed up to it; not for the view's sake alone, but because it was to her hallowed ground, sacred as the place where she had made surrender of her young heart, when she told Sir Richard Walwyn it was his. There was a pretty little summer house, with seats, and many an hour Ambrose Powell himself spent there, in the study of books and the contemplation of Nature—his delight. Not in a mere meditative way, or as an idle dreamer; but an active observer of its workings and searcher after its secrets. Nor did he confine himself to this, but also took an interest in the affairs of man, so strong as to have studied them in every aspect—probed the social and political problems of human existence to their deepest depths. Which had conducted him to a belief—a full, firm conviction—in the superiority of republican institutions; as it must all whose minds are as God made or intended them, and not perverted by prejudice or corrupted by false teachings. He was, in point of fact, a Puritan, though not of the extreme stern sort; in his ways of thinking rather as Hampden and Sir Harry Vane, or with still closer similitude to a people then scorned and persecuted beyond all others—the "Friends." It is difficult in these modern days, under the light of superior knowledge, and a supposed better discrimination between right and wrong, to comprehend the cruelties, ay barbarous atrocities, to which were submitted the "Friends," or, as commonly called, "Quakers." A people who, despite their paucity of numbers, did then, and since then have done and been doing, more to ennoble the national character of England than all the apostles of her Episcopacy, with her political boasters and military braggarts to boot. If neither the most notorious nor glorious, no names in England's history can compare in goodness and gracefulness with the Penns of 1640 and the Brights of 1880.

Though not a professed "Friend," Ambrose Powell was a believer in their faith and doctrines; and in his daily walk and life acted very much in accordance with them. But not altogether. From one of their ideas he dissented—that of non-resistance. Of a proud, independent spirit, despite his gentle inclinings, he would brook no bullying; the last man to have one cheek smitten and meekly turn the other to the smiter. Instead, he would strike back. A scene we are now called upon to record, and which occurred on that same evening, gives appropriate illustration of this phase of his character.

Chapter Nine
A Right Royal Epistle

The girls had got home, hard breathing, panting, from the haste they had made. But though supper was announced as set, they did not think of sitting down to it, but instead, entered the withdrawing-room, a large apartment, with windows facing front. In the bay of one of these, their dresses unchanged and their hoods still on, they took stand, with eyes bent down the avenue, all visible from the window. At intervals along the road they had heard behind them the trampling of hoofs, and knew from what horses it proceeded. The sounds, at first faint and distant, had grown more distinct as they reached the park gate, and they had come up the avenue with a run, to the surprise and somewhat alarm of their father, who at the time was outside awaiting their return.

Already in wonder at their being so late, he would have inquired into the cause. But they anticipated him by at once telling him where they had been, what seen, and who, as they supposed, was advancing along the Ruardean road.

This last bit of intelligence seemed greatly to excite him; and while his daughters watched from the window, he himself was also keeping vigil in the porch outside. After hearing what they had to say, he had remained there, letting them pass in.

For a time the gaze of all was fixed on the park entrance, at the lower end of the long avenue, where a massive oak gate traversed between two piers of mason-work, old and ivy-mantled. Only for a short while were they kept in suspense. The flurried girls had barely got back their breath when a grey horse was seen, with head jam up against the gate, his rider bending down in the saddle to undo its fastenings.

In an instant after it was pushed open, and they saw Reginald Trevor come riding on towards the house, for they were now sure of its being he. He was yet at too great a distance for them to read the expression upon his face; but one near enough might have noted it as strange, without being able to interpret it. All the more because of its seeming to undergo constant and sudden changes; now as one advancing reluctantly to the performance of some disagreeable duty, wavering and seeming half-inclined to back out of it; anon, with resolution restored through some opposing impulse, as anger, this shown by the fire flashing in his eyes.

Never had he ridden up that avenue swayed by such feelings, or under the excitement of emotions so varied or vivid. Those he had hitherto felt while approaching Hollymead House were of a different nature. Confident always, or, if doubting, not enough to give him any great uneasiness. Vaga Powell resist him! She, a green country girl; he, a skilled, practised Lothario, conqueror in many a love combat! He could not think of failure. Nor would he have thought of it yet, believing the sole obstruction to his suit lay in the father. But now he had to face that father in a way likely to make his hostility more determined—turn it into very hate, if it was not so already.

In truth, a *rôle* of a very disagreeable kind was Reginald Trevor called upon to play; and more than once since entering on it he had felt like cursing Sir John Wintour in his heart—the King as well.

As he drew near to the house, and saw the two fair faces in the window—a little surprised seeing hoods over their heads at that hour—he more than ever realised the awkwardness of his errand. And, possibly, if at that last moment Vaga Powell had come forth, as oft before, to give him greeting, or even bestowed a smile from where she stood, he would have risked all, forgiven the insult he had received, and left his duty undone.

But no smile showed upon the girl's face, no glance gave him welcome; instead, he saw something like a frown, as never before. Only with a glimpse of that face was he favoured; Vaga, as he drew up in front, turning her back on him, and retiring into the shadowed obscurity of the room, whither her sister had preceded her.

It may have been only a seeming rudeness on their part, and unintentional. Whether or no, it once more roused his resentment against their father; who, still in the porch, received him with a countenance stern, as his own was vexed and angry.

There was a short interval of silence after the unexpected visitor had drawn up, still keeping to his saddle. He could not well dismount without receiving invitation; and that was not extended to him, much less word of welcome. Moreover his presence there, after what had passed, not only called for explanation, but by all the rules of politeness required his giving it before aught else should be said.

He did not, however; seeming embarrassed, and leaving the master of Hollymead no choice but to take the initiative. Which the latter at length did, saying sourly, and somewhat satirically—

"What may you be wanting with me, Mr Reginald Trevor? I take it your business is with *me*."

"With you it is," brusquely returned the other, still further nettled at the way he was addressed.

"Have the goodness then to tell me what it is. I suppose it's something that can be settled by you in the saddle. If not, you may alight and come indoors."

Speech aggravating, terribly insulting, as Ambrose Powell intended it should be. He had long ago taken the measure of the man, and wished to drive him to a distance, even further off than he had already done. His last words were enough, without the contemptuous look that accompanied them. But, stung by both, the emissary of Sir John Wintour stood proudly up in his stirrups, as he replied, with a touch of satire too,—"No need, sir, to enter your very hospitable house, or even get off my horse's back. My errand can be accomplished by delivering this at your door. But, as you chance to be in it, permit me to hand it direct to you."

While speaking he had drawn from under the breast of his doublet a folded sheet, a letter, on which was a large disc of red wax, stamped with the King's seal.

The master of Hollymead was not so impolite as to refuse taking the letter from his hands; and, as soon as in his own, he tore it open and read,—

"For Ambrose Powell, Gentn.

"Trustie and well-beloved, Wee greete you well. Having obserued in the Presidents and custome of former times that all the Kings and Queenes of the Realme, vpon extraordinary occasions, haue vsed either to resort to those Contributions, which arise from one generalitie of Subiects, or to the priuate helpes of some well affected in particular, by way of loane: In which latter course Wee being at this time inforced to proceed, for supply of some portions of Treasure for diuers publique seruices, and particularly for continuing and increasing our magazins in some large proportion in our Realme of Ireland, in our Nauie, and in our ffortes: in all which greater summes have been expended of late, both in building and repairing, and in making sundry prousions, than haue bene in twentie yeares before: We haue now in Our Eye an especiall care, that such discretion may be obserued in the choise of the lenders, and such an indifferent distribution, as the summes that Wee shall receiue may be raised with an equall Consideration of men's abilities: And therefore, seeing men haue had so good experience of Our repayment of all those summes which we haue euer required in this kinde, Wee doubt not but Wee shall now receiue the like Argument of good affection from you (amongst other of Our Subiects), and that with such alacrity and readiness as may make the same so much the more acceptable, especially seeing Wee require but that of some which few men would deny a friend, and haue a minde resolued to expose all our earthly fortune for the preseruation of the generall. The summe that Wee require of you by vertue of these presents is three thousand Pounds, Which we do promise in the name of Us, our heires and successors, to repay to you or your Assignes within eighteene monethes after the payment thereof vnto the Commissioner. The person that we have appointed to receiue it is our worthy servant, Sir Jno. Wintour, To whose hands Wee do require you to send it within twelue days after you have receiued this Priuy Seale, which, together with the Commissioner's acquittance, shall be sufficient Warrant unto the Officers of our receipt for the repayment thereof at the time limitted.—Giuen under our Priuy Seale at our Pallace of Westminster.

"Carolus Rex."

So ran the curious communication put into the hands of Ambrose Powell.

A letter of "Loan by Privy Seal" even more execrable both as to grammar and diction than the documents emanating from Royalty at the present day—and that is admitting much.

Spoke the master of Hollymead, after perusing it:—

"Request for a loan, the King calls this! Beggarly enough in the beginning—a very whine; but at the end more like the demand of a robber!"

"Mr Powell!" cried he who had presented it, his back now up in anger, "though but the messenger of Sir John Wintour, at the same time I'm in the service of the King. And, holding his Majesty's commission, I cannot allow such talk as yours. It's almost the same as calling the King a robber!"

"Take it as all the same, if you like, sirrah! And apply it also to Sir John Wintour, your more immediate master. Go back, and say to both how I've treated the begging petition—thus!"

And at the word he tore the paper into scraps, flinging them at his feet, as something to be trampled upon.

At this Reginald Trevor became furious; all the more from again seeing two feminine faces in the window above, by their looks both seeming to speak approval of what their father had said and done.

He might have given exhibition of his anger by some act of violence; but just then he saw something else which prompted to prudence, effectually restraining it. This something in the shape of three or four stalwart fellows—

stablemen and servants of other sorts belonging to Hollymead House—who, having caught sound of the fracas in front, now appeared coming round from the rear.

No need for Reginald Trevor, noting the scowl upon their faces, to tell him they were foes, and as little to convince him of the small chance he and his varlet would have in an encounter with them. He neither thought of it nor any longer felt inclined to take vengeful action, not even to speaking some strong words of menace that had risen to his lips. Instead, choking them down, and swallowing his chagrin as he best could, he said, in a resigned, humble way,—

"Oh! well, Mr Powell; what you've done or intend doing is no affair of mine—specially. As you know, I'm here but in the performance of my duty, which I need not tell you is to me most disagreeable."

"*Very* disagreeable, no doubt!" rejoined the master of Hollymead, in a tone of cutting sarcasm; "and being so, the sooner you get through with it the better. I think you've made a finish of it now, unless you deem it part of this disagreeable duty to gather up those torn scraps of the King's letter, and carry them back to the Queen's obsequious servant, and your master, Sir John."

In the way of insult, taunt could scarce go farther. And he against whom it was hurled keenly felt it; at the same time felt his own impotence either to resent or reply to it. For the three or four fellows, with black brows, advancing from the rear, had been further reinforced, and now numbered nearly a dozen.

"I bid you good-evening, Mr Powell," said the emissary, as he turned his horse round, but too glad to get away from that unpleasant spot.

"Oh! good-evening, sir," returned the master of Hollymead, in a tone of mock politeness; after which he stood watching the ill-received visitor, till he saw him go out through the gates of his park.

Then over Ambrose Powell's face came a shadow—the shadow of a fear. For he knew he had offended a Royal tyrant, who, though now weaker than he had been through the restraint of a Parliament, might still have strength enough to tear him.

"My dear children," he said, as he joined them in the withdrawing-room, "the trouble I've been long anticipating has come at last. We will have to leave Hollymead, or I must fortify and defend it."

Chapter Ten
The Cousins

The sun had set as Reginald Trevor rode out of Hollymead Park. But he did not intend returning to Lydney that night; instead, purposed passing it in Ross, to which town he had also an errand. By making free use of the spur he might still reach his destination within the twilight.

Outside the park gate he was about turning in the Ross direction when he saw a party on horseback advancing from the opposite, as he had himself come. Four there were—two gentlemen in front, with their respective attendants a little behind. He could have shunned them by riding rapidly on before; but from the stylish appearance of one of the gentlemen he took it they were Cavaliers, possibly might be acquaintances; and after his long, lonely ride he was in the humour for company. It might help him some little to get over his chagrin. So he drew rein, and sate in his saddle waiting for them to come up.

There was a wide sweep of grass-grown turf between the park gate and the public road, and he had halted at the end of it on the right. Soon the party approaching reached the other, and he saw, with some surprise, and a little vexation, their horses' heads being turned in towards the gate. Whoever the gentlemen might be, they were evidently bent upon a visit to the house that had refused hospitality to himself.

With something more than curiosity he scanned them now. Were they known to him? Yes! one was; his surprise becoming astonishment, as in the more showily-attired of the two gentlemen he recognised his cousin Eustace.

"You, Eust!" he exclaimed, drawing his horse round, and trotting towards his kinsman; his glance given to the other being as that to a stranger; for he was not acquainted with Sir Richard Walwyn.

"You, Rej!" was the all-but echo of a response, and the cousins came together, Sir Richard passing on into the park. The gentleman tax-gatherer, still smarting under the rebuff given him, the smart shared by his servant, had ill-manneredly left the gate open behind them.

It was months since the cousins had met; though each knew where the other was, or ought to be. Hence Reginald's surprise to see Eustace there, supposing him to be engaged in his duties at Court. He spoke it inquiringly, as they held out to shake hands; but, before the other could make answer, he saw that which gave him a start—blood upon the hand extended to him! The white buckskin glove was reddened with it all over up to the gauntlets.

"God bless me, Eust! what's this? A wound! Have you been quarrelling?"

"Oh! nothing much. Only a little prick in the wrist."

"Prick in the wrist! But from what?"

"The point of a rapier."

"The deuce! Then you *have* been quarrelling. With whom, pray?"

"Speak a little lower, Rej. I'd rather *he* didn't hear us."

And Eustace nodded towards Sir Richard, who was not yet quite beyond earshot.

"Surely you don't mean the affair was with him?"

"I do—it was."

"He got the better of you?"

"Quick as you could count ten."

"Zounds! that's strange—you such a swordsman! But still stranger what I see now, your being in his company. Not his prisoner, are you?"

"Well, in a way I am."

"In that case, cousin, my sword's at your service. So let *me* try conclusions with him. Possibly, I may get you a *revanche*; at the same time release you from any *parole* you may be under."

Though, but the moment before, some little cowed, and declining a combat with serving men, Reginald Trevor was all courage now; and feared not to meet a gentleman in fair fight. For he saw that Trevor blood had been spilt, and, although he and his cousin Eustace had never been bosom friends, they were yet of the same family. The hot Cymric blood that ran in the veins of both boiled up in his to avenge whatever defeat his kinsman might have sustained, and without awaiting answer he asked impatiently,—

"Shall I follow, and flout him, Eust? I will if you but say the word."

"No, Rej; nothing of the sort. Thank you all the same."

"Well; if you're against it, I won't. But it edges a Trevor's teeth to see one of his kin—full cousin, too—worsted, conquered, dead—down as you seem to be. All, I suppose, from your antagonist being a bit bigger and older than you are. He's that as regards myself; for all I've no fear to face him."

"I know you haven't, Rej. But don't be angry with me for saying, if you did, it would end as it has with me—maybe worse."

The *ci-devant* gentleman-usher spoke with some pique. Notwithstanding the generous offer of his cousin to espouse his quarrel, there was that in the proposal itself which seemed to reflect on his own capability—a suggestion, almost an assertion, of patronising superiority.

"What do you mean, Eustace?" asked the other, looking a little roughed.

"That yonder gentleman," he nodded towards Sir Richard, now well out of hearing, "is a perfect master of both sword and horse. He proved himself *my* master in less than five minutes after engaging; could have thrust me in as many seconds had he been so disposed. While fighting with him I felt a very child in his hands; and he, as I now chance to know, was but playing with me. In the end he disarmed me—could have done it long before—by this touch in the wrist, which sent my rapier spinning off into the air. That isn't all. He has disarmed me in another sense; changed me from angry foe to, I might almost say, friend. That's why I've told you that I'm in a way his prisoner."

"It's a strange tale," rejoined Reginald, choking down his wrath. "All that, by sun, moon, and stars! But I won't question you further about it; only tell me why you are here. I thought you were so fixed in the Palace of Westminster, such a favourite of the grand lady who there rules the mart, you'd never more care to breathe a breath of country air. Yet here I find you in the Forest of Dean—its very heart—far away from court and city life as man could well get within England's realm. How has it come about, cousin?"

"I wouldn't mind telling you, Rej, if there was time. But there isn't. As you see, Sir Richard is waiting for me."

"Sir Richard who?"

"Walwyn."

"Oh, that's the name of your generous conqueror?"

"It is."

"I've heard of the individual, though never saw him till now. But how fell you into his company, and what brought about your quarrel?"

"Leave it, Rej, like other matters, till we meet again, and have more time to talk over such things."

"Agreed. Still there's time to say why you are going to Hollymead House."

"Hollymead House?"

"Oh, you didn't know that was the name of Ambrose Powell's place!"

"Ambrose Powell?"

"What! Nor yet the name of the man you're about to pay visit to?"

"I confess I do not."

"Nor anything else of him?"

"Nothing whatever."

He was on the point of adding, "Only that I've been told something about a pair of pretty girls," when it occurred to him he might be touching on a subject in which his cousin had a tender concern.

"'Pon my honour!" rejoined the latter, making an uphill attempt to laugh, "the tale grows stranger and stranger! You, of the King's Household, on your way to make acquaintance—friendly, of course—with one of his Majesty's greatest and most pronounced enemies—a man who hates King, Court, and Church; above all, bitter against your especial patroness, the Queen. I've heard him call her a Jezebel, with other opprobrious epithets."

"Odd in you, Rej, such a devoted Royalist, to have listened calmly to all that?"

"I didn't listen calmly; would have quickly stopped his seditious chattering, but for—"

"For what?" asked the other, seeing he hesitated.

"Oh, certain reasons I may some day make known to you. Like yourself, Eust, I have some secrets."

Eust thought he could give a good guess at one of them, but mercifully forbore allusion to it.

"But," he said, with an air of pretended surprise, "you've been just visiting this terrible king-hater yourself, Rej? If I mistake not, you came out of the park. You were up to the house, were you not?"

"I was."

"And has it shaken your loyalty, or in any way weakened it?"

"On the contrary, strengthened it. My errand to Ambrose Powell, with the reception he vouchsafed me—the ill-grained curmudgeon—has had all that effect."

"Then you've been quarrelling, too! Have you any objection to tell me what about?"

"Not the slightest. I was the bearer of a letter of Privy Seal to him—for a loan. Sir John Wintour, as you may be aware, has been appointed one of the King's Commissioners of Array for West Gloucestershire and the Forest. You know I'm in his service, which will make the matter understandable to you."

"And you haven't got the money? I needn't ask; there's the signs of refusal in your face."

"Got the money! Zounds! no. Instead, the recusant tore the letter into shreds, and flung them at his feet; defying me, Sir John, King, and all! Ah! well; that won't be the end of it. I shall be sure of having occasion to visit Hollymead again, and ere long! Next time the tables will be turned. But, cousin, after hearing what I've told you, are you still in the mind to go on to that seditious den? If you take my advice, you'll turn your back on Hollymead House, and come along with me. I'm making for Ross."

"To take your advice, Rej, would be to do as rude a thing as a man well could—ruder than I ever did in my life. Disloyal, too—doubly so; I should be traitor to gratitude, as to courtesy. Indeed, I've trenched scandalously on good manners now, by keeping yonder gentleman so long waiting for me."

He nodded towards Sir Richard, who had halted at some distance up the avenue.

"Oh, very well," sneeringly rejoined Sir John Wintour's emissary. "Of course, you can do as you like, Eust. I'm not your master, though yonder gentleman, as you call him, seems to be. Good-evening!"

And with this curt leave-taking, the sneer still on his face, he dug the spurs deep into his horse's ribs, and went off at a gallop along the road for Ross.

Chapter Eleven
Three Curious Characters

"Yee-up, Jinkum! Yee-up!"

The exclamations were accompanied by the thwack of a stick over the hips of a donkey half-hidden under a pair of panniers.

"Don't press the poor creetur, Jack. It be a hardish climb up the pitch. Gie't its time."

"But you know, Winny, the panners be most nigh empty—more's the pity."

"True o' that. But consider how fur's been the day. Seven mile to Monnerth—a good full load goin'—an' same back, whens we be home. An't han't had thing to eat, 'cept the pickin's 'long the roadside."

"All the more reezun for gittin' 'im soon home. I'd lay wager, if the anymal kud speak, 't 'ud say the same."

"Might. But, for all that, him's rightdown tired. If him want, there wud be no need yer slappin' he. Don't slap him any more, Jack."

"Well, I won't. Yee-up, Jinkum! I 'ant a-goin' to gi' ye the stick agen. 'Nother mile, and ye'll be back to yer own bit o' paster in the ole orchart, whar the grass'll be up to yer ears. Yee-up!"

At which Jinkum, as though comprehending the merciful disposition towards him, and grateful for it, seemed to improve his pace.

The speakers were a man and woman, both of uncommon appearance— the man a diminutive specimen of humanity, who walked with a jerking gait, due to his having a wooden leg. The woman was taller than he, by the head and shoulders quite; while in every other way above the usual dimensions of her sex. Of a somewhat masculine aspect, she was withal far from ill-favoured—rather the contrary. Her gown of coarse homespun, dust-stained and *délabré*, could not conceal a voluptuous outline of figure; while to have her eyes and hair many a queen would have been glad to give the costliest jewel in her crown. The complexion was dark, the features of a gipsy type—though she was not one—the hair, a very hatful, carelessly coiled around her head, black as the wing of a crow. The first thought of one beholding her would be: "What a woman, if but washed and becomingly clad?" For both skin and dress showed something more than the dust that day caught up from the road—smouches of older date. Despite all, she was a grand, imposing personage; of tireless strength, too, as evinced by her easy, elastic step while breasting that steep pitch on her twenty-second mile since morning. The journey seemed to have had little effect on her, however it may have jaded Jinkum.

Notwithstanding the disparity in size between the man and woman—a good deal also in their age, he being much her senior—they bore a certain resemblance to one another. It lay in their features and complexion; Jack having a gipsyish look, too. Nor any wonder at their being some little alike, since they were *not* man and wife, but brother and sister—both born Foresters. There was nothing in the character of either at all disreputable, though their business was such as usually brings suspicion on those who follow it. Known all over the forest, and for miles around it, as cadgers, they trafficked in every conceivable thing by which an honest penny might be made, though their speciality was the transport of fowls, with other products of the farmyard, to the markets of Ross and Monmouth— generally on freight account—taking back such parcels as they could pick up. Ruardean was their port of departure and return; their home, when they were at home, being a cottage in the outskirts of that elevated village.

Rarely, if ever, were "Jerky Jack"—the soubriquet his gait had gained for him—and his big sister seen apart; Winny, or Winifred—for such was her baptismal name—being a valuable helpmate to him. Some said she was more—his master.

That day they had been to Monmouth market, and now, at a late hour of the evening—after sunset—they were climbing Cat's Hill on their return homeward. As already said, there was then no Kerne bridge, and they had crossed by the ferry at Goodrich; a roundabout way to where they now were, but unavoidable—making good the woman's estimate of the distance.

Up the remainder of the pitch, Jerky kept his word, and no more stick was administered to Jinkum. But before reaching the summit the tired animal was treated to a spell of rest, for which it might thank a man there met, or rather one who dropped upon them as from the clouds. For he had come slithering down a steep shelving bank that bordered the road, suddenly presenting himself to their view outside the selvage of bushes.

Notwithstanding his *impromptu* appearance, neither showed sign of alarm nor surprise. Evidently they expected him; for but the minute before a sound resembling the call of the green woodpecker—the "heekul," as known to them—had reached their ears, causing them to turn their eyes toward the direction whence it came. From the wood, where, of course, they could see nothing; but there was a peculiarity in the intonation of the sound, telling them it proceeded not from the throat of a bird, but was in some way made by a man. That the woman knew how, and who the man, she gave evidence by saying, "That be Rob!" as she spoke a pleased expression coming over her countenance.

Whether Rob or no, he who so mysteriously and fantastically presented himself to their notice was a man of aspect remarkable as either of them. In size a Colossus; dark-complexioned like themselves, with full beard, and thick shock of brown-black hair standing out around his neck in curls and tangles. His coat of bottle-green cloth—amply skirted—and red plush waistcoat, showed creased and frowsy, as if he had passed the previous night, and many preceding it, in a shed or under a tree. For all, there was something majestic in his mien, just as with the woman—a savage grandeur independent of garb, which could assert itself under a drapery of rags.

As the three came together, he was the first to speak, more particularly addressing himself to Jerky. For the sister had a little side business to transact, plunging her hand into one of the panniers, and bringing forth a basket, out of which the neck of a bottle protruded.

"Well, Jack! What's the news down Monnerth way?" was the commencement of the colloquy.

"Lots, Rob; 'nough if they were wrote out on paper to fill them panners, an' load the donkey down."

Jinkum's owner was of a humorous turn, and dealt in figures of speech, often odd and varied as his bills of lading.

"Tell us some o' 'em," requested Rob, placing himself in an attitude to listen.

"Well," proceeded the cadger, "it be most all 'bout politicks there now, wi' rumours o' war, they say be a brewin'. The market war full o' them rough 'uns from Raglan side, Lord Worster's people, bullyin' everybody an' threetenin' all as wudn't cry out for the King."

"Ay;" here interposed the big sister, with a sneer, "an' you cried it, Jack—shouted till I was afeerd you'd split yer windpipe. That ye did!"

"And if I did," rejoined Jack, excusing himself, "how war I to help it? If I hadn't they'd a throttled me; may-be pulled off my wooden leg, and smashed my skull wi't. An' ye know that, Winny. A man who'd a said word there favour o' the Parlyment wud a stud good chance o' gettin' tore limb fro' limb. Tho' I han't two for 'em to tear sunderwise, I wasn't the fool to go buttin my head 'gainst a wall when no good could come o't. If I did cry 'Long live the King!' I thinked the contrary, as Rob knows I do."

"That do I, Jack, right well. A true free-born Forester, as myself, I know you ha' no leanin' like as them o' Monnerth and Lydney; Royalists an' Papists, who want to make slaves o' us, both body and soul, an' keep us toilin' for them an' their fine-dressed favourites—devil burn 'em!"

Having thus delivered himself, the free-born Forester dropped conversation with Jerky, confining it to the sister. For which Jack gave them an opportunity, shrewdly guessing it was desired. Once more saluting Jinkum with a "yee-up!" he started the animal off again up the hill, himself stumping briskly after.

Chapter Twelve
A Combat in a Quarry

The man and woman left behind, as they stood *vis-à-vis*, presented a striking appearance. Such a pair in juxtaposition were a sight not often given to the eye. He some inches the taller—though well matched as regarded the distinction of the sexes; but both of towering stature, with air so commanding that one, who could have seen them there and then, would not have given a thought to the coarseness of their apparel, or, if so, instantly forgetting it. Looking at their faces, in their eyes as they met in mutual gaze, he would have noticed something of a nature to interest more than any quality or fashion of dress—the light of love. For they loved one another warmly, and, perhaps, as purely and tenderly, as if their hearts had been beating under robes of silk.

No words of love passed between them now. If they intended speaking such, they held them in reserve till matters more pressing should be disposed of.

Upon these the man entered at once, asking,—

"Heerd you anythin' 'bout me, Win?"

"Yes, Rob."

"What?"

"They have been wonderin' how ye managed to get out o't gaol, an' blame Will Morgan for lendin' ye a hand. Day afore yesterday a party came over from Lydney wi' that young officer as be wi' Sir John Winter—Trevor I think they call him."

"Yes; that's the name. I know him well enough—too well. 'Twas he as took me in the High Meadows."

"Oh! it was. Well; he hev taked Will, too, an' carried him away to Lydney, where Sir John ha' now got a gaol o' his own. There wor some trouble 'bout it; the Lord Herbert, who's governor at Monnerth, claimin' him as his prisoner. But the other sayed as yours wor a case o' deer-stealin' in the Forest, an' Will had helped, ye ought both be taken before Sir John an' tried by him, he bein' head man o' it. Then Lord Herbert gave in, an' let them take him off. Will did help ye a bit, didn't he?"

"More'n a bit. But for him, liker than not, I'd now be in theer lock-up at Lydney. Well, if he be goed there he mayn't ha' so long to stay as they think for — won't, if what I've heerd be true."

"What's ye heerd, Rob?"

"Some news as ha' just come down from Lunnun. It's sayed the King's been chased out o't, an' the Parlyment be now havin' it all theer own way. Supposin' that's the case, Sir John Winter won't hae it all his own way much longer. We Foresters'll deal wi' him diff'rent from what we've been a doin'. An' 'bout that I ha' got word o' somethin' else."

"What somethin'?"

"A man, they say's comin' down here — from Lunnun too. One o' the right sort — friend o' the people. Besides, a soldier as ha' seen foreign service, an' is reckoned 'mong the best and kindest of men."

"I think I know who ye mean, Rob. Ain't it Sir Richard Walwyn?"

"That's the man."

"He wor at Hollymead fore he went away to the wars. I've seed him many's the time. He used to often ride past our place, an' always stopped to ha' a word an' a joke wi' Jack. That makes me remember him; an' if I beant mistook somebody else ha' remembrance o' him in a different way, an' ain't like ever to forget him."

"Who?"

"One o' the young ladies o' Hollymead — the older 'un, Miss Sabrina. I ha' heerd as much from the house sarvints theer."

Just the shadow of a cloud had shown itself on Rob's brow as Win commenced giving her reminiscences of the knight who had been visitor at Hollymead and used to crack jokes with Jerky. It passed off, however, ere her relation came to an end.

"Well, dear Win," he said, speaking more tenderly from consciousness of having harboured an unjust suspicion; "they say Sir Richard be comin' down to raise soldiers for the Parlyment. If that be so, one o' the first to join him'll be Rob Wilde; an' maybe the biggest, if not best, in the fightin' line."

"You'll be the best, Rob; I know you will. Who could equal you?"

At which she threw open her arms, then closed them around his neck, covering him with kisses.

In all probability, many soft words and much tender concourse would have succeeded this outburst of admiration. But the opportunity was not allowed them. Just then they heard a clattering of hoofs, horsemen coming down the road from Ruardean, at a gallop.

Rob, setting his ears to listen, could tell there were two of them, but nothing more—nothing to admonish him whether they were friends or enemies. But with the consciousness of having stolen deer and broken jail, twenty to one on their being the latter, reflected he. In any case prudence counselled him hiding himself, and letting the horsemen pass on.

His first impulse was to spring back up the bank, leaving the woman in the road. They could have nothing against her, whoever they were. But they were near now, still riding rapidly, and before he could scramble to the summit of the slope would be sure to see him. Just then, a hiding-place handier, and more easily accessible, came under his eye; a break in the bank just opposite, which he knew to be the entrance to an old limestone quarry, long abandoned. He would be safe enough in there, at least from observation by any one passing down the road. Whether or no, it was now Hobson's choice with him; the trampling was louder and clearer; and but for an abrupt bend of the road above he could have seen the horsemen, as they him. No alternative, therefore, but to cut into the quarry; which he did—the woman with him.

Scarce were they well inside it, when the hoof-strokes ceased to be heard. The horses had been suddenly pulled up; a colloquy ensuing.

"Hullo, Jerky!" it begun. "On your way from Monmouth market, I suppose?"

"Yes, yer honour; jist that."

"But where's your big sister? I've met you scores of times along the roads, though never without her. I hope there's nothing amiss?"

"Oh! nothin', sir. She be wi' me now, close by, coming up the pitch, only ha' legged a bit behint."

"Well, Jack, I won't detain you; as I must not be lagging myself. I want to reach Ross before the night's on. Good-bye, old cadge!"

At which the dialogue came to an end, and the hoof-strokes were again heard, now coming close.

Only for a minute or so, when a second colloquy was entered upon, this time one of the voices being different.

Rob Wilde knew them both; had long ago recognised the one that held speech with the cadger, and had reason to feel keenly apprehensive as he listened. Far more now, as the words of the later dialogue dropped upon his ears.

"Old Timber-toes said his sister was just behind. I don't see anything of her; and certainly she's not one there should be any difficulty in making out—even at a league's distance. Hey! what the deuce is that?"

And Reginald Trevor again reined up. For it was he, with his servant.

"A basket, it appears to be, Captain," answered the man, "with a bottle in it. Yes," he added, after drawing closer, lifting it from the ledge, and peering into it. "Something besides the bottle—bread, cheese, and bacon."

"Where there's so much smoke there should be some fire," reflected his master, who had halted in the middle of the road. Then, thinking it odd he saw nothing of the cadger's sister, and noticing the gap leading into the quarry, it occurred to him she might be there. Partly out of curiosity, and partly from an intuition, which the basket of provisions had done something to inspire, he headed his horse at the opening and rode in.

Soon as inside, an exclamation rose to his lips, in tone which told of more than surprise. There was triumph, exultation, in it. For there saw he, not only the woman missing from the road, but a man, the same who had been for some time missing from Monmouth Gaol. The bushes in the old quarry were not thick enough, nor tall enough, to give either of them concealment; and they were standing erect, without further attempt at seeking it.

"Ho—ho! my giant," cried the officer. "It's here you are; making love to Jerky's sister. And a pretty pair of love-birds too! Ha! ha! That explains the basket of eatables and drinkables. What a pity to interrupt your billing and cooing! But I must. So master Rob, deer-stealer and jail-breaker," he added drawing his sword. "Come along with me! You needn't trouble about bringing the basket. In the Lydney lock-up I'll see to your being fed free of expense."

"When you get me there," rejoined Rob, in defiant tone, as he spoke pulling from under the breast of his doublet a long-bladed knife, and setting himself firm for defence.

This was unexpected by the King's officer, who had not thought or dreamt of resistance. It was there, however, in sure, stern shape, and he felt himself committed to overcoming it. With a prick of his spur he sprang his horse forward, and straight at Rob, as though he would ride over him, his sword held ready for either cut or thrust.

But neither gave he, nor could. As the horse's head came close to him, the Colossus lunged out with long arm, and sent the point of his knife into the animal's nostrils, which caused it to rear up and round, squealing with pain. This brought its rider's back towards the man who had pricked it; and before he could wheel again, Reginald Trevor was in the embrace of him he had jokingly called giant—realising that he had the strength of one, as he was himself dragged out of his saddle.

But they were not the only combatants in the quarry. For, following his master, the servant had made to assist him in his assault against the big man, taking no note of the big woman, or fancying she would not interfere. In which fancy he was sadly mistaken. For in scrimmage his back becoming turned upon her, as if taking pattern by Rob, she sprang up, caught hold of the lightweight groom, and jerked him to the ground, easily as she would have pulled a bantam cock from out one of the Jinkum's panniers.

In less than threescore seconds after the affair began, Reginald Trevor and his attendant were unhorsed, disarmed, and held as in the hug of a couple of bears.

"I'll let ye go," said Rob to his prisoner, after some rough handling, "when ye say you won't take advantage o' my gen'rosity by renewin' the attack. Bah!" he added, without waiting for response, "I'll put that out o' yer power."

Saying which, he caught up the officer's sword, and broke it across his knee, at the same time releasing him. The blade of the attendant was treated likewise, and both master and man were permitted to rise to their feet, feeling vanquished as weaponless.

"You can take yourselves off," sneeringly said the deer-stealer; "an' as ye talked 'bout bein' in Ross 'fore nightfall, you'll do well to make quick time."

Not a word spoke Reginald Trevor in reply, nor thanks for the mercy shown him. Too angry was he for that; his anger holding him speechless because of its very impotence. In sullen silence he regained the bridle of his horse—like himself having lost spirit by copious bleeding of the nose—climbed back into the saddle, and continued on down Cat's Hill, his varlet behind him, both swordless, and yet more crestfallen than when they rode out through the gate of Hollymead Park.

"We're in for it now, Win," said Rob, to the cadger's sister, after seeing them depart. "An' we've got to look out for danger. I'm sorry 'bout you havin' to share it; but maybe 'twon't be so much, after all. Once Sir Richard gets here, an' the fightin' begins, as it surely must soon, trust me for takin' care o' ye."

"I will—I do, Rob!"

And again the great arms were thrown around his neck, while upon his lips were showered a very avalanche of kisses.

Chapter Thirteen
Looking Forward to a Fight

Some truth was there in the report that had reached Rob Wilde, of the King being chased out of London. Though not literally chased, after his display in the House of Commons, ludicrous as unconstitutional, he found the metropolis too hot for him. Moreover, there was a whisper about impeaching the Queen; and this arch *intrigante*, notwithstanding her high notions of Royal right, was now in a fit of Royal trembles. Strafford had lost his head, Laud was in prison, likely to lose his; how knew she but that those bloodthirsty islanders might bring her own under the axe? They had done as much for a Queen more beautiful than she. Mobs daily paraded the streets, passing the Palace; the cry, "No bishops!" came in through its windows, and Charles trembled as he thought of his father's significant epigram, "No bishop, no king." So out of Whitehall they slipped—first to Windsor to pack up; the Queen, in fine, clearing out of the country, by Dover, to Holland.

It was a backstairs "skedaddle" with her; carrying off as much plunder as she could in the scramble—chests of jewels of unknown but fabulous value, as that represented as having been found in the isle of Monte Cristo. Enough, at all events, to hold Court abroad; maintain regal surroundings; even raise an army for the reconquest and re-enslavement of the people she had plundered.

It is unpleasant to reflect on such things, far more having to speak of them. Sad to think that though England is two centuries and a half older since Charles Stuart and Henrietta de Medici did all in their power to outrage her people and rob them of their rights, this same people is to-day not a wit the wiser. The late Liberal victory, as it is called, may be urged as contradicting this allegation; but against that is to be set the behaviour of England's people, as represented by their Parliament for the last six years, sanctioning and endorsing deeds that have brought a blight on the nation's name, and a cloud over its character, it will take centuries to clear off. And against that, too, the spirit which seems likely will pervade in this new Legislative Assembly, and the action it will take. When the Long Parliament commenced its sittings, the patriots composing it never dreamt of letting crime go unpunished. Instead, their first thoughts and acts were to bring the betrayers of their country to account. "Off with his head—so much for Strafford!"

"To the Tower with Laud and the twelve recalcitrant bishops!"

"Clear out the Star Chamber and High Commission Court!" "Abolish monopolies, Loans of Privy Seal, Ship-tax, Coal and Conduit money, with the other iniquitous imposts!" And, *presto!* all this was done as by the wand of a magician, though it was the good genius then guiding the destinies of England. Off went Strafford's head; to the Tower was taken Laud; and the infamous royal edicts of a decade preceding were swept from the statute-book, as by a wet sponge passed over the score of a tapster's slate.

What do we see now? What hear? A new Parliament entering on power under circumstances so like those that ushered in the "Long" as to seem almost the same. And a Ministry gone out who have outraged the nation as much as did the Straffords, Digbys, and Lauds. But how different the action taken towards them! No Bill of Attainder talked of, no word of impeachment, not even a whisper about voting want of confidence. Instead of being sent to a prison, as the culprits of 1640, they of 1880 walk out of office and away, with a free, jaunty step and air of bold effrontery, blazoned with decorations and brand new titles bestowed on them—a very shower, as the sparks from a Catherine wheel!

Verily was the lot of Thomas Wentworth, Earl of Strafford, laid in unlucky times. Had he lived in these days, so far from losing his head, it would have been surmounted by a ducal coronet. And Laud, already at the top of the ecclesiastical tree, with no possibility of hoisting him to higher earthly honours, would have had heavenly ones bestowed on him by being enrolled among the saints.

Though merely writing a romance, who will say that in this matter I am romancing? The man that does must be what Sir Richard Walwyn pronounced him who is not a Republican; and back to Sir Richard's *dictum* I refer him.

Soon as Charles had got his Queen safe out of harm's way, he betook himself to York, there to enter upon more energetic action. For there he felt safer himself, surrounded by a host of hot partisans. In political sentiment, what a curious reversion has taken place since then between the capitals of the North and South—almost an exchange! Then York was all Royalist, and as a consequence filled with the foes of Liberty; London full of its friends. Now the former has mounted to the very hill-top of Liberal aspiration; the latter sunk into the slough of a shameful retrogression!

But the thing is easily explained. Those who dwell in the kingdom's capital are nearer to the source of contamination. There Bung and Beadledom, with their vested rights, hold sway; there the scribblers who wear plush find encouragement and promotion; while the corrupting influence of modern finance has nursed into life and strength a swarm of gamblers in stocks, promoters of bubble companies, tricksters in trade, and music-hall cads—a sorry replacement of the honest mercers and trusty apprentices of the Parliamentary times.

Once separated from his Parliament, the King had an instinct that all friendly intercourse between it and himself would soon be at an end; this nursed into conviction by the Hertfords, Digbys, and other like "chicks" who formed his *entourage*. Active became he now in adopting precautions, and taking measures to sustain himself in the struggle that was imminent. And now more industrious than ever in the way of money raising; anew granting monopolies, and sending letters of Privy Seal all over the land, wherever there seemed a chance of enforcing their demands—for demands were they, as we have seen. To Sir John Wintour had been entrusted some scores of these precious epistles, with authority to deliver them, collect the proceeds, and send them on to replenish the royal exchequer; and it was one such Reginald Trevor saw torn into scraps on the porch of Hollymead House.

This same Sir John was what Scotchmen would call a "canny chiel." Courtier, and private secretary to the Queen, he had come in for a goodly share of pilferings from the public purse; among other jobs having been endowed with the stewardship of the Forest of Dean, with all its privileges and perquisites. Appointed one of the Commissioners of Array for West Gloucestershire, he had built him a large mansion in the neighbourhood of Lydney—the White House as called—though it is not there now, he with his own hand having afterwards set the torch to it. But then, on the clearing out of the Court from London, Sir John had cleared out too, going to his country residence by Severn's side, which he at once set about placing in a state of defence. None more clearly than he foresaw the coming storm.

It seemed to him near now when Reginald Trevor returned to the White House and reported his reception at Hollymead, with the defiant message to himself and his King. But Sir John was not a man of hot passions or hasty resolves. Long experience as a courtier had taught him to subdue his temper, or, at all events, the exhibition of it. So, instead of bursting forth into a furious display, he quietly observed,—

"Don't trouble yourself, Captain Trevor, about what Ambrose Powell has said or done. It won't help his case any. But," he added reflectingly, "there seems no particular call for haste in this business. Besides, I'm expecting an addition to the strength of our little garrison. To-morrow, or it may be the day after, we shall have with us a man, if I mistake not, known to you."

"Who, Sir John?"

"Colonel Thomas Lunsford."

"Oh! certainly; I know Lunsford well. He was my superior officer in the northern expedition."

"Ah! yes; now I remember. Well; I have word of his being *en route* hither with some stanch followers. When he has reported himself, allowing a day or two for rest, we'll beat up the quarters of this recusant, and make him repent his seditious speech. As for the money, he shall pay that, every pound, or I'll squeeze it out of him, if there's stock on the Hollymead estate, or chattels in his house worth so much."

There was something in the "recusant's" house Reginald Trevor thought worth far more—one of the recusant's daughters. Of that, however, he made no mention. To speak of it lay not in the line of his duties; and even thinking of it was now not near so sweet as it had been hitherto. Little as he liked Colonel Lunsford, he would that night have been glad of him for a boon companion—in the bowl to help drown the bitter remembrance of his adventures of the preceding day.

Chapter Fourteen
A Hawking Party

"Hooha-ha-ha-ha!"

The cry of the falconer, followed by a whistle, as the hawks were unleashed and cast-off.

Away went they, jesses trailing, and bells tinkling, in buoyant upward flight. For the heron that had risen out of the sedge, intending retreat to its heronry, at sight of the enemy after it, suddenly changed direction, and was now making for upper air with all its might of wing.

The hawks were a *cast* of "peregrines" of the best strain. In perfect training, it needed no repetition of the *hooha-ha-ha-ha* to encourage them; for, as soon as their hoods were off, they had sighted the enemy, and shot like arrows after it.

At first their flight was direct—a *raking off*—but in drawing nearer the doomed bird it changed to gyrations as they essayed to mount above it. The heron, in a phrenzy of fright, uttered its harsh "craigh," disgorged the contents of its crop, with a view of lightening itself, and made a fresh effort to escape skyward. In vain! The falcons, with quicker stroke of wing, notwithstanding their spiral course, were soon seen soaring over it. Then the foremost—for one was ahead—having gained the proper height, with spread "train," and quivering "sails," poised herself for the "*stoop*." Only a second; then down swooped she at the quarry, "arm" outstretched and "pounces" set for *raking* it.

The attempt was unsuccessful. Rarely is heron touched at the first stoop. Unwieldy, and sluggish of flight as the creature may appear, it has a wonderful capacity for quickly turning, and can long elude hawk or falcon, if there be but one. When doubly assailed, however, by a *cast*, of trained peregrines, it is at a disadvantage, not having time to recover itself from the stoop of the one till the other is upon it.

So was it with this. In an instant after, the second shot down upon it with a squeal, the heron again giving out its "craigh," and then the two, hawk and heron, were seen clinging together. For this time the bird of prey had not attempted to *rake* but *bind*; and bound were they, the pounces of the falcon stuck fast in the flesh of its victim. Then followed a convulsive flapping of wings, the two pairs beating against one another, soon to be joined by a third; for, meanwhile, the first falcon having soared up again, once more poised herself and stooped, she also binding to the common quarry.

The aerial chase was now at an end, but not the combat. Unequal as this was, the heron still lived; and, when the three should come to earth, might impale either or both its adversaries on that long lance-like beak it but unskilfully wields in the air. To prevent this, the falconer hurried off for the spot towards which they were descending. Slowly they came down, upheld by the united fluttering of their wings, but reached the ground at length, luckily not far off. And when the falconer got up he gave out a loud "whoop," signal of the quarry killed. For he saw that the heron was dead, and the peregrines had already commenced depluming it.

Other voices joined in the *paean* of triumph; one of sweet, silver tones, accompanied by the clapping of a pair of pretty hands. They were the same voice and hands that on the top of Ruardean Hill had hounded on the dog Hector in his half-playful demonstration against the donkey.

"I knew my pair of 'Pers' would do it in good style!" cried Vaga in exultation, for she was the owner of the peregrines. "Did any of you ever see a kill quicker than that?"

The interrogatory was put to a trio of individuals beside her, on horseback as herself—one of them her sister, the other two Sir Richard Walwyn and Eustace Trevor. There was an *entourage* of attendants, the falconer with his helps, mounted grooms, and dogs quartering the sedge—in short, a complete hawking party from Hollymead House. For, notwithstanding his gentle inclinations, Ambrose Powell was no foe to field sports—rather favoured them when not unnecessarily cruel; and, though rarely indulging in them himself, put no restraint on his daughters' doing so. The younger was passionately fond of hawking, and the elder also relished it in a more sober way—it being then regarded as a proper pastime for ladies.

The hawking party, whose incidents we are chronicling, came off some ten days after the arrival of Sir Richard Walwyn and Eustace at Hollymead; the scene being a strip of marsh with a stream filtering through it, here and there a pool where the moor-hen coquettishly flirted her tail—a favourite haunt of the heron, as of teals, widgeons, and wild ducks. That the knight was still sojourning at Hollymead House need be no matter of surprise; but why the son of Sir William Trevor had not long ere this reported himself under the parental roof, by Abergavenny, may seem a very puzzle.

Its explanation must await the record of after events; though; an incident occurring there and then, with speech that accompanied, may throw some light upon it.

Vaga's question was rather in the way of an exclamation, to which she did not expect reply. Neither waited for it; but giving the whip to her palfrey trotted off to where the falconer was engaged in releasing the dead heron from the pounces of the hawks. She went not alone, however; Eustace Trevor having pricked his animal with the spur, and started after, soon overtaking her. The other pair stayed behind as they were.

A hundred yards or so round the edge of the marsh, and the two who had ridden off came to a halt. For, by this, the falconer having rehooded the hawks, and retrieved the quarry, met them, heron in hand, holding it out to his mistress; as would one, first up at the death of a fox, present Reynard's brush to some dashing Diana of the field.

A splendid bird it was; the white heron or great egret, a rare species, even then, though not so rate as now.

"Give it to the pers, Van Dorn!" she directed, after a short survey of it; despite its rarity, showing less interest in it than under other circumstances she might have done. "Unhood again, and let them have it. We forgot to bring the doves for them, and they deserve reward for the way they both *bound* it—so cleverly."

Van Dorn, a Hollander from Falconswaerd—whence in those days all falconers came—bowing, proceeded to execute the command, by removing their hoods from the hawks.

"Before he surrenders it to their tender mercies, may I ask a favour?"

It was Eustace Trevor who interrogated, addressing himself to the young lady.

"Of course you may. What is it, sir?"

"Leave to appropriate a few of the heron's feathers."

"Why, certainly! The falconer will pluck them for you. Van Dorn, pull out some of its feathers, and hand them to this gentleman. I suppose you mean those over the train, Mr Trevor?"

"Yes, they."

"You hear, Van Dorn."

Without that the man knew what was wanted; the loose tail coverts so much prized for plumes; and, drawing them out one by one, he bound them into a bunch with a piece of cord whipped round their shanks; then handed them up to the cavalier. After which he went off to attend upon his hawks.

There was a short interregnum of silence as the falconer turned his back on them, and till he was out of earshot. Then the young lady asked, with apparent artlessness,—

"But, Mr Trevor, what do you intend doing with the heron's feathers?"

"Pluming my hat with them."

"Why, it's plumed already! and by far showier ones!"

"Showier they may be; but not prettier, nor so becoming. And certainly not to be esteemed as these; which I shall wear as souvenir of a pleasant time—the pleasantest of my life."

There was a pleased expression in her eyes as she listened to what he said; still more when she saw what he did. This, to whip the hat from his head, pluck the *panache* of ostrich feathers from its *aigrette* and insert those of the heron in their place. Something he did further seemed also to give her gratification, though she artfully concealed it. Reproach on her lips, but delight in her heart, as she saw him tear the displaced plume into shreds, and toss them to the ground at his horse's feet.

"How wasteful you are, Mr Trevor?" she exclaimed, reprovingly. "Those foreign feathers must have cost a great deal of money. What's worse, you've spoiled the look of your hat! Besides, you forget that those now on it came from a conquered bird?"

"All the more appropriate for a plume to be worn by me."

"Why so, sir?"

"Because of my being vanquished, too."

"*You* vanquished, Mr Trevor! When? where? By whom?" she asked, at the same time mentally interrogating herself. Could he be alluding to that combat in which he received the wound brought with him to Hollymead, the story of which had leaked out, though not told by either combatant. Or, was he hinting at conquest of another kind?

There was an indescribable expression on her countenance as she sat awaiting his answer—keen anxiety, ill-concealed under an air of pretended artlessness.

"Vaga!"

It was not he who pronounced her name; though "Vaga," with "Powell" adjoined, were the words nearest to his lips. She would have given the world to hear him speak them. But it could not be then. Her sister had called to her, at that moment approaching with Sir Richard. Most ill-timed approach, for it interrupted a dialogue which, allowed to continue, might, and likely would, have ended in declarations of love—confessions full and mutual.

Chapter Fifteen
"Dear Little Mer"

"Turn and turn, sister," said Sabrina, as she rode up. "You've had sport enough with your great eagles. Suppose we go up to the hill, and give my dear little Mer a cast-off?"

"Dear little Mer" was a merlin, that sate perched on her left wrist, in size to the peregrines as a bantam cock to the biggest of chanticleers. Withal a true falcon, and game as the gamest of them.

Why its mistress proposed changing the scene of their sport was that no larks nor buntings—the merlin's special quarry—were to be met with by the marsh. Their habitat was higher up on the ridge, where there was a tract bare of trees—part pasture, part fallow.

To her sister's very reasonable request Vaga did not give the readiest assent. The petted young lady looked, and likely felt, some little vexed at her *tête-à-tête* with Eustace Trevor having been so abruptly brought to an end. It had promised to make that spot—amid reeds and rushes though it was—hallowed to her, as another on the summit of a certain hill, among hazels and hollies, had been made to her sister. Whatever her thoughts, she showed reluctance to leave the low ground, saying in rejoinder,—

"Oh! certainly, Sab. But won't you wait till the dogs have finished beating the sedge?"

"If you wish it, of course. But you don't expect them to find another heron?"

"No; but there may be a widgeon or wild duck. After such an easy victory, I'm sure my pers would like to have another flight. See how they chafe at their hoods and pull upon the jesses! Ah, my beauties! you want to hear the *hooha-ha-ha-ha* again—that do you."

"Oh! let them, then," said the more compliant Sabrina, "if the dogs put up anything worth flying them at; which I doubt their doing. We've made too much noise for that."

The conjecture of the sage sister proved correct. For the marsh, quartered to its remotest corners, yielded neither widgeons nor wild ducks; only moorhens and water-rails—quarry too contemptible to fly the great falcons at.

"Now," said Sabrina, "I suppose you'll consent to the climbing?"

Her motto might have been *Excelsior*; she seemed always urging an uphill movement.

But there was no longer any objection made to it; and the canines being called out of the sedge, all entered the forest, riders and followers afoot, and commenced winding by a wood-path up the steep acclivity of Ruardean's ridge.

When upon its crest, which they soon after reached, the grand panorama already spoken of lay spread before their eyes. For they were on the same spot from which the young ladies had viewed it that day when Hector harassed the donkey. Neither of them bestowed a look upon it now; nor did Sabrina even glance at that road winding down from the Wilderness, off which on the former occasion she had been unable to take her eyes. Its interest for her no longer had existence; he who had invested it with such being by her side. Now she but thought of showing off the capabilities of "dear little Mer," as in fondness she was accustomed to call the diminutive specimen of the *falconidae*.

Ere long Mer made exhibition of her high strain and training—for the little falcon was also a female—sufficient to prove herself neither *tercel* nor *haggard*. First she raked down a lark, then a corn bunting; and at the third cast-off overtook and bound on to a turtle-dove, big as herself. For all she speedily brought it to the earth, there instantly killing it.

Just as she had brought this quarry to ground a cry was heard, which caused interruption of the sport,—

"Soldiers!"

It was the falconer who so exclaimed; for now that they were merlin-flying his services were scarce required, and one of his aids did the whistling and whooping. Left at leisure to look around, his eyes had strayed up the road beyond Drybrook, there to see what had called forth his cry.

Instantly all other eyes went the same way, more than one voice muttering in confirmation,—

"Yes; they're soldiers."

This was evident from their uniformity of dress—all alike, or nearly—as also by the glancing of arms and accoutrements. Moreover, they were in military formation, riding in file, "by twos"—for they were on horseback.

At sight of them all thoughts of sport were at an end, and the hawking was instantly discontinued. Mer, lured back to her mistress's wrist, was once more hooded, and the leash run through the *varvels* of her jesses; while the falconer and his helps, with the other attendants, gathered into a group preparatory to leaving the field.

Meanwhile, by no accident, but evidently from previous understanding, Sir Richard Walwyn and Eustace Trevor had drawn their horses together, at some distance from the spot occupied by the ladies, the knight saying,—

"It's Wintour's troop from Lydney, I take it. What do *you* think, Master Trevor?"

"The same as yourself. Nay, more, I'm sure of it, now. That's my cousin Rej at their head, on the grey mare, with the red feathers in his hat. You remember them?"

"I do. You're right; 'tis he. Somebody beside him, though, who appears to be in command. Don't you see him turn in his saddle, as though calling back orders?"

"Yes, yes;" was the repetitive rejoinder, Eustace Trevor, despite his late sojourn at Court, still retaining some of the idiomatic forms of Welsh colloquy. "But who are those in the rear?" he added, interrogatively.

His question had reference to a number of men afoot, neither in uniform nor formation, who were seen coming behind the horse troop, pressing close upon its heels. Women among them, too, as could be told by the brighter hues and looser draping of their dresses.

"People from Mitcheldean," answered Sir Richard, "following the troop out of curiosity, no doubt."

The knight knew better; knew that, but for himself, and some action he had lately taken, the people spoken of, or at least the majority of them, would not have been there. For, since his arrival at Hollymead, he had made many excursions unaccompanied—save by his henchman, Hubert— to Mitcheldean, Coleford, and other Forest centres, where he had held converse with many people—spoken words of freedom, which had found ready and assenting response. Therefore, as he now gazed at that crowd of civilians coming on after the soldiers, though his glance was one of inquiry, it was not as to who they were who composed it, but to make estimate of their numbers, at the same time comparing it with the strength of the troop.

There was no time left him to arrive at any exactitude. The horsemen were on the way to Hollymead, for sure; and he must needs be there before—long before them.

So the hawking party made no longer stay on Ruardean Hill, but a start and return homeward—so rapid as to seem retreat; the understrappers and other attendants wondering why it was so—all save Hubert.

Chapter Sixteen
Trouble Anticipated

On return for Hollymead, the hawking party did not pass through Ruardean, as it would have been round about. Nevertheless, Sir Richard went that way. At a forking of the forest paths the knight excused himself to the ladies, leaving Eustace Trevor to escort them home; he, with his own servant, turning off towards the village.

Some matter of importance must have influenced him to deviate from the direct route; and that it was pressing might be deduced from the speed to which he put his horse. Soon as parted from the others, he and Hubert made free use of their spurs, going in reckless gallop down the steepest pitches, nor drawing bridle till they had reached Ruardean. A small place then as now, of some two hundred houses, contiguous to a fine old church, and ancient hostelry opposite, the streets all declivities, with some scattered dwellings that radiated off into quaint nooks and by-ways.

The clattering of hoofs had brought faces to every window, and figures into every door; for this had been heard long before the two horsemen made their appearance. And now, as these came to a halt in front of the inn, their horses breathing hard, all eyes were bent upon them with inquiring curiosity.

"Wind your horn, Hubert!" commanded the knight, in an undertone, without waiting for any one to come up to them.

A command which Hubert instantly obeyed by drawing a small cornet from under his doublet, clapping it to his lips, and sounding the "Assembly." He had been troop-trumpeter in "the army that swore so terribly in Flanders," and so understood the cavalry calls.

No cavalry, however, answered this one, nor soldiers of any arm; though it was answered by what looked the right material for making soldiers. Before the cornet's notes had ceased reverberating from the tower of the church, and the walls of the old castle—then in ruins—men could be seen issuing from the doors of the nearer houses, others hastening along the lanes from those more remote, all making for the spot where the horsemen were halted.

In a few seconds nearly twenty had gathered, up and grouped around the horses; the expression on their faces showing that they understood the signal in a general way, but not the reason for its having been sounded to summon them just then. All looked inquiry, one putting it in the form of speech, —

"What belt, Sir Richard?" He who interrogated was a man of gigantic size, inches taller than any of the others. But something more than his superior stature privileged him to be first spokesman, as could be deduced from Sir Richard's answer.

"A troop coming from Lydney, Rob. They're through Drybrook by this, making for Hollymead. You and your friends will, no doubt, be there, too, curious to see how the soldiers behave themselves?"

"We'll be there, sure, Sir Richard. Rob Wilde for one, an' belikes a good many more."

"So well," rejoined the knight, with a satisfied look. Then leaning over on his saddle he whispered some words of a confidential character into the ear of the deer-stealer. After which, setting himself straight in the stirrups, he again set his horse into a gallop, and rode out of the village as rapidly as he had entered it.

"I hear they're coming, Sir Richard?"

"They are, Mr Powell. By all signs, it's the party you've been expecting. Indeed, there can be no doubt about its being Wintour's troop. One of the officers at its head we made out to be Master Trevor's cousin, as you've heard, I suppose?"

"Oh, yes. And of their purpose there can be as little doubt—to levy for that 3,000 pounds the King facetiously terms *loan*. A downright robbery, I call it."

"I too."

"What ought I to do, Sir Richard? I have the money in the house, and suppose I must give it to them. But if you say the word, I'll refuse."

"Let me leave the word unsaid till I see what sort of following is after them. There appeared to be a good many from Mitcheldean, likely to be joined by more at Drybrook, to say nothing of the contingent from nearer home. Everything must depend on their numbers and the spirit we find them in."

"I understand," said the other, with an assenting nod, "and will trust all to you."

This brief dialogue was at the door of Hollymead House, its owner standing in the porch, Sir Richard still on horseback, just arrived from that passage at courier-speed through Ruardean. It ended by his dismounting and giving his horse to Hubert, with directions to take both their animals round to the stable-yard, and there keep them under saddle and bridle. Some other instructions were delivered to the same *sotto voce*. Then to the symphony of clanking spurs the knight ascended to the porch; and after a few more words exchanged with the master of the house, he passed on into the withdrawing-room.

His entrance was a welcome intrusion, as the company inside consisted of the awkward number three.

And soon they paired, each pair passing into the embayment of a window, and there taking stand. Not to talk of love, or even think of it; though something equally serious occupied their thoughts—something less agreeable. All were alike imbued with an instinct of danger drawing nigh, and so close, their eyes were now on the alert, apprehensively gazing down the oak-shadowed avenue.

A few seconds more and they saw what they were expecting—horses, plumed hats, and the glancing of armour—a troop outside the park gate halted till its fastenings could be undone. In an instant it was dashed open, and soldiers seen filing through—the same as they had descried on the hill beyond Drybrook.

On came they up the avenue, without making stop till within fifty yards of the house, where they were again brought up at the entrance to the ornamental grounds. These were enclosed by a *haw-haw*; the causeway which crossed it having a gate also. And while this was being got open all four looking from the windows had now no difficulty in identifying Reginald Trevor in one of the officers at the head of the troop; while two of them at the same time recognised the other.

"Why, bless me!" exclaimed the ex-gentleman-usher, "that's Colonel Lunsford."

"As I live, Tom Lunsford!" was the almost simultaneous exclamation of the knight.

"Colonel Lunsford?" interrogated Vaga, addressing herself to him by her side.

"Tom Lunsford?" in like manner questioned Sabrina, but with more earnestness as she saw Sir Richard's brow suddenly darken. "Who and what is he?"

"One of the most notorious—but never mind, now. By-and-by we'll talk, of him. Like enough he'll favour us with a taste of his quality before leaving Hollymead. But," he added, the cloud upon his brow becoming darker, "if he do—."

The knight did not finish what was evidently intended to be a threat, partly because he saw fear coming over the face of his betrothed, and partly that the man for whom his menace was meant had got through the gate, and, with Reginald Trevor by his side, and the soldiers filing in behind them, was now close up to the house.

Chapter Seventeen
New Faces and Old Foes

While Colonel Lunsford and Captain Trevor were waiting for the haw-haw gate to be opened, they had seen the figures of two ladies outlined in the withdrawing-room windows—one in each. As yet the two gentlemen were not visible to them; these being behind and half-hidden by the arras curtains. As the officers came closer, with eyes still upon the windows, those of Lunsford, after a hasty glance at Vaga, remained fixed upon Sabrina in steadfast, earnest gaze, as on one for the first time seen, but eliciting instant admiration.

Trevor had eyes only for the younger of the sisters, his thoughts going back to the last time he had been there. He remembered it with bitterness, for he had fancied himself slighted; and, if so, the time had come for retaliation.

"What a beautiful woman! By the Cestus of Venus, a Venus herself!"

It was the ex-Lieutenant of the Tower who thus exclaimed.

"Which?" queried Reginald Trevor, with more than common interest. Well knew he the flagitious character of the man who was once more his commanding officer.

"Which? What a superfluous question! The tall—the dark one—of course. Yellow hair isn't to be compared with her for a moment."

"Perhaps not," rejoined Trevor, pretending assent, glad to think his military superior was not likely to be his rival in love.

"*Certes*, both seem beauties in their different styles," ran on the reprobate. "Who'd ever have expected such a pair in this out-of-the-way corner of creation? I wish Sir John had given us orders to take up quarters in Hollymead House for a week or two. That may come yet when the devil!"

His final ejaculation had nought to do with what preceded. The mention of his Satanic majesty was due to his having caught sight of a face behind that he was in the act of admiring, but the face of a man. A man well-known to him—one he hated, yet feared, as could be told by the scowl instantly overspreading his countenance, along with a whitening of the lips.

Nothing of this observed Reginald Trevor, whose features changed expression at the same time, his thoughts all absorbed in what he saw for himself—the face of another man at the other window in close proximity to that of Vaga Powell.

"Eustace still here! What the deuce can that mean?"

Both exclamation and question were unspoken, though accompanied by a sharp pang of jealousy. Some presentiment of this he had felt before, on the evening when he met his handsome cousin at the gate of Hollymead Park, going on to the house. And here was Eustace yet, when by all the rules he should have been gone days ago, standing by the girl's side, apparently on terms of the most friendly familiarity!

He was not permitted to see them side by side much longer; nor Lunsford the other pair. For Sabrina, becoming indignant at the bold glances the latter was directing upon her, moved away from the window, Vaga doing the same; the two finally retiring from the room.

Another change of tableaux took place by Sir Richard appearing at the window occupied by the ex-gentleman-usher—which was that nearest the door—as he did, saying,—

"Master Trevor; I want you to be witness—see and hear for yourself how your Cavaliers and King's officers comport themselves. If I mistake not, you'll have an opportunity now."

In the words, as well as tone, was conveyed an insinuation which, ten days before, Eustace Trevor would have resented by drawing sword; all the more that his own kinsman came in for a share of it. He had no thoughts of doing so now. Since then his sentiments, social as political, had undergone a remarkable change; and he but answered the observation by pressing in to the window, till his face almost touched the glass.

By this Lunsford had halted, and formed his troop from flank to line, fronting the house. The movement brought the cousins face to face at close distance, Eustace bowing in a frank, familiar manner. The cold, distant nod vouchsafed in return would have surprised and perplexed him but for a suspicion of the cause. His own conscience had whispered it.

All this while was Ambrose Powell standing in the porch, just as when he gave reception to Reginald Trevor delivering that letter of Privy Seal so contemptuously torn up. Nor looked he now repentant for having torn it; instead, defiant as ever. For he had cast his eyes over and beyond the men in uniform, taken stock of those out of it, compared numbers, and made mental estimate of the chances for a successful resistance. A word, too, had reached him from inside; spoken from the door of the withdrawing-room by Sir Richard Walwyn. So that when Colonel Lunsford approached, in the swaggering way he had been accustomed to in the Low Country, he was met with a firm front and look of calm defiance. It all the more irritated the King's officer, thinking of him he had observed inside; and with the soldiers at his back, supposing himself master of the situation, all the more determined him to show his teeth.

"You are Ambrose Powell, I take it?" were his first words, spoken without even the ceremony of a salute, as he brought his horse's head between the supporting columns of the porch.

"Ambrose Powell I am, sir," responded the Master of Hollymead. "If you doubt my identity," he added, in his old satirical tone, "I refer you to the gentleman by your side. He knows me, if I mistake not."

This was a shaft shot at Reginald Trevor, further stinging him, too. But it was not his place to reply; and he bore it in sullen silence.

"Oh!" lightly ejaculated Lunsford, "it don't need the formality of Captain Trevor's endorsement. I'll take it for granted you're the man I want."

He spoke as might a policeman of modern days about to "run in" some unfortunate infringer of the laws.

"The man you want! And pray what for?"

"Only to pay your debts."

"Debts, sirrah! I have no debts."

"Oh, yes, you have. And right well you know it, Master Powell. Maybe you'd prefer my calling it your dues. Be it so."

"Nor dues, neither; I owe no one anything."

"There I beg leave to contradict you. You owe the King three thousand pounds; just dues for maintenance of the State; your share of Supply for its necessary expenses. As I understand, you've been asked for payment already, and refused. But now—"

"Now I do the same. The King will get no three thousand pounds from me?"

"He will."

"No—never!"

"Yes, now! This day; this very hour. If you don't give it willingly, why I must take it from you; must and shall. Possibly you haven't so much money in the house. No matter for that. We can levy on your plate, of which, I'm told, you've got good store—glad to know it. I'm in earnest, Master Ambrose

Powell, and mean what I say. When Tom Lunsford has a duty to do, he does it. So make no mistake; I'm not the man to go back empty-handed."

"If you be Tom Lunsford," sneeringly retorted the Master of Hollymead, "not likely. I've heard of you, sir. Robbers as you rarely leave any place empty-handed."

"Robbers!" cried the colonel, now furious. "How dare you apply such epithet to me—an officer of the King?"

"I dare to the King's self—if he stood there beside you."

"A curse upon you, caitiff! You shall rue your rash words. Know, sir, that I have the power to punish sedition as recusancy. But I won't palter speech with you any longer. Do you still refuse to lend the money—pay it, I should rather say?"

"Oh! you needn't have taken the trouble to correct yourself. It's a demand all the same. The 'stand and deliver' of a highwayman. But you shall have an answer. I still refuse it."

"Then it shall be taken from you, sirrah?"

"If so, *sirrah*, 'twill be under protest."

"Under protest be it. As you like about that; devil care I. Ha-ha-ha!" and Lunsford laughed again. Then turning to the troop, he called out to his first sergeant,—

"Dismount, Robins, and follow me with a couple of files?"

Saying which, he flung himself out of the saddle, and made to ascend the steps of the porch.

"You don't enter my house by an open door," cried the Master of Hollymead, stepping backward. "You'll have to break it in first," he added, gliding into the hallway, dashing the door to behind him, and double-bolting it inside.

Almost immediately after strong oaken shutters, moved by invisible hands, were seen to close upon all the windows of the lower story, till Hollymead House looked as though its inmates had suddenly and mysteriously abandoned it.

Chapter Eighteen
"Resist!"

In his defiant refusal the Master of Hollymead, as already said, had received encouragement by a word spoken from the withdrawing-room. It was after the ladies had passed out of it; Sir Richard, who had followed them to the door, simply saying, "Resist!" It was said in a significant tone though, and loud enough to be heard by him who stood in the porch. For the knight had now made up his mind to some sort of action, as yet known only to himself; and but returned to the window to get further informed of the chances in favour of it.

Judging by the sparkle of his eyes, they seemed satisfactory, each moment becoming more so. He had already taken stock of the soldier troop, counted its files—less than twenty—saw that half of them were but "Johnny Raws" in uniform; while the crowd beyond them numbered nigh two hundred. Not all men; but such women as were among them had the look of being able to do man's work, even in the way of fighting. Nor were they all unarmed, though no warlike weapons were conspicuously displayed. Here and there could be seen hands holding hedge forks, or grasping hatchets, bill-hooks, and hay-knives; others carrying long-shafted hammers and mattocks—tools of the mining industry peculiar to the Forest. All implements denoting peace; but readily convertible into weapons with which could be dealt deadly blows.

Sir Richard had taken all this in, as the soldiers came to a halt at the haw-haw gate. And now that they were inside it, looking over their heads from the high window, he saw something else, for which he had been anxiously watching—another crowd on its way up the avenue, smaller than that already arrived, but more compact, and apparently under discipline. All men these, with one at their head, taller by inches than any of those behind him, easily recognisable as Rob Wilde.

The deer-stealer had been true to his promise, and done his work well; for not only was the Ruardean contingent a large one, but carried real war weapons—here and there a matchlock and *snap-hans*, with pikes and halberds held high above their heads—a bristling array of them.

It was just then, on catching sight of these, that Ambrose Powell retreated from the porch, and in, dashing to his door. For Sir Richard's doings in the days past were all known to him, and why he had gone out of his way, and lingered behind the hawking party at Ruardean.

At the same moment the knight made a hasty movement away from the window, as he did so saying, —

"Now, Master Trevor! Time's come for action. I'm not going to let our good host be plundered without an effort to prevent it. Of course you can do as you like — remain neutral if it so please you."

"But it don't so please me," promptly responded the ex-gentleman-usher. "If there's to be fighting, I draw swords too."

"On which side?"

"Oh, Sir Richard! Why do you ask that? After what I've just seen and heard, you might know. Never was I aware that the King sanctioned such doings as these, nor will I be the one to abet them. Besides, you seem to forget my debt to yourself — my life; and I've been longing for an opportunity to pay it. My sword is at your service, as my heart, ever since you conquered both."

"Eustace Trevor!" exclaimed the knight, with more than ordinary warmth, "I now know that you are not only my friend, but the friend of our cause, which is that of country and humanity. Your generous offer of alliance delights me, and I am grateful for it. But all the more reluctant you should compromise yourself with your father — your people. Reflect before drawing you sword! Among those we are to fight with — if it come to that — is your own kinsman, your cousin, and you may have to cross blades with *him*."

"Be it so. I have reflected, and well, before espousing your cause. 'Tis now more to me than cousin — a matter of conscience. Reginald's on the wrong side — I the right one; and if we must cross swords, let him take the consequences as will I."

Not often in man's face might be seen such expression as came over that of Sir Richard Walwyn while listening to these determined words. The handsome youth he had made chance acquaintance with on the road, liking him at first sight; continuing to like him notwithstanding their adverse political faith; reluctant to quarrel with him; refusing it till there was no alternative with honour — this youth, now no more enemy either to him or his cause, but friend of both, professed and sure of proving true — at thought of all this the eyes of the soldier knight sparkled with an ecstatic joy which they alone can feel who fight for country, not king.

"Enough!" he said, grasping the youth's hand and warmly pressing it. "Glad am I to think you will be with us. Swords such as yours were an accession to any cause; and ere long, even now, there may be fine opportunity for you to prove it—baptise your new faith in the blood of Freedom's foes. Come with me!"

Their dialogue had occupied but a brief interval of time; and as the knight brought it to an end, he strode hastily out into the hall, spurs still on and clanking. There to encounter their host, also hurrying about, and shouting to his domestics to shutter the windows. The door he had already made secure.

In the hallway the three came together, but only for a few moments to remain so. The occasion called for quick, instant action, allowing scant time for speech. Nor was there much said; Sir Richard hurriedly saying to their host,—

"Tell the ladies not to be alarmed. Say that Mr Trevor and I have gone out to reason with those rude visitors of yours, and see what terms we can make with them. If they won't listen to—"

Whatever the alternative meant he left it unspoken, for chancing to turn his eyes up the stairway, he there saw that he was being listened to already. On its lowest landing were the sisters, who had overheard all.

They were coming down, and now came on; Sabrina gliding forward to the knight, and laying her hand on his shoulder. He had stepped a little apart to receive her, with anticipation of something she might have to say confidential, and with her, he, too, wanted a word of that kind.

"Oh, Richard!" she tremblingly exclaimed, "what are you going to do? Nothing rash, I hope?"

"Certainly not, dearest. Have you ever known me to act rashly?"

"No; but now—"

"Well, now. I'm not likely to change my ways. In what I intend there may be no danger after all. A little risk true, but for a big stake. No less than three thousand pounds these royal miscreants demand from your father, and will have it if we don't do something. But we will, and they won't get it—not this day, unless I'm mistaken about the men who are gathering outside. Ah! we'll match them, never fear."

He then spoke some words in a whisper, not to be overheard by the servants still rushing to and fro, which seemed further to reassure her.

"Now, love! let me go," he said, in conclusion. "There isn't a second to spare. Mr Trevor and I must out."

She neither questioned nor tried to detain him longer. Whatever he meant doing, she could confide in him; if to fight, believed him capable of conquering the whole world, and wisely ruling it after. For the woman who loves there is no fancy too wild, no feat seeming impossible to him who has her heart.

More constrained was the speech passing neat at hand, for there were three taking part in it. Yet not less anxious than her sister seemed Vaga,—if anything in greater distress about the danger apprehended. Possibly but for her father being beside her, she would have addressed Eustace Trevor in a strain similar to that of Sabrina appealing to Sir Richard. As it was her looks were eloquent of fear for him, mingled with a confidence in his power to hold his own, whatever was to happen.

The scene was short—of not more than a minute's duration—and ended by the two gentlemen guests of Hollymead House making all haste out of it—not by the front door, but one at back, which opened into the stable-yard.

Soon as on its stoop, Sir Richard called out,—"Horses, Hubert! Quick!" And quick they came. In an instant after, Hubert was seen leading two out of their stalls, another pair being led behind by the servant of Eustace Trevor. Saddled and bridled all; for word had been sent out before, and everything was ready—even to the varlet having been warned by the veteran and gained over to the good cause, now his master's.

In twenty seconds' time all four were in the saddle, men as masters setting themselves firm in the stirrups, taking tight hold of the reins, with a look to their swords to see there was no entanglement against unsheathing them.

Then, at a word from Sir Richard, the yard gate, hitherto shut, was thrown open, and out they all burst, spurring to a brisk canter as they rode round for the front of the house.

Chapter Nineteen
In the Midst of a Mob

The people who had followed the soldiers were still outside the haw-haw; a file of troopers having been stationed by its gate to prevent their passing through. They could easily have sprung over out of the *fosse*, but for some reason seemed not to care for it.

Lunsford, after dismounting, had rushed up into the porch, but too late to hinder the shutting of the door; at which he was now thundering and threatening to adopt the alternative he had been dared to.

"We shall certainly break it in," he cried out in a loud voice, "if not opened instantly."

This eliciting no response from inside, he added,—

"Burst it in, men! Knock it to pieces!"

At which the sergeant and a file of troopers, now also in the porch, commenced hammering away with the butts of their dragon-muzzled muskets. But they might as well have attempted to batter down the walls themselves. Not the slightest impression could they make on the strong oaken panels. They were about to desist, when something besides that caused them suddenly to suspend their strokes, Lunsford himself commanding it. He at the same time sprang down from the porch and back to his saddle, calling on them to do likewise.

Odd as might seem his abrupt abandonment of the door-breaking design, there was no mystery in it. A cry sent up by the crowd of people had given him notice of something new; and that something he now saw in the shape of four horsemen sweeping round from the rear of the house. These were also outside the haw-haw, having crossed it by another causeway at back. A second shout greeted them as they got round to the front, and drew bridle in the midst of the crowd—a cheer in which new voices joined; those of the Ruardean men, just arrived upon the ground.

"Foresters?" cried Sir Richard, as they gathered in a ring around him, "will you allow Ambrose Powell to be plundered—your best friend? And by Sir John Wintour—your worst enemy?"

"No—never! That we won't?" answered a score of voices.

"Well, the soldiers you see there are Sir John's, from Lydney, though wearing the King's uniform?"

"We know 'em—too well!"

"Have seen their ugly faces afore."

"Curse Sir John, an' the King too?" were some of the responses showered back. Then one, delivering himself in less disjointed but equally ungrammatical phrase, took up the part of spokesman, saying,—

"We've niver had a hour o' peace since Sir John Wintour ha' been head man o' the Forest. He've robbed us o' our rights that be old as the Forest itself, keeps on robbin' us; claims the mines, an' the timber, an' the grazin' as all his own. An' the deer, too! Yes, the deer; the wild anymals as should belong to everybody free-born o' the Manor o' Saint Briavel's. I'm that myself, an' stan' up here afore ye all to make protest agaynst his usurpins."

That the speaker was Rob Wilde might be deduced from allusion to the deer, pronounced with special emphasis. And he it was.

"We join you in your protest, Rob; an'll stan' by you!" cried one.

"Yes! All of us!" exclaimed another.

"An' we'll help enforce it," came from a third. "If need be, now on the spot. We only want some 'un as'll show us the way—tell us what to do."

At this all eyes turned on Sir Richard. Though personally a stranger to most of them, all knew him by name, and something more—knew how he had declared for Parliament and people, against King and Court, and that it was no mere private quarrel between him and Sir John Wintour which had caused him to speak as he had done.

"Theer be the gentleman who'll do all that," said Rob, pointing to the knight. "The man to help us in gettin' back our rights an' redressin' our wrong. If he can't, nobody else can. But he can and will. He ha' told some o' us, as much."

Another huzza hailed this declaration, for they knew Rob spoke with authority. And their excitement rose to a still higher pitch, when the knight, responding, said,—

"My brave Foresters! Thanks for the confidence you give me. I know all your grievances, and am ready to do what I can to help you in righting them. And it had best begin now, on the spot, as some one has just said. Are *you* ready to back me in teaching these usurpers a lesson?"

"Ready! That we be, every man o' us."

"Try us, an' see!"

"Only let's ha' the word from you, sir, an' well fall on 'em at once!"

"We're Foresters; we an't afeerd o' no soldiers—not sich raws as them, anyhow."

"Enough!" cried the knight, his eyes aglow as with triumph already achieved; for he now felt assured of it. Over two hundred of the Foresters against less than a sixth of that number of Lunsford's hirelings, he had no fear for the result, if fight they must. So, when he placed himself at their head, with Eustace Trevor by his side, their two armed attendants behind, and rode up to the gate guarded by the two troopers, he made no request for these to open it and let them pass in, but a demand, with sword unsheathed, and at back a forest of pikes to enforce it.

The guards at once gave way. Had they not, in another instant they would have been hoisted out of their saddles on the blades of weapons with shafts ten feet long. Alive to this danger, they briskly abandoned their post, giving the Foresters free passage through the gate.

During all this time the ex-Lieutenant of the Tower had scarce moved an inch from the spot where he remounted his horse. When he saw the four horsemen coming around the house, heard the enthusiastic shout hailing them, at the same time caught sight of the pikes and barbed halberds, whose blades of steel gleamed above the heads of the huzzaing crowd, his heart sank within him. For this brutal monster, "Bloody Lunsford" as he afterwards came to be called, was craven as cruel. He had swaggered at the front door as inside the Parliament House by the King's command; but there was no King at his back now, and his swaggering forsook him on the instant. He knew something of the character of the Foresters—his raw recruits knew them better—at a glance saw his troop overmatched, and, if it came to fighting, would be overpowered. But there was no fight, either in himself or his following; and all sat in their saddles sullen and scowling, but cowed-like as wolves just taken in a trap.

Chapter Twenty
"No Quarter!"

Straight on to the soldiers rode Sir Richard Eustace Trevor by his side, their mounted servants behind; the men afoot following close after in a surging mass. These, soon as well through the gate, extended line to right and left, turning the troop until they had it hemmed in on every side. Nor was it altogether the movement of a mob, but evidently under direction, Rob Wilde appearing to guide it more by signs and signals than any spoken words. However managed, the troopers now saw themselves environed by pikes and other pointed things—a very *chevaux de frise*—held in the hands of men whose faces showed no fear of them. For the country had not yet been cursed by a standing army, and in the eyes of the citizen the soldier was not that formidable thing as since, and now. Rather was the fear on the side of Lunsford's party, most of whom, Foresters themselves of the inferior sort, knew the men who stood confronting them.

Up to this moment no word had been spoken by their commanding officer, save some muttered speech he exchanged with Reginald Trevor. Nor did he now break the silence, leaving that to the intruders.

"Captain, or, as I understand you are now called, Colonel Lunsford," said Sir Richard, drawing up in front of him, "by the way you're behaving you appear to think yourself in the Low Countries, with rights of free forage and plunder. Let me tell you, sir, this is England, where such courses are not yet in vogue; and to be hoped never will be, even though a King authorise, ay, command them. But I command you, in the name of the people, to desist from them, or take the consequence."

Under such smart of words it might be supposed that a professional soldier and King's officer would have dared death itself, or any odds against him. It was of this the muttered speech had been passing between him and Reginald Trevor, the latter urging him to risk it and fall on. Whatever else, *he* was no dastard, and, though he had once given way on that same spot, it was not from cowardice, but ruled by a sentiment very different.

In vain his attempt to inspire his superior officer with courage equalling his own; no more would he have been successful with their followers, as he could see by looking along the line of faces, most of them showing dread of that threatening array of miscellaneous weapons, and a reluctance to engage them.

In fine, the ex-Lieutenant of the Tower made up his mind to live a little longer, even at the risk of being stigmatised as a poltroon. But, not instantly declaring himself—too confused and humiliated for speech—Sir Richard went on,—

"No doubt, sir, your delicate sense of humanity will restrain you from a conflict in which your soldiers must be defeated and their blood spilled uselessly—innocent lambs as they appear to be."

The irony elicited laughter from the Foresters; for a more forbidding set of faces than those of the troopers could not well have been seen anywhere.

"But," continued the knight, "if you decline to withdraw without showing how skilfully you can yourself handle a sword, I'm willing to give you the opportunity. You've had it from me before, and refused. But you may be a braver man, and think yourself a better swordsman now; so I offer it again."

The taunt was torture itself to the man in whose teeth it was flung. All the more from the cheering and jibes of the Foresters, who seemed thoroughly to enjoy seeing Sir John Wintour's bullies thus brought to book. And still more that in the window above were two feminine faces, one of them that he had been so late admiring, the ladies evidently listening.

Notwithstanding all, Lunsford could not screw up courage for a combat he had once before declined, and now the second time shunned it, saying,—

"Sir Richard Walwyn, I am not here for the settlement of private quarrels. When the time fits for it I shall answer the challenge you say is repeated, but which I deny. My business at present is with Mr Ambrose Powell, as Deputy-Commissioner of Array, to collect the King's dues from him. Since he's refused to pay them, and I have no orders, nor wish, to use violence, so far as shedding blood, it but remains for me to take back his answer to my superiors."

It was such a ludicrous breakdown of his late blustering, and withdrawal of demand, that the Foresters hailed it with a loud huzza, mingled with laughter and satirical speech.

When their cheering had ceased, so that he could be heard, Sir Richard rejoined,—

"Yes; that is the best thing you can do. And the sooner you set about it the better for both yourself and your men, as you may be aware without further warning."

It was like giving the last kick to a cur, and as a cur Tom Lunsford took it, literally turning tail—that of his horse—upon Hollymead House.

Out through the haw-haw gate rode he, his troop behind, every man-jack of them looking cowed and crestfallen as himself.

Alone Reginald Trevor held high front, retiring with angry reluctance, as a lion driven from its quarry by hunters too numerous to be resisted. But he passed not away without holding speech with his cousin, on both sides bitterly recriminative.

"So you've turned your back upon the King!"

It was Reginald who said this, having spurred up alongside the other before parting.

"Rather say the King has turned his back upon the people," was Eustace's rejoinder. "After such behaviour as I've just been witness to, by his orders and authority, I think I am justified in turning my back upon him."

"Oh! that's your way of putting it. Well; it may justify you in the eyes of your new friends here—very warm friends all at once?"—this with a sneer—"but what will your father think? He won't like it, I'm sure."

"I daresay he won't. If not, I can't help it."

"And don't seem to care either! How indifferent you've grown to family feeling! and in such a short space of time. You used to pass for the most affectionate of sons—a very paragon of filial duty; and now—"

"And now," interrupted the ex-courtier, becoming impatient at being thus lectured, "whatever I may be, I'm old enough, and think myself wise enough, to manage my own affairs, without needing counsel from any one—even from my sage cousin, Reginald."

"As you like, Eust. But you'll repent what you're doing, yet."

"If I should, Rej, it won't be with any blame to you. You can go your way, as I will mine."

"Ah! Yours will bring you to ruin—like enough your neck upon the block or into a halter!"

"I'll risk that. If there's to be hanging and beheading—which I hope there will not—it needn't be all on one side. So far, that you are on hasn't had the advantage in the beheading line, and's not likely. They who struck off Strafford's head might some day do the same with the King's own. And he would deserve it, going on in this way."

"By Heaven?" cried Reginald, now becoming infuriated, "the King will wear his head, and crown too, long enough to punish every traitor—every base renegade as yourself."

The angry bitterness of his speech was not all inspired by loyalty to King or throne. Those fair faces above had something to do with it; for the ladies were still there, listening, and he knew it.

Never was Eustace Trevor nearer to drawing sword, not to do it. But it was his kinsman—cousin; how could he shed his blood? That, too, late so freely, generously offered in his defence! Still, to be stigmatised as a "base renegade," he could not leave such speech unanswered, nor the anger he felt unexpressed.

"If you were not my cousin, Rej, I would kill you!"

He spoke in a low tone, trembling with passion.

"*You* kill *me*! Ha-ha! Then try, if you like—if you dare!"

And the King's officer made a movement as if to unsheath his sword.

"You know I dare. But I won't. Not here—not now."

It was with the utmost effort Eustace Trevor controlled himself. He only succeeded by thinking of what had been before. For it was no feeling of fear that hindered him crossing his sword with his cousin, but the sentiment hitherto restraining him.

"Oh, well!" rejoined Reginald. "We'll meet again—may be on the field of battle. And if so, by G—! I'll make you rue this—show you no mercy!"

"You will when you're asked for it."

"You needn't ask. When you see my sword out, you'll hear the cry, 'No Quarter!'"

"When I hear that, I'll cry it too."

Not another word passed between them, Reginald wheeling round and galloping off after the soldiers. And from that hour, in his heart, full of jealous vengeance, the resolve, should he ever encounter his cousin in the field of fight, to show him no quarter!

Chapter Twenty One
War in Full Fury

An interval of some weeks after the scenes described, and the war, long imminent, was on. All over England men had declared cause and taken sides; the battle of Edgehill had been fought, and blood spilled in various encounters elsewhere. For besides the two chief forces in the field, every shire, almost every hundred, had its parties and partisans, who waged *la petite guerre* with as much vigour, and more virulence, than the grand armies with generals commanding. Many of the country gentry retired within the walled towns; they who did not, fortifying their houses when there was a plausibility of being able to defend them, and garrisoning them with their friends and retainers. The roads were no longer safe for peaceful travellers, but the reverse. When parties met upon them, strangers to one another, it was with the hail, "Who are you for—King or Parliament?" If the answers were adverse, it was swords out, and a conflict, often commencing with the cry, "No Quarter!" to end in retreat, surrender, or death.

Looking at the allegiance of the respective shires to the two parties that divided the nation, one cannot help observing the wonderful similitude of their sentiments then as now—almost a parallelism. In those centres where the cavaliers or malignants held sway, their modern representatives—Tories and Jingoes—are still in the ascendant. With some changes and exceptions, true; places which have themselves changed by increase in population, wealth, refinement, and enlightenment—in short, all the adjuncts of civilisation. And in all these, or nearly all, the altered political sentiment has been from the bad to the better, from the low belief in Divine rights and royal prerogatives to a higher faith in the rights of the people, if not its highest and purest form—Republicanism.

From this standard rather has there been retrogression since that glorious decade when it was the Government of England. At the Restoration its spirit, with many of its staunchest upholders, took flight to a land beyond the Atlantic, there to breathe freely, live a new life, call into existence and nourish a new nation, ere long destined to dictate the policy and control the action of every other, in the civilised world. This "sure as eggs are eggs;" unless the old leaven of human wickedness—not inherent in man's heart, as shallow thinkers say, but inherited from an ancestry debased by the rule of prince and priest—unless the old weeds of this manhood's debasement spring up again from the old seeds and roots, despite all tramplings down and teachings to the contrary.

It may be so. The devil is still alive on the earth, busy as ever misleading and corrupting the sons of men; in many places and countries, alas! too triumphantly successful, even in that land *outre mer*, over the Atlantic.

At the breaking out of our so-called, but miscalled, "Great Rebellion," in the belt of shires bordering Wales, the Royalists were in the majority; perhaps not so much in numbers as in strength and authority. The same with Wales itself; not from any natural belief in, or devotion to, the thing called "Crown," but because this spirited people were under the domination of certain powerful and wealthy proprietors of the Royalist party, who controlled their action, as their political leanings. Of this Monmouthshire offers an apt illustration, where the Earl of Worcester, Ragland's lord, held undisputed sway to the remotest corners of the county.

Still, Wales was not all for the King; and where such influence failed to be exerted, as in Pembroke and Glamorgan in the south, and some shires and districts of the north, the natural instincts of the Welsh prompted them to declare for liberty, as they have lately done at the polls. From any stigma that may have attached to them in the seventeenth century they have nobly redeemed themselves in the nineteenth.

Of the bordering counties, Salop, as might be expected, stood strong for the King. The subserviency of its people—for centuries bowing head and bending knee to the despotic Lords of the Marches, who held court at Ludlow—had become part of their nature; hence an easy transfer of their obeisance to Royalty direct.

The shire of Worcester, closely connected with Salop in trade and other relationships, largely shared its political inclinations; the city of Worcester itself being noted as a nest of "foul malignants," till purged of them by the "crowning mercy."

As for Hereford county, with its semi-pastoral, semi-agricultural population, it espoused the side natural to such; which, I need hardly say, was not that of liberty. Throughout all ages, and in all countries, the bucolic mind has been the most easily misled, and given strongest support to tyranny and obstruction. But for it the slimy Imperialism of France would never have existed, and but for the same the slimier imitation of it in England would not have been attempted. Luckily, on this side of the English Channel there is not so much of the base material as on the other. When the Jew of Hughenden travestied country squire, patronising and bestowing prize smock-frocks on poor old Dick Robinson, he mistook the voting influence of Dick's farmer-master. It no longer controls the destinies of this land, and will never more do so if the Parliament now in power but acts up to the spirit which has so placed it. *Nous verrons!*

Returning to the times of England's greatest glory, and the shire of Hereford, this, though strongly Royalist, was not wholly so. Many of the common people, especially on the Gloucester shire side, were otherwise disposed, and among the gentry were several noble exceptions, as the Kyrles, Powells, and Hoptons; and noblest of all. Sir Robert Harley, of Brampton Bryan—relentless iconoclast. If the name of Sir Richard Walwyn be not found in the illustrious list, it is because the writer of romance has thought fit to bestow upon this valiant knight a fictitious *nom de guerre*.

But the western shire entitled to highest honours for its action in this grand throe of the nation's troubles was undoubtedly Gloucester—glorious Gloucester. When the lamp of liberty was burning dim and low elsewhere over the land, it still shone bright upon the Severn's banks; a very blaze in its two chief cities, Gloucester and Bristol. In both it was a beacon, holding out hope to the friends of freedom, near and afar, struggling against its foes, in danger of being whelmed, as mariners by the maddened ocean.

To the latter city, as a seaport, the simile may be more appropriate, though the former is equally entitled to a share in its credit. But Bristol most claims our attention now, as it was in 1642, under the mayoralty of Aldworth. A main *entrepôt* and emporium of commerce with the outside world, it was naturally emancipated from the narrow-minded views and prejudices of our insular nationality; not a few of its citizens having so far become enlightened as to believe the world had not been created solely for the delectation of royal sybarites, and the suffering of their subjects and slaves. Indeed, something more than the majority of the citizens of Bristol held this belief; and, as a consequence, showed their preference for the Parliament at the earliest hour that preferences came to be declared. So, when Colonel Essex, son of the Earl of like name—Lord General of the Parliamentary army—was sent thither commissioned as its military governor, no one offered to dispute his authority; instead, he was received with open arms.

But ere long the free-thinking Bristolians made a discovery, which not only surprised but alarmed them. Neither more nor less than that the man deputed by the Parliament to protect and guard their interests showed rather the disposition to betray them. If living in these days, Colonel Essex would have been a Whig, with a leaning towards Toryism. As Governor of Bristol in 1642 he inclined so far to Cavalierism as to make boast of not being a Crophead, while further favouring those who wore their locks long and prated scornfully of Puritans and Quakers. At the time there was a host of these long-haired gentry in Bristol, prisoners whom Stamford had taken at Hereford, under *parole*, and the indulgent colonel not only kept their company, but joined them over their cups in sneers at the plebeian Roundheads, who lacked the gentility of blackguardism.

Luckily for the good cause, the tongue of this semi-renegade outran his prudence; his talk proving too loud to escape being heard by the Parliament, whose ears it soon reached, with the result that one fine evening, while in carousal with some of his Cavalier friends, he was summoned to the door, to see standing there a man of stern mien, who said,—

"Colonel Essex! 'Tis my disagreeable duty to place you under arrest."

"Place me under arrest!" echoed the military governor of Bristol, his eyes in amazement swelling up in their sockets. "What madman are you, sirrah?"

"Not so much madman as you may be supposing. Of my name, as also reason for intruding upon you so inopportunely, I take it this will be sufficient explanation."

At which the stern man handed him a piece of folded parchment, stamped with a grand seal—not the King's, but one bearing the insignia of the Parliament.

With shaking fingers Essex broke it open and read:—

"This to make known that our worthy and well-trusted servant, Colonel Nathaniel Fiennes, has our commission to undertake the government of our good and faithful city of Bristol, and we hereby direct and do command that all persons submit and yield due obedience to the lawful authority so holden by him.

"Signed, Lenthal."

The astonished colonel made some vapouring protest in speech, but not by action. For the son of Lord Saye and Sele had not come thither unattended. At his back was a *posse* of stalwart fellows—soldiers, who, that same morning, were under the orders of him now being placed in arrest, but, having learnt there was a change of commanding officers, knew better than to refuse obedience to the new one.

So the deposed governor, forced to part company with his *convives*, was carried off to prison as a common malefactor. He, too, the son of the Earl of Essex, Lord General of the Parliamentary army—the Parliament itself having ordered it! Verily, these were days when men feared not to arraign and punish—unlucky times for tyrants and traitors! To have concealed a deficit of four thousand pounds in the national exchequer *then* would have been a more dangerous deception than to waste as many millions *now*, without being able to render account of them.

Chapter Twenty Two
The Cadgers on Dangerous Ground

"Yonner be the big city at last! Glad I am. Ain't you that, Jinkum?"

It was Jerky Jack who spoke, the exclamation meant for his sister, who was with him, the interrogation addressed to the donkey.

They were not upon any of the Forest roads, but quite on the other side of the Severn, trudging along towards Bristol, the big city whose spires Jack had caught sight of.

One could almost fancy that the dumb brute comprehended the question facetiously put; at the words elevating its head, giving a wallop or two with its long ears, and mending the pace.

"It be good three mile to go yet," rejoined the woman. "Just that frae the cross roads—a bit forrard."

"Well, Winny; us ought to get theer by seven o' the clock?"

"So us ought, if nothin' stop we," and she cast an anxious glance along the road ahead.

"Don't think theer be much danger o' gettin' stopt now. The Governor o' Glo'ster sayed when's we got well on maybe we'd meet some o' the Bristol sodgers patrollin' about. Weesh we did. 'Tain't noways comfortable travellin', all o' the time in fear o' being pulled up and knocked about by them Cavalières. Ha! ha! If that party we passed at Berkeley cud a' seed through my wooden leg, 'tain't likely I'd be stumpin' along here?"

"True. But 'tain't wise to cry safe till one be sure o' it. Ye know they told us in Glo'ster that the King's dragoneers ha' it all their own way in the country places; him's they call Prince Roopert, goin' about like a ragin' lion, runnin' people through, an' shootin' 'em down wi' pistols as if they were no better than dogs. It's a big risk us be runnin', Jack!"

"Right you bees, theer. But then—the reward, Winny! If us only get safe inside, it ought be worth mor'n the profits on a twelvemonth o' cadgin'. Don't ye think 'twill?"

"Coorse I do."

She spoke in all sincerity. Whatever the money reward Jerky Jack was looking forward to, the woman had another in view, also contingent on their safe arrival inside the city,—one she thought worth far more than money. For there she would, or should, meet a man she had not seen for months, though ardently longing to see him. Scarce necessary to say, Rob Wilde was the individual, when it was known that the erst deer-stealer of Dean Forest was now a soldier—first sergeant of a troop forming part of the force then garrisoning Bristol.

"Yee-up, Jinkum?" cried Jack, encouraged by his sister's words, at the same time conscious as she of the danger alluded to, and the probability of their yet encountering obstruction. It was just after the capture of Cirencester by Prince Rupert; a massacre, sparing neither man nor woman, friend nor foe; they who survived it having been carried, or rather dragged, off to Oxford in triumphal train, a feast for the eyes of the King. To meet it, he, with his *entourage* of courtiers and sycophants, sallied forth from the city of colleges—but not of education or manners—supreme capital of conceit and snobbery, almost as much then as now. They were met miles out, coming from Witney, by hundreds of half-naked people, shivering in the chill frost of a winter's day, weary and footsore, covered with mud from the roads they had been driven over as cattle to market!

An impartial historian, or certainly not one who favours the Parliament, thus records the cruel episode:—"Tying them in pairs, they were marched to Oxford. The King, with many nobles and commanders and people of the city, went forth to witness their arrival. They formed a long line upon the road, escorted by two troops of cavalry. Among them were gentlemen and ministers, and a mixed multitude of soldiers, husbandmen, and townsmen. The ways were foul with the trampling of horses; the captives had gone sometimes knee deep in mire, beaten and driven along like jaded beasts, all of them weary, and many of them wounded. In this wretched train appeared a ghastly figure, naked, and, because he was unable to march with the rest, mounted upon the bare back of a horse. His form was manly and handsome; though exhausted, he sat upright with an undaunted air, and the remarkable fairness of his bodily complexion was heightened, where it was not concealed, by gore from many a gaping wound. As he drew near the King, a brawling woman cried aloud to him—'Ah, you traitorous rogue! You are well enough served.' He turned upon her a scornful look, retorted a term of base reproach, sunk from his seat, and expired."

Such was the spectacle to which the ruffian Rupert treated his uncle after the taking of Cirencester at the expense of its unfortunate citizens. And the "kind-hearted King" looked upon it without showing a spark of pity, while his courtiers gloated over it in a very exuberance of joy, even insulting the wretched captives by ribald speech, while giving gleeful and fulsome congratulations to their inhuman captors.

The fall of Cirencester was the prelude to that of Tewkesbury, Malmesbury, and Devizes, all hitherto held by Parliamentary forces; while the strong castles of Sudley and Berkeley had also to be evacuated by them, changing garrisons and showing new flags above their *donjons*. So close pressed at this time were the partisans of the Parliament in the border shires that Massey was all but cooped up in Gloucester, while the new governor of Bristol was almost equally engaged within the Seaport of the Severn.

Not strange, then, Jerky and his sister having fear to encounter the "Cavalières," as Jack called them. Though as humble cadgers, they would not be exempt from outrage at the hands of the Royalists; one of whom, Hastings, son of an aristocratic nobleman, had obtained such notoriety in this line as to be called "Rob-carrier." The princely plunderer, Rupert, had set the fashion, and wherever he and his troopers had control, the routes were only passable for travellers at the risk of being stripped, as by highwaymen, and butchered in cold blood on the slightest show of resistance.

It was no market commodity, however, about which Jerky and his sister were apprehensive, nor aught else carried in Jinkum's panniers—these being absolutely empty. What it was could not be learnt from anything seen upon the donkey or the persons of its owners; though Jack's allusion to his wooden leg, with certain eventualities contingent on its being seen through, seemed to point to some mysterious matter. Whatever it might be, no more speech was heard concerning it then, Jerky with another "Yee-up!" adding,—

"Three mile more, Jinkum, and ye'll be in the snug corner o' an inn stable-yard, wi' a measure of barley or beans at your nose. Think o' that!"

Despite the evident hurry the cadger was in, no thwack of stick accompanied the words. Nor was any needed; the night was well-nigh on, the air piercingly cold, the road frost-bound, with nothing on either side that even an ass could eat, and Jinkum, hungry enough, seemed to know something of that snug stable-yard which promised barley or beans. So, setting ears as if determined to reach the city soon as possible, it again briskened its pace.

The firm frozen ground favoured speed, enabling Jinkum to go gingerly along. It was equally favourable to Jack, with his timber leg, or he would have had ado to keep up with the donkey. As it was, no time was left him for aught else than quick tramping, the rough and now darkened path calling for all the attention he could bestow on it to save him from a tumble. But he had no need to trouble himself with any look-out ahead. That was left to the big sister, who, stepping out some paces in advance, scanned the road at every turn and corner. She saw nothing, however, to be apprehended. If there were any "Cavalières" in the neighbourhood, either the hour—between day and night—or the pinching cold, kept them confined to their quarters. At all events, neither Cavaliers, nor wayfarers of any other speciality, were encountered by them, and for their last three miles of trudge towards Bristol they had the road all to themselves.

Chapter Twenty Three
A Grand Sergeant of Guard

Getting within sight of the city's gate, the cadgers could see it was shut, drawbridge up, and portcullis down. Bristol was then a walled town, with an *enceinte* of ancient fortifications that had lately been repaired and strengthened. Night had now come on, and it was pitch dark. But a lamp set high on one of the gate towers threw its light across the moat, revealing to the eyes of the sentry who held post overhead the party seeking admittance. At sight of their humble mien, he thought of the bitterly cold night, and hearing of their reasonable request, called to the guard-sergeant below; then, to the inquiry of the latter, gave description of them in brief soldierly phrase—"Woman, man, and donkey."

Whether his reversing the usual rule, by putting the woman before the man, was due to her superior stature, or because of her being better under the lamplight, his words seemed to produce a singular effect on the sergeant. Starting suddenly up from his seat by the guard-house fire, he rushed out and on to the wicket. There, placing his eye to the peep-hole, he saw what influenced him to give instant orders for the lowering of the bridge.

By this he was taking a great responsibility on his shoulders, though they seemed strong and broad enough to bear it; for the guard-sergeant was no other than Rob Wilde. As it chanced, the captain of the guard was just then out of the way; and Rob had reason to think he would be pardoned for the little stretch of vicarial authority.

"Ha' patience, Win!" he shouted across. "We won't be more than a minnit."

Then with a will he set on to assist the others in letting the bridge down.

Win was patient; could well be, after hearing that voice, at once recognised by her. She thought nothing of the cold now; no more feared the raiding "Cavalières."

Never was drawbridge more promptly made passable. The creaking of a windlass; with a rattling of chains, and it was down in its place. The wicket was at the same time drawn open, and the cadger party passed over and in.

"Lor, Win!" said Rob, drawing the great woman aside under the shadow of the guard-house wall, and saluting her with a kiss, "where be yees from?"

"Glo'ster east," she responded, soon as her lips were released from the osculation.

"An' what ha' brought ye to Bristol?"

"Business o' diff'rent kinds."

"But ye don't appear to ha' any ladin' on the donkey?"

"Us may goin' back—hope to."

The cadgeress was prevaricating. No commercial speculation was the cause of their being there; and if in passing through Gloucester they had picked up a commission, it was quite a windfall, having nought to do with the original object of their extended excursion. Neither on leaving Ruardean, nor up to that moment, was Jerky himself aware of its purpose, Winny having been its projector. But he could trust her, and she, in her usual way, insisting upon the tramp, he had no alternative but to undertake it. He knew now, why his sister had brought him to Bristol, and that Rob Wilde was the lure which had attracted her thither.

Rob had some thought of this himself, or at least hoped it so; the unburdened donkey helping him in his hope.

"But ye bean't goin' back, surely?" he said.

"Why not?"

"The danger o' the roads now. If I'd a known you war on them, Win, dear, I should ha' been feelin' a bit uneasy."

Her game of false pretence was now nearly up. It had all been due to a fear which had suddenly come over her on seeing him again. Months had elapsed since they last met, and the rough Forester, erst in coarse common attire, his locks shaggy and unkempt, was now a man of military bearing, hair and whiskers neatly trimmed, in a well-fitting uniform resplendent with the glitter of gold. He was only a sergeant; but in her eyes no commanding officer of troop or regiment, not even the generalissimo of the army, could have looked either so grand or so handsome. But it was just that, with the thought of the long interval since they had last stood side by side, that now held her reticent. How knew she but that with such change outwardly, there might also have come change within his heart, and towards herself? A soldier too, now; one of a calling proverbial for gallantry as fickleness, living in a great city where, as she supposed, the eyes of many a syren would be turned luringly upon her grand Rob.

Had he yielded to their lures or resisted them? So she mentally and apprehensively interrogated. But only for a short while; the "Win, dear," in his old voice, with its old affectionate tone, and his solicitude for her safety, told he was still true.

Doubting it no longer, she threw aside the reserve that was beginning to perplex him, at the same time flinging her arms round his neck, and in turn kissing *him*.

That was her grateful rejoinder, sufficiently gratifying to him who received it, and leading him to further expressions of endearment. Glad was he they had arrived safe; and as to their errand at Bristol, which she cared no longer to keep from him, he forbore further questioning.

"Ye can tell me about it when we ha' more time to talk," he said. "But where do you an' Jack 'tend passin' the night?"

"The old place us always stop at,—Bird-in-the-Bush Inn."

"That be over Avon's bridge?"

"Yes; just a street or two the other side." Bristol was no strange place to her. She, Jerky and Jinkum had made many a cadge thither before.

"I'd go 'long wi' ye to the Bird-in-the-Bush," said the guard-sergeant, "but, as ye see, I'm on duty at this gate, and musn't leave it for a minnit. If the captain was here—unlucky he isn't just now—he'd let me off, I know—seein' who it be."

"Why for seein' that, Rob?"

"Because o' his knowin' ye. He ha' seen you and Jack at Hollymead House."

"It be Sir Richard?"

"No, no," hastily responded the ex-deer-stealer, in turn, perhaps, experiencing a twinge of jealousy as when by the quarry on Cat's Hill. "Sir Richard be in Bristol, too; but he's a colonel, not captain."

"Who be the captain, then?"

"That young Cavalier gentleman as comed to Hollymead 'long wi' Sir Richard, after fightin' him. He changed sides there, an's now on ours. Ye heerd that, han't you?"

"Deed, yes. An' more; heerd why. 'Twas all through a sweet face him seed there—so be the word 'bout Ruardean."

"Well; I hope her won't disappoint he, after his doin' that for her. Better nor braver than he an't in this big town o' Bristol. But, Win, dear," he added, changing tone, and slinging an arm round her neck, "'tan't any consarn o' ours. Oh! I be so glad to see ye again."

She knew he was now.

"Hang it!" he went on, "I only weesh my turn o' guard was over, so's I could go 'long wi' ye. Maybe when the captain come back he'll let me off for a hour or so. Sit up late, if ye ain't too tired. Ye will, won't ye?"

"I will; for you all night, Rob. Ay, till the sun o' morning shines clear in the sky."

Her passionate and poetic words were succeeded, if not cut short, by a thumping on the pavement. Jerky's wooden leg it was; its owner approaching in the darkness, the rapid repetition of the thumps telling him to be in great haste.

"Winny!" he called to her in urgent tone, "us maunt linger here any longer. Ye know somethin' as needs our bein' quick about it."

"Yes, yes," she answered, excitedly, as if recalled to a duty she felt guilty of having trifled with or neglected. "I be ready to go on, Jack."

The guard-sergeant looked a little puzzled. There was a secret, after all, which had not been confided to him. What could it be?

Rough Forester though he had been, bold soldier as he now was, he lacked the courage, or rather the rudeness, to ask. It might be a question unwelcome.

Divining his thoughts, the woman said in a whisper,—

"Something Rob, us have sweared not to tell o' to anybody, 'till't be all over an' done. When's I see you at the inn 'twill be over, an' ye shall hear all about it."

"That be enough, Win?" said in rejoinder the trusting Rob; and the two great figures went apart in the shadowy night, the separation preceded by their lips once more meeting in a resonant smack.

On along the streets passed the cadger party; Jack urging Jinkum to haste by a succession of vociferous "yee-ups," and now and then a sharp touch of the stick. He seemed angry with himself, or perhaps more at Winny, for having tarried so long by the gate.

"Good gracious!" he exclaimed in a troubled tone, "what if us get theer too late? Ye know, the Glo'ster governor told we not to waste one second o' time. Maybe better keep on straight to the castle. What d'ye say, Winny?"

"It be but a step to Bird-in-the-Bush, now. Won't take we mor'n ten minnits; that can't a make much difference. An' us can go faster when's we've left Jinkum in the inn yard."

Thus counselled and controlled, Jack, as was customary with him, gave way; and the trio continued on for the Bird-in-the-Bush.

Chapter Twenty Four
On the Bridge

The river Avon bisecting the city of Bristol was spanned by a bridge; one of those quaint structures of the olden time, with a narrow causeway, high *tête-de-pont*, and houses along each side. There were shops and dwellings, with a church of rare architectural style and rarer proportions—being but twenty-one feet in width, while over seventy in length!

A conspicuous and important part did this bridge of Bristol play in the political action of the time; for it was invested with a political character. Creditable, too; the dwellers upon it—the "Bridgemen," as called—being all warm partisans of the Parliament. As a consequence, it was a favourite assembling-place for the citizens so disposed; especially in evening hours, after the day's work had been done.

Though dark and keenly cold that seventh of March night, it did not deter a number of them from congregating, as was their wont, about the bridge's head, to talk over the news and events of the day, with the prospects and probabilities for the morrow. The fervour of their patriotism rendered them regardless of personal discomfort or exposure; just as one may see at a political meeting in the present time the thronging thousands, packed thick as mackerels in a barrel, standing thus for hours, up till midnight—ay, morning, if leave be allowed them—eagerly listening to hear words of truth and promise, with the hope of the promise being fulfilled.

I know no more pleasing or grander spectacle than that to be witnessed from a Liberal platform, a sea of faces—the faces of the people—by their expression giving proof of man's natural inclinations to what is good and right, and abhorrence of what is wicked and wrong.

Nor can I conceive any shabbier spectacle than the crowd which usually displays itself before a platform where Toryism is preached. For there assemble all who are the foes of liberty, the enemies and oppressors of mankind.

Among the friends of liberty that night gathered upon the bridge of Bristol were several men armed and wearing uniform; soldiers, though not belonging to any regiment of the regular army. Volunteers, they were; a force then for the first time heard of in England, taking the place of the militia or "trained bands." They were on guard with a young officer in command, one who afterwards made name and fame in the annals of his Country, and his sword sharply felt by its enemies. For it was Captain John Birch—the merchant-soldier.

The writers of the Restoration have flung their defiling mud at this brave man—which did not stick, however—by representing him as of humble birth, and mean calling—a common carrier, the driver of a pack-horse,—stigmas similar to that cast at Cromwell, the brewer of Huntingdon. But it should be remembered that in those days trade was not deemed degrading; and if here and there aristocratic noses were turned up at it, here and there also aristocratic people took a hand in it. What were the Coningsbys, those types of the Cavalier idea, but soap-boilers and soap-chandlers, holding a monopoly from the King for the making and selling of this useful commodity? As for John Birch, he was neither base-born nor of humble occupation; instead, engaged in honourable merchandise, and, for the times, on a somewhat extensive scale. His correspondence, extant, so far from proving him coarse or illiterate, shows both refinement and education beyond most of his contemporaries—soldier or civilian—even superior to that of the King himself.

In intelligence and courage few were his equals, while, as a partisan leader, he is entitled to first place; some of his feats in the *guerilla* line reading more like the fictions of troubadour romance.

One of the earliest and most ardent espousers of the Parliamentary cause, he had enrolled this company of Bristol volunteers—most of them "Bridgemen"—with a detail of whom on the bridge itself he was now keeping guard; not so much against an outside enemy, but one within the city's walls. Bristol was full of Cavalier officers, prisoners in its gaols, but many of them freely circulating through the streets *on parole*—ready to break it if they but saw the chance, as some of them, to their eternal disgrace, actually did; though it failed to disgrace them in the eyes of their Royal master, who rather, the more favoured them after—as with Vavasour—promoting them to higher command!

The treason not only winked at, but fostered, by the deposed governor—now in the prison of Berkeley Castle—had not all been trodden out, but was still rampant, and ready to raise its Hydra head; so that Colonel Nathaniel Fiennes had his hands full in keeping it under. But he could not have had a better man to help him than John Birch. The young captain of Volunteers was especially prepared for this duty; since he had himself suffered from the late governor's delinquency—the insult of having been placed under arrest. So, tempered to vigilance, if not revenge, he held guard upon the bridge-head, watchful and wary, carefully scrutinising all who passed over it.

While thus engaged he saw a party approaching of such singular composition as to attract him more than common. Little man with a wooden leg; tall woman nearly twice the man's height; between the two a donkey, with pair of panniers—Jack, Winny, and Jinkum.

If Birch was not himself a pack-horse carrier, in his capacity of trading merchant he was well acquainted with all the country routes, and the modes of traffic and transit thereon. At a glance he took in the character of the cadgers; saw they were rustics fresh from the country; and, by the direction from which they were approaching, concluded they must have made entry at the gate towards Gloucester. On the bridge there was light in plenty, both from lamps and shops; and, as they came close, a scrutiny of their features gave the sharp-witted captain an idea that they, too, were of quick wit, especially the woman. She looked like one who did not tramp the roads without seeing what was to be seen, and hearing all that could be heard; one, moreover, capable of forming a correct estimate of how things stood, social, political, or military. If from Gloucester, or even Berkeley, she or the man might have picked up some scraps of news worth extracting from them.

Stepping out into the middle of the causeway, he confronted the cadger party, and brought it to a stop, with the interrogation:

"Whence come you, my worthy people?"

"Frae Gloster, yer honner," responded Jack, spokesman by right of sex and seniority.

"And what's your business in Bristol?"

"Only our reg'lar business, sir. As ye see, us be cadgers."

"But your panniers appear to be empty!" said the officer, peeping into and giving them a shake. "How is that?"

The question was awkward, nonplussing Jerky, and, the second time, calling for explanation from his sister; who, however, promptly vouchsafed it.

"Ye see, master, us be come to Bristol to take back some things Gloster way, an' far ayont. Us belong to the Forest o' Dean."

"Ah! All that way off. And when left you the Forest country?"

"A good week agone, yer honner," Jerky giving the response.

"At least that, I should say," rejoined the officer, with a look at the wooden leg. "Well, you must have seen and met many people upon the road, especially between this and Gloucester. Can you tell me whether—"

He ceased speech abruptly, seeing it was overheard by the street passengers, who, attracted by the oddness of the group, had begun to gather round it.

He was about to demand of the cadgers, *sotto voce*, where they intended putting up, with a view to further conference, when a man of herculean stature—soldier in cavalry uniform—made appearance inside the circle of bystanders, going straight up to the woman, and speaking some words, as one who had familiar acquaintance with her,—

"Ah! Sergeant Wilde," said the Volunteer officer, "you know these people, do you?"

"I ought to, Captain. All o' us war born an' brought up in the Forest o' Dean, not very far apart."

"Enough," said, or rather thought, Birch, who, after a whispered word with the colossal trooper, gave permission for the cadger party to pass on over the bridge.

Rob went with them; soon as beyond earshot of the crowd, saying:

"Dear Win! I ha' got leave o' guard duty for the whole o' an hour. Captain Trevor coined back to the gate 'most the minnit ye left it. When I tolt him who'd passed through, it war, 'Rob, go and see to their bein' stowed in comfortable quarters.' Kind o' him, warn't it?"

"Deed war it," answered Win, but without thinking it strange; her woman's instinct told her the why and wherefore of Captain Trevor's kindness.

Jerky seemed less satisfied than either of the other two; for a reason he knew of, equally known to his sister. That detention on the bridge's head had been torture to him; it might forfeit the reward promised and expected. She cared less for it, hers already gained, in having her beloved Rob once more by her side.

The two, talking of old things and times, might have lagged upon the way, had Jack given them time and opportunity, which he did not; on the contrary, urging greater haste than ever, while persuading Jinkum to make still better speed by a multiplication of "gee-ups," and a storm of solid thwacks administered by the cudgel.

But they had not reached the Bird in the Bush—were scarce beyond sight of the people who saw them depart from the bridge—when he who had just held speech with them was accosted by one whose speech and air told that she, too—for it was a woman—had a secret to communicate; but, unlike the cadgeress, wanted—was impatient—to reveal it. And altogether unlike the latter otherwise was the new applicant for converse with Captain Birch—so far as could be seen of her—for she was cloaked and hooded. But when the hood was tossed back, so that she could herself see and speak freely, a face was revealed, beautiful and of delicate outlines, unmistakably that of a lady.

That she was not unknown to the young Volunteer officer might be told from the start of surprise at seeing her. Still better proof of their being acquainted in the words she addressed to him, spoken in panting haste and excitedly. He had said, interrogatively:

"What's brought you hither, Marian?" to get for response, "You, John; your life's in danger."

"How? From what?"

"Treason. Even now—at this minute—there are conspirators armed and ready to start out into the streets, with a cry for the King."

"But where?"

"Some in the house of Yeomans, others at Boucher's. They have expectation of help from the outside; that's why they're gathered now."

"How do you know it, Marian?"

"Don't ask me, John; God help me! To think my own father is one of them—my brother, too! But your life is dearer to me than either. And you will lose it if you don't listen to my warning."

"Dearest Marian, I not only listen to, but believe in it. More, I'll take instant action to stop this conspiracy you speak of, trust me for that."

She could trust him, and did; saw that to leave him unfettered, and free for the action intended, she should no longer remain there; and pulling the hood down over her face, though not till after two pairs of lips had met under it, she lightened the cloak around her shoulders, and hurried away from the bridge-head.

Heart full of sweet thoughts, thrilled by them, the young merchant-soldier stood looking after the graceful figure till it waned and was lost in the dim light of distant lamps. No wonder he should so long continue his gaze. She was one of Bristol's fairest daughters; daughter, too, of one of its richest merchants, and proudest; her father a man who would have seen her hurled from the parapet of that bridge, and drowned in Avon's stream, rather than know of her having stood upon its head, and said what she had said to John Birch.

Whatever the reflections of John Birch himself about this jealously-guarded daughter, they seemed to pass away soon as she was out of sight; though not the warning she had given. This was with him still; and so vividly realistic, he lost not a moment in acting up to it. A word or two with his sergeant of guard—orders earnestly enjoined—and away went he from the bridge, with face turned towards the Castle, and step hurried as man could make, almost a run!

Chapter Twenty Five
In Council of War

The man who had succeeded Colonel Essex in the governorship of Bristol was well, even enthusiastically, affected to the Parliamentary cause. Beyond that, he was altogether unfitted for the trust reposed in him. A lawyer before becoming soldier, he better understood the marshalling of arguments than armies, and, though a man of grave, serious thought, his passionate temper gave offence to friends as foes, oft thwarting his best intentions. Fortunately he had around him men of greater military capacity and experience, by whose counsels he was, to some extent, controlled — officers who had seen service in the Low Countries, Sweden, and Germany — among them Sir Richard Walwyn.

How the knight came to be in Bristol — Eustace Trevor too — may need making known. At the breaking out of hostilities, when blood began to flow, the Dean Foresters were, in a way, taken by surprise, and for a time overpowered. In addition to their old enemy, Sir John Wintour, threatening them on the south, they had to contend with the strong and well-disciplined force of Lord Herbert on the west; while Harry Lingen, a man of more capability than either — as a partisan leader unsurpassed — had commenced harassing them from the Herefordshire side.

Seeing he would be unable to hold ground against such odds, Sir Richard, who had hastily got together a body of horse, withdrew it from the Forest, and joined the main force of the Parliament, which confronted that of the King. At the time the two armies were manoeuvring in Worcestershire, Warwick, and Salop, every day expecting to come into collision, which they did soon after at Edgehill — a drawn battle, with feats of daring on both sides, and on both displays of abject cowardice.

The men commanded by Sir Richard Walwyn were not chargeable with this last; instead, on that day distinguishable by the first, having performed prodigies of valour. Since then he and his Foresters had shown themselves on other fields, and done other gallant deeds, till the troop of horse, with the "big sergeant," had become a name of terror to the Royalist soldiers. Even Rupert's pick Cavaliers would have shied encounter with it, unless they knew themselves in the proportion of two to one.

By the drift of events, this small but efficient body became part of the garrison of Bristol—disagreeable duty to the Foresters, but forced upon them by the chances of war.

So in Bristol we now find them, with their commanding officer Sir Richard, their "big sergeant" Rob Wilde, and for one of their captains the ex-gentleman-usher, Eustace Trevor. To explain his presence there and position it needs but referring back to his words spoken in that hour when Lunsford was hammering at the door of Hollymead House.

Reverting to the new governor, we must give him the credit of endeavour to do his best—that at least. Entering upon the office full of hope and spirit, he was correspondingly vigorous in the execution of its duties. And as there had been no time for his enthusiasm to get cool, or his vigour to become relaxed, before that 7th of March—but a few days after Essex had been clapped under arrest—Fiennes was in the very blush of energetic activity. Not dining, wining, and dancing, as his predecessor would have been, in the company of gay Cavaliers, and light-hearted, as light-headed, ladies; but within one of the reception rooms of the castle, holding counsel with half-a-score of grave men—chiefly commanding officers of the troops that composed the garrison of the city.

All were impressed with the seriousness of the situation, feeling themselves, if not actually besieged, likely soon to be. From without, reports were pouring in, daily, hourly, of reverses sustained by the Parliamentarians. The capture and massacre at Cirencester, the surrendering of Malmesbury, Tewkesbury, and Devizes, with the abandonment of Sudley and Berkeley Castles,—all adverse events, following in quick succession as the blows of a hammer,—were enough to alarm the new governor and the men in consultation with him.

The more, from their belief that in all likelihood Bristol would be the next point aimed at by the now victorious Royalists. For they knew it was the quarry these would most like to stoop at and kill. Ever since the commencement of hostilities, it and Gloucester had been very thorns in the side of the Royalist party; both cities being storehouses of war material, and other effects conducive to the supply of its sinews. But chiefly the great seaport, at once door of entry and key to the rich Severn Valley—

with its towns and villages up to Shrewsbury—while also commanding the commerce and intercourse with South Wales.

Rupert, now at the head of a considerable body of troops, held all the open country from the Severn up to Oxford, raiding over and ravaging it at will. But the rumour had got ground that he meant soon to engage in something more than mere skirmishing warfare, by making a dash at Bristol, either to attempt taking that city by assault, or laying siege to it.

The assemblage of officers at the Castle was in consequence of this rumour, which had just reached the Governor's ears, and he had hastily called them together to have their views and advice upon what steps had best be taken in the contingency—should it occur.

But, as already made known, something more than the enemy without called for their consideration. The egg of treason, which had been hatching under Essex's too lenient rule, was not an addled one. The vile bird was still vigorous within it, threatening to break the shell. A gleam of warmth and hope, the touch of a helping hand, and it would burst forth full fledged, ready to tear with beak and talons.

On this night Nathaniel Fiennes was unusually excited; angry at the difficult task left him by his predecessor, just as might the Earl of Ripon be with Lord Lytton, that ass in lion's skin—now politically defunct—for demising him the legacy of Afghanistan.

But the lawyer-soldier, however worried and over-weighted, was not either dismayed or discouraged. After listening to what his fellow counsellors had to say, and giving his own views, he exclaimed in conclusion, and determinedly:

"Before our enemies enter Bristol they'll have to pass over my dead body!"

"And mine, too!" "And mine!" were echoes of like patriotic resolve.

All emphatic, though not all sincere; for the loudest of them came from the lips of a man who least meant what he said. Even then, Colonel Langrish was contemplating the treason he afterwards perpetrated.

No one present so quietly declared himself as Sir Richard Walwyn. A man more of deeds than words, such pompous proclamation was averse to his nature, and pompous, so far as regarded Fiennes, it afterwards proved. For the enemy *did* enter Bristol, not over his dead body, nor even fiercely fighting with him, but by surrender, facile, and so much like being criminal, that the lawyer-soldier was himself cast into prison, not by foes, but those hitherto his friends; afterwards tried for his life, and let off as the son of Lord Saye and Sele, though without leave to play at soldiering any more. But we anticipate.

Returning to the conference in the Castle, it had well-nigh reached conclusion, when the usher in charge of the door entered to announce a party seeking audience of the Governor, to whom alone the communication was made.

"Who are they?" demanded Fiennes.

"I don't know, your Excellency. They're still outside the gate. The guard-corporal brought the message—he's at the door."

"Bring him in!"

The abrupt order was with promptness executed; and in twenty seconds after, the corporal of the castle guard stood before the Governor, saluting in military style.

"Who are these wishing to speak with me?" asked the latter.

"I only know one of them, your Excellency," returned the corporal. "That's Sergeant Wilde, of the Forest of Dean troop—Sir Richard Walwyn's. The other two are a short man and a tall woman—very tall she is. The man has a wooden leg."

"If I'm not mistaken, Colonel Fiennes," interposed Sir Richard, who, standing by, overheard what the corporal had said, "I know all the party. And as my sergeant, Wilde, appears to be one of them, I'll answer for the honesty of their purpose in seeking an interview with you, whatever it be."

"Let them be brought in?" commanded the Governor—"all three."

At which the guard-corporal, once more saluting, made "about face," and with the usher disappeared from the room.

"Who are they, Sir Richard?" asked the Governor, as the door was again closed.

"By the description," answered the knight, "I identify the short man and the very tall woman as cadgers, who follow their humble calling around the Forest of Dean; despite the reversed proportions in stature, being brother and sister."

"But what, think you, can they be wanting with me?"

"That I can't say, your Excellency. Though likely something of grave concern, or Rob Wilde wouldn't be with them as their introducer. He isn't the man to intrude, without serious purpose."

Their dialogue was interrupted by sounds in the hallway outside; a scraping and shuffling of heavily-shod feet, with something that resembled the strokes of a wooden mallet upon the stone flags, administered in regular repetition. It was no mystery, however, either to the Governor or the knight, both already aware that they were to see a man with a wooden leg.

Which they did, as the door was again pushed open, and the usher entered for the third time, conducting in Jerky Jack and his sister, the sergeant bringing up the rear.

Chapter Twenty Six
A Despatch Cunningly Conveyed

The officers had separated into two groups, one on each side the Governor, as the odd trinity of personages was presented to him; these, as they came up, falling into line—Rob on the right, the woman left, and Jack central, as a pollard between two tall trees.

Not yet aware of his colonel being in the room, the sergeant, as introducer of the other pair, was about to make known their business—of which Winny after all had given him a hint—when Sir Richard stepped forward to interrogate them. The knight had received instructions for this, on account of his acquaintance with the party.

"Well, sergeant," he said, after nodding recognition to Jack and his sister, "what may your Forest friends be wanting? I hope they haven't got into any trouble with our soldiers, or the Bristol folk?"

"No, Sir Richard; nothin' o' that sort whatsoever. They ha' just entered the city, comin' frae Gloster, an' wi' a message from Colonel Massey to his honner here." The speaker, by a look, indicated the head figure of the listening assemblage; then added, "They think it be somethin' o' very great consarn, seein' how the Colonel ha' told them not to lose a minnit in the deliverin' o't."

At this all eyes turned eagerly upon the cadgers. A message from Massey, who commanded at Gloucester, and at such a crisis! It should mean something of importance.

"Perhaps your Excellency would prefer hearing it in private?" suggested Sir Richard, with a feint at withdrawing, imitated by the other officers.

"No, no!" rejoined the *ci-devant* lawyer, who, unlike his confraternity, was of aught but secretive habit. "Stay, gentlemen! Whatever it be, we're all equally interested in it. Now, my worthy friends," he continued, his glance alternating between the little man and big woman, "what is this matter with which Colonel Massey has entrusted you? You may speak out openly and without fear."

The words of encouragement were superfluous. Neither Jerky Jack nor his sister were of the stuff to be affrighted, though they stood in the presence of Royalty itself. They had travelled too far, and seen too much of the world for that.

"It be wrote, yer honner." The woman it was who spoke. "The thing be's all put down on paper; an' Jack—my brother, sir—ha' got it on him, hid away, as there was a fear us might meet the Cavalières."

"Well, you needn't fear meeting them here. So let Jack produce it."

Which Jack did, though not *presto*, on the instant. It took some time, with an amount of manipulation, before the secreted despatch could be laid open to the light. The cadger's artificial leg had to be unstrapped and separated from what remained of the real one; then a cavity in the former, being uncorked, disclosed to view a roll of paper, bearing resemblance to a cartridge.

This, drawn forth by Jerky himself, was handed to Sir Richard, and passed on to the Governor; who, having directed the temporary withdrawal of the messenger party, unrolling it, read—

> "Gloucester, March 7.—Report here of Rupert, with 8,000 men, on march for Bristol. Expected to arrive before your gates early in the night. Be careful to keep them shut. Sorry I can do nothing for you in the way of diversion. Myself pressed on Monmouthshire side. Brett and Lord John Somerset, with their Popish crew, have crossed the Forest, and are now threatening us from Highnam. But I'll hold Gloucester at all hazards, as I know you will Bristol.
>
> "Massey."

"That will I!" cried Fiennes, in a fresh burst of enthusiasm, inspired by the last words of the despatch. "Hold and defend it to the death. We will, gentlemen!"

Needless to say, they all again echoed his resolve loudly and determinedly as before.

While their responses were still ringing through the room, the door was once more pushed open by a man who entered in haste, without announcement of usher, or introduction of any kind. The expression upon his features was sufficient apology for intrusion, but better the words that leaped from his lips, soon as he was inside:

"Your Excellency—gentlemen all—we're standing upon a mine!"

"'Standing upon a mine!'" echoed the Governor. "Explain yourself, Captain Birch!"

"Treason in our midst—a conspiracy—the conspirators met at this very moment."

"Where?" demanded several voices. "I heard first of a party in the house of Robert Yeomans, and another at George Boucher's. But I've since been told about more of them at Edward Dacre's."

"And they're assembled now, you think?"

"I'm sure of it, your Excellency. Armed, too; ready for rising."

In view of the contents of Massey's despatch, now hastily communicated to the Volunteer captain, this seemed probable as intelligible. Rupert to assault from outside, aweing the loyal citizens by an attack, sudden as unexpected; the disloyal ones, these conspirators, to take advantage of it and act in concert—the programme beyond a doubt!

Withal, Langrish and one or two others were disposed to discredit it. For in that confidential council itself was a leaven of treason. Luckily not enough to control it; and when Fiennes put the question, "Shall we arrest these men?" a majority of voices declared promptly and decisively in the affirmative.

"Captain Birch!" said the Governor, once more turning to the young officer of Volunteers, "you hear our determination. I commit this matter to you, who best know the guilty parties, and the places. Take your own men, and whatever other force you think necessary. This gentleman will go with you as my authority for the requisition."

He referred to an aide-de-camp by his side, who, after receiving some directions in undertone, parted from him, and, with Birch, hastily left the room.

Scarce were they outside, when another officer presented himself in the council-chamber; in haste also, and unannounced, on the plea of pressing matter. A Volunteer captain, too; for Bristol had already raised more than one company of these citizen soldiers. Captain Jeremiah Buck, it was—the "busy mercer," as the Restoration writers contemptuously style him. But whatever he may have been otherwise, he was a busy soldier, too busy that night for Royalist likings, and brought further intelligence of the conspiracy, obtained from other sources—confirming that of Birch.

And, as the latter, he also received instant commands to proceed on the arrest of the conspirators. As there were several distinct "clatches" of them, more than one force was needed to catch them simultaneously.

So commissioned, off went Buck, to all appearance greatly elated, and possibly indulging himself in the thought of satisfying some private spite.

Whether or no, the door that had closed behind him was still vibrating to the clash, when one who needed no usher to announce him caught hold of its handle and pushed it open, with an alacrity which proclaimed him also the bearer of tidings that would not brook delay.

"What is it, Trevor?" asked Sir Richard Walwyn, advancing to meet his troop captain. "Why have you left your guard at the gate?"

"Because, Colonel," panted out the young officer, "I've thought it better to come myself and make sure of the news reaching you in good time, as the Governor here."

"What news?"

"Prince Rupert and the Royalist army reported outside the city. A countryman just come in says they are pitching tents on Durdham Down. And his report's confirmed by what I've myself seen from the top of the gate tower."

"What saw you, Captain Trevor?" asked the Governor, who, with the other officers, had been all the while anxiously listening.

"A glare of light, your Excellency; such as would proceed from the blaze of camp-fires."

This was confirmation full, of Massey's warning despatch, the conspiracy, everything. But, for better assurance of it, the Governor, with the assembled officers, rushed out of the council-chamber and up to the Castle donjon; there to see the horizon lit up with a yellowish glare which, as soldiers, they knew to be the reflection from bivouac fires. And a wide spread of them, the sky illumined all over Durdham Down, away to King's Weston.

"Rupert it must be—he, and his plundering host!"

Captain Birch made quick work of the duty assigned to him. In less than twenty minutes after receiving the Governor's commands, he stood before the door of Robert Yeomans's house, demanding admission. He had the strength at his back to enforce it—his own Volunteers afoot, with a body of horse, lest the conspirators should escape by flight. And some of both, distributed round the house, already enfiladed it.

It was a large house, its owner being one of the wealthy citizens of Bristol. Forty men were within it, all armed, as the Volunteer officer had been told. At word of what was without they sprang to their arms, some of the more courageous counselling fight. But when they looked through the windows, saw that formidable array, and heard the stern summons "Surrender!" their hearts failed them, and they surrendered. Wisely, too. Had they resisted, instant death would have been their fate. For, among the men with Birch, were some fresh from the affair of Cirencester; themselves escaped, but leaving behind friends, relatives, even brothers, butchered in cold blood. Exasperated, maddened, by the memory of that slaughter—some of them with wounds still unhealed from it—Birch, who was moderate as brave, had a difficulty to restrain them from dealing out death to the malignants. The troopers who accompanied him, smarting under late reverses, would have gladly hailed the order to "fall on." But the cowed conspirators submitted like sheep, and were marched off to the Castle, every man-jack of them; there to meet other batches brought in by Buck and the different officers who had been detailed for their arrest.

In houses here and there throughout the city, parties of them were found and picked up; all armed, waiting for a signal to sally forth and shed the blood of their fellow-citizens. This has been denied, but a letter from the barbarous Lord Byron to Prince Rupert puts the design beyond doubt. But for the vigilance of the merchant-soldier Birch, and the activity of the "busy mercer" Buck, that night the streets of Bristol would have run blood, and every house in it belonging to a Parliamentarian been sacked and plundered. For the head plunderer, Rupert—he who introduced the word to the English language—stood at that very hour on the top of King's Weston hill, awaiting a triple signal—the bells of three churches to be rung—Saint John's, for summoning the Royalist sailors; that of Saint Nicholas, to call out the butchers for butchers' work congenial to them; while from the tower of Saint Michael's he expected to hear a peal more especially meant for himself and his freebooters, as it were saying, "You may come on! The gates of Bristol are unbarred for you!"

But he heard it not. They who had been entrusted with the ringing of that fatal peal never rang it. Instead of bell ropes in their hands, they now had manacles around their wrists, and grim sentries standing guard over them.

Rupert waited, watched, and listened, till the break of day showed him the great seaport of the Severn still calm; its gates close shut; its walls and towers bristling with armed men, in attitudes that told them determined on its defence.

Thinking he had been made a fool of, and fearing further betrayal, he hastily beat retreat from Durdham Down to seek the pillage of some city more easy of being entered.

The rising sun saw his back turned upon Bristol; he and his Cavaliers venting loud curses—reviling their partisans inside, whose misleading correspondence had lured them to an expedition ludicrous as bootless.

Chapter Twenty Seven
A City of Refuge

Of the Foresters who figure in our tale, Rob Wilde, Jerky Jack, and Winny were not the only ones who had found their way into Bristol. Most of Sir Richard Walwyn's troopers were Foresters. But the master of Hollymead was himself there, with his daughters, their maid Gwenthian, and others of the family servants.

Why he had exchanged his Forest home for a residence in town—that, too, in a city under military occupation, threatened with siege and all its inconveniences—has been already in part explained. With the commencement of hostilities country life became unsafe, more especially for people of quality and those who had anything to lose. Parties of armed men penetrated into the most remote districts, demanding contributions and levying them—at first in the name of the King. Naturally, this aroused the spirit of retaliation, and dictated reprisals; so that in time both sides became more or less blamable for *filibusterism*. The weight of evidence, however, shows that, as a rule, the Parliamentarian officers did all in their power to restrain, while those of the Royalist army not only encouraged but gloried in it—themselves taking a hand. A Prince had set them the lesson, making robbery fashionable, and they were neither backward nor slow in profiting by it.

As a sample of the spirit in which the Cavaliers made war, thus wrote Sir John, afterwards Lord Byron—the same truculent ruffian already alluded to, commanding a body of the King's horse—"*I put them all to the sword, which I find to be the best way to proceed with these kind of people, for mercy to them is cruelty.*"

The gallant defenders of Barthomley Church were "these kind of people," whom this monster, ungrammatical as inhuman, had massacred to a man!

Fighting under such faith, no wonder the *lex talionis* soon displayed itself on both sides, and in bitterest, most relentless form. Not only had the main routes of travel become unsafe, but sequestered country roads; while the sanctity of private houses was invaded, and women subjected to insult, oft even to the disregarding of their honour. This was conspicuously the case in the districts where the Cavaliers had control, no decent woman daring to show herself abroad. Even high-born ladies feared encountering them, if having father or brother on the Parliamentary side. Some dames, however, who favoured their side, were bold and free enough with them; and a very incarnation of female shamelessness was the strumpet following of Rupert.

As known, Ambrose Powell had at first thought of fortifying Hollymead, and holding it with his servants, retainers, and such of the Foresters as he could rally around him; of whom he had reason to believe many would respond to his call. The *haw-haw* around the house was suggestive of his doing so—itself an outer line of defence, which could be easily strengthened. It but needed a parapet of *gabions*, or *fascines*, to render it unassailable, save in the face of a scathing fire. And he had the wherewith to deliver this, having long expected the coming storm, and stored up materials to meet it. One of the chambers of Hollymead House was a very armoury and ordnance room, full of the best weapons of the time, which his great wealth had enabled him to provide—muskets of the *snap-hans* fire, pistols, pikes, and halberds. They but wanted putting into hands capable of making efficient use of them.

And he himself had but waited for Sir Richard Walwyn's advice, as to whether he should attempt holding Hollymead, or abandon it. He knew he must do one or the other. His partisanship, long since proclaimed and known beyond the borders of the Forest, with the echoes returning, so admonished him.

"Could it be held, think you?" he asked of the soldier knight, on the evening of his arrival with Eustace Trevor—Sir Richard and his host alone closeted in conversation.

"Impossible!" was the answer, backed up by convincing reasons. "Were it a structure of stone, I might say Yes, easily enough; with a force numerous enough to garrison it. But those wooden beams, and roofs dry as tinder—they'd be set ablaze by the first arrow sent at them."

The reader may fancy Sir Richard's allusion to arrows was a figure of speech, or anachronism. It was neither. For this primitive weapon, almost universal among savage men, was not then obsolete, or out of the hands of the civilised. In the army of Essex—the Lord General himself—was a corps of bowmen; and others elsewhere. The belief in the bent yew stick and feathered shaft, that had gained for England such renown at Cressy and Agincourt, was still strong in the days of her more glorious struggle—the Great Rebellion.

But it was not to shafts of this kind the knight had reference; instead, arrows projected from muskets and arquebusses for setting fire to assailed forts and houses—a species of ordnance which then formed part of the equipment of every well-appointed *corps d'armée.*

With the master of Hollymead the argument was conclusive. He saw his house could not be held, with any hope of successful defence, if attacked by a force strong and determined. And that such would come against it he had been as good as sure, ever since that hour when Reginald Trevor placed in his hands the letter of Loan by Privy Seal—altogether sure, when Lunsford, later, came to make the levy itself.

Only a day or two longer had he remained in it, to pack up his plate, with other cherished penates, and have them transmitted to a place of safety—to Gloucester—the nearest city promising asylum to the harried partisans of the Parliament—going thither himself with his family.

He had, however, made but short stay there. The seaport of Bristol beyond was a "city of refuge" more to his mind, because of a house in it that offered him hospitality—a sister's—and under its roof he and his were sojourning on that night of dread danger, averted almost as soon as apprehended.

Nor in that crisis was the refugee from Dean Forest himself inactive. When men stood gazing with eyes full of keen apprehension at the fire-glare over Durdham Down, Ambrose Powell was moving briskly through Bristol's streets, urging its citizens to arm and defend it. Along with him a clergyman, who added his appeal with eloquent tongue and passionate speech. He was Tombes, of Leominster, who had been mobbed in that town of woolstaplers, and driven out of it by drunken roughs; no doubt the progenitors of those who in the late Parliamentary election in like manner dishonoured themselves.

To Darwin's transmutation and improvement theory, the human animals of Leominster seem to be an exception; especially as regards the improvement, for its Jingo cur of to-day is rather a falling off from the quality of his prototype—the Cavalier wolf of the Great war time.

Chapter Twenty Eight
A Home Gayer than Congenial

Madame Lalande, *née* Powell, was the widow of a West Indian planter, late deceased. Her husband, during life, had held commercial intercourse with Bristol, then chief port of communication with all the Transatlantic colonies. Though a Creole of French descent, the isle of his nativity, in the Antilles, had come under British rule; and he himself rather affected English tastes and habits, often visiting England and making short sojourns in it. At a Bristol ball he had first met Gwendoline Powell, Ambrose's sister; had married in Bristol, and there designed spending the evening of his days in retirement from the cares of business life. And when the time at length came for carrying this design into execution, he sold off his West Indian plantation—an extensive one, with its human chattels, some hundreds in number—and invested the proceeds in Bristol property, part of it being a handsome dwelling-house meant for his future home:

Into this he had entered about a year before the commencement of the civil strife, which he lived not to see. The cold, moist climate of our island, so different to that of the tropical Antilles, was fatal to him, and in less than twelve months after settling on the Avon's banks he was buried there, having succumbed to an attack of pleurisy. Possibly fast living may have had something to do with it. He was a man of social inclinations and sumptuous habits, which his great wealth enabled him to indulge without stint; and he had recklessly disregarded the care of his health.

Fortunately for those who inherited his property, his life of extravagance had not been long enough to dissipate it, and Madame Lalande was still one of the wealthiest women in Bristol, with no one to share her wealth, save an only daughter, a girl of some eighteen summers, or, to speak more correctly, one summer of eighteen years in length. For the occasional visits to England with her father and mother had been made in this season, the rest of her life spent in a land where winter is unknown. All summer her life in every sense; from her cradle not a wish denied, or taste ungratified, but everything lavished upon her which money could purchase or parental fondness bestow.

As a consequence, Clarisse Lalande had grown up a spoilt child; and now that she was almost a woman, the fruits of such folly made themselves manifest. Imperious and capricious, she had a temper which would not brook restraint. For this it had never known, accustomed all her life to the obeisance of black slaves, and the flattery of mulatto hand-maidens.

Flattery from others she had received too—a very incense of it—which her beauty, without thought of her prospective wealth, commanded. For a beauty she was, of the true Creole type, with all its characteristics; the golden brown tint of skin, the crimson flush of cheeks, the brilliancy of dark eyes, with a luxuriance of hair that defied confinement by ordinary clasp or comb. There was the suspicion of a "wave" in it; and report said that the blood in her father's veins had not been pure Circassian, but with a slight admixture of Ethiopian. All the more piquant were the charms it had transmitted to his daughter, as the star-like fire in her brown-black eyes, and a figure of grandly voluptuous outline. Some of her mental characteristics, too, may have come from it—a certain sensuousness, with the impatience of control already adverted to.

Such being Clarisse Lalande, it scarce needs saying that between her and her cousins Powell there was little congeniality either of tastes or sentiments. Though in person more resembling Sabrina, the two were mental antipodes; while sunbright Vaga, who looked altogether unlike her dark-skinned Creole cousin, had yet certain similar traits of temper; the which made mutual antipathy, at first sight, as when alkali and acid come into contact. It afterwards became heart-hatred, inspired and nursed by the most powerful of influences.

Considering that Madame Lalande was Ambrose Powell's sister, and that her late husband had been a Protestant of Huguenot ancestry—at least four-fifths of him—one would naturally expect her to be on the Parliamentary side—supposing her to take a side at all—with ardent inclinings thereto. Ardent inclinings had she, and side she took; but, strange perversity, *against* the Parliament, not *for* it!

And it was like mother, like daughter, for Clarisse, with all her frivolousness of character, had political leanings too, or more properly caprices, the frivolity itself their cause. In the eyes of the imperious young lady Roundheadism and Puritanism were things of reproach, and the terms themselves often scornfully on her lips. Kingly form of government was the only one fit for gentlepeople; and Cavaliers alone worthy to associate with such as she—those curled darlings, "dear delightful creatures," as, in her fond partiality, she was accustomed to call them.

Wonderfully hospitable was Madame Lalande; that is, in a fashionable way. She gave grand entertainments, which was indeed but continuing what had been done before the death of her husband. Nor was it so long after that event they were recommenced, and carried on with greater *éclat* than ever. For Clarisse had become a toast and now an heiress—sole and safe from any possibility of late-born brother or sister to share the demised wealth. There was keen competition for the favour of her smiles. Knights and baronets were flitting about in plenty, with here and there an earl; and as her ambitious mother aimed at having a titled son-in-law, so spread she the banquet to allure them.

During the brief rule of the gay Essex, as a matter of course Madame Lalande's house was open to him; and so frequently was he its guest, there had been talk of an attraction in it beyond the delights of the dinner table or the joys of the dance. He was not a lord; but, as the son of one, in all probability some day would be.

Alas! for any matrimonial designs Madame Lalande might have upon the rollicking Colonel for her daughter, her chances of showing him further hospitality were brought to an abrupt end, by his heels getting kicked up in a different way, and himself carried off a prisoner to Berkeley Castle.

Withal the festivities in the house of the planter's relict went on as usual—nearly every night something of dinner party, and during the day receptions. If there was suffering in other homes of Bristol through the state of semi-siege in which the place was then held, nothing of this affected the home of the rich West Indian widow. There all was gaiety and splendour.

Yet it had inmates who took little delight in its joys, and one who detested them—that one Ambrose Powell. A new style of life, with a companionship altogether uncongenial, was it to him; and, but for its being forced upon him by the necessity of circumstances, he would not have continued it a single day—not an hour. It was many long years since he had last met his sister; and, remembering her as a guileless country girl—almost portionless too—seeing her now a sharp woman of the world, wealthy and devoted to ideas of frivolity and fashion,—above all, finding her changed from the political faith of their common father and family, he was alike surprised and shocked—angry, moreover, to the point of reproaching, even scolding her; and would have done so, but for the question "*Cui bono?*" which had negative, though silent, answer in all he saw around. His dear sister Gwen, who in earlier days would have humbly listened to his counsels, and been controlled by them, would now resent the meekest suggestion as to her way of life or the conduct of her affairs.

Many a time, after becoming her guest, did he regret having passed on, and beyond Gloucester, to seek an asylum in Bristol. But he was in Bristol now, he and his; and how to get out of it was not a mere question of inconvenience, but a matter of great difficulty, attended with danger. Though not so close to the door, after that 7th of March night, the wolves were still without, on the roads—ravening everywhere.

Chapter Twenty Nine
The Night Owl

The conspiracy having been nipped in the bud, and the conspirators in prison, Bristol again breathed freely. The approaches to it were once more open, the thwarted Royalists having withdrawn to a distance; so that Jerky Jack might have made the return trip to Gloucester with a despatch stuck in the band of his hat safe as it inside his wooden leg.

But swifter messengers traversed that road now, cleared of the enemy at both ends, and on both sides of the river Severn.

He who had effected this clearance was Sir William Waller, jocularly styled "William the Conqueror," from the succession of victories he had late achieved. Also was he known as the "Night Owl;" a sobriquet due to his habit of making nocturnal expeditions that oft took the Royalists by surprise. No Crophead he, but a Cavalier in the true sense; a very Paladin — withal a Christian gentleman. He had separated from slow-going Lord General, and made one of his bold dashes down to the shires bordering Wales; first relieving Gloucester, which was in a manner besieged by the Monmouthshire levies of Lord Herbert. The besiegers were not only brushed off, but the main body of them either killed or captured; only a scant residue escaping to their fastnesses beyond the Wye; whither the "Conqueror" followed, chastising them still further.

Returning across the Forest of Dean, he outwitted the Royalist troops under Prince Maurice; and, once were setting face westward, raided through Herefordshire on to its chief city — which he captured, with a flock of foul birds that had been roosting there ever since its abandonment by the Parliamentarians under the silly Stamford.

But the "Night Owl" himself was not the bird to remain long on perch anywhere; and, gathering up his captured game — a large bag, including some of Herefordshire's best blood, as the Scudamores, Conningsbys, and Pyes — he rounded back to Gloucester, and on to Bristol.

Not to tarry here, either. Soon as he had disembarrassed himself of his captive train — committed to the keeping of Fiennes — he was off again into Somersetshire, there to measure swords with Maurice and the Marquis of

Hertford. As he rode out through the Bath gate at the head of a troop of steel-clad cuirassiers—"Hesselrig's Lobsters"—the citizens of Bristol felt more confident of safety than ever since the strife began. For now they were assured against danger, outside as within. Internal treason had been awed, the traitors cowed and crushed, by what had befallen the conspirators of March the Seventh. The two chiefs of them, Yeomans and Boucher, had been tried, found guilty, and sentenced to death—a sentence soon afterwards carried into execution. Grand efforts were made to get them off; the King himself, by letter, threatening to retaliate upon the poor captives taken at Cirencester—such of them as remained unmurdered. Old Patrick, Earl of Forth, his Majesty's Lieutenant-General, was put forward as the writer of the barbarous epistle. But canny Scot and accomplished soldier as his lordship might be, in a polemical contest he was no match for the lawyer, Fiennes, who flung the threat back in his teeth, saying:

"The men we have tried and condemned are not soldiers, but spies and conspirators. The prisoners you took at Cirencester are prisoners of war. I would have you observe the distinction. And know, too, that for every hair of their heads that falls, I will hang ten of your curled Cavaliers—make Bristol a shambles of them."

Though not Nathaniel Fiennes's exact words, they convey his meaning very near. And he could and would have acted up to them, as the King and his counsellors knew. So, whether or not they deemed his argument rational, it was unanswerable, or at all events unanswered, by a counter-threat; and the Cirencester prisoners were spared execution, while the Bristol conspirators went to the scaffold.

Much has been made of the King's forbearance in this affair by those who did not, or would not, comprehend the motive. It was pure fear, not humanity—fear of a still more terrible retaliation. At that time the Parliament held ten prisoners for one in the hands of the Royalists—men of such rank and quality, his Majesty dared not put their lives in peril, much less let them be sacrificed. He had his revenge in secret, however, since under his very nose at Oxford many of the hapless captives from Cirencester miserably perished, through the torturing treatment of the Royal Provost-Marshal, Smith.

Finally, the "two State martyrs"—as Yeomans and Boucher have been styled by the Royalist writers—were strung up, protesting their innocence to the last, for all they were little believed. The evidence adduced at their trial clearly proved intent to shed the blood of their fellow-citizens; else why were they and their co-conspirators armed? Independent of this, their design of handing over Bristol to the rule of Prince Rupert and his ruffians meant something more than the mere spilling of blood in a street conflict—it involved the sack and pillage of peaceful homes, the violation of women, rapine and ruin in every way. It was only on getting the details of the trial that the Bristolians became fully sensible of the danger they had so narrowly escaped; convinced then, as Captain Birch worded it, that they had been standing upon a mine.

Notwithstanding all these occurrences and circumstances running counter to the Royal cause, against which the tide seemed to have turned, within Montserrat House—as the late Monsieur Lalande had named his dwelling—was no interruption of the festive scenes already alluded to. Its guests were as numerous, its gaieties gay and frequent as ever. For, to speak truth, the political *bias* of the planter's widow, as that of her daughter, was but skin deep. Hair had much to do with it; and, like enough, had the Parliamentarian officers but worn theirs a little longer, submitted it to the curling tongs, and given themselves to swearing and swaggering, in a genteel Cavalier way, they would have been more welcome to the hospitality of her house.

Still not all of them were denied it; for not all were of the Roundhead type. Among them were many gentlemen of high birth and best manners, some affecting as fine feathers as the Cavaliers themselves. For the "Self-denying Ordinance" had not yet been ordained, nor the Parliamentary army moulded to the "new model."

In view of certain people sojourning in Montserrat House, it need scarce be said that Sir Richard Walwyn and Eustace Trevor were visitors there. Even without reference to the predilections of Madame or Mademoiselle, they could not well be excluded. But there was no thought of excluding them; both were unmistakably eligible, and one of them most welcome, for reasons that will presently appear. They had arrived in Bristol only a short while antecedent to its state of semi-siege, the Powells having long preceded them thither. And now that the approaches were again open, most of their time was spent keeping them so; the troop with the "big sergeant," and standard showing a crown impaled upon a sword, once more displaying its prowess in encounters with the Cavaliers. After Rupert had disappeared from that particular scene, Prince Maurice, with his *corps d'armée*, began to manoeuvre upon it, swinging round southward into Somersetshire to unite his force with that of Hertford. To hang upon his skirts, and harass his outposts, was the work of Sir Richard Walwyn; a duty which often carried him and his Foresters afar from the city, and kept them away weeks at a time.

He was just returning to it when Waller passed through. But, entering by a different route and gate from that taken by the latter going out, he missed him. Like enough but for this he would have been commanded along. For the "Conqueror" had carried off with him the *élite* of the troops quartered in Bristol, almost stripping it of a garrison, to the no small annoyance of Nathaniel Fiennes. Glad was the Governor that the troop with the "big sergeant" had escaped such requisition—overjoyed his eyes to see that banner, bearing the emblem of a crown with sword stuck through it once more waving before the Castle gate.

Chapter Thirty
A Mixed Assembly

If Waller's passage through Bristol caused general rejoicing, there was joy in a certain private circle at the re-entry of Sir Richard Walwyn with his troop. Three of the inmates of Montserrat House hailed his return with a flutter of delight; though not all on his account, nor any of them its mistress, the Madame herself. She was pleased, however, to see the gallant knight again, as also his young troop captain, so much, that within a week after their return she sent out invitations to a grand ball, to be given, if not professedly for them, at least so understood.

Many of the invited who were of the King's party wondered, not at her giving a ball, but giving it at such a time, and in honour of their enemies; one of these Eustace Trevor, formerly in the service of the Court itself, whom they regarded as the basest of renegades. Madame Lalande, hitherto such an enthusiastic Royalist, making merry, while the State Martyrs were scarce cold in their graves, and things looking black generally! Waller's unopposed marchings through the surrounding districts had, in a manner, made good the belief in his being invincible; and that he would be equally victorious in the shires of the "West," whither he was now gone. If so, the Royal cause, hitherto ascendant in that quarter, would come under a cloud, if not be extinguished altogether.

Among the Cavalier acquaintances of the planter's widow, therefore, were heard sneering allusions to the "worship of the rising sun," as the reason for her seeming defection.

It was not the correct one, though. Nor, if called upon, could she herself have stated the precise *motif*. Alone her daughter could do that; since it was she had suggested the entertainment; or rather commanded it. Though but turned eighteen, this young lady, child of a precocious clime and race, was a full-grown woman, intellectually as physically; wont to have her own way in Montserrat House, as in her native isle of the Antilles; and was in reality more its mistress than her mother. Her father's will had been read to her, and she quite comprehended its provisions—all in her favour. Little cared she for slanderous whispers, whether by the tongues of Cavaliers or Cropheads; though it was no worship of rising sun inspired her in this particular matter. Instead, a wish to shine herself in the eyes of society; but chiefly those of one for whom she had begun to feel adoration, beyond that to sun, moon, or stars. She could dance like a Bayadere, and knew it.

There need be no difficulty in getting together an assemblage of guests, numerous, and of the right *ton*. Bristol was then an ancient city, second only to London itself; the mushroom Liverpools, Manchesters, and Birminghams having barely a mark upon the map. Besides, in those days, the gentry were more resident in towns; the state of the roads—where there were any—and the scarcity of wheeled vehicles, cumbersome at that, making travel irksome and country life inconvenient. In times of peace the city on Avon's banks had its quota of England's upper crust; but now that war raged around it was crowded with such—fugitives from the adjoining villages and shires, even from beyond the Welsh border, who, as Ambrose Powell and his family, had repaired thither to escape exaction and insult—it might be outrage— from the marauding Cavaliers.

In addition, Bristol, just at this time, contained a goodly sprinkling of the Cavaliers themselves, both military and civilian; not voluntarily there, nor as political refugees, but prisoners. Waller had flung some threescore into it, brought all the way from Monmouth and Hereford, most of them men of high rank, and most as many *on parole*—allowed free range about the city and circulation in its best society, if they had the *entrée*.

So, in sending out her invitations, Madame Lalande had not only a large, but varied list to select from; and to do her justice—or it may have have been Clarisse—on this occasion the names were pricked with impartiality; short hair and long being alike honoured by circulars of complimentary request. In this there might have been an eye to the changing times.

Few were the refusals. No ball had ever come off at Montserrat House unaccompanied by a sumptuous supper. This was lure enough for the elder *invitées*, especially in a city still straitened if not besieged; while to the younger the dancing itself offered attraction sufficient. Since the deposition of the festive Essex there had been but little gaiety in Bristol; under the stern administration of his successor the dance being discouraged, if not altogether tabooed; so that youthful heels were itching for it, of both sexes, and belonging to families on both sides of the political question.

As a result, over two hundred responded to Madame Lalande's invitations by presenting themselves at Montserrat House. Twice the number would not have inconveniently crowded it; since, in addition to several ample reception rooms, there was plenty of space in the ornamental grounds outside, which had been prepared for the occasion by a setting and festoonery of lamps. A summer's night—for it was July, and sultry too—this was an advantageous arrangement, the open air being more enjoyable than that inside.

But another advantage was derived from it; one that may be thought strange enough. It gave Madame Lalande's guests an opportunity of *shunning* one another! With many of them a thing most desirable; for men met there who had been enemies outside—were so still, even to hating—the fugitives from persecution and their very persecutors; the last, now their prisoners, humbled and abashed. Seemingly a fine chance for the former to indulge spites; but good manners forbade that.

Still something more interposed to prevent awkward encounter or recognition. On the ball notes of invitation was marked "Fancy costume at pleasure," which left the invited free to wear masks, or appear without them. But then, even in ordinary street promenade, masks had not been altogether abandoned, at least by ladies, many wearing them to a still later period.

As a consequence of this allowed latitude, numbers of both sexes who attended the Lalandes' ball came in fancy costumes, and masked. But ladies reliant on their charms were careless about the fastenings of the masks, and, somehow or other, the detested screens soon disappeared, giving the gentlemen an opportunity for the scrutiny and comparing of faces.

Many were remarkable for their beauty—some of Bristol's fairest daughters. And as a great seaport, with much foreign element in it, the types were varied. Three, however, attracted special attention—all entitled to the epithet lovely. They had been observed from the beginning, as they were in the withdrawing-room, unmasked, beside Madame Lalande, assisting her in the reception of the guests. Which identifies them as Madame's daughter, and her two nieces, Sabrina and Vaga Powell. So were they.

A connoisseur in female beauty would have found it difficult to decide which of the three deserved the palm. Paris himself would have been puzzled to award it. Clarisse, at home, and helping her mother in the duties of introduction stood prominently forward, and so first met the view of the incoming guests. Few who looked upon her would have thought of looking farther, nor cared to take their eyes off. But beyond her face with features of French type, tinted olive and carmine, was another of English outline, all roses set in a framework of gold—Vaga's. In front of this that of the Creole brunette, despite its piquant beauty, was but the shadow of a partial eclipse vainly endeavouring to hide the light of the sun.

Beside this, still another face in retirement, which many admired as much as either—Sabrina's. Notwithstanding the preference shown by the frivolous Trojan, stately, queenly Juno had her charms too.

Among the gentlemen received by Madame Lalande, and the fair triune forming her staff, were three who had peculiar relations with them—at least with the young ladies—Sir Richard Walwyn, Eustace and Reginald Trevor. They came not in together; the last by some minutes preceding the other two. But, without bettor knowledge of antecedents, it may seem strange his being there at all. Nothing much of this, however, was there about it; nor did Eustace show any surprise at seeing his cousin in the room, which he did soon as entering. He knew Reginald was in the city, and the reason—no voluntary sojourner, but one of the prisoners enjoying "parole." As a captain in Sir John Wintour's troop of horse he had been with Lord Herbert's Monmouthshire levies in their farcical siege of Gloucester, so abruptly raised by Waller; where he escaped death by being made captive, and sent for safe keeping to Bristol. Though Colonel Lunsford was not there also, that worthy had been served the same way at an earlier period. Having cried "quarter" at Edgehill, and there surrendered up his precious person, it was now being taken care of by the gaoler of Warwick Castle. But for that adverse incident he might have been in Bristol too, and figuring, as other fine Cavaliers, at the Lalandes' ball.

Though Reginald Trevor had been now some weeks in the city, and on parole, before that night he and his cousin had not met. As known, Eustace was for a time absent on scout with Sir Richard. But even after his return Reginald had shunned him, and neither had seen aught of the other since that angry parting at Hollymead. Now that chance had brought them together again, it was to meet with no increased cordiality; instead diminished, what had occurred since having but widened the gap between them. Still the hostility was all on Reginald's side, by him felt keenly and bitterly. He had suffered humiliation; a soldier of fortune he was now, not only thrown out of employ but a prisoner. And, if not one of his captors, there among them in amicable association was his cousin, to whom he had sworn giving "No Quarter!" should they ever cross swords in the field of fight.

By good fortune they had not done so yet; and whether he desired it, the other did not—had no such wish. Instead, would have been willing there and then to shake hands with him, and be friends again.

With a half-formed resolve to make offer of reconciliation Eustace approached his cousin. To get a reception which flung him back upon himself, and his sensibilities.

Though few their words exchanged, they were sharp and cutting, as might have been their swords.

"So you've done what you said you would?"

It was Reginald who spoke.

"Done what?"

"Turned traitor to your King. And to your father too?"

"But not to my conscience, nor my God. They are more to me than loyalty to any King, as you call it—even more than affection for my poor deluded father, however much I feel for him."

"Feel for him, indeed! Ha, ha! But you can go on as you've begun. Your Cropheads have it all their own way here, and now; but the tide will turn sooner than you may think for. As for yourself, Eust, you may thank your stars you weren't among the rabble that overpowered me at Highnam. I sent half-a-dozen to their long account, and like as not you'd have been one of them."

The implied superiority, even without the cruelty, was an impertinence. But Eustace Trevor, instead of taking it in that sense, and making angry retort, treated it rather as a joke, with a light laugh rejoining—

"Possibly had I been there, Rej, you wouldn't be here."

At which he turned away, leaving his dark-browed cousin to count the change in satire that had been given him in full.

Chapter Thirty One
A Labyrinth of Jealousies

No more on that night came the cousins together. If by chance they met, it was to pass one another as strangers unacquainted, exchanging neither speech nor look. Further attempt at reconciliation Eustace meant not to make now; he rather regretted having gone so far already.

As for Reginald, he would not have listened to it. A sentiment inspired hostility to his cousin, far stronger than any vexation at his having forsaken the King's cause—altogether different. For it was jealousy; the same he had first felt during that exciting scene at Hollymead, and since brooded over till it had become an all-pervading passion. Eustace had replaced him in the affections of Vaga Powell—or he at least suspected it—that was provocation enough for antipathy, even hatred. And almost this he now entertained for him.

Whatever the political disagreement among the others assembled at Montserrat House, there was no open exhibition of it Royalists and Roundheads stood in groups, or moved about, chatting in a familiar, many of them friendly, way. Officers who had been face to face on the battlefield, and done their best to take one another a lives, here met in mutual good humour, with laughing allusion to the changed circumstances. And when the dancing commenced, gentlemen might be seen, noted adherents of the Parliament, some wearing its uniform, with ladies as their partners strongly affected to the King's cause; while, in the couples *vis-à-vis* to them, the political sentiments would be reversed.

But the majority of those who danced, being the gay *jeunesse*, had no thought of politics, nor care for them one way or the other. They left, that to their elders, and those more seriously disposed; to themselves the delights of the dance being the controlling influence of the hour.

Still there were some, even of the youthful, with whom this was but a secondary consideration. Sabrina Powell preferred strolling about the grounds with Sir Richard Walwyn, for they had much to say to one another. Of late their opportunities of meeting had been few and far between, and they were *fiancée*.

Different with Vaga. She was an ardent worshipper of Terpsichore, and few equalled her in the accomplishment of dancing—scarce any excelling. She was up in every set; and, could she have multiplied herself to count a score, would have found a partner for every unit. A very host sought, with eagerness, to engage her.

There was one who observed this with a secret vexation—Clarisse. Not that she was without her share of aspiring partners; she had them in numbers equalling those of her "country cousin." But even that did not satisfy her; craving universal incense she wanted all.

Possibly, she would have cared less had the rival belle been any other than Vaga Powell. But already between the two had sprung up rivalry of a nature different from any competition as to who should shine brightest at a ball. In a word, they were both in love with Eustace Trevor, and each knew, or suspected it, of the other.

On this night Clarisse had the advantage. Though her mother ostensibly gave the entertainment, she herself was the promoter of it—in a manner mistress of the ceremonies. As such, commanding the music, the arrangement of the dances, and, to a certain extent, who should dance with whom. Not much cared she, however, to exercise this control over other than Eustace Trevor, which she did so effectually, that the two danced together oftener than seemed consistent with ballroom etiquette, and far too frequently to escape observation.

Remarks were made about it, and by the partisans of both sides. "That explains Madame Lalande's defection from our cause," said the Cavaliers. "We now know why this entertainment is being given," remarked the Parliamentarians; "clearly for Captain Eustace Trevor."

And Vaga Powell! What thought she? How did she feel about it? As one at first perplexed, then sorely pained. She who, on the summit of Ruardean Hill, had talked so lightly of love—almost boasted of never having experienced the sentiment—was now within its toils and suffering its torments.

And but little of its delights had she yet known—nothing beyond hopes and vague anticipations. For from the hour when Eustace Trevor plucked the ostrich feathers from his hat, replacing them by those of the egret, she and he had never another opportunity of taking up the thread of the dialogue her sister had so inopportunely interrupted. Several interviews between them since, but all under surveillance or constraint. This, however, had failed to change or weaken the sentiment with which he had inspired her; perhaps strengthened it. True to her profession of constancy, when she said—"If I ever had loved a man, I think I should love him still," she did love him still; on that night with a passion burning as it was bitter.

And the very thing that was filling her heart with gloom gave joy to another. Glad was Reginald Trevor to see his cousin Eustace paying attentions in the quarter where he seemed paying them—to Clarisse Lalande. During all the intervening time since he himself had suffered rebuff, or fancied it, despair had never quite mastered him. As most young Cavaliers, he believed himself a lady—slaughterer irresistible; and to the belief of his having made a conquest of Vaga Powell he would still have confidently clung; but his cousin, of late having better opportunity, had destroyed his chances. And now, seeing Eustace apparently neglectful of her, while all attention to Clarisse Lalande, the old confidence returned to him: he had been labouring under a misconception, and Vaga Powell loved him after all!

Indeed, but for a lingering belief in this, he would not have been there. No thought of ball or supper had brought him to Montserrat House, but the hope of holding speech with her. For, notwithstanding all that had occurred, he entertained such hope. True, he had offended her father; but that was in the exercise of his duties, and under some provocation. Perhaps it was forgotten, or might be forgiven; perhaps she had more than forgiven it already. This night he would know.

An opportunity of speaking with her soon offered. There was little difficulty in his obtaining that. Madame Lalande kept no guard over her nieces, having enough to do in looking after her *chère Clarisse*. And their father was not with them. If within the house he was not a partaker in its gaieties. With no relish for such, he had declined taking part in them. But liberal in this, as in everything else, he placed no constraint on the inclinations of his girls. They were free to dance, as to walk, ride, or go hawking.

The two were standing together as Reginald Trevor approached them. He had but bowed as he was received on entering, and felt gratified at having his salutation returned. Still more now when permitted to enter into conversation with them; finding, if not affability, anything but the distant coldness he had half anticipated. The truth was they had heard many things about him in the interval; that, though fighting for a cause they detested, he had fought gallantly, and gained renown. It is woman's nature to look leniently on the faults of a man who comports himself with courage; and these girls were both of generous disposition. Besides, he was now a defeated man; if not humiliated, a prisoner. Enough that to claim their compassion, and he had it.

Only a few words were exchanged between him and Sabrina—commonplace, and relating to things of a past time. There was one she more desired conversing with; and, turning away, left Reginald Trevor alone with her sister. Long ere then she had learnt where Vaga's predilection lay, and could trust this young lady to take care of herself.

"I suppose you've quite forgotten me, Mistress Vaga?" he said, when Sabrina was out of hearing.

"You give me credit for a very short memory, Captain Trevor," she promptly returned, but in no unkindly tone. "Why should you think I've forgotten you?"

"Oh! so many matters and events since I last had the pleasure of seeing you. And you've met so many other people, more interesting than myself, I could hardly hope for your bearing me in mind."

He spoke in a subdued, humble way, unlike his old swagger; which had the effect of still farther inclining her to kindness. As yet, however, it was but sympathy for his misfortunes.

"But, Captain Trevor, all that would not justify me in forgetting a friend; as I think you were, and would have continued, but for these troubles that have turned so many friends to foes."

"No one regrets them more than I; and for the best of reasons."

He had a reason for regretting them in the fact of his being a prisoner. No light matter just then; for, though not kept confined in a prison, he might at any moment be cast into one, only to be led forth from it to execution. The King had not yet ceased fulminating his threats of retaliation; and, should these be carried out, he, in all likelihood, would be among the foremost of its victims.

He was not speaking the truth, however, in saying he regretted the troubles. As a soldier of fortune they were bread to him, promising fame with promotion. He might look to regaining his liberty by exchange, or otherwise, and once more get upon the ladder of ascent.

Nor had the reasons he spoke of aught to do with his being a prisoner; though she seemed, or affected, so to understand them.

"Indeed, yes," she rejoined, "you have been very unfortunate, Captain Trevor. I'm sorry you should have been taken; still more, fighting on the side you were."

"Oh, thank you!" he returned, encouraged by her kind words, and without heeding the last clause. "But 'tis not for that I care. What makes me regret the war is the loss of friendships. And," he added, speaking in a lower tone, but more impressively, "the fear of having lost yours."

"But you have not, sir—so much as it is worth. My father was angry in those days; so were we all. But, then, you were not to blame—we could not think that, did not—knowing you acted under orders."

"Ah! never had I an order to execute so much against my wish, never one with such disagreeable consequences, separating me so long from—"

He hesitated to say whom or what. But, mistaking her look of simple inquiry for one of a more interested nature, he completed the speech with one other word—"yourself."

She started, looking a little confused, but remained silent; which he, again misinterpreting, took as a permission to go on, which he did, with increased fervour.

"Yes, Mistress Vaga! that was my chief regret, never out of my mind for a moment since. Many the night on watch and guard have I thought of you. Sleepless they would have been, even without duty to keep me awake."

"But why all this, sir? Why should I be a cause to keep you awake?"

She spoke in a tone that suddenly checked and chilled him. For the question recalled a fact he seemed to overlook, or had forgotten—that Vaga Powell had never acknowledged him in the light of a lover; never before given him permission to address words to her such as he was now speaking.

"Ah!" he answered, with a disappointed air, "if you do not know why, 'tis not much use my telling you." Then adding, with a sigh, "I had hopes you would have understood me."

She did understand him perfectly; knew his aspirations and their hopelessness. And never was she less inclined to give heed to them than at that moment. For close by she saw her cousin Clarisse by the side of his cousin Eustace, the two standing up as partners for a dance about to begin.

If Reginald Trevor suffered the pangs of an unrequited love, Vaga Powell was in a very torment of jealousy. For the air and attitude of the other two seemed to speak of something more than the mere indifference of dancing partners. The Creole had hold of his arm, was hanging upon it, her eyes upturned to his face with a languishing, loving smile, which he appeared to reciprocate.

Rather a pleasing sight to Reginald, for reasons that just then presented themselves. But a painful one to her with whom he was conversing—torture itself.

All at once a thought occurred to her, which promised something, if not relief. Anyhow, it gave this and more to Reginald Trevor. For of the many seeking her hand for the dance, he was the one preferred, and with an alacrity that somewhat surprised, while delighting him.

His delight would have been less could he have fathomed her motive and design. Little dreamt he of either, or that he was about to be utilised solely as a pawn for playing the game of *piques*.

Chapter Thirty Two
A Contradanza

It was a *contredanse*; the "contradanza" of Spain transmitted through France to England, where it had become naturalised, and by a misapprehension of terms called "country dance" It was the *pièce de resistance* of the time, before the introduction of the cotillon, quadrille, and other "square" dances.

The assemblage being a large one, several sets danced at the same time, inside the house and without, the music in a central position availing for all.

The set in which figured Mademoiselle Lalande was, of course, the select one, comprising the *élite* of the family's friends and resident gentry, with the strangers of greatest distinction, military and civilian. It was formed on the lawn outside, in front of the withdrawing-room windows, where a spread of smooth, firm turf afforded ample space, and a floor for dancing good as that of any ballroom. Better, slips and tumbles considered. Around and overhead were strings of lamps suspended from the trees, while a profusion of flowers, now in full blow, filled the air with incense. A warm summer's night, with such surroundings, the Creole girl might have fancied herself back in her native isle of the Antilles, under the palms and amidst the flashing *cocuyos*.

As if she had such a fancy, her grand dark eyes were aglow with delight—triumph in them too. But neither had to do with any thought of scenes or things transatlantic. The cause was by her side, and she took no pains to conceal it. Impassioned child of the tropics, never in her life gainsaid, she had needed not the resorts of subterfuge; instead openly demanding and having whatever she desired. And now desiring Eustace Trevor, she believed she had secured him.

Certainly it seemed so; and as if with her wiles and witchery—bold ways the sober Bristolians called them—she had succeeded in weaving a spell around him. Once already had he been her partner, and now for the second time was he standing up with her, to all appearance absorbed in what she said, making impressive responses, partaking of her joy and triumph.

This was what Vaga Powell supposed; and no wonder at her jealousy stung to the highest, bitterest pitch. But the green-eyed monster sees with eyes that distort and exaggerate, as hers were doing then. She was putting a wrong interpretation on what she saw, reading it reversely to the truth. A disinterested spectator, with skill in physiognomy, could have told that Eustace Trevor, so far from being taken up with Clarisse Lalande, would have been glad to get disembarrassed of her. He too was at that moment suffering pangs of jealousy equal to those he inflicted. This from seeing his cousin the partner of Vaga Powell, thinking of Reginald's acquaintance with her older than his own, and recalling something he had heard of between them antecedent to the time of his introduction at Hollymead. Only a rumour it was—a vague whisper—but it spoke of relations of a nature warmer and more confidential than those of mere friendship.

Could it have been so, and was there a renewal of them? These were the questions self-asked by the *ci-devant* gentleman-usher. Seemingly answered in the affirmative by what he now saw. For, young as was the younger daughter of Ambrose Powell, she was no child of simplicity, but could play at coquetting with the oldest and cleverest coquette there. If he in her eyes seemed too assiduously attentive to Clarisse, she in his appeared the same with Reginald.

An odd position of affairs it was with this *quartette* of cousins as regarded their feelings towards one another—a play of cross purposes, triangularly twisted and sinister, but in a manner symmetrical. The two men in love with the same woman, the two women loving the same man, yet two of the four not loved at all—as it were, left out in the cold. And these last the ones that were joyous and exultant, the others despondent and sad.

Could hearts see into hearts, and read the writing therein, all this would have been reversed; the glad ones would have ceased to be gay, and on the instant, while the sad ones would as suddenly have found joy. But the people so perversely astray could not comprehend one another. Not likely with everything done to hinder it—glances, attitudes, gestures, all meant to deceive.

And so the mutual misconception remained throughout the night. Dance succeeded dance, but in none was Eustace Trevor the partner of Vaga Powell.

And yet the fault was not with him, though it may appear so. His dancing the first set with Clarisse was quite accidental so far as he was concerned. He had not sought to engage her; on the contrary she seeking him—in a manner commanding him. Officially privileged, she might do so without incurring censure or challenging remark. But when the thing was repeated, and for the second time in succession they were seen standing up together, a whisper went round that it meant something more than mere inadvertency—in short, a decided preference.

And so was it with her at least, he neither feeling it nor conscious of her design. For, in truth, he had been on the way to seek Vaga Powell and ask her for the second set, when once more encountering Clarisse, as by chance, she exclaimed, in a half patronising, half-coaxing way,—

"How well you dance, Captain Trevor! So different from all the others."

Rather surprised by such a plain-spoken compliment, flattery in fact—he was about to give it this name—but, without waiting his rejoinder, she rattled on,—

"And I hope you're enough satisfied with *my* dancing to have me for your partner again—you will, won't you?"

Solicitation seeming bold, almost to shamelessness. It would have been this in an English girl; but one knowing Clarisse Lalande, her impulsive nature, and the way she had been brought up, could better pardon it.

"It will give me the greatest pleasure," was his response. He would not have been man—less gentleman—to answer otherwise. Both gallantry and good manners enforced an affirmative.

"Consider yourself engaged then!"

"By all means, Mademoiselle. For which set?"

"Oh! now—the next. I wish it."

Another surprise to him, anything but agreeable. It interfered with his intentions, spoiling his own programme. But there was no help for it, no gain saying a wish so plainly expressed, and he stammered out assent with the best grace possible.

As the music for the second set was just commencing, she thrust her jewelled fingers inside his arm, and conducted him, rather than he her, back to the place of dancing.

It was then Vaga Powell experienced that jealous pang which determined her to the line of action she was pursuing. But it was a jealousy neither new, nor born of that hour; only in that hour reaching the climax and acme of its keenness. Eustace Trevor twice dancing with her cousin, and never coming near herself! Never once, even to say a word, since the one or two of ceremony exchanged between them at his first entering and reception. No wonder at her being a prey to jealousy!

But she was not alone in the experience of its misery. He, in his turn, was tasting of it too. When at length released from his engagement with the Creole, inopportune as irksome, and he again sought Vaga Powell, it was to find her in a mood aught but amiable. And with Reginald still by her side—she had no difficulty in retaining *him*—the two seemingly engrossed with one another. Well and skilfully—too well and too skilfully—was the damsel of Dean Forest playing her part.

As Eustace approached them, Reginald drew back a pace, and stood in an attitude of dignified stiffness, with a perceptible triumph in his eyes, and something like a sneer on his lips. No word of salutation passed between the cousins now—not even nod of recognition—and one seeing who knew them not would have supposed them utter strangers. Eustace but bowed to the lady; and, as the music was just sounding the prelude to another dance, he asked, in rather a timid, doubting way,—

"May I have you for a partner, Mistress Vaga?"

At another time, even earlier that night, he might have addressed her differently and more familiarly—ay, would have been safe in saying—"Let us dance, dear Vaga!" But he had neither thought nor confidence to "dear" her now, nor she the desire to be deared. Curt, and almost disdainful was her answer,—

"Sorry; but I'm engaged."

He did not need being told to whom, the triumphant bearing of his cousin declared that; and, with a bow of feigned resignation, and much bitterness of heart, he withdrew, leaving them to themselves.

And so the jealous fire, just kindled in his breast, burned on in hers, not that night to be extinguished.

Chapter Thirty Three
A Pas-Seul

Wide the breach now between Vaga Powell and Eustace Trevor, growing wider as the moments passed. Though the evolutions of the dance often brought them near one another, no more speech exchanged they that night; nor glances either. If by chance their eyes met there was a retirement on both sides, quick and subtle, as though each felt caught in some criminal act. For all they were mutually observant, and when only one looked, the other unconscious, it was with gaze continued, regard telling the tale of love and jealousy plainer and truer than could words.

What had caused the rupture was still there to hinder its healing— on one side Clarisse, practising all her arts and seductions; on the other Reginald doing the same. And both, so far as they themselves believed, and general appearance might be trusted, with sinister success.

Between these two, aiming at like ends, there was much similitude otherwise. Equally vain, Creole girl as Cavalier, they had grand reliance in their respective powers, each over the opposite sex. Though no Adonis, Reginald Trevor was a fairly handsome man—of the martial type, whom many a woman would have fancied, as many had. So favoured, and conscious of it, not so strange his restored confidence that he still possessed the affections of Vaga Powell. He had entertained this belief, and then partially lost it, but now it was back with him again, her behaviour seeming to justify it.

There was less in the past to cloud the hopes of Clarisse—less known to her. For the antecedent circumstances between Eustace Trevor and her cousin had as yet been revealed to her only in a scant desultory way. She had heard of his having spent some days at Hollymead; had been told also of his sudden conversion there, and half suspected the cause. But she had herself observed nothing to confirm her suspicions. He had been several times on visit to Montserrat House, but always in the company of his colonel, Sir Richard; and while there his interviews with Vaga were under her own eyes and others. They might have met outside without her having knowledge of it. But it was in truth the brilliant beauty of her country cousin, which more than aught else troubled and had given rise to her jealousy. Still what was it to her own, with her powers of fascination? Nothing that night, thought she; and thus confident in herself, she noticed not the strange distraught air of her partner, as now and then his eyes turned furtively to the partner of his cousin.

Thus unobservant, the two who cared not for one another danced joyously on little dreaming of that mad jealousy between the other two, but for which there would have been a quick change in the arrangement of the couples.

"What next? What now?"

The questions passing from lip to lip, late on in the night, and after another *contredanse* had come to a close. A whisper had got wing of something to succeed, altogether different—a dance of a special character, introduced to the Bristolians by the daughter of Madame Lalande.

In those days, the era of the morris and other picturesque dances, excellence in the Coryphean art was esteemed a qualification; not lightly held as now, and deemed rather degrading. The French Queen had encouraged this, and noble dames oft vied with each other in saltatory displays.

To show her superiority, Clarisse Lalande had prepared a surprise for the assembly at Montserrat House—a dance of the Antilles, in which she could have no competitor, nor need fear any if she had. It was also of Spanish origin, much practised in the West India islands; where, then as now, dancing was a thing of every night, and often of the day—even the negroes giving half their off-labour hours to it, jigging with a grace unknown to the peasantry of European lands. Their white "massas" were, many of them, perfect *maîtres-de-danse*, and their young mistresses very Odalisques. Monsieur Lalande had prided himself on this accomplishment, and, as a matter of course, his daughter did the same—hence the resolve to make display of her proficiency.

The music had been prearranged; the time too—after supper, when the excitement which comes of the wine cup would make it more attractive in the eyes of the spectators; though Clarisse Lalande was thinking of only one of them, and how it would affect him.

It was new to most of the people present, but not all. The familiars of Montserrat House had witnessed it before, and were aware of its peculiarities. A *pas-seul* it was, danced only by a lady, though a gentleman had something to do with it at the termination. The lady commences in slow movement and gentle step, accompanied by pantomimic gestures; as she passes on every now and then stooping down, or reaching upward, to take hold of some object that has caught her eye. It is, in fact, a representation, in dumb show, of an Indian girl straying along a forest path in the act of gathering flowers. Nor does she pause while plucking them, only poising an instant on one limb, and, with a whirl, or *pirouette*, continuing onward. The step admits of many changes and every variety of attitude; according to whether the blossoms tempting her be on the right or left, down upon the earth, or overhead among the branches of the trees. All which affords fine opportunity for displaying the graces of figure and movement, with skill or cleverness in the pantomimic representation. After this has gone on for a time, the flower gatherer is seen to start, her features changing expression. Some sound in the forest has caught her ear. She pauses, bends low, and listens. At first interrogatively; then with apprehension, ending in alarm. Flight follows, the lines of if hither and thither in irregular zigzags, as if the affrighted girl, in her confusion, knows not which way to go. The movement is now violent, the gesticulation excited. At length the retreat takes a steadier course, around the outer edge of the arena, not by forward steps, but the whirling gyrations of a waltz. This being kept up for a turn or two, fatigue is counterfeited, with continued fear of the pursuing enemy, and by looks and gestures appeal is made to the spectators for help. These know, however, that only one is privileged to offer it—he whom she will designate by tossing to him a riband, kerchief, glove, or some such token. His *rôle*, then, is simply to step forth and place himself in the attitude of a rescuer, when the fugitive flings herself into his arms, looking all gratitude.

When Clarisse Lalande took the floor, or, to speak more correctly, the turf,—for it was outside in the place already described,—there were few knowing the character of the novel dance but could give a guess as to who would be summoned to the rescue. Too soon to be thinking of that yet, however; all thoughts being engrossed by the Creole herself, all eyes fixed upon her, as she appeared in the open space, around which the spectators were now standing two deep. The whole company was there; the other dancing places, inside and out, for the time deserted.

It was seen that she had changed her dress—this done during the interlude of supper—and was now in the costume of a Carib queen, short skirt and low boddice. Robes rather gauzy and transparent; at which some present were not slow to speak disapprovingly. But these were in the minority; the wonderful beauty of the girl, with a knowledge that her ways and bringing up had not been as theirs, made the majority large and something more than lenient. And when she became engaged in the innocent occupation of flower-gathering, like a brilliant butterfly flitting from one to another, satire was silent; even the most Puritanical seeming to forget all about the thinness and scantiness of her attire.

Then came the start, the listening attitude, the affectation of alarm, followed by the confused flight; in grand *voltes* in side-bounds, as an antelope surprised by a panther. At length the circling retreat, round and round the ring of spectators, at first in a rapid whirl, till feigning exhaustion, her movements gradually became slower and feebler, as though she would drop to the earth.

Every eye was now on the alert; they knew the *finale* was near, and the recipient of the favour would soon be declared. It often means nothing beyond mere compliment; and as oft for delicate reasons, the favoured one is not the one wished for. But no such influences were likely to affect the present case, and the *dénouement* was looked for with a rare intensity of interest.

The girl had drawn off one of her jewelled gloves—in those days they were so adorned—and held it with arm astretch, ready to be flung. Still, she went undulating on, at each turn of her face toward the spectators seeming to search among them. Many a one had wishes, and more than one a hope of seeing that glove tossed to him. For Clarisse Lalande had a large following of lovers. All save one to suffer disappointment, with more or less chagrin. And yet giving no gratification to him at whose feet it eventually fell, as the wise ones knew it would—Eustace Trevor.

With less show of alacrity than resignation he took it up; this an exigency of the performance. After which, with open arms, he received the exhausted *danseuse*, her breasts heaving and panting as though they would burst the silken corset that so slightly confined them.

Cold-blooded man he, many might have thought him. But had other breasts been thus near his own, another heart beating so close to his, he would have shown warmth enough.

Chapter Thirty Four
Guardian Angels

"The swift Rhone cleaves his way between
  Heights which appear as lovers who have parted
In hate, whose mining depths so intervene
  That they can meet no more, though broken-hearted;
Though in their souls, which thus each other thwarted,
  Love was the very root of the fond rage
Which blighted their life's bloom, and then departed —
  Itself expired, leaving them an age
Of years, all winters - war within themselves to wage."

Was it to be thus with Eustace Trevor and Vaga Powell?

Verily, it seemed so on that night; and never more than at that moment, when he, with her cousin—Indian queen in counterfeit—strolled off arm in arm along the lamplit walks. A sight to tear her heart. And it tore it; might have altogether rent and ruined it had the mutual misunderstanding continued. Ay, "blighted the life's bloom" of both, "leaving them an age of years, all winters."

But kind fate decreed it otherwise; before another night shadowed Avon's banks, whatever of confidence had hitherto been between them was reestablished, and true love triumphed over jealousy.

Partly by accident was the happy result brought about; though it might have come without that. For on the side of each was a watchful monitor, who understood the situation better than either of themselves.

The guardian angels were Sir Richard Walwyn and Sabrina Powell; his friendship, and her sisterly solicitude standing the younger lovers in stead.

"Why has your sister not danced with Captain Trevor—I mean my Captain Trevor?" queried the soldier knight of his betrothed. "I haven't seen him near her all the night. Has there come a coolness between them, think you?"

"Something of the sort, I fear."

"But from what cause? Have you any idea?"

"Oh! the cause is clear enough! though she hasn't made me her *confidante*."

"The Creole cousin?"

"Just so."

"But Vaga has nothing to fear from her; nor need being jealous, in the least."

"Why do you say so, Richard?"

"Because Trevor don't care a straw for Mademoiselle Lalande."

"Then what means the way he's been carrying on with her?"

"Rather, say, the way she's carrying on with him. It don't—signify, however. Let her practise all her arts; she'll have her pains for nothing. I know he's madly in love with your sister; has been ever since first setting eyes upon her at Hollymead. That much he has confided to me."

"He may have changed. Clarisse is very beautiful—very attractive?"

"True, she is. But not the style to attract him. Nor is he of the fickle sort. At Whitehall he bore the reputation of having a heart of adamant; with no end of sighing damsels doing their endeavour to soften it. Indeed, scandal spoke of its very obduracy being the cause of his dismissal from Court; a certain Royal lady having assailed it unsuccessfully, and for that reason turned against him. Such a man once in love, as I know he is with your sister, is not likely to veer about so suddenly."

"But, you remember with what suddenness he changed sides, politically?"

"Ah! that's different, and to his credit. It was not of his own choosing that he was on the wrong one. And, soon as finding it so, he espoused the right one. All the more likely his standing firm, and proving true in an affair of the heart. But are you sure the fault is not on Vaga's side? I've observed her a good deal in the company of the other Trevor, and several times dancing with him. What does that mean?"

"I cannot tell. He may be forcing his company upon her; and she, offended at Eustace's behaviour, accepts it."

"Likely then they are playing at spite—that is, my captain and your sister. It's a dangerous game, and we must do something to stop it."

They thus exchanging confidences were engaged lovers of long standing, who, but for the war coming on, would now have been man and wife. Hence their interest in the two who were in danger of going astray was of a protecting character. Sabrina, especially anxious about the upshot on the score of her sister's happiness, rejoined with alacrity, —

"We must. Are you sure Eustace loves Vaga?"

"Sure as that I love you, dearest. I had evidence of it, not many hours ago, and from his own lips. On the way hither—we came together you may know—he spoke of a heaviness at his heart, and that he had never started to go to a ball with less anticipation of pleasure. On my asking for explanation, he said it was on account of your sister. It was weeks since he had seen her; and something seemed to whisper she would not be the same to him as she had been. Trying to laugh away his fancies, and pressing him for a more tangible reason, he merely added 'Reginald.' I know he has always had a suspicion, if not jealousy, about his cousin's relations with Vaga, before he himself came to know her. When he returned the other day, and he learnt that Reginald was in Bristol—had been for some time—he took it for granted he would also be often here in this house. That, of course, considering the Cavalier inclinings of your aunt and cousin. No doubt the thought, or fancy, of Master Rej being restored to Vaga's favour is what affects him now."

"It's but a fancy, then. Master Rej couldn't be restored to favour he never had. As for Vag—"

She broke off abruptly at the sound of voices and footsteps. Two persons in conversation were coming along the gravelled walk. The place was a pavilion, trellised all round, the trellis supporting a thick growth of climbers that formed a curtain to it. There was a lamp suspended inside, but its light had gone out, either through neglect or because the day would soon be dawning. The dialogue given above took place within the pavilion; that to follow occurring just outside by the entrance.

It was between two of the four, about whom they inside had been conversing—Clarisse and Eustace. She was still upon his arm, as he had conducted her off the dancing ground; she now rather conducting him towards that quiet spot, whither she had no idea of any one having preceded them.

"It seems so strange, Captain Trevor, you fighting for the Parliament?"

"Why strange, Mademoiselle?"

"Because of your father, and all your family, being on the King's side; your brave cousin too. Besides, you're so different from these plebeian Puritans and Roundheads; unlike them in every way."

"Not every way, I hope, and would be sorry to think I was. Rather would I resemble them in their ways of truth and right—their aspirations for liberty, and the self-sacrificing courage they have shown to achieve it."

"But the Cavaliers show courage too; as much, and more than they."

"Neither more, nor as much. Pardon me, Mademoiselle, for contradicting you. Hitherto they've been better horsed, by robbing the poor farmers, emptying every stable they came across. That's given them the advantage of us. But there'll be a turn to it soon, and we shall pay the score back to Rupert and his plunderers."

"Oh, Captain Trevor! To speak so of the gallant Prince—calling him a plunderer. For shame!"

"He's all that, and more—a ruthless murderer. Nor is the King himself much less, after his doings of the other day with the wretched captives of Cirencester."

"You naughty, naughty rebel!" she rejoined, with a laugh telling how little the misfortunes of the Cirencestrians affected her, adding—"And I feel inclined to call you renegade as well."

"Call me that, and welcome. 'Tis no disgrace for a man to turn coat when he discovers he has been wearing it wrong side out; not put on so by himself but by others. For what I've done, Mademoiselle Lalande, I feel neither shame nor repentance; instead, glory in it."

"What a grand, noble fellow!" thought Sir Richard, as also the other listener inside the pavilion; the latter with added reflection how worthy he was to mate with her sister.

It was less his reasoning, than the defiance flung to her in tone so independent, that caused the Creole to shrink back from what she had said. Fearing it might have given offence, she hastened to heal the wound by the salve of self-humiliation.

"O sir! I but spoke jestingly; and please don't think I meant reproaching you. As you know, we women have but little understanding of things political; of English politics I less than any, from being a stranger to the country—almost a foreigner. In truth, I know not clearly which party may be in the right. Nor do I care either—that is, enough to quarrel with my friends, and certainly not with yourself, Captain Trevor. So please pardon what I've said—forget it. You will, won't you?"

Her *naïve* admission and submission inclined him to a better opinion of her than he had hitherto entertained. "After all," thought he, "she has a woman's heart true, but led astray by sinister surroundings." So reflecting, he returned kindly,—"There's nothing either to be pardoned or forgotten, *chère Mademoiselle*. And if there was, how could I refuse a request made as you make it?"

He spoke more warmly than had been his wont with her; addressed her as "chère Mademoiselle"—that also unusual. It was all on the spur of the moment, and without thought of its being taken in the way of endearment. But it was so taken, and had the effect of misleading her.

"I'm so glad we're to continue friends," she exclaimed, impressively; then in changed tone adding—"About my glove? Is it to be returned? Or do you wish to keep it?"

Questions that took him by surprise, at the same time perplexing him. For, though offering a choice of ways, it was a delicate matter which should be taken. The glove was still in his hand, as he had picked it up. To retain it would imply something more than he was in the mind for; while returning it implied something else, equally against his inclinations. It might give offence—be even regarded as a rudeness.

A happy thought struck him—a compromise which promised to release him from his dilemma. The glove was a costly thing, embroidered with thread of gold, and beset with jewels.

"It is too valuable," he said; "I could not think of keeping it. Oh, no!" and he held it out towards her.

But she refused to take it, saying with a laugh,—

"Very considerate of you, sir; and thanks! But I'm not so poor, that it will be impossible for me to replace it by one of like value."

Foiled, he drew back his hand; now with no alternative but to keep the token he cared not for.

"Since you are so generous, Mademoiselle, I accept your gift with gratitude."

Even the cold formality of this speech failed to dispel the illusion she had been all the night labouring under. Unused to discomfiture of any kind, she thought not of defeat in the game of passion she was playing.

"Oh! it's nothing to be grateful for," she lightly rejoined. "Only your due for rescuing me from the pursuing enemy. Ha-ha-ha!"

He was about to stow the favour under the breast of his doublet, when he saw her glance go up to the crown of his hat, over which still waved the feathers of the egret, plucked by the base of Ruardean hill.

"Perhaps you wouldn't care to carry it there?" she said, half jestingly. "It might spoil the look of that pretty plume."

He was doubly perplexed now. To place the glove in his hat meant letting it remain there, meant more—a symbol to show that the giver of it was esteemed beyond all others. And that in her case would not be true. Besides, what would *she* say—what think—whose favour, not proffered but asked for, was already there? Despite all the contrarieties of the night, Eustace Trevor was not prepared to break with Vaga Powell by offering her such a slight—an insult. With much to make him sad and angry, he was neither sad nor angry enough for retaliation as that. Sure, moreover, to recoil upon himself—a reflection which needed no other to determine him.

But the challenge had been thrown out, and called for instant response—a yes or a no. Subterfuge was no longer possible, even had it been of his nature, and he resolved upon making a clean breast of it.

"Mademoiselle Lalande, however proud of the trophy you've been good enough to bestow on me, there's a reason why I cannot wear it as you suggest?"

"A reason, indeed!" the voice in a tone half vexed, half surprise. "May I know it?" Then, as if repenting the question, she quickly added, "Oh, never mind! Give me back my glove, sir. Good-night!"

They, listening inside the pavilion, heard no more words, only the sound of footsteps passing away; first light ones in rapid repetition; then others heavier and slower; after which silence profound.

Chapter Thirty Five
A Complete Eclaircissement

"Mademoiselle's game is up. You see, Sabrina, I was right, and he's loyal to his love—true to the *guage* of the egret's plume."

"Indeed, yes! What a tale for Vaga! And I shall tell it her soon."

"'Twill gladden her, you think?"

"I'm quite sure of it. Though I haven't evidence of her heart's inclinings in speech plain as that we've just—Hish! Another couple coming this way! Really, Richard, we ought not to stay here; 'tis bad as being eaves-droppers."

"Never mind about the eavesdropping. It will sit light on my conscience, after leading to such good results. Who may be the pair approaching now, I wonder?"

They listened. To hear music, with the hum of many voices afar off; but two near, and drawing nearer.

"My sister!" said Sabrina, almost instantly recognising one of them; then, after another brief interval of silence, adding, "and Reginald Trevor!"

Continuing to advance, the two were soon up to the pavilion; and made stop, on the same spot where but five minutes before stood their respective cousins.

Now, however, it was the gentleman who spoke first—after their coming to a stand—and as if changing the subject of the dialogue already in progress.

"My cousin Eust seems beside himself with Mademoiselle Lalande. I never saw man so madly in love with a woman. I wonder if she reciprocates it?"

He was pouring gall into Vaga Powell's heart, and apparently without being conscious of it. For, by this, he had reached full confidence that his own love was reciprocated by her with whom he was conversing.

"Like enough," was the response, in tones so despairingly sad, that, but for his being a fool in his own conceit, he might have drawn deductions from it to make him suspect his folly. More, could he have but seen the expression upon her features at that moment—pain, almost agony. The pantomimic dance—just over, all its acts, incidents, and gestures were still fresh before her mind—the latest the most vivid—the dropping of the glove; its being taken up, as she supposed, with eager alacrity; then, the man she loved throwing wide open his arms to receive into them the woman she hated! All this was in her thoughts, a very tumult of trouble—in her heart as a flaming fire.

The darkness favoured her, or Reginald Trevor could not have failed perceiving it on her face. But, indeed, she would have little cared if he had. Dissembling with him all the night, she meant doing so no more. Though the play was not with him, the game had gone against her; she had lost the stakes, as she supposed, irretrievably; and now would retire into the shadow and bitterness of solitude.

Little dreamt he of how she was suffering, or the cause. Knowing it, he might have sprung away from her side, quickly and angrily as had Clarisse from that of Eustace.

Continuing the conversation, he said, insinuatingly,—

"On second thoughts, I'm wrong, Mistress Vaga. I *have* known a man as much in love with a woman as my cousin is with yours—know one now?"

"Indeed?"

The exclamatory rejoinder was purely mechanical, she who made it not having enough interest in what had been said to inquire who was the individual he alluded to. Yet this was the very question he courted. He had to angle for it further, saying,—

"May I tell you who it is?"

"*Oh*, certainly; if you desire to do so."

Even this icy response failed to check him. He either did not perceive its coldness, or mistook it for reticence due to the occasion. Several times, since his first abortive attempt, he had been on the eve of making fuller declaration to her—in short, a proposal of marriage. But she had been dancing with others besides himself, and no good opportunity had as yet offered. That seemed to have come now. So, taking advantage of it, and her permission, he said, in an impressive way,—

"The man is Reginald Trevor—myself."

If he expected her to give a start of feigned surprise, and follow it up by the inquiry, "Who is the woman?" he was disappointed. For he but heard repeated the laconic exclamation she had already used, and in like tones of careless indifference.

"Indeed!" That, and nothing more.

Still unrepulsed he returned to the attack; again, as it were, begging the question,—

"Shall I name the woman?"

"Not if you don't wish it, sir." Response that should have made him withhold the information, if not driven him from her presence. A very rebuff it was; and yet Reginald Trevor looked not on it in this light. Instead, still strong in his false faith and foolish hope, he persisted, saying,—

"But I do wish it, and will tell you; though you may little care to know. I cannot help the confession. She I love is yourself—yourself, Vaga Powell; and 'tis with all my heart, all my soul!" The avowal, full and passionate, affected her no more than the hints he had already thrown out. In the same calm tone, firm, and with the words measured, she made response,—

"Captain Trevor, you've told me almost as much before. And if I never gave you answer to say the feeling you profess for me was not reciprocated, I say it now. It is not—never can be. Friends, if you wish, let us remain; but for the other—"

"You needn't go on!" he interrupted, impatiently, almost rudely. "I've heard enough; and now know what's the obstacle between us. Not your father, as I once supposed, but my cousin. Well, have him, if you can get him. As for myself, I'm consoled by thinking there are as good fish in the sea as ever were caught out of it, and I go to catch one of them. Adieu, Mistress Vaga Powell!" Saying which, he strode off in true Cavalier swagger, humming a gay *chanson*; having left her alone in the darkness of night, and the gloom of despair.

Only for an instant was she thus. Then she felt arms flung around her, tenderly, lovingly, while listening to speech which promised to relieve her of her misery.

"I was so glad, Vag," said Sabrina, "hearing what you said. And I've heard something said by another, at which you'll be glad, when I tell it you."

Almost at the same instant of time, though in a different part of the grounds, Sir Richard Walwyn was in like manner promising to let light into the heart of Eustace Trevor.

Chapter Thirty Six
After Roundway Down

An hundred horsemen riding at their hardest—not in any military formation, but strung out in a straggled ruck—horsemen steel-clad from crown to hip, some with helmets battered; others bare-headed, the head-piece gone; cuirasses showing dints, as from stroke of halberd or thrust of pike; on back and breastplate blood splashes, dried and turned purple-black; boots, mud-bespattered and *délabré*—this damaged cohort all that remained of "William the Conqueror's" army!

They were the remnant of Hesselrig's Horse, the "Lobsters" in retreat from Roundway Down, where the chivalrous, but too reckless, too confident Waller, had given battle to the outnumbering enemy under Byron and Wilmot; been defeated, and put to utter rout.

It was the wind up of a series of sanguinary engagements with the Marquis of Hertford and Prince Maurice, commencing with an encounter on the low-wooded bottom between Tog and Friznoll hills, so hotly contested that veterans there engaged, who had gone through all the Low Country and German campaigns, declared the most furious fights they ever had abroad were but sport to it.

Carried up to the adjacent height of Lansdown, from which, after another fierce conflict, the Parliamentarians were forced to retire, the two armies—what remained of them—again came face to face on the elevated plateau of Roundway Down; the final scene of the struggle and Waller's discomfiture.

Hesselrig's Cuirassiers had especially suffered. With ranks broken, and many of them unhorsed, they were all but helpless in their unwieldy armour, and scores got tumbled over the cliffs of the Down. Of a well-appointed regiment, over five hundred strong, which but a few days before had filed out through the gates of Bristol, only this straggling troop—less than a fifth of the force, still kept the saddle.

Waller was himself along with it—for the "Lobsters" formed his body-guard—so too Hesselrig, severely wounded. Crestfallen both—it could not be otherwise—but with no cowed or craven look. The blood upon their gauntlets and sword-hilts, on their blades still unwiped, told both had been where cowards would not be—in the thick of the fight. Only to superior numbers had they yielded, and were now retiring sullenly as disabled lions. If they rode hard and fast it was through the urgency of their followers, who feared pursuit behind with the fiendish cry, "No Quarter!"

Morn was just dawning as the retreating troop caught sight of Bristol's towers—glad to their eyes, giving promise of refuge and rest. This last they needed as much as the first. For days and nights they had scarce ever been out of the saddle; looked wan for the want of sleep, and were weak from fatigue and hunger. Their horses blown and dead-beat, many of them staggering in their gait. No wonder the sight of that city was welcome to them.

But what a spectacle they themselves to those inside it, to the hundreds, nay thousands, who gazed off and out from turret, wall, and window! The first glimpse got of them was by the warder in the Castle's keep, just as the brightening sky enabled him to descry objects at a distance. Then other sentries saw them from the watch towers of the gates on that side; and the signal of alarm ran along the line of fortification, round and round. Soon bells rang, trumpets brayed, and drums beat all over the city, startling the citizens out of their sleep and beds. Before the sun had yet shown above the horizon, not one but was awake, and most out of doors. Men rushed wildly through the streets—women too—or stood aperch, clustering on every eminence, every pinnacle and parapet thick as bees, with eager, anxious glances scanning the country outside. At length to fix them on the long, glittering line—for the sheen of the cuirasses were not all gone—that now approached in slow, laboured pace, as the crawl of a scotched snake.

When near enough for the bare heads and battered helmets to be distinguished, the blood smouches on dress, arms, and accoutrements, the gloom on brows and in eyes, with lips compressed and features hard set as in sullen anger—when these sure insignia of disaster were fully before them, a feeling of despondency came over the hearts of the Bristolians. Intensified, doubled, when at the head of this figment of a force, crushed and shattered, they saw Sir William Waller, and by his side Sir Arthur Hesselrig—the two leaders so long victorious as to be deemed invincible! They had seen them ride out with an army numbering nigh 6,000 men, and now saw them returning, in retreat, with but a bare hundred! These so down-looking and dispirited, that, as Waller himself—candid as he was brave—confessed in his report to the Lord General, "a corporal with an ordinary squadron could have routed them."

To many who witnessed their re-entry within Bristol's gates it was as much spectre as spectacle—the presentiment of misfortune for themselves.

But not all viewed it in this light. There were eyes into which it brought a sparkle of gratification; some even the glow of anticipated vengeance. During Fiennes's iron rule, the "malignants" had been much humiliated, and the prospect of a change, themselves to have the upper hand, made them jubilant. And there were the relatives and friends of the so-called "State Martyrs," with the fate of these fresh in their mind, burning for revenge. Citizens affected to the King's cause, Cavaliers, whether prisoners on parole or otherwise, the tapsters, gamesters, and tricksters of every speciality; in a word, all the reprobacy and blackguardism of Bristol, high and low, male and female, were gleeful at a sight giving them forecast of that for which they had long been yearning—an opportunity of pillage and plunder. It was just with them, as it would be with their modern representatives the Jingoes, at any mischance to Liberalism, likely to give the Jew of Hughenden another spell at despoiling and dishonouring England. For they, too, were doughty champions of beer and Bible, with whom national honour was but a name, the nation's glory an empty boast. They, as Tories now, cared not for the wrongs and sufferings of an over-taxed people, any more than recks Arab slave-trader the tears and lamentations of the poor human beings with black skins he drives, brute-like, across the burning sands of Africa. For is not the whole history of Toryism, from its commencement up to the latest chapter and verse, a record of sympathy with the wronger and unpitying regardlessness for the wronged—an exhibition of all the ferocity known to the human heart, with all its falsehood and meanness?

By a coincidence in no way singular, but simply from two events chancing to occur at the same time, they were dancing at Montserrat House, while Waller was riding in retreat from Roundway Down. Madame Lalande's ball was on the night after the battle, July 13th.

It was about to break up, for day was dawning, and cheeks growing pale. Less than a month after mid-summer, the hour was not so much into morning, and there were some tireless votaries of Terpsichore inclined for still another *contredanse*, by way of wind up. This came, however, in a manner more sudden and unexpected. First, the call notes of a distant bugle, taken up and responded to by others, till a very chorus of them sounded all over the city. Then a *tantara* of drums, and the jangling of church bells, with the boom of a great gun from the Castle!

Too early for the *reveillée*—before the hour of *orisons*—what could it all mean? So queried they in the grounds of Montserrat House, gathering into groups. Certainly, something unusual; as the fracas not only continued but seemed growing greater. To the instrumental sounds were added human voices, shouting in the streets, calls and responses, with a hurried trampling of feet—men rushing to and fro!

Only for a short while were Madame Lalande's guests in suspense. Nor had they to go outside for explanation. There was an eminence in the grounds which commanded a view of most part of Bristol, with the country beyond the fortified line, south-eastward. On its summit stood a pavilion; the same which on that night had been the means of revealing more than one secret. And now from this spot an anxious crowd—for scores had rushed up to it—learnt the cause of the excitement. Close in to the city's walls, about to enter one of the gates, was the shattered remnant of Hesselrig's Horse—all that was left of Waller's defeated army!

If the dresses of those who clustered round the pavilion—most in fancy costume—were diversified, varied also were the feelings with which they regarded this new spectacle presented to them. A surprise to all; to many an unpleasant one, but most viewing it with delighted eyes. For, unlike as with the crowds clustering other eminences outside, within that precinct, hitherto almost sacred to Cavalierism, this was, of course, in the ascendant. And what they saw seemed sure evidence of a crushing defeat having been sustained by their adversaries; so sure, that many who had all the night behaved modestly, and worn masks, now pulled them off and began to swagger in true Cavalier fashion.

Sir Richard Walwyn, Eustace Trevor, and other Parliamentarian officers present were compelled to listen to observations sufficiently offensive. Had they been themselves unmannerly, or even without it, they could have stopped all that, being still masters in Bristol. But there was no need for their showing spite by taking the initiative; as this was forced upon them, whether or no, by command and the simple performance of duty. While Madame Lalande's guests were hastening to take their departure, a man, newly arrived, made appearance in their midst; an officer, wearing *sabretasche* and other insignia of an aide-de-camp. Entering unannounced at the outer gate, without ceremony he strode on up to the house, inquiring for Sir Richard Walwyn.

"Here!" responded the knight, himself about to leave the place; and he stepped forth to meet the new comer.

"From the Governor, Colonel Walwyn," said the aide-de-camp, saluting, and drawing a slip of folded paper from his sabretasche, which he handed to the Colonel of Horse, adding, "In all haste."

Tearing it open, Sir Richard read:—

"Re-arrest all prisoners on parole, whether soldiers or civilians. Search the city through, and send them, under guard to the Castle.

"Fiennes.

"To the Colonel Walwyn."

"Here's a *revanche* for us, Trevor," said the knight, communicating the contents of the despatch to his young troop captain, "if we are ill-natured enough to care for such. Anyhow, we'll stop the speech of some of those fellows who've been making themselves so free of it. Haste down to quarters, and bring Sergeant Wilde with half a dozen files. We may as well begin our work here. Why, bless me! there's the man himself, and the soldiers, too!"

This, at the sight of the big sergeant, who was just entering the gate, and behind him a score of dismounted troopers. Rob had already received orders from the Castle to report himself with a detachment at Montserrat House.

A scene followed difficult of description. Kings, Sultans, Crusaders— in costume only—with many other disguised dignitaries, were unceremoniously stopped in their masquerading; each taken charge of by a common trooper, and pinned to the spot. Many repented the imprudence of having thrown aside their masks. By keeping these on they might have escaped recognition. It was too late to restore them; and in a few minutes' time the paroled prisoners were picked out, and ranged in line for transport to the Castle's keep.

In all this there was much of the comic and grotesque; on both sides even badinage and laughter. But there was anger too—Madame Lalande and her daughter especially indignant—while among the faces late unmasked were some showing serious enough, even rueful. To them it might be no jesting matter in the end.

On the countenance of Reginald Trevor—of course one of the re-arrested—the expression was singularly varied. As well it might, after so many changes quick succeeding one another—jealousy of his cousin; confidence in his sweetheart restored soon to be lost again; and now that cousin confronting him, as was his duty, with a demand terribly humiliating. Yet Eustace had no desire to make it so; instead the reverse. For, meanwhile, Sir Richard had whispered a word in his ear which went far to remove the suspicions late tormenting *him*. He but said,—

"I've orders to take you to the Castle, Reginald."

Then to avoid speech, which might be unpleasant to both, he turned away, leaving the prisoner to be looked after by Rob Wilde, who had commands to conduct him to his prison.

"Come, captain!" said the big sergeant patronisingly, "we han't a great ways to go. Not nigh sich a distance as ye 'tended takin' me—frae Cat's Hill to the lock-up at Lydney."

The Royalist officer keenly felt the satirical jibe flung at him by the Forester, but far more the play of a pair of eyes that were looking down upon him from one of the upper windows. For there stood Vaga Powell, a witness to all that was passing below. In a position almost identical he had seen her twice before, with the expression upon her face very similar. It puzzled him then, but did not vex him as now. For now he better understood it; and, as he was marched off from Montserrat House, he carried with him no sustaining faith or hope, as when riding away from Hollymead.

Eustace also saw her at the window, as he was passing off. But different was the look she gave him, and his given back. In their exchanged glances there was a mutual intelligence, which told that their respective guardian angels had kept promise by whispering sweet words to both.

Chapter Thirty Seven
Fiennes Shows the White Feather

Waller's stay in Bristol was of the shortest, only long enough to rest his wearied men and their jaded horses. The "Night Owl" was not the bird to relish being engaged in a beleaguered city, which he anticipated Bristol would soon be. The field, not the fortress, was his congenial sphere of action; and though sadly dispirited, his army all gone, he had not yet yielded to despair. He would recruit another, if it cost him his whole fortune. So "To horse!" and off again without delay—Hesselrig along with him.

London was his destination, and to reach it, with such feeble escort, a dangerous enterprise. For it was but continuing his retreat through a country swarming with the triumphant enemy. With a skill worthy of Cyrus he made it good, however; going round by Gloucester, Warwick, and Newport Pagnell, at length arriving safe in the metropolis.

But what of the citizens of Bristol he left behind? If they had been despondent on seeing the shattered Cuirassiers re-enter their city not long after these left, they saw another sight which filled them with dismay. Also a body of horsemen approaching the place; not a skeleton of a regiment in retreat, but the vanguard of a victorious army—that which had won the day at Roundway Down. For as the defeated one had suffered utter annihilation, the western shires, now overrun by the Royalists, were completely at their mercy. The only Parliamentarian forces that remained there were the garrisons of Gloucester and Bristol, and it was but a question as to which should be first assaulted.

The former had already experienced something of a siege, and, thanks to its gallant Governor, successfully resisted it; while its bigger sister, farther down the Severn, only knew what it was to be threatened. But the Bristolians also knew their city to be better game—a richer and more tempting prize— and that they might expect the plunderers at any moment. So when they beheld the Light Horse of Wilmot and Byron scouring the country outside, and up to their very gates, they had little doubt of their being the precursors of a larger and heavier force—an army on the march to assail them.

Soon it appeared in formidable array, and leaguer all round. For there was more than one army left free to enfilade them. First came up the conquering host of Hertford and Maurice, fresh from the field of Lansdown. Then, on the Oxford side, appeared Rupert with his freebooters, fire-handed from the burning of Birmingham, and red-wristed from the slaughter at Chalgrove; where, by the treachery of the infamous Urrey, they had let out the life-blood of England's purest patriot.

In a very revel of Satanic delight they drew around the doomed city, as eagles preparing to stoop at prey, or rather as vultures on quarry already killed. For it had neither strength of fortification, nor defending force sufficient to resist them. As already said, Waller going west had almost stripped it of its defenders, numbers of whom were now lying dead on the downs of Wiltshire, as the Royalist leaders well knew. So there was no question as between siege and assault, Rupert, soon as arrived on the ground, determining to storm.

And storm it was, commenced the next morning at earliest hour. Successful on the Gloucester side, where Rupert himself attacked, and the traitor Langrish, with the timid Fiennes, defended. After all his boasting, the lawyer-soldier let the enemy in, almost without striking a blow. Nor did they pass over his dead body either. He survived the sad day, but never more to be trusted with sword in the cause of a struggling people.

Very different was the defence on the southern side, and of different stuff the defenders. There Sir Richard Walwyn with his Foresters, and Birch with his Bridgemen, held the ramparts against Hertford and Maurice, not only foiling the attack, but beating them off. In that quarter had been blows enough, with blood flowing in rivers. The Cornish men were cut down by scores, among them some of their best leaders, as Slanning and Trevannion. Alas! all in vain. Alike to no purpose proved the gallantry of the soldier knight and the stanch courage of the merchant-soldier! Unavailable their deeds of valour; for while they were fighting the foe in their front—in the act of putting him to rout—behind they heard a trumpet sounding signals for parley! And turning, beheld a white flag, waving from a staff, within the city's walls! Saw and heard all this with amazement. On their side the assailants were repulsed, and Bristol still safe. Why then this show of surrender? Could it be treason?

Birch believed it was, though not on the part of Fiennes. He was but vacillating and frightened, Langrish playing the traitor, as the events proved, ending in capitulation. But while Sir Richard and his troopers were still in doubt about the purport of the signals, they saw an aide-de-camp galloping towards them—the same who brought the despatch to Montserrat House at the breaking up of the ball. A verbal message he carried now — command for them to cease fighting.

"And why?" demanded the astonished knight, other voices asking the same, as much in anger as astonishment. "For what reason should we cease fighting? We're on the eve of victory!"

"I know not the reason, Colonel Walwyn," responded the aide-de-camp, evidently ashamed of the part he was constrained to play; "only that they've beaten us on the Gloucester side, and got into the works. The Governor asked for an armistice, which Prince Rupert has granted."

"Oh! you have Rupert round there, have you? I thought as much. This is Langrish's doing. Gentlemen," he observed to the officers now gathering around him, "we may guess how 'twill end — in a base, traitorous surrender. Possibly to be delivered over to the tender mercies of this princely freebooter. Are you ready to risk it with me, and cut our way out?"

"Ready — yes!" responded Eustace Trevor, and the men of the Forester troop, loudest of all their sergeant.

"We, too!" cried the Bridgemen, Birch giving them the cue; while others here and there echoed the daring resolve.

But the majority were silent, and shrank back. It was too hopeless, too desperate, running the gauntlet against countless odds. With the whole garrison agreeing to it, there might have been a chance. But they knew this would be divided, in view of the treason hinted at.

While they were still in debate as to what should be done, another mounted messenger came galloping up with news which quickened their deliberation, bringing it almost instantly to a close. The enemy had offered honourable terms, and Fiennes had accepted them. It was no longer a question of surrender, but a *fait accompli*.

"What are the conditions?" every one eagerly asked.

To get answer: "No prisoners to be taken, no plundering. Soldiers, and all who have borne arms against the King, left free to march out and away. Citizens the same, if they wish it. Three days to be allowed the disaffected for clearing out of the city, and removal of household effects." After that — ay, and before it, as the wise ones believed — it would be "'ware the pillager!"

On its face the bond was fair and reasonable enough, and many were rather surprised at its leniency. Certainly, to one unacquainted with the circumstances, such conditions of surrender might seem more than generous. But knowing the motives, all idea of generosity is at once eliminated. Around to Rupert had come the report of repulse on the southern side—Slanning killed, Trevannion, too; with slaughter all along the Cornish line, and a likelihood of utter rout there. Besides, two or three scores of distinguished prisoners inside Bristol had to be considered; these no longer on parole, but jailed, and still held as hostages. With, these *guages* against any attempt at cruel extortion, none could be safely made; and the keys of Bristol were handed over to Prince Rupert by Nathaniel Fiennes in a quiet, consenting, almost amicable way, as might the seals of office from a going-out mayor to his successor.

How the son of the Elector Palatinate honoured the trust, and kept faith with his word, is matter of history. He did neither one nor the other; instead, disregarded both, basely, infamously. Soon as his followers were well inside the gates, as had been predicted, there was pillage unrestrained; insult and outrage to every one they encountered on the streets, women not excepted. This was the way of the Cavaliers—the self-proclaimed *gentlemen* of England.

Chapter Thirty Eight
Insulting a Fallen Foe

A very saturnalia of riot and rapine followed the capture of Bristol. For the conditions of surrender were broken before the ink recording them was dry, and the soldiers fell to sacking, unrestrained. There were plenty of spiteful "malignants" to point out who should be the victims, though little recked the royal hirelings what house they entered, or whose goods appropriated. All was fish to their net; and so the plundering went on, with scenes of outrage indescribable.

Fiennes has left testimony that Rupert did his best to stay his ruffian followers, cuffing and striking them with the flat of his sword. Light blows they must have been, administered more in jest than earnest, with aim to throw dust in the eyes of the now ex-Governor and his staff standing by. The men on whose shoulders they fell paid little heed to them; for had they not been promised the sacking of Bristol? An intercepted letter from Byron, of massacre memory, to Rupert himself, puts this scandalous fact beyond the possibility of contradiction or denial.

That promise was kept faithfully enough, and the licence allowed in full. Every house of a Parliamentarian, noted or not, received a domiciliary visit, and was stripped of its valuables—all that could not be hidden away— while ladies of highest respectability were subjected to insult. It was Bristol's first experience of victorious Cavalierism; and even they who had conspired to introduce the sweet thing had their surfeit of it ere long.

By the terms of capitulation the soldiers of the vanquished garrison were to march out unmolested. But they must go at once, so as to vacate quarters for the in-coming conquerors. To civilians three days were allowed for decision as to staying or going, with the implied right of removing their effects. This last clause may seem a sorry jest, since there was not much left them for removal. Of course, all who knew themselves compromised, and had the means, decided on going.

Among these, it need scarce be said, was the Master of Hollymead. Under royal ban already, he knew Bristol would no longer be a safe place of residence, either for himself or his daughters. Perhaps he feared more for them under the aegis of such an aunt, and the companionship of such a cousin. The Cavalier wolves would now be ravening about free from all restraint—admitted to Montserrat House, and there made more welcome than ever. Sad he had been at finding his sister so changed; irksome the sojourn under her roof; and now that opportunity offered to take departure he hastened to embrace it. So eager was he to get away from the surrendered city, that he would not avail himself of the three days' grace, but determined to set forth on the morning after the surrender.

Luckily he had but few effects to embarrass him, having left his plate and other Penates in Gloucester, whither he intended repairing. It remained but to provide transport in the way of saddle-horses, just then a scarce and costly commodity in Bristol. But cost what they might, Ambrose Powell has the means of obtaining them; and that night, ere retiring to rest, he had everything ready, His daughters had been warned and were prepared for the journey; both of them eager as himself to set out upon it—neither caring ever to set eyes on Aunt Lalande or Cousin Clarisse again.

Still another sunrise, and the people of Bristol were treated to a spectacle different from any that had preceded, or they had ever witnessed. They saw the late defenders of their city, now disarmed and half-disbanded, marching away from it, out through its gates, and between files of their foes, these last lining the causeway for some distance outside.

In such cases, among the soldiers of civilised countries, it is a rule, almost universal, that no demonstration be made by the conquerors to insult or further humble the conquered. More often may be heard expressions of sympathy even deeds of kindness done. But all was different at this the first surrender of Bristol. As the defeated soldiers marched out, many with yes downcast and mien dejected, no word nor look of pity was bestowed on them. Instead, they were assayed with taunts and derisive cries, some even getting kick or cuff as they ran the gauntlet between the lines of their truculent enemies. And these were "the gallants of England," ready to "strike home for their King," as one of their songs puts it; but as ready to be spit upon by King, or Prince, if it so pleased him. Gallants indeed! As much desecration of the term applied to the Cavalier of Charles's time as to the music-hall cad of our Victorian era.

The chief exodus of the departing Parliamentarians was by the gate, and along the road leading to Gloucester. There was nothing in the articles of capitulation to hinder them again taking up arms. For reasons already stated they were not prisoners, not bound by *parole d'honneur*, but free to turn round and face the foe now exulting over them whenever opportunity should offer. As a consequence, most took the route for Gloucester, where the stanch Massey still held his ground, and would be glad to avail himself of their services.

But not all making away were soldiers. In the stream of moving humanity were citizens, men and women, even whole families who had forsaken their homes, dreading ill-treatment at the hands of the Royalist soldiery; fleeing from Bristol as Lot from the doomed cities of the plain. Among these fugitives many a spectacle of wretchedness was presented, at which the unfeeling brutes who were witnesses but laughed.

Outside, and not far from the gate through which the motley procession was passing, Rupert sat in his saddle, the central figure of a group of splendidly uniformed officers. They were his personal staff, with the *élite* of his army, gathered there to gloat over the humiliation of adversaries who had oft humiliated them. *Gentlemen* as they deemed themselves, some could not resist gratifying their vengeful spleen, but gave exhibition of it, in speech coarse and ribald as any coming from the lips of their rank-and-file followers. In all of which they were encouraged by the approving laughter of their Prince and his high-toned *entourage*.

Never merrier than on that morn were these jovial gentry; believing as they did that the fall of Bristol was the prelude to their triumph over all England, and henceforth they would have it their own way.

While at the height of their exultation a troop came filing along the causeway, the sight of which brought a sudden change over the countenances of the jesters. It was composed of men in cavalry uniform, but afoot and without arms; only some half-dozen—the officers—on horseback. Its standard, too, taken from it, and, perhaps, well it had been. Flouted before the eyes of that Cavalier crew, alike regardless of oath and honour, the banner, showing Crown impaled by Sword, would have been torn to shreds; they bearing it set upon and cut to pieces.

But it needed no ensign, nor other insignia, to tell who the dismounted and dismantled troopers were. Many around Rupert had met, fought with, and fled from them; while all had heard of Sir Richard Walwyn's Horse, and his big sergeant.

These they were, but in woefully diminished numbers—worse than their sorry plight. They had borne the brunt of battle on the southern side; and although they had slain hundreds of the Cornish men, it was with a terrible thinning of their own ranks.

But their gallant leader was still at their head and by his side Eustace Trevor, with his veteran trumpeter Hubert; while, though marching afoot, almost as conspicuous as the mounted ones, there too was the colossal sergeant erst deer-stealer, Rob Wilde. All proudly bearing themselves, notwithstanding what had transpired. No thought of having been conquered had they; instead, the consciousness of being conquerors. And less angry at the men with whom they had been fighting than at him for whom they had fought. Nathaniel Fiennes had either betrayed them and their cause, or proved incapable of sustaining it. It was on that account they looked scowling and sullen, as they filed past Rupert and his surrounding.

But if their black looks were given back by the Royalist officers, these forbore the taunting speech they had hitherto poured upon others. Something of shame, if not self-respect, restrained them. They knew it would but recoil on themselves, as with curs barking at lions.

As Sir Richard and his troop captain came opposite, two officers alongside Rupert exchanged looks with them of peculiar significance. Colonel Tom Lunsford and Captain Reginald Trevor these were. Both released from their imprisonment—the latter but the day before—they were now not only free, but in full feather and favour, appointed to the Prince's staff.

The interchange of glances between the *quartette* was each to each; the ex-lieutenant of the Tower alone regarding the soldier knight, and with a sneer of malicious triumph. He would have added words, but dreaded getting words back that might rake up old scores, as when they last met at Hollymead, exposing his poltroonery. So he contented himself with a sardonic grin, to get in return for it a look of contempt, too scornful and lordly to care for expression in speech.

The play of eyes between the cousins was alike full of meaning, and equally unintelligible to lookers on who knew not the antecedents. But they passed words as well; only a remark with rejoinder, the former even unfinished. Reginald, still smarting from the incidents of that night at Montserrat House, could not restrain his tongue; and, as the other came close, he said, with his old affectation of superiority,—

"If I'd only had the chance to meet you on the ramparts yesterday morning, I would—"

"*You* would be there now, without me," was the interrupting retort. "Down among the Cornish dead men. That's what you intended telling me, isn't it?"

Thus again getting the better in the encounter of words, with a light laugh Eustace rode on, leaving his cousin angrier than ever, more than ever desirous of crossing swords with him to the cry of "No Quarter!"

Chapter Thirty Nine
A Princely Admirer

"Mein Gott, what a sweet *fraülein*! A pair of them! *Wunderschön*!"

It was Prince Rupert who so exclaimed, his eyes turned upon two young girls in a gaze of more than ordinary interest.

Ladies they were, as grace, garb, and other surroundings proclaimed them. On horseback, an elderly gentleman along with them, riding in front; and behind a small retinue of servants, male and female. They had just issued out of the gate as part of the stream of people hastening away from the city, and were coming on towards the spot occupied by the Royalist commander and his staff.

Still looking after the Forest troop, not yet out of sight, Reginald Trevor faced round on hearing the Prince's exclamatory words. Chafed already by the sharp retort of his cousin, what he saw now gave him a fresh spasm of chagrin. Ambrose Powell and his daughters setting off on a journey, evidently for Gloucester, whither Eustace was going too!

Lunsford had also caught sight of them, showing almost as much excitement, with more surprise. Just out of Berkeley Castle, where he had been incarcerated ever since the affair of Edgehill, he had not heard of the Powell family being in Bristol. And now beholding the woman whose beauty had so impressed him while tax-collecting in the Forest of Dean, it gave him a start, succeeded by a feeling of vexation to see she was going away, again to be beyond his reach.

By this the travelling party had got opposite, and were passing on. Poorly mounted all, on horses very different from those they would have been riding around Ruardean. But the sorriness of their nags made no difference as regarded the looks of the ladies. Dignity as theirs was not dependent on extraneous trifles, and for their beauty the very contrast, with the excitement of the situation, but rendered it the more piquant and conspicuous.

The cheeks of both flushed burning red as they came opposite the group of officers. No wonder, with so many eyes bent in bold gaze upon them. They heard words, too, offensive to female ears.

"It's a pity, Vag," said Sabrina, in an undertone, "we didn't think of putting on our masks."

"Oh! I don't care," rejoined the younger sister, with a jaunty toss of the head. "They may look their owlish eyes out—it matters not to me."

Just then her own eyes encountered another pair, which brought a change over her countenance—Reginald Trevor's. He was gazing at her with an intensity of expression that ill bore out the indifference he pretended when parting with her at the Lalandes' ball. A frown it was now, equally affected, as she knew. And just because of knowing this she did not return it; instead, gave him a look half-kind, half-pitying. If a little coquettish, she was not cruel; and she felt repentful, remembering how on that night she had misled him.

At the same time there was a crossing of eyes between her sister and another officer close by Sabrina saw the man who had so impudently ogled her at Hollymead, knowing him to be Colonel Lunsford. In a similar manner was he acting now, only to get from her a glance of contemptuous scorn, which would have rebuked any other than a brazen Cavalier.

He did quail under it a little, feeling in his heart that if he ever received favour from that lady it would have to be a forced one.

"Who are they?" interrogated the Prince, after they had passed, still following them with his eyes. "You appear to know them. Colonel?"

It was Lunsford to whom he addressed himself, observing the look of recognition with which the latter was regarding them.

"Those ladies? Is it they your Royal Highness deigns to inquire about?" And he pointed to the party which had so interested all.

"*Ya!* Or only one of them, if you like—she with the golden locks. I care not to know the other."

Reginald Trevor had overheard this with a singular revulsion of feeling. Bitter as it was to him to see Vaga Powell depart, it would now have been worse, the thought of her remaining in Bristol. Angry he was with her, but not so spiteful nor wicked, as to wish her a fate like that. Well knew he what danger there was to any woman whose beauty tempted Rupert.

Diametrically opposite were the feelings of Lunsford as he listened to the Prince's declared preference. He had feared it was for the elder sister, which would spoil his own chances should such ever come. Relieved, he made answer,—

"They are sisters, your Royal Highness; the daughters of the gentleman you see along with them."

"Egad! a rich father in the way of womankind. I wouldn't mind pilfering a part of his wealth. That bit of saucy sweetness, with cheeks all roses, ought to be pleasant company. I haven't seen anything to equal her in all your England."

"Then, your Royal Highness, why do you allow them to go?" said Lunsford, speaking in an undertone. "As you see, they're setting off for Gloucester, and it may be some time before an opportunity—"

"Ah! true," interrupted the Prince, reflectively.

"If your Highness deign to say the word, they'll be brought back. It's not yet too late."

The suggestion was selfish as it was base. For he who made it but wished them detained on his own account.

For a moment Rupert seemed inclined to fall in with it; and might have done so, but for a reflection that got the better of him.

"*Nein*, Colonel!" he said at length. "We dare not."

"What dares not your Royal Highness?"

"That you propose. You forget the terms of capitulation? To infringe them would cause scandal, and of that we Cavaliers have had accusation already—as much as we can well carry. Ha-ha-ha!"

The laugh told how little he cared for it, and how lightly it sat upon his conscience.

"Your Highness, I'm aware of all that," persisted Lunsford. "But these are excepted people—that is, the father."

"How so?"

"Because of his being one of the King's worst and bitterest enemies. But that's not all. He's been a *recusant*—is still. I myself attempted to levy on him for a loan by Privy Seal—three thousand pounds—the King required. I not only failed to get the money, but came near being set upon, and possibly torn to pieces, by a mob of Dean Foresters—very wolves—his adherents and retainers. Surely all that should be sufficient justification for the detaining of him and his."

Prompted by his vile passions again, the Royal Sybarite seemed inclined to act upon the diabolical counsel. But, although the war's history already bristled with chronicles of crime, nothing quite so openly scandalous, as that would be, had yet appeared upon its pages. Many such there were afterwards, when this Prince and his gallants had more corrupted England's people, and better accustomed them to look lightly on the breaches of all law and all decency.

At a later period Rupert would not have regarded them, as indeed he did not twelve months after in this same city of Bristol. Of his behaviour then thus wrote one of his attached servitors to the Marquis of Ormonde,—

"Prince Rupert is so much given to his ease and pleasure that every one is disheartened that sees it. The city of Bristol is but a great house of bawdry."

Things were not so on that day succeeding its surrender, and public opinion had still some restraint upon him. Enough to deter him from the outrage he would otherwise willingly have perpetrated.

"Never mind, Colonel," he at length said resignedly. "We must let the birds go, and live in hopes of seeing them again. You know their roosting place, I suppose?"

"I do, your Royal Highness."

"So, well! When we've settled things with the sword, which we soon shall now, I may want you to pilot me thither. Meanwhile, *laszt es gehen.*"

At which the dialogue ended, unheard by all save Reginald Trevor. And he only overheard snatches of it; still enough to make him apprehensive about the fate of Vaga Powell. If he wanted her for himself it was not in the way Prince Rupert wanted her.

Chapter Forty
The Cadgers on the Kymin

"Laws, Jack! fear us be takin' back bad news to Sir Richard. An worse for the poor young lady at Glo'ster. Rob's tolt me her wor well-nigh deestract when her heerd he wor took pris'ner. What'll it be as her get to hear o' his bein' bad wounded too? Her knows nothin' o' that."

"Maybe 'tant so much o' a wownd after all, nothin' for he to go dead on. Folks allays zagerates sich things. An' if he live it through, like 'nough 'twon't be very long fores they git un free o' his 'prisonment. I ha' an idea, Winny dear, the letter us ha' got be relatin' to that same. Else-wise why shid the Colonel Kyrle, who wor onct on the Parlamenteery side, an's now on t'other why shid him be writin' to Sir Richard, or Sir Richard to he? Beside, all this queery business us be a doin'. It seem to mean somethin' 'bout gittin' the young gen'lemen out o' gaol; maybe by changin' he for another. Don't ee think so?"

"Like it do."

She knew it meant that, and more. For Rob Wilde had given her a hint of why they had been sent to Monmouth market—ostensibly cadging on their own account, but in reality as messengers in the pay and employ of Sir Richard Walwyn. Though Jack was personally the bearer of the secret despatches, Winny was the one entrusted with the diplomacy, and knew more than she thought necessary to confide to him.

They were on return from the market—for it was afternoon—and once more climbing a steep hill; this time not the *Cat's* but the *Kymin*—the old Roman Road (Camen), which, crossing the Wye at Monmouth (Blestium), led up to the Forest table-land by Staunton. The ascent commences at the bridge, winding for miles through romantic woods and scenery unsurpassed in England. The bridge as then was a quaint, massive structure, having a towered gate on its *tête de pont*, with portcullis, draw-arch, and guard-house. A guard of Royalist soldiers were stationed on it; for ever since the breaking out of the war Monmouth had been kept for the King. But the cadgers had found no difficulty in passing this guard, either at going in, or coming out. It was market day, and Jinkum was laden with marketable commodities—a motley collection of farmyard fowls—hens, ducks, and geese—making a very pandemonium in the panniers. Had the soldiers upon the bridge but known what the little limping man carried inside his wooden leg, like enough they would have pitched him over the parapet. It was after getting clear of them, and well uphill, that the brother and sister were unburthening themselves to one another, as above described. The dialogue had commenced by Jack chuckling over the way they had outwitted the bridge guards, and referring back to how they had done the same, some fifteen months before, with the "Cavalières," encountered on the Bristol road by Berkeley. He was in high glee, jesting about and praising his artificial leg—which had proved worth more to him than the real one—again in pleasant anticipation of a like remunerative result. The sister, however, was not joyous as he; her thoughts just then dwelling on that poor young lady described by Rob Wilde as having been "well-nigh deestract." That was it which had turned their conversation into the channel it had taken.

There was a short interregnum of silence after Winny's assenting rejoinder. Broken by Jack with an observation bearing on the same topic of discourse, but about a different place and time.

"'Twor a pity the Captain goed back to Hollymead wi' so few o' his sodgers along. I cud a tolt he that wan't safe, seein' the Colonel Lingen ha' his quarters so near by, in Goodrich Castle. Him be a dangerous neighbour, an' master o' all round about theer now."

"Ye be right, Jack; 'twor a pity," she answered, echoing his first reflection. "But theer wor a good reason for 't, Rob's gied me. Seems Master Powell had somethin' at Hollymead—him wanted gettin' to Glo'ster, so's to be safer theer. 'Twor a thing o' great value him had hid away, fores leavin' for Bristol that time, an' the Captain volunteered like to go for it. How could him know o' the danger frae Goodrich? That wor brought about by treezun; one o' his men, who stepped away in the night an' warned the Colonel Lingen. So him got tooked by surprise."

"Well, they didn't take he, 'ithout gettin' a taste of his steel; a sharp taste, too; beside more frae his sodgers, few as they wor. Jim Davis, who wor up to the house, mornin' after, seed blood all 'bout the place; more'n could a' comed o' them as lay killed. The Cavalières had carried away the wounded a' both sides, wi' theer own dead; as Jim think a good dozen."

"That be true enough; more nor a dozen, I ha' myself heerd. But what do it signify how many o' Lingen's wolves be gone dead, if that handsome young gentlemen ha' to die, too? Sure as we be on Kymin hill, 'twill break Mistress Vaga's heart."

"Stuff an' nonsense! Hearts beant so eezy broke."

"Ah! that's all *you* know about it."

She could make the remark with confidence in its truth. There was no record of Jerky ever having had sweetheart, or feeling the soft sentiment of love. And for herself, some pangs of jealousy which Rob Wilde had occasioned her, though unconsciously, made her a believer that hearts *could* be broken. For this great Forest woman loved like a lioness, and could be jealous as a tigress.

"Oh, well!" rejoined the amiable brother, without taking notice of the slur on his lack of his amatory experience, "it mout be as ye say, sister Winny; supposin' the young gen'leman's wounds to prove mortyal. But that an't like, from all us ha' heerd the day. So let's we live in hope. An' I wudn't wonner," he added, in a more cheerful tone; "wudn't a bit wonner, if, inside this timmer leg o' mine, theer be somethin' to tell Sir Richard the Captain an't in any great danger. Maybe to say him will soon be out o' prison, an' bade in his saddle, to cut down another Cavalière or two."

"Hope that's the news us be takin' to High Meadow. Whativer 'tis, let we get theer quick's us can. Whack on the creetur."

The final admonition referred to Jinkum; and his master, in obedience to it, gave out the customary "yee-up!" accompanied by the less usual application of cudgel.

A good deal of this last the donkey now needed. The morning had been hot, with the panniers full and heavy, toward the market. Now, on return, it was still sultry, and the wicker weighted as ever, Sir Richard Walwyn was not the strategist to let his scheme have a chance of miscarrying; and Jinkum was bearing back into the Forest country a large consignment of grocery goods; for which the consignee would care little, save as to the time of delivery. But about this he would be particular to an instant, as the cadgers knew; and so, on up the Kymin, Jinkum caught stick, in showers thick as had ever rained upon his hips, even when climbing the sharper and more familiar pitches of Cat's Hill.

Chapter Forty One
By the "Buckstone"

On the highest point of the Forest of Dean district—just one thousand feet above ocean's level—is a singular mass of rock known as the "Buckstone." An inverted pyramid, with base some fifteen feet in diameter, poised upon its apex, which rests on another rock mass of quadrangular shape as upon a plinth. Into this the down-turned apex seems indented so far as to make the apparent surface of contact but a few square feet. In reality the two masses are detached, the superimposed one so loose as to have obtained the character of a "rocking stone." Many the attempt to rock it; many the party of tourists who had laid shoulders against it to stir it from its equilibrium; not a few taking departure from the place fully convinced they had felt, or seen it, move.

And many the legend belonging thereto, Druidical and demoniac; some assigning it an artificial, others a supernatural, origin.

Alas for these romantic conjectures! the geologist gives them neither credence nor mercy. Letting the light of science upon the Buckstone, he shows how it comes to be there; by the most natural of causes—simply through the disintegration of a soft band of the old red sandstone interposed between strata of its harder conglomerate.

From beside this curious eccentricity of the weather-wearing forces is obtained one of the finest views of all England, or rather a series of them, forming a circular panorama. Turn what way one will the eye encounters landscape as lovely as it is varied. To the east, south-east, and south can be seen the far-spreading champaign country of Gloucester, Somerset, and Devon, here and there diversified by bold, isolated prominences, as the Cotswolds and Mendips, with a noble stream, the Severn, winding snake-like along, and gradually growing wider, till in funnel-shape it espouses the sea, taking to itself the title of Channel.

From the shores of this, stretching away northward, but west from the Buckstone, is a country altogether different. No plains in that direction worth the name, but hills and undulating ridges, rolling up higher and higher as they recede, at length ending in a mountain background, blue black, with a horizontal line which shows many a curious *col* and summit.

The greater portion of this view is occupied by the shire of Monmouth, its foreground being the valley of the Wye, where this river, after running the gauntlet between English Bicknor and the Dowards, comes out surging and foam-crested as a victorious warrior with his plumes still unshorn. And as he in peaceful times might lay them aside, so the fretted and writhing river, clot after clot, casts off its snowlike froth, and, seemingly appeased, flows in tranquil current through the narrow strip of meadow land on which stands the miniature city of Monmouth.

Although below the Buckstone, at least nine hundred of the thousand feet by which this surmounts the sea's level, the point blank distance between them is inside the range of modern great guns. And so well within that of a field-glass that from the overhanging Forest heights men could be distinguished in the streets of the town, or moving along the roads that lead out of it.

As already said, one of these is the Kymin, then the main route of travel to Gloucester, by Coleford and Mitcheldean. Near where it attains the Forest elevation, at the picturesque village of Staunton, a lane branches off leading to the higher point on which stands the Buckstone; a path running through woods, only trodden by the tourist and others curious to examine the great balanced boulder.

On that same afternoon and hour when the cadgers were toiling up the Kymin Hill, two personages of very different appearance and character— both men—might have been seen entering into the narrower trackway, and continuing on up towards the rock-crowned summit.

On reaching it one of them drew out a telescope, and commenced adjusting the lens to his sight. If his object was but to view the scenery there was no need for using glass. Enough could be taken in by the naked eye to satisfy the most ardent lover of landscape, though in September the woods still wore their summer livery; for on Wye side it is late ere the foliage loses its greenery, and quite winter before it falls from the trees. Here and there only a dash of yellow, or a mottling of maroon red, foreshadowed the coming change; but no russet-grey as yet. The afternoon was one of the loveliest; not a cloud in the azure sky save some low-lying fleecy cumuli, snow-white but rose-tinted, towards which the sun seemed hastening as to a couch of repose. A cool breeze had succeeded the sultriness of the mid-day hours; and, aroused from its torpor, all animated nature was once more active and joyous. Out of the depths of the High Meadow woods came the whistling call of stag and the bleat of roebuck; from the pastures around Staunton the lowing of kine, mingled with the neighing of a mother mare, in response to the "whigher" of unweaned foal, while in Forest glade might now and then be heard shrill cries of distress, where fierce polecat or marten had sprung upon the shoulders of some hapless hare, there to clutch and cling till the victim dropped dying on the grass.

All the birds were abroad, some upon the trees, singing their evensong, or making their evening meal; others soaring above, with design to make a meal of them. Of these a host; for nowhere are the predatory species more numerously represented than along the lower Wye. More numerous then than now; though still may be seen there the fish-eating osprey; oftener the kite, with tail forked as that of salmon; not unfrequently the peregrine falcon in flight swift as an arrow, and squeal loud as the neigh of a colt; and at all times the graceful kestrel, sweeping the air with active stroke of wing, or poised on quivering pinions, as upon a perch.

In those days, eagles were common enough on the Wye; and just as the two men had taken stand by the Buckstone, a brace of these grand birds came over; the owners of an eyrie in the Coldwell rocks, or the Windcliff. After a few majestic gyrations around the head of Staunton-hill, with a scream, they darted across the river to Great Doward, and thence on to quarter Coppet Wood.

But he using the telescope, as his companion, took no more notice of them than if they had been but skylarks. Nor looked they on that lovely landscape with any eye to its beauties. They were neither tourists nor naturalists, but soldiers; and just then, man, with his ways alone, had interest for them.

Both were in uniform; the elder—though there was no great difference in their ages—wearing that of a Colonel in the Parliamentary army; a rank which, in these modern days, when military titles are so lavishly bestowed, would seem as nothing. But in those times of a truer Conservatism, even though the social fabric was being shaken to its foundation, a colonel held as high command as a major-general now. So with him who had the telescope to his eye; for it was Colonel Edward Massey, the military Governor of Gloucester.

And the other was a colonel, too, on the Parliamentary side; though in uniform of a somewhat irregular kind. Dressed as a Cavalier, but with certain insignia, telling of hostility to the Cavalier's creed; one especially proclaiming it, with bold openness—this, a bit of gold embroidery on the velvet band of his hat, representing a crown, thrust through and through by a rapier. Fair fingers had done that deft needlework, those of Sabrina Powell. For he who displayed the defiant symbol was Sir Richard Walwyn.

Why the two colonels were together, and there, needs explanation. Many a stirring event had transpired, many a bloody battle been fought, since the surrender of Bristol to Rupert; and among them that most disastrous to him as to the King's cause—Marston Moor. It had changed everything; as elsewhere, freeing the Forest of Dean from the Royalist marauders, who had been so long its masters. Massey had himself dealt them a deadly blow at Beachley; routing Sir John Wintour's force, caught there in the act of fortifying the passage a crass the Severn.

That occurred but three days before, and the active Governor of Gloucester having hastened on to Staunton, was now contemplating a descent upon Monmouth.

There was one who had pressed him to this haste, having also counselled him to attempt the capture of the town. This, the man by his side. But a woman, too, had used influence to the same end. Before sallying forth from Gloucester, for Beachley, a girl—a beautiful girl—had all but knelt at his feet, entreating him to take Monmouth. Nor did she make any secret of why she wished this. For it was Vaga Powell, believing that in Monmouth Castle there was a man confined, whose freedom was dear to her as her own. But she feared also for his life, for it had come to that now. The *lex talionis* was in full, fierce activity, and prisoners of war might be butchered in cold blood, or sent abroad, and sold into slavery—as many were!

Luckily for the young lady, her intercession with Massey was made at the right time, he himself eagerly wishing the very thing she wanted. Ever since becoming Governor of Gloucester, Monmouth had been a sharp thorn in his side, compared with which Lydney was but a thistle. And now, having laid the latter low—as it were, plucked it up by the roots—he meant dealing in like manner with the former. To capture the saucy little city of the Wye would be a *coup*, worth a whole year's campaigning. With it under his control, soon would cease to be heard that cry hitherto resonant throughout South Wales, "For the King!" To still the hated shibboleth—alike hated by both—he and Sir Richard Walwyn were now by the Buckstone, with eyes bent upon Monmouth.

Chapter Forty Two
A Reconnaissance

Instead of viewing the rural scenery, the two colonels had come there to make a reconnaissance. The town itself, its fortified *enceinte*, the gates piercing it, and the roads around, were the objects to which their glances were given. And, for a time, all their attention was engrossed by them, neither speaking a word.

At length Massey, having made survey of them through the telescope, handed it to the knight, saying,—

"So you think there's a chance of our taking the place?"

Sir Richard but ran the glass around hastily. He had been up there before, and more carefully reconnoitred, their chief object being to ascertain the strength of the garrison.

"Yes, your Excellency," he rejoined, "a chance, and something more, if Kyrle prove true; or rather should I say, traitor. And," he added, with a significant smile, "I think we can trust him to do that."

"As it wouldn't be the first time for him, no doubt we can. He has twice turned coat already. And's no doubt itching to give it another shift, if he can but see the way without getting it torn from his back. Marston Moor has had its effect on him, too, I suppose."

"It has, and our affair at Beachley will strengthen it. He'll want to be back on what he believes the winning side now more than ever. His communication to me, though carefully worded, means that, if anything. But we'll be better able to judge when our despatch-bearers report themselves at High Meadow House. I think we may look for a letter from him."

It was at High Meadow House their men were encamped; the main body under Massey having just arrived, while Sir Richard, with his troopers in advance, had been there overnight. And that same morning the cadgers, hastily summoned from their home at Ruardean, had been despatched to Monmouth market: Jack, or rather the sister, with secret instructions, and Jinkum with full panniers.

"They ought to be back soon now," added Sir Richard, again raising the glass to his eye, and turning it on the town, his object to see if the market people had all gone away.

When he last looked, they were streaming out through the gates, the commercial business of the market being over long ago. And now there were only some stragglers on the outgoing roads, men who had lingered by the ale-houses in gossip, or standing treat to the ever-thirsty soldiery.

Just then there came within his field of view a group composed of elements altogether different from the home-returning rustics.

"What do you see?" asked Massey, observing the telescope steadied, and the knight looking through it with fixed, earnest gaze.

"A party of horse, carrying the lance—most of them."

"Where?"

"Just coming out of the northern gate."

"A patrol, perhaps?"

"No; something more. There are too many of them for that. Over a hundred have passed out already. And—yes; prisoners with them?"

"Let me have a look," said the Governor, stretching out his hand for the telescope, which, of course, the other surrendered to him. Reluctantly though, as Sir Richard felt more than a common interest in the prisoners so escorted.

"You're right," said Massey, soon as sighting them. "Prisoners they have. But whither can they be taking them? That's the road to Ross."

"To Hereford also, your Excellency. The route; are the same as far as Whitchurch."

"Ah, true. Still it's odd their starting out at such an hour! And why carrying prisoners away to Hereford? Surely Monmouth Castle affords gaol room enough. I hope it's not so full. If so, all the more reason for our doing what we can to empty it."

"I don't think they're for Hereford, either. If I'm not mistaken, I saw something which tells of a different destination. If your Excellency will allow me another look through the telescope, perhaps—"

"Oh, by all means, take it!" said the Governor, interrupting, and again handing over the glass.

"Yes! just as I supposed they were—Harry Lingen's Horse!" exclaimed Sir Richard, after viewing them for a second or two. "And those poor fellows, their prisoners, likely enough are my own men—one of them, though I can't identify him, my unfortunate troop captain, young Trevor. They're *en route* neither for Ross nor Hereford, but Goodrich Castle, where Lingen has his headquarters. It's but a short six miles, which may account for their setting out so late."

"But Trevor's party was taken at a place near Ruardean—Hollymead House, if I recollect aright."

"True; the house of Master Ambrose Powell. It was there Lingen surprised them, through a scoundrel who turned traitor."

"Then why were they brought to Monmouth at all? Ruardean's but a step from Goodrich."

"Just so, your Excellency, I was puzzled about that myself up till this morning. Now I know why, having got the information from our cadger friends. It appears that when Lingen made his swoop on Hollymead he was on the way to join Wintour at Beachley, so kept straight on through Monmouth, where he dropped his *impedimenta* of prisoners. On return he's now picked them up again, and's taking them on to his own stronghold."

"That's it, no doubt," assented Massey. "But," he added, with a smile of triumphant satisfaction, "whoever those captives be, pretty sure none of them have been brought up from Beachley. Nor is their escort as large as it might have been had Lingen left Wintour to himself. We gave their ranks a good weeding there—all round."

"Yes, indeed," rejoined the knight, rather absently, and with the telescope still at his eye. He was endeavouring to make good the identity of the captive party, and assure himself whether it was really what he had conjectured it to be.

But he could have little doubt, as he had none about the soldiers forming their escort—Lingen's Horse to a certainty—a partisan troop, variously armed, but most carrying the lance. And while he still continued gazing at them, they commenced the ascent of the Ley's *pitch*, which passes over the col between Little Doward and the Table Mount, the road running through woods all the way. Under these they were soon lost to his sight, and as the last lance with its pennon disappeared below the tops of the trees, he lowered his telescope with a sigh, saying,—

"What a pity the river's between, with a flood on! But for that we might have crossed at Huntsholme, and caught up with them ere they could—"

He broke off abruptly at sound of footsteps: the tread of heavy boots, with the chink of spurs, and the louder clank of a steel scabbard striking against them.

He making all these formidable noises was Sergeant Rob Wilde, seen ascending the steep pitch, and evidently on some errand that called for haste.

Sir Richard, advancing to meet him, saw that he had something in his hand, with a good guess as to what it was.

"Jerky Jack ha' brought this, colonel," said the sergeant, saluting, as he held out a slip of paper, folded and sealed. "He ha' just got up fra Monnerth; an', accordin' to your command, I took it out o' his leg."

"You did quite right, sergeant. Was there nothing more in the leg?"

"Only some silver, colonel; the difference o' the money he got for the fowls an' what he gied for the grocer goods. He stowed it theer, afeerd o' the King's sodgers strippin' him o't."

"A wise precaution on Jerky's part," observed the knight, with a smile. "And called for, no doubt."

Then, returning to where Massey stood awaiting him, he said, —

"We shall know now, your Excellency, what Kyrle means doing. This is from him—I recognise the script."

The superscription on the letter was only the initials "R.W.," Sir Richard's own, who otherwise knew it was for himself, and while speaking had broken open the seal.

Unfolding the sheet, he saw what surprised and at first fretted him— that device borne on his hat and the standard of his troop—the sword-pierced crown. It appeared at the head of the page, in rough pen-and-ink sketch, and might be meant ironically. But no; the writing underneath gave the explanation:—

> "By the symbol above R.W. will understand that K. abjures the hatred thing called 'Kingship' henceforth and for ever. After this night he will never draw sword in such a cause, and this night only to give it a back-handed blow. R.W.'s proposal accepted. Plan of action thus:—M. at once to retire troops from High Meadow, news of which a messenger already warned will bring hither post haste. But good reason must be given for retiring, else K. might have difficulty

getting leave to go in pursuit. Withdrawal appearing compulsory, there will be none. H., who commands here, is a conceited ass, ambitious to cut a figure, and will rush into the trap as a rat after cheese. R.W. may show this to M., and himself feel assured that if the sword of his old comrade-in-arms be again employed in the service of the P., it will cut keen enough to make up for past deficiencies, which K. hopes and trusts will be forgiven and forgotten."

No name was appended to the singular epistle nor signature of any kind. It needed none. Sir Richard Walwyn knew the writer to be Robert Kyrle, a lieutenant-colonel in the Royalist army, who at the beginning of the war had drawn sword for the Parliament. In days gone by they had fought side by side in a foreign land,—more recently in their own,—and Kyrle could well call Sir Richard an "old comrade-in-arms." Now they were in opposite camps; but if that letter could be relied upon as a truthful exponent of the writer's sentiments, they were likely soon to be in the same again. Already there had been a passage of notes between them, and the knight had now a full comprehension of what his anonymous correspondent meant, knew to whom the various initials referred—in short, understood everything purposed and proposed.

"What's your opinion of it, Colonel Walwyn?" asked the Governor, after hearing the letter read, and receiving some necessary explanations. "Do you think we can trust him?"

"I do, your Excellency; feel sure of it now. I know Kyrle better than most men, and something of his motives for going over to the other side. Nothing base or cowardly in them; instead, rather honourable thin otherwise. For, in truth, it was out of affection for his old father, whose property was threatened with wholesale confiscation. Walford, up the river, this side Ross, is their home. It is within cannon range of Goodrich Castle, right under, and Lingen would have been sure to make a ruin of it had Kyrle not gone over to the King. Now that the chances of war are with us again, and he thinks that danger past, his heart bounds back to what it once warmly beat for. I know it did, as he has oft told me, in tent and by camp fire."

"To what?" asked Massey, himself a veteran of the Low Country campaigns, and feeling interest in souvenirs of sentiment.

"This?" answered the knight, pointing to the device inside the letter, still in his hand. "I believe he will be true to it now, as he promises; and if we get nothing more by it than his sword, it's one worth gaining, your Excellency. Than Kyrle I don't know braver or better soldier."

"Well, Colonel, since you seem so disposed to this thing, and confident of success, I'm willing we should make the attempt. At the worst we can but fail, though, indeed, failure may cost us a good many of our best men. Best they must be to form the forlorn hope."

"If your Excellency permit, I and my Foresters will form that. With my confidence in them, and faith in Kyrle, I have no fear of failure—if the details of our scheme be carried out as designed."

"They shall be, Sir Richard, so far as I can effect it. You may rely upon me for that. Nay, I leave the ordering and arrangement of everything to yourself."

"Thanks, your Excellency. But the sooner we set about it the better. Kyrle, as you see, counsels the withdrawal at once."

"But what about the reasons for doing so? Without that, he tells us—"

"I've thought of that, too," interrupted Sir Richard, now all haste. "It's part of my plan already arranged. But it will take a little time to procure this reason, so that it may appear plausible—the time it will take a man, mounted on a good horse, to gallop to Coleford and back."

"I don't quite comprehend you, Colonel. For what purpose this galloping to Coleford?"

"To get news from Gloucester—telling us it is threatened by Rupert."

The Governor gave a start, as if actually being told it was so. Then, recovering himself, as he saw the smile on Sir Richard's face, at the same time catching the purport of his dubious words, he smiled, too, admiringly upon the soldier knight, as he rejoined,—

"An admirable idea! It will do! But, as you say, Colonel, there must be no time lost. The messenger must be despatched at once. So let us back to High Meadow House."

Saying which, he started off down the hill.

Sir Richard was about to follow when his big sergeant, who had been all the while standing near, stepped up to him, and saluting, said,—

"There be a woman as wants a word wi' ye, Colonel."

"A woman! Who, Rob?"

"Cadger Jack's sister."

"Where is she?"

"A little ways down the lane. I didn't like bringin' she up, fears you or the Governor mightn't wish bein' intruded on. Besides, her business be more wi' yerself, Colonel."

"Well, Wilde," half jocularly returned the knight, "your discretion seems on a par with your valour. But let us down, and hear what the cadgeress has to say. If it be a question of squaring the market account, you can take that upon yourself. I give you *carte blanche* to settle scores; and if they've brought back groceries, you may distribute them among the men."

"It bean't nothin' o' that Win want to speak ye about?"

"What is it, then? You seem, to know."

"There be herself, Colonel. Her can tell you better'n me."

He pointed to the Forest Amazon, who but a short distance below stood by the trunk of a tree, from behind which she had just stepped, Massey having passed without seeing her.

"Well, Mistress Winifred," said the knight, when near enough to commence conversation, "my sergeant tells me you've something to say."

"Only a word, your honour; an' I be's most feered to speak it, since it ant a pleasant one."

"Out with it, anyhow."

"Him be wounded."

"Who?"

"The young officer as wor took at Hollymead—Captain Trevor."

"Ha! Wounded, too! Who told you that?"

"'Twor all about Monnerth the day, wheres him be in prison. I tried get a chance to speak wi' he, but couldn't, bein' watched by the sodgers roun' the Castle."

"Did you hear whether his wound be serious?"

"No, Sir Richard; nothin' more than that it wor from a gunshot, an' had laid he up. Hope it won't signify no great deal; but I thought it better you be told o't fores it reach the young lady at Gloster—so's yer honour might break it to her a bit easier."

"Very thoughtful of you, Mistress Winifred, and thanks! I'll endeavour to do that."

He passed on with quickened step and shadowed countenance. Eustace Trevor, whom he had grown to regard as a brother, wounded! This was news to him. And a gunshot wound which had laid him up—that looked grave.

All the more reason for taking Monmouth, and soon. But however soon, he had a presentiment, and something more, it would be too late—so far as finding Eustace Trevor there. He felt almost sure that, whether slightly or severely wounded, his troop captain had been taken on to Goodrich.

Chapter Forty Three
High Meadow House

High Meadow House, where Massey's troops were quartered, was but a step from the Buckstone. A first-class mansion it was, belonging to a gentleman, by name Benedict Hall, and inhabited by him till within a few days before. A large landowner, with estates both in the shires of Gloucester and Hereford, he commanded some influence throughout the Forest country, and being a bigoted Papist, he, of course, went for the King and the devil, as those of his sort have ever done since Vaticanism became a power upon the earth.

But in something more than a mere sentimental way had the master of High Meadow shown his political inclinations. Second only to those of the silly old Marquis of Worcester, and the wicked Sir John Wintour, were his services to the Royal cause in that quarter, his great wealth enabling him to pay for soldiers, if he could not himself handle them. More than one well-appointed squad had he armed and equipped at his own expense, now sending subsidies to Wintour at Lydney, and now helping Lord Herbert on the Monmouth side. Moreover, at the breaking out of hostilities he had fortified High Meadow House, and ever since held it with his own servants and hired retainers.

His wife, a priest-ridden woman, had been prime inspirer and chief instigator to all this, herself moving about among the men employed on the defensive works, encouraging them with speech, and promises of reward for devotion to the King's cause.

There came a time, however, when this ultraloyal couple began to get tired of the bauble which was costing them so dearly. For over two years it had been a constant drain upon their resources: all output and nothing returned, save the scantiest of thanks—such gratitude as might be expected from princes, above all, one like Rupert. Had Benedict Hall better held by his Bible, it would have warned him against the hollow trust. The battle of Marston Moor did that more effectively than the sacred Book; showed him the fool's part he had been playing, and that likely a day was on the dawn when England's people would no longer be the consenting slaves of

Royal caprice. So, bitter Papists and malignants as were he and his wife, their worship for Pope and King did not blind them to coming events; and they had now turned their thoughts to the rising sun. When the news came from the North of the Royalist rout, and was followed by other adverses to the King's cause, Benedict Hall, like many others of higher rank, hastened to change sides, or, at all events, save himself by "compounding." Which, in reality, he afterwards did, the wife, clever woman, conducting the negotiations with the Parliamentary Committee.

Ere this, however, on hearing of Wintour's defeat by the Wye's mouth, they had forsaken their fortified mansion at High Meadow, betaking themselves to Bristol; just as the master of Hollymead with his family had fled to it many months before—both seeking it as a city of refuge, but from enemies the very opposite!

Even more abruptly, and in greater haste, had the Halls abandoned their home, leaving behind, not only their furniture, but some of their most cherished household gods. Provisions, too, in plenty—eatables and drinkables, with the still undischarged staff of domestics. Snug quarters for the Parliamentarians, fatigued after their sharp conflict at Beachley, and difficult march through the Forest, with its tortuous routes and steep pitches.

As already said, Colonel Walwyn and his troopers had come on in advance, Massey's men having but just arrived, when, forsaking saddle, he and Sir Richard started off to the Buckstone to reconnoitre.

Now returned from it, they looked upon a spectacle which, though of a striking character, was not new to either of them. Huge fires blazed up everywhere, with great joints of meat spitted and sputtering over them; soldiers, with doublets off and shirt sleeves rolled up to the elbow, knife in hand, still engaged in cutting up the beeves they had butchered; hundreds of horses, with saddles off, standing haltered along the walls, munching corn, which the master of High Meadow House had been hoarding up for visitors who would have been more welcome. For, up to a late period, he had been expecting Rupert and his Cavaliers to come that way.

The soldiers were in high glee, congratulating one another on the comfortable quarters into which they had dropped. For at High Meadow House they found not only full granaries, but a well-stocked larder and cellar containing various potables. A portion of the last had been already dealt out to them, and they were quaffing and laughing, one giving ironical thanks to the absent host for having so thoughtfully provided the entertainment, another in like strain drinking his health.

The arrival of the Governor on the ground caused but a momentary suspension of their boisterous mirth. Though a strict disciplinarian in a military sense, Massey was aught but puritanical, and rather liked seeing his soldiers enjoy themselves in a harmless way. Besides, he and Colonel Walwyn—who, hurrying after, had overtaken him—at once went inside the house, where dinner, already prepared, was awaiting them and the other officers.

Before sitting down to it, the Governor called for pen, ink, and paper, and writing to Sir Richard's dictation, hastily scratched off a note, which he handed to the latter, as they exchanged some words in undertone.

The knight, on taking it, passed hurriedly out to see close to the door a horse under saddle and bridled with a trooper standing by his head. That he expected this was evident by his saying,—

"You can mount now. Take this to Coleford. Give it to Major Rowcroft,— into his own hands, mind you,—and stay there till he sends you back. Don't spare your horse: ride whip and spur all the way."

The soldier, an orderly, simply saluted as he took the folded sheet, then slipping it under his doublet, sprang to the saddle, and went off at a gallop through the gate.

The bivouackers, inside the courtyard and without, having commenced their Homeric repast, paid little heed to an incident so slight and of such common occurrence. They were more interested in the roast beef, with which the pastures around High Meadow House had provided them, and the beer drawn from its subterraneous depositories. Good store of sack had been found there too, with claret, metheglin, and other dainty drinks. But these were reserved for the officers, who, in a somewhat similar fashion, were making merry inside.

For the better part of an hour was the feasting kept up, amid jest and laughter, then, interrupted by the hoof-stroke of a horse in gallop, afar off in the Forest when first heard, but at each repetition louder and nearer, till at length the sound abruptly ceased.

All listening knew why. The fast-riding horseman, whoever he was, had pulled up by the out-picket, whose challenging hail could be faintly heard through the trees.

Time enough elapsed for the necessary parley and permission to pass on, when the trampling recommenced, and soon after horse and rider were in sight, still at a gallop, making direct for the gate of the fortified mansion.

Some who were expecting to see the orderly that had late ridden off saw a different man, though to many of them no stranger. A dragoon orderly too, but acting with the detachment at Coleford. His horse was in a lather of sweat, tossing clots of froth from the champed bit back upon his counter, as dashing in through the outer gate, he was drawn up at the house door.

On the stoup were several officers, who had just stepped out after finishing dinner, Massey himself in their midst.

"What is it?" he demanded, as the dragoon, springing down from the saddle, advanced towards him. He was feigning ignorance, for he well knew what it was.

"Despatch from Major Rowcroft, your Excellency," answered the orderly, presenting it. "H. commanded it brought in all haste, saying 'twas of great importance."

"Yes!" exclaimed the Governor, after tearing the sheet open, and giving but a glance to the writing. "Major Rowcroft is right: it *is* of great importance. Gentlemen," he added, turning to his officers, and speaking loud enough to be heard all over the place, "this is a serious matter. Rowcroft advises me of news just reached Coleford that the Princes Rupert and Maurice have united their forces, taken Stroud, Cirencester too, and are supposed to be *en route* for Gloucester. Our own city threatened, we mustn't think more of Monmouth. Glorious old Gloucester, that has so long defied all the strength of Cavalierism, with all its malevolent spite! But we shan't let it fall; no! Let us get back there without a moment's delay. So each of you to your respective commands. Have your men in marching order within twenty minutes. I give you that, and no more."

No more was needed. The troops under Massey were too well-disciplined, too often summoned into action with like suddenness, to go bungling about getting ready for the route.

Quick after his words came the notes of a bugle sounding the "assembly," with other calls taken up by the trumpeters of the respective corps, followed by a hurrying to and fro—horses un-haltered, bitted and saddled, men buckling on swords, grasping lances, or adjusting accoutrements; then trumpets once more commanding the "march," and in less than the prescribed time neither trooper nor soldier of any sort could be seen within the precincts of High Meadow House, or anywhere around.

But the place was not altogether deserted. The domestics and outdoor servants of its absent owner were still there. In greater numbers now, as many—came stealing from holes and corners, where they had been all day hiding in fear of rough treatment by the Roundheads.

Hall's head man, the steward of the estate, was among them, he too having come from a place of concealment as soon as warned that the troops had taken departure. Different from the rest, he was on horseback. Nor did he alight. Instead, after getting their report, from such of the house-servants as had been there all the while and heard everything, he reined about and rode off again. Not to follow the retiring Parliamentarians, but in quite the contrary direction.

So, while Massey and his troops were on the march from High Meadow, apparently *en route* for Gloucester, a man—this same steward—was riding down the Kymin at a breakneck pace, the bearer of glad news to the Governor of Monmouth.

Chapter Forty Four
Out in the Storm

Though clear and placid had been the sky when the two colonels stood by the Buckstone, in a few hours after it was all clouded. Night had descended, but in addition to its natural darkness, the white fleecy cumuli along the western horizon had turned black at the setting of the sun; then rolled upward, overspreading heaven's whole canopy as with a pall. But the obscurity was not continuous. The extreme sultriness of the day had disturbed the electrical equilibrium of the atmosphere, resulting in a thunderstorm of unusual violence. At intervals vivid sheets of lightning illumined the firmament, while red zig-zagging bolts, like arrows on fire, pierced the opaque clouds, bringing down rain as at the Deluge.

Between the flashes all was darkness; so dense that a traveller on the Forest roads must needs stop till the blaze came again, else run the risk of straying from the track, possibly to bring up against the trunk of a tree. But it was a night on which no traveller would think of venturing forth, and one already on the road would make for the nearest shelter.

Yet were there traveller abroad, or at least men on horseback, who neither sought this nor seemed to regard the raging elements. About a mile from High Meadow House, on the Coleford Road, a party of four might be seen seated in the saddle under a spreading tree. That they were not sheltering from the rain could be told by its pouring down upon them through the leaves quickly as elsewhere, and their being already wet to the skin. Shadow, for concealment, was evidently their object, though at intervals the lightning interfered with it. But they were in such position as to command a view of the road, and any one coming along it, before being themselves observed. As now and then the blue electric light gleamed around them, it could be seen that they were in uniform—an officer and three common troopers, one with trumpet in hand—while their attitude of listening proclaimed them on picket duty. A vidette it was, stationed to watch the approaches and give warning to a larger force.

Another might have been found at no great distance off, in a sequestered glade of the forest, some hundreds of horsemen, who, as the party under the tree, were all in their saddles, and alike disregarding the rain. Silent as spectres were they, here and there only a muttered word, with the champing of bits, and occasionally the louder clink of scabbard against stirrup as some horse shied at the blinding flash.

They, too, seemed listening, as indeed were they—especially a group of officers near the outgoing of the glade—listening for a signal preconcerted, and expected to come from the trumpeter under the tree.

Nor were these the only soldiers abroad and voluntarily exposing themselves to that drenching storm. While it was at its worst, a party of Horse issued out of Monmouth, and, crossing the Wye bridge, took the route up Kymin Hill. A small body it was, about forty in all, with but two officers—he who commanded and a cornet, their arms and accoutrements, as the light caparison of their horses, proclaiming them on scout.

As the lightning flashed upon a banneret carried by the cornet, it could be seen to bear the emblem of a crown, while other specialities of uniform and equipment betokened the little troop as belonging to the army of the King, and therefore hostile to those halted in the forest glade, whose insignia told them to be of the opposite party.

It wanted an hour or more of midnight when the party from Monmouth, after surmounting the Kymin steep, entered Staunton—to find the villagers still awake and stirring. They had received news of Massey's departure from the neighbourhood, so hastily as to seem a retreat, and, indeed, knew the reason, or supposed they did, from the contents of that Coleford despatch. Most of them being of Royalist proclivities, they were sitting up in jubilance over the event.

The soldiers made but short halt among them; just long enough to get answer to some inquiries; then on to High Meadow House.

Why thither none of the rank and file knew, not even the cornet. Alone their commanding officer, who kept the true reason to himself, giving a spurious one—that his object was to make sure of the place being in reality abandoned. A weak force as they were, it would not do to advance farther along the Coleford road, should there chance to be an enemy in their rear.

This seemed reasonable enough, nor were the men loth to accept it. On such a night shelter was above all things desirable, and they were sure to find snug quarters at the mansion of High Meadow, hoping their commander would let them stay there till the storm came to an end.

Just as they turned off the high road, or scarce a minute after, a solitary figure came gliding along from the Staunton side, and passed on towards Coleford. Afoot it was, wrapped in a cloak, with hood, which, covering the head, left visible only a portion of the face. Tall, and of masculine proportions, otherwise it might have been taken as the figure of a man, but for a certain boldness, yet softness of outline, which betokened it that of a woman. And a woman it was—the cadgeress.

She had followed the Royalist troopers from Staunton, silently, stealthily, and at safe distance behind. But as they turned off the main road, she, still keeping to it, broke into a run, not slowing again till she stood under the tree where the four Parliamentarians were on picket. By the fitful flashes these had seen her making approach, at least three of the four knowing who it was—Sir Richard Walwyn; he who had the trumpet, Hubert; and one of the troopers, wearing the *chevrons* of a sergeant, Rob Wilde.

That she in turn recognised them, and had been expecting to find them there, was evinced by her behaviour. For when she thought herself within hearing, she called out,—

"Cavalières turned off and goed for High Meadow House. 'Bout forty theys be in all."

"Sound the signal, Hubert!" said Sir Richard, in command to his trumpeter, adding to the big sergeant, "Ride back, Rob, and tell Captain Harley to bring on our men as rapidly as possible."

The lightning still flashed and forked, with loud thunder, now in quick claps, now in prolonged reverberation. But between came the notes of a cavalry bugle, in calls, which, reaching the glade where Massey's men sat waiting in their saddles, caused a pricking of spurs, and a quick forward movement at the command, "March!"—word most welcome to all.

Meanwhile, the soldiers from Monmouth had reached Hall's house to find no enemy there, only some servants, who at first took them for a returned party of Parliamentarians. But the steward, who had been detained on the way, riding up the instant after, reassured the frightened domestics.

Besides what these had to tell, there were other evidences of the hurried evacuation. On tables everywhere was a spread of viands only partially consumed, with tankards of ale unemptied, and inside the house bottles of wine, some yet uncorked.

The Cavalier soldiers were not the sort to hasten away and leave such tempting commodities untouched. And, as their commanding officer seemed not objecting, they were out of their saddles in a trice, eating and drinking as though they had that day gone without either breakfast or dinner.

The stable mangers, too, were full of beans and barley, left uneaten by the horses of the Parliamentarians, to which their own animals fell with a hungry voracity equalling that of their masters.

Short time was allowed them for this greedy gormandising. Scarce had they taken seat by the tables when a trampling of hoofs was heard all around the house, louder on the stone pavement by the gate, from which came the shout "Surrender!" the same voice adding, "'Twill be idle for you to resist. We are Massey's men, and fifty to your one. If you wish your lives spared, cry 'Quarter,' or we cut you to pieces."

The carousing Royalists were taken completely by surprise. In fancied security, thinking the Parliamentarian force *en route* for Gloucester, and far on the way, they had neither placed picket nor set sentry; and the house being fortified, there was no exit from it save by the one gate, now blocked up, as they could see, by a solid body of horse. They were literally in a trap, with no chance to get out of it, for, by the multitudinous hoof-clattering outside, they knew the words "fifty to one" were not far from the truth.

Alone, the cornet got off afoot by a desperate leap into the ditch at back; stealing away unseen in the darkness. The rest made no attempt, either at escape or resistance. They but stood, terror-stricken, to hear the threat—

"Speak, quick, or we open fire on you!" Then, at least, half of them called out "Quarter!" without waiting word or sign from their leader.

What followed, however, showed that he sanctioned it. As the Parliamentarian troopers came riding in through the gate he advanced to meet them, with drawn sword, hilt outward, which he handed to the officer at their head.

As the latter took it, a smile of peculiar significance was exchanged between the two, with words equally strange, inaudible save to themselves.

"Glad to have you back with us, Kyrle."

"Not more than I to get back, Walwyn. God knows! I've had enough of Rupert, and his rascals."

Chapter Forty Five
A Town Cleverly Taken

About an hour after the capture of Kyrle's party, a body of horse, numbering over one hundred, might have been seen descending the Kymin towards Monmouth. The fury of the storm had worn itself out, the downpour of rain being succeeded by a drizzle, while the lightning only flickered faintly, and at long intervals, the thunder muttering low and distant. But the darkness was deep as ever, and the horsemen rode down the steep incline at a slow, creeping pace, as if groping their way. In silence too, neither word of command, nor note of bugle, directing their march.

Had there been light enough to give a good view of them, it might have been guessed that something other than the darkness and difficulty of the path was causing them to advance in this noiseless, deliberate manner. For at their head would have been seen Kyrle himself; no prisoner now, on parole or otherwise, but with sword restored, and in every way acting as their commanding officer! And by his side one who carried a troop flag, with a crown upon its field, the same which had been left behind by the escaped cornet. The captured troopers were there too—as at first glance any one would suppose—forming a half-score files in front of the marching line, with a like number in rear. Only in seeming, however—only their uniforms and equipments—for they themselves were at that moment shut up in a cellar of High Meadow House, where Benedict Hall had erst incarcerated many a rebel and recusant.

A different set of men were now wearing their doublets and carrying their accoutrements in the descent of the Kymin Hill, and any one familiar with the faces of Sir Richard Walwyn's Foresters would have recognised some forty of them thus partially disguised, with nigh twice as many more in their uniforms there, the last apparently disarmed and conducted as prisoners, their place being central in the line!

In rear of all was the knight himself, with his new troop captain, Harley; Sergeant Wilde and Hubert the trumpeter constituting the file immediately in front of them—all four, as the others, seemingly without arms.

That his oddly composed cohort had some strategic scheme in view was evident from the cautious silence in which they advanced. And at intervals, Kyrle, reining his horse to one side, would wait till the rearmost file came up; then, after exchanging a word or two with Colonel Walwyn, spur back to his place in the lead.

Thus noiselessly they descended the long, winding slope; but when near its bottom, and within some three or four hundred yards of the bridge, all was changed. The troopers began to talk to one another, Kyrle himself having given them the cue. Loudly and boisterously, with a tone of boasting, their speech interspersed with peals of light, joyous laughter. All this meant for the ears of those on guard at the bridge gate.

A sufficiently strong force was stationed there, and with fair vigilance were they guarding it. For although Massey had been reported as on hurried return to Gloucester, the fugitive cornet, having found his way back, had brought with him a different tale. Afoot, and delayed by losing his way, he had but just passed over the bridge and on to the castle, after saying some words that left the guard in a state of alarm.

It was more bewilderment, as the men seemingly so merry drew near, invisible through the pitchlike darkness. At least a hundred there must be, as told by the pattering of their horses' hoofs on the firm causeway. Kyrle's scouting party had gone out not half this number, yet there was Kyrle himself, talking and laughing the loudest. Many of the guard—officers and soldiers—knew his voice well, and could not be mistaken about it. What then meant the sooner return of the cornet, without his standard, and with a tale of disaster? Had he retreated from a conflict still undecided, afterwards ending in favour of the Royalist forces? It might be so.

By this the approaching party had got nearly up to the gate, in front of which the causeway showed a wide gap, and through it, far below, the flooded river surging angrily on. The officer in command of the guard was about to call out, "Who comes?" when anticipated by a hail from the opposite side, pronounced in tone of demand,—"Hoi over there! Let the drawbridge down!"

"For whom?"

"Kyrle and party. We've taken prisoners threescore Roundheads, and sent as many more to kingdom come. Be quick, and let us in. We're soaking wet, and hungry as wolves!"

"But, Colonel Kyrle," doubtingly objected the officer, "your cornet has just passed in, with the report that you and your party were made prisoners! How is it—"

"Oh, he's got back, has he?" interrupted the ready Kyrle, though for an instant non-plussed. "The coward! And double scoundrel, telling such a tale to screen himself! Why, he dropped his standard at sight of the enemy, and skulked off before we had come to blows! Ah! I'll make short work of it with him."

While he was speaking there came a flash of lightning more vivid than any that had late preceded, bright enough and sufficiently prolonged for the soldiers on guard to see those on the other side of the chasm throughout the whole extended line. In front some half-score files of Kyrle's Light Horse, whose uniform was well-known, with a like number in the rear, and between, with heads drooped, and looking dejected, the prisoners he had spoken of.

The spectacle seemed to prove his words true. Under the circumstances who could think them false? Who suspect him of treason?

Not the officer in command of that guard, anyhow; who, without further hesitation or parley, gave orders for the lowering of the bridge.

Down it went, and over it rode a hundred and odd men, counting the supposed Royalists and their unarmed prisoners. But soon as inside the gate, all seemed to be armed, prisoners as well as escort, the former suddenly bristling with weapons, which they had drawn from under their doublets to the cry, "For God and Parliament!" The opposing shout, "For God and the King?" was stifled almost soon as raised, the bridge guard being instantly overpowered, many of them cut down, and killed outright.

Then a larger and heavier force, that had been following down the Kymin Hill, Massey's main body, came on at full gallop, over the drawbridge and through the gate. There, taking up the cry, "God and Parliament!" they went rattling on through the streets of the town, clearing them of all hostile opposition, and capturing everybody who showed a rag of Royalist uniform.

When the morning's sun rose over Monmouth, from its castle turrets floated a flag very different from that hitherto waving there. The glorious standard of Liberty had displaced the soiled and blood-stained banner of the Stuart Kings.

Chapter Forty Six
Awaiting War News

"What a life we've been leading, Sab! Shut up in cities as birds in a cage! Now nearly two years of it, with scarce ever a peep at the dear, delightful country. Oh! it's a wretched existence."

"It's not the pleasantest, I admit."

"And in this prosaic city, Gloucester."

"Ah, Vag, don't speak against Gloucester. Think what her citizens have suffered in the good cause. And how well they have borne themselves! But for their bravery and fidelity, where might we be now? Possibly in Bristol. How would you like that?"

"Not at all," returned Vag, with a shrug and grimace, the name of Bristol recalling souvenirs aught but agreeable to her.

"Well," resumed Sabrina, "life there is not prosaic, anyhow—if there be poetry in scandal. Very much the reverse, I should say, supposing half of what's reported be true. But I wonder how our foolish aunt, and equally foolish cousin, are comporting themselves under the changed circumstances?"

"Oh! they're happy enough, no doubt; everything just as they wished it. Plenty of titled personages flitting and figuring around—at least three princes of the blood royal, with an occasional chance of their seeing the King himself. Won't Madame open wide the doors of Montserrat House. As for Clarisse, I shouldn't be surprised at her making a grand marriage of it, becoming baroness duchess, or something of that sort. Well, I won't envy her."

Vaga Powell could afford to speak thus of her Creole cousin, with light heart now, all envy and jealousy having long since gone out of it.

"Let us hope nothing worse," rejoined the elder sister, with a doubting look, as though some painful thought were in her mind. "Clarisse is very, very imprudent, to say the least of it."

"And very wicked, to say nothing more than the most of it. But what need we care, Sab, since we neither of us ever intend going near the Lalandes again? After the way they behaved to us, well—"

"Well, let us cease speaking of them, and turn to some pleasanter subject."

"Ay, if that were possible. Alas! there's none very pleasant now—every day new anxieties, new fears. I wish this horrid war were at an end, one way or the other, so that we might get back to dear old Hollymead."

"Don't say one way or the other, Vag. If it should end in the King being conqueror, Hollymead will be no more a home for us. It would even cease to belong to us."

"I almost wish it never had."

"Why that?"

"You should know, Sab. But for my father sending him there after those worthless things, he would not now be—"

"Dear Vaga!" interrupted the elder sister entreatingly. "For your life do not let father hear you speak in that strain. 'Twould vex him very much, and, as you yourself know, he has grieved over it already."

"Ah, true. I won't say a word about it again, in his hearing, anyhow— you may trust me. But it's hard to think of my dear Eustace being in a prison—shut up in a dark dungeon, perhaps hungering, thirsting, and, worse than all, suffering ill-treatment at the hands of some cruel jailer."

She was justified in calling him her "dear Eustace" now, and giving him all her sympathies. Since that night of perverse misconceptions at Montserrat House there had been many an interview between them; the thread of their interrupted dialogue by Ruardean Hill had been taken up again, and spun into a cord which now bound them together by vows of betrothal.

Of their engagement Sabrina was aware, and under the like herself, she could well comprehend her sister's feelings. True, her betrothed was not in a prison, but she knew not how soon he might be—or worse, dead on the battlefield. Invincible as she believed him, war had its adverse fates, was full of perils, every day, as the other had said, fraught with new anxieties and fears. Concealing her own, she essayed to dispel those of her sister, rejoining,—

"Nonsense, Vag. Nothing so bad. Why should they treat him with cruelty?"

"You forget that they call him renegade. And they on the King's side are most spiteful against all who turn from them. Think how his own cousin acted towards him; and 'tis said his father disowned him. Besides, other prisoners have been scandalously treated by the Cavaliers, some even tortured. And they may torture him."

"No fear of their doing that. Even if disposed they're not likely to have the opportunity."

"But they have it now."

"Not quite."

"I don't comprehend you, Sab."

"It's very simple. Heartless as many of the Royalists leaders are, and vindictive, they will be restrained by the thought of retaliation. At this time our people hold two prisoners to their one. A large number of these Monmouth men, with their officers, have been taken at Beachley, and that will insure humane treatment to your Eustace. So make you mind easy about him."

It became easier as she listened to the cheering words, almost reassured by others spoken in continuation.

"In any case," pursued Sabrina, "his captors are not likely to have the time for *torturing*, as you put it. Richard's last letter says he and his troops were at High Meadow House—the Halls', near Staunton, you know?"

"That Papist family; great friends of Sir John and Lady Wintour. I remember their place. Well?"

"He was there in advance, awaiting the Governor to come up, with every hope of their being able to take Monmouth. If they succeed, and they will—I feel sure they will, Vag—then Eustace will be a free man, and all of us go back to Hollymead, with not much danger of being again molested."

"Oh?" exclaimed the younger sister, overjoyed by the prospect thus shadowed forth, "wouldn't that be delightful! Back at the dear old place. Once more our walks and rides through the Forest. Our hawking, too. Bless me! my pretty Pers and your Mer, I suppose they won't know us! I trust Van Dom hasn't neglected them, nor my Hector either."

And so she ran on, in the exuberance of her new-sprung hopes seemingly forgetting him around whom they all centred. Only for an instant though. Without Eustace Trevor by her side the Forest walks and rides, with Hollymead and its hawking,—would have less attraction for her now. Wherever he might be, that were the place of her choice, thenceforth and for ever. So soon the thought of his being in a prison, with fears of something worse, came back in all its bitterness.

And the shadow of returned anxiety was again visible on the brow of Sabrina. A fortified town to be taken there would needs be fighting of a desperate kind—her lover in the thick of it. A forlorn hope for storming, who so like as her soldier knight to be the leader of it? He had been so at Beachley, and proud was she on hearing of his achievements there. But at the thought of his now again undergoing such risk, with all the uncertainties of war—that he might fall before the ramparts of Monmouth, even at that moment be lying lifeless in its trenches—her heart sank within her.

For a time both were silent. Then Sabrina, with another effort to cast-off the gloomy reflections, which she saw were also affecting her sister, said,—

"Richard promised to write again last night, or early this morning, if there should be anything worth writing about. He hasn't written last night, or the letter would have been here now. If this morning, I may soon expect it. His messengers are never slow, and a man on a swift horse should ride from High Meadow House to Gloucester in two hours, or a little over."

From her belt she drew a quaint, three-cornered watch to ascertain the correct time. Correct or not, its hands pointed to 10 a.m. A messenger from the High Meadow could have been there before if sent off at an early hour, and on an errand calling for courier-speed.

Perhaps no reason had arisen for such, and consoling herself with this reflection, she resumed speech, saying,—

"Anyhow, we may make sure of getting news before noon, some kind or other. The Governor will be sending a despatch to the Committee, and one may have already reached them. We shall know when father returns."

The last remark had reference to the fact of Ambrose Powell being one of the Parliamentary Commissioners for the Gloucester district, and just then in committee.

But the anticipated news reached them without being brought by him. As they stood conversing in an embraced window, which, terrace-like, overhung the street, they heard a clattering of hoofs, almost at the same instant to see a horseman coming on at quick pace. When opposite the house in which they were, he halted, flung himself out of the saddle, and disappeared from their sight under the projecting balcony. Long ere this they had recognised Sir Richard's henchman Hubert.

There was a loud rat-tat-tat at the street door, and soon after a gentle tapping against that of their room, which both recognised as from the knuckles of Gwenthian, simultaneously exclaiming, "Come in."

In came she with a letter that seemed terribly soiled and crumpled.

"Hubert has brought this, my lady," she said, holding it towards Sabrina, for whom the sharp-witted Welsh maid knew it was meant. "Poor man! he be wet to the skin, and all over mud, and looks as if just dropped out of a duck pond."

The "poor man" was but a mild, evasive form of expressing her sympathy. Had she put it as she felt, it would have been "dear man," for long ago had Gwenthian entered into tender relations with the trumpeter.

Neither of the sisters gave ear to what she was saying, for the elder had snatched the letter out of her hand, and torn it open on the instant, while the younger stood by in eager, anxious attitude.

There was contentment in Sabrina's eyes as she glanced at the superscription. It became joy on reading the first words written inside, and she cried out, in tone of enthusiastic triumph,—

"Glorious news, sister! They've taken Monmouth?"

"They have! Heaven be praised!" Sabrina was about to read the letter aloud, when some words caught her eye which admonished first running it over to herself hastily, as the other was all impatience. It ran:—

"My love,—We are inside Monmouth, thanks to little strategy I was able to effect, with the help of an old Low Country comrade, Kyrle, of Walford, whom you may know. For all, we had some sharp fighting by the bridge gate, where Kyrle proved himself worthy of his ancient repute as soldier and swordsman. Had we failed there this letter would not have been written, unless, perhaps, inside a prison. And now on that subject I'm sorry to say E. Trevor is still in one, but, unluckily, not at Monmouth. Taken by Harry Lingen from the Hereford side, they have carried him off that way, likely to Goodrich Castle. What's worse, he has been wounded; whether severely or not, I haven't yet been able to ascertain. Soon as I can learn for certain where he is, and what the nature of his hurt, you shall hear from me, as I know your sister will be in a sad state of anxiety. We've made many prisoners, and now, commanding Monmouth, may hope to gather in a good many more. If we succeed in clearing the Wye's western bank of the wolves so long infesting it you may all safely return to Hollymead."

The letter did not conclude quite so abruptly. There were some expressions tenderer and of more private nature, which she was scarce permitted to read, much less dwell upon. For Vaga, all the while gazing in her face with a look of searching interrogation, saw a shadow pass over it, and unable longer to bear the suspense, cried out,—

"There's something wrong? Ah! it's Eustace; I know it is!"

"Nothing wrong with him more than we knew of already. He is still a prisoner; but, of course, not at Monmouth, or he'd have been released. They have taken him away from there, as Richard thinks, to Goodrich Castle."

There was that in her manner, with the words and their tone of utterance, which led to a suspicion of either subterfuge or reticence. And Vaga so suspecting, with another searching look into her eyes, exclaimed,—

"You've not told me all. There's something in that letter you fear to communicate. You need not, Sab. I'll try to be brave. Better for me to know the worst. Let *me* read it."

Thus appealed to the elder sister gave way. The thing she desired to conceal must become known sooner or later. Perhaps as well, if not better, at once.

Tearing off that portion of the sheet on which were the words of tenderness concerning only herself, she passed the other into the hands of her sister, saying,—

"All's there that interests you, Vag; and don't let it alarm you. Remember that wounds are always made more of than—"

"Wounded!" came the interrupting cry from Vaga's lips, intoned with agony. "He's wounded—it may be to death! I shall go to Goodrich. If he die, I die with him!"

Chapter Forty Seven
Old Comrades

"Well, Dick, for a man who's just captured a city, you look strangely downhearted—more like as if you'd been captured yourself."

It was Colonel Robert Kyrle who made the odd observation; he to whom it was addressed being Colonel Sir Richard Walwyn. The time was between midnight and morning, some two hours after Monmouth had succumbed to their strategic *coup-de-main*; the place Kyrle's own quarters, whither he had conducted his old comrade-in-arms to give him lodgment for the rest of the night.

Snug quarters they were, in every way well provided. Kyrle was a man of money, and liked good living whether he fought for King or for Parliament. A table was between them, on which were some remains of a supper, with wines of the best, and they were quaffing freely, as might be expected of soldiers after a fight or fatiguing march.

"Yet to you," added Kyrle, "Massey owes the taking of Monmouth."

"Rather say to yourself, Kyrle. Give the devil his due," returned the knight, with a peculiar smile.

Notwithstanding his serious mood at the moment, he could not resist a jest so opportune. He knew it would not offend his old comrade, as it did not. On the contrary, Kyrle seemed rather to relish it, with a light laugh rejoining,—

"Little fear of him you allude to being cheated of his dues this time. No doubt for all that's been done I'll get my full share of credit, however little creditable to myself. They'll call me all sorts of names, the vilest in the Cavalier vocabulary; and, God knows, it's got a good stock of them. What care I? Not the shaking of straw. My conscience is clear, and my conduct guided by motives I'm not ashamed of—never shall be. You know them, Walwyn?"

"I do, and respect them. I was just in the act of explaining things to Massey up by the Buckstone when your letter came—that carried in the cadger's wooden leg."

"Most kind of you, Dick; though nothing more than I expected. Soon as I heard of your being at the High Meadow, I made up my mind to join you there, even if I went alone as a common deserter. Never was man more disgusted with a cause than I with Cavalierism. It stinks of the beerhouse and *bagnio*; here in Monmouth spiced with Papistry—no improvement to its nasty savour. But the place will smell sweeter now. I'll make it. Massey has told me I'm to have command."

"You are the man for it," said the knight approvingly. "And I am glad he has given it to you. Nothing more than you're entitled to, after what you've done."

"Ah! 'tis you who did everything—planned everything. What clever strategy your thinking of such a ruse!"

"Not half so clever as your carrying it out."

"Well, Dick, between us we did the trick neatly, didn't we?"

"Nothing could have been better. But how near it came to miscarrying! When they flung that Cornet in your teeth I almost gave it up."

"I confess to some misgiving myself then. It looked awkward for a while."

"That indeed. And how you got out of it! Your tale of his cowardice, and threat to make short work with him, were so well affected I could scarce keep from bursting into laughter. But what a simpleton that fellow who had command of the bridge guard! Was he one of those we cut down, think you?"

"I fancy he was, and fear it. Among my late comrades there were many I liked less than he."

"And the Cornet, to whom you gave credit for making such good use of his heels. Has he escaped?"

"I've no doubt he's justified what I said of him by using them again. He's one that has a way of it. I suspect a great many of them got off on the other side—more than we've netted. But we shall know in the morning when we muster the birds taken, and beat up the covers where some will be in hiding. Hopelessly for them, as I'm acquainted with every hole and corner in Monmouth."

There was a short interval of silence, while Kyrle, as host, leant over the table, took up a flagon of sack, and replenished their empty cups. On again turning to his guest he could see that same expression, which had led to him thinking him downhearted. Quite unlike what face of man should be wearing who had so late gained glory—reaped a very harvest of laurels—

on more than one battlefield. The exciting topics just discoursed upon had for a time chased it away, but there it was once more.

"Bless me, Walwyn! what is the matter with you?" asked Kyrle, as he pushed the refilled goblet towards him. "You could not look more sadly solemn if I were Prince Rupert, and you my prisoner. Well, old comrade," he went on, without waiting for explanation, "if what's troubling you be a secret, I shan't press you to answer. A love affair, I suppose, so won't say another word."

"It *is* a love affair in a way."

"Well, Walwyn! you're the last man I'd have looked for to get his heart entangled—"

"You mistake, Kyrle. It has nothing to do with my heart—in the sense you're thinking of."

"Whose heart then, or hearts? For there must be a pair of them."

"You know young Trevor?"

"I know all the Trevors—at least by repute."

"He I refer to is Eustace—son of Sir William, by Abergavenny."

"Ah! him I'm not personally acquainted with; though he's been here for several days—in prison. Lingen's men took him at Hollymead House, near Ruardean; brought him on to Monmouth on their way to Beachley; and going back have carried him with them to Goodrich Castle. They left but yesterday, late in the evening. He's got a wound, I believe."

"Yes. It's about that I'm uneasy. Can you tell me anything as to the nature of it? Dangerous, think you?"

"That I can't say, not having seen him myself. Some one spoke of his arm being in a sling. Likely it's but a sword cut, or the hack of a halbert. But why are you so concerned about him, Dick? He's no relative of yours."

"He's dearer to me than any relative I have, Kyrle. I love him as I would a brother. Besides, one, in whom I am interested, loves him in a different way."

"Ah, yes! the lady of course; prime source and root of all evil."

"In the present case the source of something good, however. But for the lady, in all likelihood Monmouth would still be under Royalist rule—nay, I may say surely would."

"How so, Walwyn? What had she to do with the taking of Monmouth?"

"A great deal—everything. She was the instigator; her motive you may guess."

"I see; to get young Trevor out of prison. Well!"

"I had some difficulty in convincing Massey the thing was possible; and, but for her intercession with him, I might have failed doing so. Our success at Beachley, however, settled it; especially when I laid before him the scheme we've been so fortunate in accomplishing."

"Well, we should thank the lady for it. May I know who she is?"

"Certainly. The daughter of Ambrose Powell, of Hollymead."

"Ah! That explains why Trevor was there when taken?"

"In a way, it does."

"I've but slight acquaintance with Powell, myself; though, as neighbours, we were always on friendly terms. He and his family are now in Gloucester, are they not?"

"They are. For a time they stayed at Bristol—up to the surrender."

"Luckily they're not there now. A sweet place that for anything in the shape of a young lady. Master Powell may thank his good star for getting him and his out of it. Two daughters he has, if I remember rightly, with names rather singular—Sabrina and Vaga?"

"They are so named."

"With whom is young Trevor in relations?"

"The younger, Vaga. Poor girl! she'll be terribly disappointed when she hears of his having been carried on out of our reach, and so near being rescued!"

"Out of our reach!" said Kyrle, an odd expression coming over his features, as if some thought had struck him. "Is that so sure?"

"Why not? He's in Goodrich Castle. You don't think it possible for us to take it?"

"Not at present; though, by-and-by, it may be within the possibilities. No man wishes more than I to see the proud pile razed to the ground, and Henry Lingen hanged over the ruins. Many the fright he has given my poor father with his cowardly threats. But I hope getting quits with him before the game's at an end."

"What chance then of rescuing Trevor? Have you thought of any?"

"I have. And not such a hopeless one either. You're willing to risk something to get him free?"

"Anything! My life, if need be."

"That risk will be called for; mine too, if we make the attempt I'm thinking of."

"An attempt! Tell me what it is. For heaven's sake, Kyrle, don't keep me in suspense!"

"It's this, then. Lingen, it appears, don't intend lodging any prisoners in Goodrich Castle. Since the affair at Beachley he has some fear of his castle being besieged; and in a siege the more mouths the worse for him. By the merest accident I heard all this yesterday; and that the party he took away from here will be sent on to Hereford under escort first thing to-morrow morning—that is this morning, since it's now drawing up to it."

"I think I comprehend you, Kyrle."

"You'd be dull if you didn't, Walwyn."

"You mean for us to strike out along the Hereford Road, and intercept the escort?"

"Just so. 'Twill be venturing into the enemy's ground dangerously far; but with a bold dash we may do it."

"We *will* do it!"

"What about leave from Massey? Do you think there will be any difficulty in our getting that?"

"I don't anticipate any. In my case he can't object. My command is independent of him; the troop my own; and, though now numbering little over a hundred, they are Foresters, and I've no fear to match them against twice their count of Lingen's Lancers—the gentlemen of Hereford, as they style themselves."

"Then you agree to it? We go if Massey gives permission?"

"I go, whether he gives it or not. In fact, I don't feel much caring to ask him."

"Egad! that may be the best way, and I'm willing to risk it too. Suppose we slip out without saying a word? Time's everything. Our only chance with the escort will be to take them by surprise—an ambuscade. For that we'll have to be well along the Hereford road before daylight. I know the very spot; but we must be into the saddle at once."

"Then at once let us into it!"

Chapter Forty Eight
Between Two Prisons

In Parliamentary war times English roads were very different from what they are of to-day. Those of the shires bordering Wales were no better than bridle paths, generally following the routes of ancient British trackways, regardless of ups and downs. Travel over them was chiefly in the saddle or afoot, traffic by pack-horse, wheels rarely making mark on them save when some grand swell of the period transported his family from town to country house. Then it was a ponderous coach of the chariot order, swung on leathern springs—such as the gossipy Pepys and Sir Charles Grandison used to ride in—calling for at least four horses, with a retinue of attendants. These last armed with sword and pistol for protection against robbers, but also, pioneer fashion, carrying spade and axe to fill up ruts, patch broken bridges, and cut down obstructing trees.

Where the routes ran over hills, the causeway, sunk below the level of the adjacent land, was more like the bed of a dry watercourse than a highway of travel; this due to the wear of hoof and washing away by rains. There was no Macadam then to keep the surface to its normal height by a compensating stratum of stone; and in many places the tallest horseman, on the back of a sixteen-hands horse would see a cliff on either side of him, its crest barely touchable with the stock of his whip. Often half a mile or more of this ravine-like road would be encountered, so narrow that vehicles meeting upon it could not by any possibility pass each other; one of them must needs back again, perhaps, hundreds of yards! To avoid such *contretemps*, the husbandman who had occasion to carry corn to the mill, or produce to the market town, in his huge lumbering wain, was compelled by law to announce its approach by a jangle of big bells, or the blowing of a horn!

Yet over these ancient highways—many of them still in existence—the Roman legionaries of Ostorius Scapula had borne their victorious eagles; and along them many a Silurian warrior, standing erect in his scythe-winged chariot, was carried to conquest or defeat.

At a later period had they echoed the tramp of armed men, when Henry the Fourth, father of Agincourt's hero, made war upon the Welsh. Later still, twice again, in the days of the gallant Llewellyn and those of the bold Glendower; and still farther down the stream of time were they stained with blood as of brother shed by brother, when England's people—those of Wales as well—King-mad and King-cursed, took a fancy, or frenzy, to cut one another's throats about the colour of a rose.

And now, on these same roads, two centuries later, they were again engaged in a fratricidal strife, though not as before with both sides infatuated through kingcraft. One was fighting for a better cause—the best of all—a people's freedom. The first time they had struck blow for this or themselves; their stand for Magna Charta, so much vaunted, being a mere settling of disputes between barons and king; no quarrel of theirs, nor its results much gain to them. Neither would it be far from the truth to say, it was the *last* time for them to draw sword on the side of human liberty; indeed difficult to point out any war in which Great Britain has been engaged since not undertaken for the propping up of vile despotisms, or for selfish purposes equally vile, to the very latest of them—Zululand and Afghanistan *videlicet*.

But the rebellion against Charles Stuart had a far different aim, all who upheld it being actuated by higher and nobler motives; and, though the war was internecine, it need never be regretted. For on the part of England's people it brought out many a display of courage, devotion to virtue, and other good qualities, of which any people might be proud.

Nor was it all fruitless, though seeming so. From it we inherit such fragment of liberty as is left us, and to it all such aspirations turn. Not all stifled by the corruption which came immediately after under the rule of the Merry Monarch; nor yet by what followed further on, during the foul reign of "Europe's first gentleman;" and let us hope still to survive through one foreshadowing, nay, already showing, corruption great as either.

Though in the Parliamentary wars no great battle occurred in the counties of Monmouth or Hereford, in both there was much partisan strife, at first chiefly along their eastern borders. Their interior districts, save during the Earl of Stamford's brief occupation, and Waller's sweeping raid, had been hitherto in the hands of the Royalists; and no traveller thought of venturing on their roads who was not prepared upon challenge to cry "For the King!"

Two routes were especially frequented; but more by warlike men than peaceful wayfarers. One of them ran due north and south between their respective capitals. The other passed through the same, but with a bow-like bend eastward, keeping to the valley of the Wye, and about midway communicating with the town of Ross. Between them lay a wild-wooded district of country, the ancient kingdom of Erchyn, to this day known as the Hundred of Archenfield. Through this was a third road, leading from Goodrich Castle north-west; which, on the shoulder of a high hill, Acornbury, some six miles south of Hereford, met the more direct route from Monmouth—the two thence continuing the same to the former city.

On the morning of the capture of Monmouth, at the earliest hour of dawn, a cavalcade was seen issuing from the gates of Goodrich Castle, and turning along this road in the direction of Hereford. It numbered nigh an hundred files, riding "by twos," a formation which the narrow trackway rendered compulsory. Most of the men comprising it carried the lance, a favourite weapon with Colonel Sir Henry Lingen, its commanding officer. But some twenty were without arms of any kind, though on horseback: the prisoners of whom Kyrle had spoken as likely to be transferred from Goodrich to the capital. The information accidentally received by him was correct; they were now in transit between the two places, escorted by nearly all the castle's garrison, Lingen himself at the head.

Had he known of Monmouth being in the hands of the enemy, he would not have been thus moving away from his stronghold. But, by some mischance, the messenger sent to apprise him of the disaster, did not reach Goodrich till after his departure for Hereford.

Nor was his errand to the latter place solely to see his prisoners safely lodged. He had other business there, with its Governor, Sir Barnabas Scudamore; hence his going along with them. For taking such a large retinue there was the same reason. Sir Barnabas contemplated an attack on Brampton Bryan Castle; so heroically defended by Lady Brilliana Harley, who had long and repeatedly foiled his attempts to take it.

The High Sheriff of Hereford county—for such was Lingen—took delight in a grand Cavalier accompaniment—many of his followers belonging to the best families of the shire—and along the route they were all jollity, talking loud, and laughing at each *jeu d'esprit* which chanced to be sprung. Just come from hard blows at Beachley, and crowded quarters in Monmouth, they were on the way to a city of more pretension, and promising sweeter delights. Hereford was at the time a centre of distinction, full of gentry from the surrounding shires; above all, abounding in the feminine element, with many faces reputed fair. Lingen's gallants meant to have a carousal in the capital city, and knew they would there find the ways and means, with willing hosts to entertain them.

Different the thoughts of those whom they were conducting thither as captives. No such prospects to cheer or enliven them; but the reverse, as their experience of prison life had already taught them.

Most of all was Eustace Trevor dejected, for he was among them. It had been a trying week for the ex-gentleman-usher. Captured, wounded—by good fortune but slightly—transported from prison to prison, taunted as a rebel, and treated as a felon, he was even more mortified than sad. Enraged also to the end of his wits; he the proud son of Sir William Trevor to be thus submitted to ignominy and insult; he to whom, at Whitehall Palace, but two short years before, earls and dukes had shown subservience, believing him the favourite of a Queen!

Harrowing the reflections, and bitter the chagrin, he was now enduring, though the Queen had nought to do with them. All centred on a simple girl, in whose eyes he had hoped to appear a hero. Instead, he had proved himself an imbecile; been caught as in a trap! What would she—Vaga Powell—think of him now?

Oft since his capture had he anathematised his ill-fate—oft lamented it. And never more chafed at it than on this morning while being marched towards Hereford. While at Monmouth he had entertained a hope of getting rescued. A rumour of the affair at Beachley had penetrated his prison; and he knew Massey had been long contemplating an expedition across the Forest and over the Wye. But Hereford was in the heart of the enemy's country, a very centre of Royalist strength and rule. Not much chance of his being delivered there; instead, every mile nearer to it the likelier his captivity to be of long continuance.

Hope had all but forsaken him; yet, in this his darkest hour of despondence, a ray of it scintillated through his mind, once more inspiring him with thoughts of escape. For something like a possibility had presented itself, in the shape of a horse—his own. The same animal he bestrode in his combat with Sir Richard Walwyn, and that had shown such spirit after a journey of nigh fifty miles. Many a fifty miles had it borne him since, carried him safe through many a hostile encounter.

He was not riding it now, alas! but astride the sorriest of nags. "Saladin," the name of the tried and trusty steed, had been taken from him at Hollymead, and become the property of a common soldier, one of those who had assisted in his capture, the same now having him in especial charge. For each of the prisoners was guarded by one of the escort riding alongside.

It was by a mere accidental coincidence that the late and present owners of Saladin were thus brought into juxtaposition; and at first the former only thought of its singularity, with some vexation at having been deprived of his favourite charger, which he was not likely to recover again. By-and-by, however, the circumstance became suggestive. He knew the mettle of the horse, no man better. Perhaps, had Sir Harry Lingen, or any of his officers, known it as well, a common trooper would not have been bestriding it. But as yet the animal's merits remained undiscovered by them, none supposing that in heels it could distance all in their cavalcade, and in bottom run them dead down.

On this, and things collateral, had Eustace Trevor commenced reflecting; hence his new-sprung hope. Wounded, with his arm in a sling, he was not bound—such precaution seeming superfluous. Besides, badly mounted as he was, any attempt at flight would have been absurd, and could but end in his being almost instantly retaken. So no one thought of his making it, save himself; but he did—had been cogitating upon it all along the way.

"If I could but get on Saladin's back!" was his mental soliloquy, "I'd risk it. Three lengths of start—ay, one—and they might whistle after me. Their firelocks and lances all slung, pistols in the holsters buckled up; none dreaming of—Oh! were I but in that saddle!"

It was his own saddle to which he referred, now between the legs of the trooper, who had appropriated it also.

Every now and then his eyes were turned towards the horse in keen, covetous look; which the man at length observing, said,—

"Maybe ye'd like to get him back, Master Captain? He be precious good stuff; an' I don't wonder if ye would. Do ye weesh it?"

It was just the question Saladin's ci-devant owner desired to be asked, and he was on the eve of answering impressively, "Very much." A reflection restraining him, he replied, in a careless indifferent way,—

"Well, I shouldn't mind—if you care to part with him."

"That would depend on what ye be willin' to gie. How much?"

This was a puzzler. What had he to give? Nothing! At his capture they had stripped him clean, rifled his pockets, torn from his hat the jewelled clasp and egret's plume—that trophy of sweet remembrance. Even since, in Monmouth gaol, they had made free with certain articles of his attire; so that he was not only unarmed and purseless, but rather shabbily dressed; anything but able to make purchase of a horse, however moderate the price.

Would the man take a promise of payment at some future time—his word for it? The proposal was made; a tempting sum offered, to be handed over soon as the would-be purchaser could have the money sent him by his friends; but rejected.

"That's no dependence, an' a fig for your friends?" was the coarse response of the sceptical trooper. "If ye can't show no better surety for payin', I hold on to the horse, an' you maun go without him. 'Sides, Master Captain, what use the anymal to ye inside o' a prison, where's yer like to be shut up, Lord knows how long?"

"Ah, true!" returned the young officer, with a sigh, and look of apparent resignation. "Still, corporal,"—the man had a *cheveron* on his sleeve—"it's killing work to ride such a brute as this. If only for the rest of the way to Hereford, I'd give something to exchange saddles with you."

"If ye had it to gie, I dare say ye would," rejoined the corporal, with a satirical grin, as he ran his eye over the bare habiliments of his prisoner. "But as ye han't, what be the use palaverin' 'bout it? Till ye can show better reezon for my accommodatin' you, we'll both stick to the saddles we be in."

This seemed to clinch the question; and for a time Eustace Trevor was silent, feeling foiled. But before going much farther a remembrance came to his aid, which promised him a better mount than the Rosinante he was riding—in short, Saladin's self. The wound he had received was a lance thrust in the left wrist—only a prick, but when done deluging the hand in blood. This running down his fingers had almost glued them together, and the kerchief hastily wrapped round had stayed there ever since, concealing a ring which, seen by any of the Cavalier soldiers, would have been quickly cribbed. None had seen it; he himself having almost forgotten the thing, till now, with sharpened wits, he recalled its being there; knew it to be worth the accommodation denied him, and likely to obtain it.

"Well, corporal," he said, returning to the subject, "I should have liked a ride on the horse, if only for old times' sake, and the little chance of my ever getting one again. But I'd be sorry to have you exchange without some compensation. Still, I fancy, I can give you that without drawing upon time."

The trooper pricked up his ears, now listening with interest. He was not inexorable; would have been willing enough to make the temporary swop, only wanted a *quid pro quo*.

"What do you say to this?" continued the young officer.

He had slipped his right hand inside the sling; and drawn forth the golden circlet, which he held out while speaking. It was a jewelled ring, the gems in cluster bedimmed with the blood that had dried and become encrusted upon them. But they sparkled enough to show it valuable; worth far more than what it was being offered for. And there was a responsive sparkle in the eyes of him who bestrode Saladin, as he hastened to say,— "That'll do. Bargain be it?"

Chapter Forty Nine
An Uphill Chase

At sight of the glistening gems a sudden change had come over the features of the trooper, their expression of surliness being displaced by that of intense cupidity. But for this he might have considered why the offer of such valuable consideration for so trifling a service. As it was, he had no suspicion of it; though on both sides the dialogue had been carried on in guarded undertone. For this their reasons were distinct, each having his own. That of the prisoner is already known; while a simple instinct had guided the corporal—a fear that the negotiation between them might not be altogether agreeable to his superiors.

More cautious than ever after declaring it a bargain, he glanced furtively to the front, then rearward, to assure himself they had not been overheard, nor their *tête-à-tête* noticed by any of the officers.

It seemed all right, none of these being near; and his next thought was how to effect the exchange agreed upon. The files were wide apart, with very little order in the line of march—a circumstance observed by Eustace Trevor with satisfaction, as likely to help him in his design. They were passing though a district unoccupied by any enemy and where surprise was the last thing to be thought of. But even straggled out as was the troop, any transfer of horses, however adroitly done, would not only be remarked upon, but cause a block in the marching column, the which might bring about inquiry as to the reason, and the guard, if not the prisoner, into trouble.

"Ye maun ha' patience for a bit," said the former, in view of the difficulty. "'Tan't safe for me to be seen changin' horses on the road. But ye won't ha' long to wait; only till we get to the bottom o' that hill ye see ahead, Acornbury it be called. There we can do the thing."

"Why there?"

The question was put with a special object, apart from the questioner's impatience.

"Cause o' an inn that be theer. It stand this side o' where the pitch begins. The Sheriff always stops at it goin' from Goodrich to Hereford, an' he be sure o' makin' halt the day. When's we be halted—ye comprehend, Captain?"

The man had grown civil almost to friendliness. The prospect of becoming possessed of a valuable ring for but an hour's loan of his new horse had worked wonders. Could he but have known that he was hypothecating the more valuable animal with but slight chance of redeeming it, the bargain would have been off on the instant. His avarice blinded him; and his prisoner now felt good as sure he would soon have Saladin once more between his knees.

"I do comprehend—quite," was the young officer's satisfied response; and they rode on without further speech, both purposely refraining from it.

The corporal might have saved his breath in imparting the situation of the inn under Acornbury Hill. Eustace Trevor knew the house well as he; perhaps better, having more than once baited his horse there. Familiar was he with the roads and country around, not so far from his native place by Abergavenny. Besides, he had an uncle who lived nearer, and as a boy, with his cousins, had ridden and sported all over the district. This topographical knowledge was now likely to stand him in stead; and as he thought of the Monmouth road joining that he was on near the head of Acornbury pitch, he fairly trembled with excitement. Could he but reach their point of junction on Saladin's back he would be free.

How he longed to arrive at the roadside hostelry! Every second seemed a minute, every minute an hour!

It was reached at length, and his suspense brought to an end. True to expectation, a halt was commanded; and the extended line, closing up, came to a stand on the open ground before the inn. A scrambling house of antique architecture, its swing sign suspended from the limb of an oaken giant, whose spreading branches shadowed a large space in front.

Under this Lingen and his officers made stop, still keeping to their saddles, and calling to Boniface and his assistants to serve them there. It was only for a draught they had drawn up, the journey too short to need resting their horses. Nor was there any dismounting among the rank and file rearward, save where some trooper whose girths had got loosened took the opportunity to drop down and tighten them.

Seeming to do the same was the corporal in charge of Eustace Trevor, his prisoner too, both on the ground together. Only an instant till they were in the saddle again, but with changed horses, and the blood-crusted ring at the bottom of the corporal's pocket. Meanwhile the officers under the tree had got served, and, cups in hand, were quaffing joyously. In high glee all; for the sun, now well up, promised a day gloriously fine, and they were about to make entry into Hereford with flying colours. Nearly twenty prisoners, it would be as a triumphal procession.

A cry, strangely intoned, brought their merriment to an abrupt end; a chorus of shouts, quick following with the clatter of hoofs. Turning, they saw one on horseback just parting from the troop, as if his horse had bolted and was running away with him!

But no. "Prisoner escaping!" came the call, as every one could now see it was. The man in rich garb, but soiled and torn; the horse a bit of blood none of their prisoners had been riding. One of the officers they had taken— which?

The question was answered by the High Sheriff himself—

"Zounds! it's that young renegade, Trevor! He mustn't escape, gentlemen. All after him!"

Down went tankards and flagons, dashed to the ground, spilling the wine they had not time to drink; and off all set, swords drawn, and spurs buried rowel deep.

The common men, save those cumbered with prisoners, joined in the pursuit; some unslinging lances or firelocks, others plucking pistols from their holsters.

"Shoot!" shouted Lingen. "Bring him down, or the horse!"

It was the critical moment for the fugitive, and in modern days would have been fatal to him. But the old *snap-hans* and clumsy horse pistol of the Stuart times were little reliable for a shot upon the wing, and as a winged bird Saladin was sweeping away. Both volley and straggling fire failed to stay him; and ere the pursuers were well laid on, the pursued was at least fifty lengths ahead of the foremost.

Up the hill, towards Hereford, was he heading! This a surprise to all. In that direction were only his enemies; and he could as easily have gone off in the opposite, with hope of getting to Gloucester. At starting he had even to pass the group of officers under the tree. And why setting his face for Hereford—as it were rushing out of one trap to run into another?

He knew better. Fleeing to the capital of the county was the farthest thing from his thoughts. His goal was Monmouth; but first the forking of the roads on the shoulder of Acornbury Hill. That reached, with no *contretemps* between, he might bid defiance to the clattering ruck in his rear.

The distance he was so rapidly gaining upon them told him he had not been mistaken about the superior qualities of his steed. If the latter should show bottom as it already had heels, his chances of escape were good. And the omens seemed all in his favour: his own horse so oddly restored to him; the luck of that ring left un-pilfered during his imprisonment; and, lastly, to have come unscathed out of the shower of bullets sent after him! They had whistled past his ears, not one touching him or the horse.

He thought of these things when far enough ahead to reflect; and the farther he rode the greater grew his confidence. Saladin would be sure to justify his good opinion of him.

And Saladin seemed to quite comprehend the situation. He at least knew his real owner and master was once more on his back, which meant something. And having received word and sign for best speed—the first "On!" the last a peculiar pressure of the rider's knees—he needed no urging of whip or spur. Without them he was doing his utmost.

Up the pitch went he as hare against hill; up the channel-like trackway between escarpments of the old red sandstone that looked like artificial walls; on upward, breasting the steep with as much apparent ease as though he galloped along level ground. No fear of anything equine overtaking him; no danger now, for the pursuers were out of sight round many turnings of the road; the hue and cry was growing fainter and farther off, and the stone which marked the forking of the routes would soon be in sight.

Eustace Trevor's heart throbbed with emotions it had long been a stranger to, for they were sweet. He now felt good as sure he would get off, and to escape in such fashion would do something to restore his soldierly repute, forfeited by the affair of Hollymead. Nothing had more exasperated him than his facile capture there; above all, the light in which a certain lady would regard it; but now he could claim credit for a deed —

"Not done yet!" was his muttered exclamation, interrupting the pleasant train of thought, as he reined his horse to a sudden halt.

He was approaching the head of the pitch, had almost surmounted it, when he saw what seemed to tell him his attempt at escape was a failure; all his strategy, with the swiftness of his steed, to no purpose. A party of mounted men, just breaking cover from among some trees, and aligning themselves across the road. At the same instant came the customary hail, — "Who are you for?"

The dazzle of the sun right before his face, and behind their backs, hindered his seeing aught to give a clue to their character—only the glance of arms and accoutrements proclaiming them soldiers. And as no soldiers were like to be there save on the Royalist side, to declare himself truthfully, and respond "For the Parliament," would be to pronounce his own doom.

Yet he hated in his heart to cry "For the King." Nor would the deception serve him. They coming on behind would soon be up, and lay it bare.

He glanced to right and left, only to see that he was still between high banks of the sunken causeway. On neither side a possibility of scaling them to escape across country. It was but a question, then, to which he should surrender—the foe in front, or that he had late eluded?

There was not much to choose between them; in either case he would be returned to the Sheriff of Hereford; but to cut short suspense he decided on giving himself up at once. The road was blocked by the party of horse, and, weaponless, to attempt running the gauntlet of them would be to get piked out of his saddle, or cut to pieces in it.

These observations and reflections occupied but an instant, to end in his responding,—

"For the Parliament?"

He might as well make a clean breast of it, and tell the truth.

"We see you are. Come on!"

Surprised was he at the rejoinder as at the voice that gave utterance to it, which seemed familiar to him. But his surprise became astonishment when the speaker added, "Quick, Trevor! we're in ambuscade;" and drawing nearer, the sun now out of his eyes, he saw that well-known banneret, with sword-pierced crown in its field, waving above the head of Sir Richard Walwyn!

Chapter Fifty
An Ambuscade

Steaming at the nostrils Saladin was for the second time brought to a stand, head to head with old stable comrades that snorted recognition. For with Colonel Walwyn was Rob Wilde and others of his troop.

A hurried explanation ensued, Sir Richard first asking, —

"Your guards? You were being escorted?"

"Yes; I've given them the slip."

"Where are they now?"

"Coming up the hill—you hear them?"

"Hush!" enjoined the knight, speaking to those around him; and all became silent, listening.

Voices, with a quick trample of hoofs, and at short intervals a call as of command, from far below and but faintly heard. The road was almost subterranean, and wound up through a dense wood.

"What's their number?" again questioned the knight.

"Nigh two hundred—nearly all Lingen's force—and about twenty prisoners."

"Is Lingen with them?" eagerly asked an officer by Sir Richard's side, who seemed to share the command with him.

"Colonel Kyrle—Captain Trevor," said the knight, introducing them. "I suppose you're aware we've taken Monmouth?"

"I was not; but am happy to hear it. Yes, Colonel," replying to Kyrle, "Lingen is with them; coming on in the pursuit."

Over the features of the ex-Royalist came an expression of almost savage joy, as one who had been longing to confront an old and hated foe, and knew the opportunity near.

"I'm glad?" he exclaimed, as in soliloquy; then seemed to busy himself about his arms.

"His presence was near being a sorry thing for me—the inhuman scoundrel!" rejoined the escaped prisoner.

"How so?"

"I heard him give the order to fire on me, as I was making off."

"And they did?"

"Yes. Every one who could get piece, or pistol, ready in time."

"That explains the shots we heard, Walwyn. Well, young sir," to Trevor, "you seem to bear a charmed life. But we must back into ambush. You take the right, Dick; let me look to the left and give the cue to fall on. I ask that from my better knowing the ground."

"So be it!" assented Sir Richard, and the two commanders, parting right and left, rode back a little way within the wood, where each had a body of horse drawn up, and ready for the charge.

The conversation, hurriedly carried on, had consumed but a few seconds' time; and in an instant after the causeway was clear again, only a vidette left under cover to signal the approach of the pursuers. Captain Trevor, of course, went with his colonel, but now carrying a sword and pistols; supernumerary weapons which had been found for him by Sergeant Wilde.

A profound silence succeeded; for the horses of the Parliamentarians, after two years' campaigning, had become veterans as the men themselves, and trained to keeping still. Not a neigh uttered; no noise save the slight tinkle of curb or bit, and an occasional angry stamp at bite of the *bree* fly. But the one could not be distinguished, even at short distance, amid the continuous screeching of jays, and oft-repeated *glu-glu-gluck* of the green woodpecker, whose domain was being intruded on; while the other might be mistaken for colts at pasture.

To the surprise of all in ambuscade, the pursuing party appeared to be coming on very slowly; and in truth was it so. Two reasons retarded them. Their horses were not Saladins, and the best of them had become blown in their gallop against the steep acclivity more than a mile in length. But the riders themselves had grown discouraged. In their last glimpse got of the fugitive he was so far ahead, and his mount showing such matchless speed, it seemed idle to continue the chase. They but hoped that some chance party of Scudamore's men from Hereford might be patrolling the road farther on, and intercept him. So, instead of pressing the pursuit with ardour, they lagged on it; toiling up the steep in straggled line, and at a crawl.

Some twenty of the best horsed, however, had forged a long distance ahead of the others, who were following in twos and threes, with wide intervals between. And among the laggards was Lingen, instead of in the lead, as might be expected in the commander of a partisan troop. Fond of display, and that day designing exhibition of it, he rode a charger of superb appearance; one of the sort for show, not work. As a consequence, after the first spurt of the pursuit, he had fallen hundreds of yards behind, and was half-inclined to turn round and ride back to the inn, under pretence of looking after his other prisoners.

But there was no going back for those who had pushed on, nor much farther forward. Having surmounted the summit of the pitch, they heard a heavy trampling of hoofs, with the dreaded slogan, "God and the Parliament!" and saw two large bodies of horse, one on each flank, simultaneously closing upon them. At a charging gallop these came on, so quick the surprised party had no time either to turn back or make a dash onward, ere seeing the road blocked before and behind.

A surround complete as sudden, accompanied by the demand "Surrender!" made in tone of determination that would not brook refusal.

Of the score of Cavaliers so challenged, not one had the heart to say nay. They had left their courage below with their spilled wine cups, and now cried "Quarter!" in very chorus, delivering up their arms without striking blow, or firing shot.

"Where's Harry Lingen?" cried Kyrle, spurring into their midst with drawn sword. "I don't see his face among you." Adding, with a sneer, "Such a valiant leader should be at the head of his men!"

Then fixing on one he knew to be a cornet of Lingen's Light Horse, he vociferated,—

"Say where your colonel is, sirrah! or I'll run you through the ribs."

"Down the hill—behind somewhere," stammered out the threatened subaltern. "He was with us when we commenced the pursuit."

Riding clear of the crowd Kyrle glanced interrogatively down the road. To see the tails of horses disappearing round a corner; some of the pursuers, who, catching sight of what was above, had made about face, and were galloping back.

"Let us after them, Walwyn! What say you?" hurriedly proposed Kyrle.

"Just what I was thinking of. Trevor tells me most of their prisoners are my own men, those taken at Hollymead. They shall be rescued, whatever the risk."

"Not much risk now, I fancy. Lingen's lot are so demoralised they won't stand a charge. We needn't fear following them up to the gates of Goodrich Castle. And we can get back to Monmouth that way, well as the other."

"That way we go," then said the knight determinedly; and down the pitch started the two colonels with their respective followers, a detail having been hastily told off to guard the prisoners just taken.

Meanwhile the Sheriff had been balancing between advance and return. Vexed with the cause which retarded him, he was vowing he would never again bestride the showy brute, when he saw several of his men coming back down the pitch at breakneck speed, as they approached calling out, "Treason! A surprise!"

"Treason! What mean you?" he demanded, drawing his sword, and stopping them in their headlong flight. "Are you mad, fellows?"

"No, Colonel; not mad. Some one has betrayed us into an ambuscade. The Roundheads are up the hill; hundreds—thousands of them?"

"Who says so?"

"We saw them, Sir Henry."

"You couldn't have seen Roundheads. There are none on these roads. It must be some of Scudamore's men from Hereford. Fools! you've been frightened at your own shadows."

"But, Colonel, they've taken a party of ours prisoners; all that were ahead of us. We heard the 'Surrender!' and saw them surrounded."

"I shall see it myself before I believe it. About, and on with me!"

The men thus commanded, however reluctant to return towards the summit, knew better than to disobey. But their obedience was not insisted upon. In the narrow way, ere he could pass to place himself at their head, a horseman came galloping from below, and pulled up by his side. A courier with horse in a lather of sweat, showing he must have ridden far and fast. But the slip of paper, hurriedly drawn from his doublet and handed to the Sheriff, told all.

Unfolding it, he read,—

"Kyrle has betrayed us. Massey in Monmouth. Large body of Horse—several hundred—Walwyn's Forest troop, and some of Kyrle's old hands with the traitor himself, gone out along the Hereford road this morning before daybreak. Destination not known. Be on your guard."

The informal despatch, which showed signs of being written in great haste, was without any signature. None was needed; the bearer, personally known to Lingen, giving further details *vivâ voce*; while its contents too truly confirmed the report just brought by the soldiers from the other side.

Among Cavaliers Sir Henry Lingen was of the bravest, and would not cry back from any encounter with fair chances. But he was not foolhardy, nor lacking prudence when the occasion called for it. And there seemed such occasion now. He knew something of Sir Richard Walwyn and his Foresters, as also of Kyrle and his following, and what he might expect from both. They would not likely be out that way unless in strong force. Several hundred, the despatch said—pity it was not more exact—while his own numbered less than two. Besides, if the returning soldiers were not mistaken, twenty of them had been already snapped up; and the rest would make but a poor fight, if they stood ground at all. He rather thought they would not now; and so reflecting reined his unwieldy charger round, and rode back down the pitch, at a much better pace than he had ascended it.

Picking up all stragglers on the way, he meant doing the same with his prisoners left at the inn. But before he had even reached it, he heard hoof-strokes thundering down the hill behind in a multitudinous clatter, that bespoke a large body of horse coming close upon his heels. So close, he no longer thought of cumbering himself with prisoners, but swept on past those at the hostelry in a *sauve qui peut* flight, their guards going along, and leaving them there in a state of supreme bewilderment.

Not long, however, till they understood why they had been so abruptly abandoned. In less than five minutes after, broke upon their view the banner of the sword-stabbed crown, and beneath it coats of Lincoln green, with hats plumed from the tail of Chanticleer, the uniform of the Forest troop—their own.

In a trice they were freed from their fastenings, and armed with the weapons taken from the party of Cavaliers that had been caught by the head of the pitch. Riding their horses, too, after a quick exchange—in short, everything reversed—then away from their halting-place with cheers and at charging gallop, no longer prisoners, but pursuers!

Never did the chances and changes of war receive better or more singular illustration than upon that autumn's morn along the road between Acornbury and Goodrich. At early daybreak a Royalist host, in noisy jubilance, conducting a score of dejected captives towards Hereford; and, before the sun had attained meridian height, a like number of prisoners going in the opposite direction, under guard of Parliamentary soldiers!

Some difference, however, in the mode of march and rate of speed: the former leisurely slow, as a triumphal procession; the latter a hot, eager pursuit that permitted no tarrying by the way. Nor was there on the return passage either jesting or laughter; instead, now and then shouts in stern, angry tone—the demand, "Surrender!" as some fleeing Cavalier, cursed with a short-winded horse, had to pull up, and call out "Quarter!"

So on to the gates of Goodrich Castle, into which Lingen, *malgré* his indifferent mount, contrived to enter, quick closing them behind.

The pursuit could go no farther, nor the pursuers make entrance after him. In that strong fortress he might bid defiance to cavalry—even the best artillery of the time. Famine only had he to fear.

But to so shut him up—so humiliate him—was a triumph for Kyrle, his ancient foe; and as the latter turned away from the defying walls, the smile upon his face told how greatly it gratified him. A *revanche* he had gained for some wrongs Lingen had done his father; and, now that he was himself to rule in Monmouth, he had hopes, ere long, to make a real revenge of it, by razing Goodrich Castle to its foundation stones.

Chapter Fifty One
In Carousal

"We'll drink - drink,
And our goblets clink,
Quaffing the blood-red wine;
The wenches we'll toast,
And the Roundheads we'll roast,
The Croppies, and all their kind."

"A capital song! And right well you've sung it, Sir Thomas. *Herrlich!*"

"Your Highness compliments me."

"*Nein—nein.* But who composed the ditty? It's new to me."

"Sir John Dertham. He who wrote the verses about Waller, and their defeat at Roundway Down—

"'Great William the Con-
So fast did he run,
That he left half his name behind him.'

"Your Highness may remember them?"

"Ha-ha-ha! That do I; and Sir John himself. A true Cavalier, and no better company over the cup. But come, gentlemen! Let us act up to the spirit of the song. Fill goblets, and toast the wenches!"

"The wenches! The wenches!" came in responsive echo from all sides of the table, as the wine went to their lips.

No sentiment could have been more congenial to those who had been listening to Colonel Lunford's song. For it was this man of infamous memory who had been addressed as "Sir Thomas." He had late received knighthood from his King; such being the sort Kings delight to honour, now as then. And among the *convives* was a King's son, the embryo "Merry Monarch," taking lessons in that reprobacy he afterwards practised to the bestrumpetting England from lordly palace to lowly cot.

It was not he, however, who had complimented Lunsford on his vocal abilities; the "Highness" being his cousin, Prince Rupert, in whose quarters they were carousing; the place Bristol; the time some weeks subsequent to the taking of Monmouth by Massey. But the occasion which had called them together was to celebrate a success on the opposite side; its re-capture by the Royalists, for Monmouth had been retaken. A sad mischance for the Parliamentarians; through no fault of Kyrle, who, on active duty, was away from it, but the *lache* of one Major Throgmorton, left in temporary charge.

Riotous with delight were they assembled within Rupert's quarters. They had that day received the welcome intelligence, and were in spirit for unrestrained rejoicing. Ever since Marston Moor the King's cause had been suffering reverses; once more the tide seemed turning in its favour.

But nothing of war occupied their thoughts now; the victory on the Wye had been talked over, the victors toasted, and the subject dismissed for one always uppermost at a Cavalier carousal.

Several songs had been already sung, but that of Lunsford — so indecent, that only the chorus can be here given — tickled the fancies of all, and an *encore* was demanded. A demand with which the festive Lunsford readily complied, and the ribald refrain once more received uproarious plaudits.

"Now, gentlemen!" said the host, on silence being restored, "fill again! We've but toasted the wenches in a general way. I'm going to propose one in particular, whom you'll all be eager to honour. A fascinating damsel, who, if I'm not mistaken, Cousin Charles, has put a spell upon your young heart."

"Ha-ha!" smirked the precocious reprobate, in a semi-protesting way. "You *are* mistaken, coz. None of womankind can do that."

"Ah! if your Royal Highness has escaped her witcheries, you're one of the rare exceptions. *Mein Gott!* she has turned the heads of more than half my young officers, and commands them as much as I do myself. Well, she's worthy of obedience, if beauty has the right to rule, and we Cavaliers cannot deny it that. So let us drink to her!"

By this all had replenished their cups, and were waiting to hear the name of her whose charms were so extolled by their princely host. A good many could guess; and more than one listened to what he had been saying with a feeling of unpleasantness. For he but spoke the truth about the fascinations of a certain lady, and more than one present had felt their spell to the surrender of hearts. Not from this came their pain, however, but from whisperings that Rupert himself had set covetous eyes on the lady in question, and well knew they what that meant — a thing fatal to their own aspirations. Where the sun deigns to shine the satellite stars have to suffer eclipse.

And just as these jealous subordinates anticipated, the damsel about to be toasted was Mademoiselle Lalande.

"Clarisse Lalande?" at length called out the Prince, adding—"To the bottom of your cups, gentlemen!"

And to the bottom of their cups drank they, honouring the toast with a cheer, in which might be detected some tone of irony.

The usual brief interval of silence, as lull in the midst of storm, was succeeded by a buzz of conversation, not about any common or general subject, but carried on by separate groups, and in dialogue between individuals.

Into this last had entered two gentlemen, who sate near the head of the table; one in civilian garb, the other wearing the uniform of a cavalry officer. Both were men of middle age, the officer somewhat the older; while a certain gravity of aspect distinguished him from the gay roysterers around. But for the insignia on his dress, he would have looked more like Parliamentarian than Royalist.

The demeanour of the civilian was also of the sober kind, and marked by an air of distinction which proclaimed him a somebody of superior rank.

"'Tis no more than the truth," he said, turning to the officer, after the toast had been disposed of. "The Creole *is* a fascinating creature. Don't you think so, Major Grenville?"

"I do, my Lord. Her fascination is admitted by all. But, perhaps, some of it is due to her rather free manners. With a little more modesty she might not appear so attractive—certainly would not to most of the present company."

"Ah! true. There's something in that."

"A good deal, my Lord; despite the old adage. For modesty is a quality that does *not* adorn Mademoiselle Lalande. A pity, too! The want of it may ruin her reputation, if it hasn't done that already."

"What a moralist you are, Major! Your ideas have a strong taint of Puritanism. I hope you're not going to turn your back on us gay Cavaliers. Ha-ha-ha!"

The laugh told his Lordship to be in jest. He knew Major Grenville to be a devoted adherent of the King, else he would not have bantered him.

"But," he continued, reverting to the topic with which they started, "morals apart, I've never seen a thing to give one such an idea of woman's power as she does—in that curious Indian dance. 'Tis a wonderful picture, or rather embodiment, of feminine voluptuousness."

"All that I admit," returned the Major. "But for true womanly grace—ay, *abandon*, but of a very different kind—you should see a cousin she has, a real English girl, or, to speak more correctly, Welsh."

"All the same. But who is the cousin so highly endowed?"

"A Miss Powell, the daughter of a wealthy gentleman, who, I'm sorry to say, is not on our side; instead, one of our bitterest enemies."

"Might you mean Master Ambrose Powell, of Hollymead House, up in the Forest of Dean?"

"The same. Your Lordship seems to know him?"

"Certainly I do, or did; for it's several years since I've seen him. But he had two daughters then, Sabrina and Vaga. One is not likely to forget the names. Are not both still living?"

"Oh yes."

"The elder, Sabrina, was nearly grown up when I saw them last, the other but a slip; but both promised to be great beauties."

"If your Lordship saw them now, you'd say the promise has been kept. They are that, beyond cavil or question."

"But from what you've said, I take it you regard one of them as superior to the other. Which, may I ask? At a guess I'd say Sabrina. As a girl I liked her looks best; came near liking them too well. Ha-ha! Have I guessed correctly?"

"The reverse, my Lord; that is, according to my ideas of beauty."

"Then you award the palm to Vaga?"

"Decidedly."

"Well, Major, I won't question your judgment, as I can't till I've seen the sisters again. No doubt they will be much changed since I had the pleasure of last meeting them. But they should now be of an age to get married; Sabrina certainly. Is there no talk of that?"

"There is, my Lord."

"Regarding which?"

"Regarding both."

"Ah! And who the respective favourites?"

"Say respective *finances*, your Lordship. They're engaged. So report has it."

"And who are to be the Benedicts? Who is Mistress Sabrina to make happy?"

"Sir Richard Walwyn, 'tis said."

"Dick Walwyn, indeed! An old classmate of mine at Oxford. Well, she might do worse. And the little yellow-haired sprout? She was a bright blonde, I remember, with wonderful tresses, like a Danäe's shower. Who's to be the possessor of all that auriferous wealth?"

"One of the Trevors."

"There's one of them on the Prince's staff, I understand. Is it he?"

"No; a cousin — son of Sir William of Abergavenny."

"What! the young stripling who used to be at Court — one of the gentlemen ushers?"

"The same, my Lord."

"Quite an Adonis he; so the Queen thought, 'twas said. Mistress Vaga must have all the fascinations you credit her with to have made conquest of him. But he's not with the King now?"

"No; nor on the King's side neither. He turned coat, and took service under the Parliament, in Walwyn's troop of Horse. 'Tis supposed the Danäe's shower your lordship speaks of had a good deal to do with his conversion."

"Very likely that. Cupid's a powerful proselytiser. Well, I should like to see the Powell girls again; their father too, for old friendship's sake. By the way, where are they?"

"I am not well informed about their present whereabouts. Some twelve months ago they were here in Bristol, staying at Montserrat House with Madame, his sister. When we took the place, Master Ambrose thought it wise to move away from it, for reasons easily understood. He went hence to Gloucester, where, I believe, he has been residing ever since — up till within the last few days. Likely they're at Hollymead just now; at least I heard of Powell having returned thither, thinking he would be safe with Monmouth in Massey's hands. Since it isn't any longer, he may move back to Gloucester; and the sooner the better, I should say. He has sadly compromised himself by acting on one of the Parliament's Committees; and some of ours will show him but slight consideration."

"Indeed, I should be sorry if any serious misfortune befell him, or his. An odd sort of man with mistaken views politically; still a man of sterling good qualities. I hope, Major, he may not be among the many victims this unnatural war is claiming all over the land."

"I echo that hope, my Lord."

And with these humane sentiments their dialogue came to a close, so far as that subject was concerned.

Two men had been listening to it with eager ears—Prince Rupert and Colonel Lunsford, who sate by his side. Amidst the clinking of goblets, and the jarring din of many voices, they could not hear it all; still enough to make out its general purport.

They seemed especially interested when the Major spoke of the Powells having returned to Hollymead. It was news to them; glad news for a certain reason. Often since that morning after the surrender of Bristol had the princely voluptuary given thought to the "bit of saucy sweetness, with cheeks all roses," he had seen passing out of its gates for Gloucester. Just as at first sight her sister had caught the fancy of the brutal Lunsford, so had she caught his; and the impression still remained, despite a succession of *amours* and love escapades, with high and low, since.

In more than one of his marauds through the Forest of Dean, Lunsford along with him, he had paid visit to Hollymead House; only to find it untenanted, save by caretakers—the family still in the city of Gloucester. Many the curse hurled he, and his infamous underling, at that same city of Gloucester; where the Cavalier who had not cursed it?

Overjoyed, then, were the two by what had just reached their ears, the Prince interrogating in undertone,—

"You hear that, Lunsford?"

"I do, your Highness."

"*Gott sei dank*! Just what we've been wishing and waiting for. We may now visit Hollymead, with fair hope of the sweet *fraüleins* being there to receive us. Then, *mein* Colonel, then—*nous verrons!*"

After delivering himself in this polyglot fashion, he caught hold of his goblet, and clinking it against that of Lunsford, said in a confidential whisper,—

"We drink to our success, Sir Thomas?"

There had been a third listener to the dialogue between Major Grenville and the nobleman, who also overheard the words spoken by Rupert to the new-made knight. But, instead of gladdening, the first gave him pain; which the last intensified to very bitterness. His name made known, the reason will be divined. For it was Reginald Trevor.

Chapter Fifty Two
At Home Again

There was rejoicing at Ruardean. After two years of forced absence, the master of Hollymead had returned to his ancestral home, and the faces of his beautiful daughters once more gladdened the eyes of the villagers.

Out of the world's way as was this quaint little place, it too had suffered the severities of the war. More than one visit had been paid to it by patrols and scouting parties of the Royalist soldiery; which meant very much the same as if the visitors had been very bandits. They made free with everything they could lay hands on worth the trouble of taking—goods, apparel, furniture, even to the most cherished household goods; invading the family sanctuary, and at each re-appearance stripping it cleaner and cleaner.

Ruardean had, indeed, become an impoverished place, as all the rural district around. The "chimney tapestry" had disappeared from the farmer's kitchen, neither flitch nor ham to be seen in it; empty his pigsties, unstocked his pastures; and if a horse remained in his stable it was one no Cavalier would care to bestride. The King's Commissioners of Array had requisitioned all, calling it a purchase, and paying with bits of stamped paper, which the reluctant vendor knew to be worth just nothing. But, *nolens volens*, he must accept it, or take the alternative, sure of being made severe for him.

So afflicted ever since the surrender of Bristol to Rupert, no wonder the Forest people had grown a-weary of the war, and were glad when they heard of Wintour's defeat at Beachley, and soon after of Monmouth being taken by the Parliamentarians. It seemed earnest of a coming peace; while to the people of the Ruardean district Ambrose Powell once more appearing among them was like the confirmation of it.

Something besides gave them security, for the time at least. A squadron of horse had taken up quarters in their village; not the freebooting Cavaliers, bullying and fleecing them; but soldiers who treated them kindly, paid full price for everything, in short, behaved to them as friends and protectors. For many of them were their friends their own relatives, the body of horse being that commanded by Colonel Walwyn, with Rob Wilde as its head sergeant.

Alike secure felt the ladies in Hollymead House, safe as within Gloucester. How could it be otherwise, with Sir Richard having his headquarters there and Eustace Trevor under the same roof?

The happy times seemed to have returned; and the sisters, after their long irksome residence in walled towns, more than ever enjoyed that country life, to which from earliest years they had been accustomed.

And once again went they out hawking, with the same cast of peregrines and the same little merlin. For Van Dorn, living in a sequestered spot, and unaffected by the events of the war, had kept the falcons up to their training.

Once more to the marsh at the base of Ruardean Hill, the party almost identical with that which had repaired thither two years before. And as before rang out the falconer's *hooha-ha-ha-ha*! and shrill whistle, as a heron rose up from the sedge; again a *white* heron, the great egret! Singular coincidence, and strangely gratifying to the fair owner of the peregrines, for she especially wanted an egret. How she watched as it made for upper air, with the falcons doing their best to mount above it; watched with eager, anxious eyes, fearing it might get away. Not that she was cruel, only just then she so desired to have a *white* heron; would give anything for one.

She did not need to have a fear. Van Dorn had done his duty by the hawks, and, the chased bird had no chance of escaping. Soon its pursuers were seen above it, with spread trains and quivering sails; then one *stooped, raked*, and rose over again; while the other stooped to *bind*; both ere long becoming bound; when all three birds came fluttering back to earth.

With triumphant "whoop?" the falconer pronounced it a kill; but this time, seemingly without being told, he plucked out the tail coverts, and handed them to his young mistress. Days before, however, Van Dorn had received injunctions to procure such if possible. There was a hat that wanted a plume.

"To replace that you lost, dear Eustace," she said, passing them over to him.

"'Tis so good of you to think of it, darling?"

How different their mode of addressing one another from the time when they were last upon that spot! No painstaking coyness now; but heart knowing heart, troth plighted, and loves mutually reliant.

"I shall take better care of this one," he added, adjusting the feathers into a *panache*. "Never man sadder than I when the other was taken from me. For I feared it would be the loss of what I far more valued."

"Your life. Ah! so feared I when I heard you were wounded—"

"No, not my life," he said, interrupting. "Something besides."

"What besides?"

"Your love, Vaga; at least your esteem."

"Eustace! How could you think that?"

"From having lost my own, along with my character as a soldier. To be taken as in a trap."

"Never that, dearest! All knew there was treason. If you were taken so might a lion, with such numbers against you. And how you delivered yourself!"

She had learnt all the particulars of his escape—a deed of daring to be proud of. And proud was she of it.

"Do you know, Eustace," she continued, without waiting his rejoinder, "that you spared me a journey, and perhaps some humiliation?"

"A journey! Whither?"

"To Goodrich Castle first; and it might have been anywhere after."

"But why?"

"To throw myself at Sir Henry Lingen's feet, and crave mercy for you."

"That would have been humiliation indeed, darling. And I'm glad that chance hindered you from it."

"Chance! No love: your courage did it, and—"

"My horses's heels, rather say. But for them I should not be here."

He was upon that horse's back then; she on a palfrey by his side.

"Noble Saladin!" she exclaimed, drawing closer, and passing her gloved hand caressingly over his arched neck. "Dear, good Saladin! If you but knew how grateful I am!"

Saladin did seem to know, as in soft, gentle neighing he turned his head round to acknowledge the caress.

A fair picture these betrothed lovers formed as they sate in their saddles under the greenwood tree. Some change was there in them since they had been there before. He handsome as ever, perhaps handsomer. His cheeks embrowned with two years' campaigning, his figure braced to a terser, firmer manhood; on Saladin's back he seemed the personification of a young crusader just returned from the Holy Wars.

She lovelier than of erst, if that were possible. A woman now, her girlhood's beauty had done all Major Grenville said of it, and more. Sager had she grown, made so by the vicissitudes and trials of the time; and it became her. Not now clapped she her hands, and echoed the falconer's "whoop!" when the hawks struck their quarry down. Instead, took it all quietly; so different from former days!

But there was another cause now sobering, almost saddening, her, one which affected both. The war was not yet at an end. At any hour, any moment, might come a summons which would again separate them, perchance never more to meet! In that tranquil sylvan scene they felt as on the deck of a storm-tossed, wreck-threatened ship, in the midst of angry ocean! Cruel war, to beget such reflections—such fears!

And, alas! they were realised almost on the instant. Following the old course, the hawking party had ascended to the summit of the hill to give the merlin its turn. The game of its pursuit, more plentiful, was easily found and flushed, so that soon the courageous creature made a kill—a landrail the quarry.

But ere it could be cast-off for a second flight, just as once before, the sport was interrupted by, their seeing a horseman on the opposite hill coming down the road from the Wilderness to Drybrook.

He might not have been noticed but for the pace, which was a rapid gallop. This down the steep declivity told of some pressing purpose, while the sun's glitter upon arms and accoutrements proclaimed him a soldier.

More definite was the knowledge got of him through a telescope, which one of the attendants carried. Glancing through it, Sir Richard recognised the uniform of a Parliamentarian dragoon—one of Massey's own regiment. Coming that way, and at such a speed, the man must be a messenger with despatches; and for whom but himself?

Separating from his party, and taking Hilbert with him, the knight trotted off to the nearest point where the Ruardean road passed over the shoulder of the hill, there halting till the dragoon should come up. Nor had he long to wait. As conjectured, the man was a messenger, bearing a despatch that called for all haste in the delivery, and therefore came galloping up the slope without lessening his pace. He seemed some little disconcerted at seeing two horsemen drawn up on the road before him, but a word from Sir Richard reassured him, as he perceived it was the knight himself.

As the despatch was for Sir Richard, this brought his gallop to an end; and, drawing up, he handed over the document, simply saying—

"From Governor Massey, Colonel."

Addressed "Colonel Walwyn," it read,—

> "Gerrard has slipped through out of South Wales, by Worcester, and now *en route* to join the King at Oxford. I've got orders from the Committee to march out and intercept him, if possible at Evesham, or before he can cross the Cotswolds. I shall want every man of my command. So draw off from the Ruardean, for Gloucester, and reinforce its garrison. Start soon as you get this—lose not a moment. Time is pressing.
>
> "E. Massey."

When Sir Richard returned to the hawking party his hurried manner, with the serious expression upon his features, admonished Vaga Powell that her presentiment was on the eve of being fulfilled. Sure was she of it on hearing his answer to Sabrina, who had anxiously questioned him on his coming up.

"Yes, dearest! A courier from Massey at Gloucester. I'm commanded to proceed thither in all haste. We must home."

And home went they to Hollymead, hurriedly as once before. But not to stay there; only to leave the ladies within a few minutes in getting ready for the "route." Then back down to Ruardean to order the "Assembly" sounded; soon after "Boots and saddles"; in fine, the "Forward, march!" and before the sun had sunk over the far Hatteral Hills, the sequestered village had resumed its wonted tranquillity, not a soldier to be seen in its streets, nor anywhere round it.

Chapter Fifty Three
Again Presentiments

"Don't you wish we were back in Gloucester, Sab?"

"Why wish that, Vag?"

"It's so lonely here."

"How you've changed, and in so short a time! While in the city you were all longings for the country and now—"

"Now I long to get back to the city."

"The prosaic city of Gloucester, too!"

"Even so. And am sorry we ever came away from it."

"You've got yourself to blame. Father was all against it, you know, and only yielded to your solicitations. As you're his favourite he couldn't refuse you."

"But you approved of it yourself, for another reason."

Sabrina had approved of it for another reason thus hinted at. After the taking of Monmouth by the Parliamentarians, Sir Richard Walwyn had orders to keep to the Hereford side of the Forest and guard the approaches in that direction. Hence his having his Horse quartered at Ruardean, and hence the desire of the sisters to be back at Hollymead House. Now that he was gone to Gloucester—so unexpectedly summoned thither—all was different, and to Vaga the country life she had so enthusiastically praised seemed no longer delightful.

"Well, Vag, we're here now, and must make the best of it. Though I confess to feeling it a little lonely myself. I wish father had taken Richard's advice."

At his hurried departure Colonel Walwyn had counselled their leaving Hollymead, and going back to reside at Gloucester, if not at once, soon as the removal could be conveniently made. The knight, without wishing unnecessarily to alarm them, had yet some apprehensions about their safety in that remote place. But they were not shared in by his intended father-in-law, who, although not absolutely rejecting the advice, still delayed following it. So secure felt he that, even on the very day when Sabrina was speaking of it, he had himself gone to Gloucester, on Committee business, and left his daughters at Hollymead alone.

Vaga echoed her sister's wish, then added,—"It may be worse than lonely. Don't you think there's some danger?"

"Oh, no! What danger?"

"Why, from the enemy—the King's people."

"There are none nearer than Bristol and Hereford."

"You forget Goodrich Castle?"

"No, I don't. But with Monmouth in the hands of our soldiers the Goodrich garrison will have enough to do taking care of itself, without troubling us."

Monmouth had not yet been retaken by the Royalists; at least no word of that had reached Hollymead House.

"Besides," she continued. "Sir Henry Lingen would not likely molest us. You remember before the war he was very much father's friend, and—"

"And before he was married very much yours," interpolated the younger sister, with a glance of peculiar significance. "I remember that too. For the which reason he might be the very man to molest us. There's such a thing as spitefulness, and he could scarce be blamed for feeling it a little."

"T'sh, Vaga! Don't say such silly things. There never was aught between Sir Henry and myself, nor any reason for his being spiteful now. We have nothing to apprehend from that quarter."

"Still we may from some other."

"What other are you thinking of?"

"Not any in particular. Only a vague sense of somebody—a foreboding— as when we were out hawking, just before that courier arrived. I had the same feeling then, and it came true."

"Admitting it did, what evil came of it? None; only an ordinary event, Richard and Eustace being separated from us. So long as the war lasts we must expect that, and be patiently resigned to it."

Though sager grown, Vaga was still not equal to the strain of any prolonged resignation. Of a subtle, nervous nature, she was easily affected by signs and omens, felt presentiments and had belief in them. One was upon her at this same moment, and in an instant after she saw that which seemed likely to justify it.

"Look!" she cried; "look yonder?" They were in the withdrawing-room, having entered it after eating breakfast, she herself standing at one of the windows, with eyes bent down the long avenue. What had elicited her exclamation was a figure that, having passed inside the park gates, was coming on for the house. A woman, but of man's stature, and by this easily identifiable. For at the first glance Vaga recognised the sister of Cadger Jack.

It was not that which had caused her to exclaim so excitedly. Winny was an almost everyday visitor at the big house, having much business there, and nothing strange would be thought of her coming to it at any time. The strangeness was the way in which she was making approach, hurriedly and in long strides—almost at a run!

"What can it mean?" mechanically interrogated Sabrina, who had joined the other at the window. "So unlike Winifred's usual stately step! Unlike her manner too—she seems greatly excited. Something amiss, I fear."

"Oh, sister! I'm sure of it. Just what I've been thinking and saying. She has news for us, and sad news—you'll see."

"I trust not. Stay! this is Monmouth market day, possibly she has been to the market and heard something there. In that case it's not likely to affect us much, all we care for being on the other side of the Forest. And yet the cadgers could scarce have been to the market and back again already? 'Tis too early. But we shall soon know."

By this the cadgeress was pushing open the wicket-gate of the *haw-haw*, and, now near, they could read the expression upon her features, which showed full of concern.

Though the month of October, the morning was warm, and the window in which they, stood, a casement, had been thrown open. Stepping into a little balcony outside, and leaning over the rail, Sabrina called out interrogatively—"You have some news for us, Win?"

"'Deed yes, my lady. That hae I, an' sorry be's I to say't."

"Bad news, then?" exclaimed both sisters in a breath, their hearts audibly beating.

"Is it anything from Gloucester?" gasped out the elder one, the other mentally echoing the question.

"No, my ladies. It be all 'bout Monnerth."

This some little relieved them, and more tranquilly they waited to hear what the news was.

"Them be's bad, as ye ha' guessed," continued the cadgeress. "Him have been took by the Cavalières."

"Him! Who?" simultaneously exclaimed the sisters, again greatly excited.

"Monnerth, mistresses; I sayed Monnerth, didn't I?"

"Oh! yes, yes." They were too glad to give assent, without noticing her ungrammatic provincialism. "Monmouth taken by the Cavaliers, you say?"

"Yes, my ladies. They's be back into it, an' ha' shut up the Parliamentaries in prison—all as didn't get away."

"Where have you heard this, Win? You haven't been to Monmouth yourself, have you?"

"No, Mistress Sabrina. Only partways. Jack an' me started for the market; but fores crossin' the ferry at Goodrich us heerd as how the Sheriff wor down at Monnerth, an' had helped them o' Ragland to capter the town. Takin' the hint, us turned back an' hurried home, fast as ever we could; an' I han't lost a minnit in comin' to tell ye."

"'Twas thoughtful of you, Winifred," said Sabrina. "And we give you thanks. Now go round to the cook and have something to eat. But stay! I'm forgetting. You haven't told us what time it happened—I mean the taking of Monmouth. You heard that, didn't you?"

"Yes, mistress. Night afore last, or early yester morn. Whens day broke the King's flag be seen over the Castle, an' there wor great rejoicins in the town. So tolt we the ferryman o' Goodrich."

"What should we do?" inquired Vaga, after the cadgeress had parted company with them, retiring to the kitchen.

"What can we do? Nothing, till father comes home. As they must have had the intelligence at Gloucester, yesterday evening at latest, we may look for him soon. I suppose we must give up all thought of hawking to-day? Some one had better go to Van Dorn's lodge, and tell him not to come."

"Too late! There he is now."

The falconer was seen approaching by a side path, with an attendant who carried the hawks on a *cadge*, a couple of dogs following. At the same instant saddled horses, in the charge of grooms, were being brought round from the rear of the house. All this had been ordered beforehand, the ladies having sate down to breakfast costumed and equipped for the sport of falconry.

"Shall we send them back?" queried Sabrina, irresolutely.

"Why should we?"

Vaga was passionately fond of hawking; and, now that she knew the worst of that foreboding late felt, was something of herself again. The taking of Monmouth was but one of the many incidents of the war; no misfortune had happened to any in whom they had special concern.

"I suppose we'll have to leave Hollymead now," she added, "once more to take up our abode in cities. In which case it may be long before we have another day with hawks. If we don't go, Van Dorn will be so disappointed."

"If we do, then," rejoined Sabrina, half assentingly, "it mustn't be far—not outside the park."

"Agreed to that. No need for our going out of it. Inside we'll find plenty of things to fly your Mer at. As for my Pers, if better don't turn up, we can whistle them off at a cushat."

So it was settled, and in twenty minutes after they were in their saddles, and away beyond sight of the house, listening to the *hooha-ha-ha-ha*, the whistle and the whoop.

Chapter Fifty Four
A Glittering Cohort

It was getting late in the afternoon when a party of horsemen, numbering about two hundred, commenced the ascent of Cat's Hill, going in the direction of Ruardean.

Soldiers they were, in scarlet doublets, elaborately laced; their standard flag, with the Royal arms in its field, and a crown upon the peak of its staff, proclaiming them in the service of the king.

That it was no common cavalry troop could be told by other distinctive symbols. Beside the three or four subalterns in their places along the line, half a score other officers were at its head; in gorgeous uniforms, and with hats grandly plumed, as on the personal staff of a general. And such were they; the rank and file rearward being his escort. No ordinary general either, but the commander-in-chief of the King's armies—Prince Rupert himself.

His own garb in splendour outshone all; a blaze of jewels and gold, from the *aigrette* in his hat to the spurs upon his heels—costume more befitting court than camp.

But he was not now on any war expedition; instead, on the way to seek conquest of other kind than by the sword.

It was the day succeeding that night of revelry at his quarters in Bristol; and the words there exchanged between him and Colonel Lunsford will explain his presence on the Cat's Hill, with face turned towards Ruardean. For in that direction also lay Hollymead House whither he was proceeding.

Quick work and a rapid ride had he made of it; evincing the strong passion of fancy with which the "bit of saucy sweetness" had inspired him.

Lunsford was with him, by his side; the two some lengths in the lead, and apart from the others, conversing as they rode on.

"You think, *mein* Colonel," said the Prince, interrogatively, "we shall find the *fraüleins* at home this time!"

"Pretty sure of it, your Highness. Since the Goodrich ferryman heard of their being at Hollymead yesterday, it's scarcely probable they can have taken departure since."

"But the news from Monmouth will have reached them. How about that?"

"It will affect them somewhat, I dare say. Still, Master Powell is not a man to be easily frightened. As your Highness will be aware, Ruardean is not under the Monmouth Commissioners. Sir John Wintour on the Gloucester side, is the one Powell has most reason to apprehend a visit from. And as he will know of Sir John's being held in check by Massey, he won't be much alarmed, just yet. Still, no doubt, he'll be for moving back again to Gloucester; though not in such hot haste, but that your Highness will have an opportunity of holding speech with him."

"*Gott*! Sir Thomas; that should be the reverse of pleasant, from what you've told me about the old Roundhead's tongue. He may give it me as he did yourself."

"No fear of that, your Highness."

"Why not, pray?"

"The circumstances are quite different. He had backings about him then—these ugly fores fellows, five to our one. Besides a Royal Prince—Puritan though he be—he'll have respect for that. But what matters it about his prating? Your Highness intends laying him by the heels."

"That will depend on circumstances. We must try the *suaviter* before the *fortiter*. If fair words fail, then—the extremities."

"Our present visit to the Master of Hollymead is to be of a friendly character then? Is that your Highness's intention!"

"Ceremoniously so; all the politeness to be observed by every one of our escort. You will see to that, Colonel?"

"It shall be seen to. But does your Highness propose taking them all to the house? It might be convenient to leave some at the village, to wait your coming back."

"*Nein, nein!*" impatiently exclaimed the Prince. "All go on with me." Astute schemer as was Lunsford himself, he was not aware of certain motives actuating his master. Anything but an Adonis was the son of the Elector Palatinate. Yet such he dreamed himself, with a confidence in his power of fascinating the fair sex almost illimitable. The type and boast of Cavalierism, he wielded sway uncontrolled wherever he went, or the Royal cause was triumphant; women, as men, either willingly submitting to his caprices, or not daring to oppose them. Many a conquest had he made over weak creatures consenting. For the achievement of such he well knew the advantage of stately show and regal surroundings, nowhere more effective than in the country he was defiling with his presence. Even at this day as then, where the proverbial indemnity for the wrong-doing of kings is extended to princes and princelets, their social backslidings gaining them credit, rather than blame, under the facetious title, geniality.

No man better than Rupert knew woman's weakness in this regard. Hence the shining retinue he had summoned to attend him in this ride through the Forest of Dean—one of the pleasure excursions he was accustomed to make under the plea of a military reconnaissance. For, although the future pirate of the West Indian seas was quite indifferent to English public opinion, there were reasons then for him not too openly outraging it. By his defeats and failures he had lost the countenance of the court, and intrigue was there busy against him.

"In that case, your Highness," rejoined Lunsford, "there's no necessity for our going through the village. A path leads through the woods by which it can be avoided."

"Is it a roundabout?"

"Not much, if any. It comes back into this again, near Hollymead Park gates. If we pass through the village your Highness's escort will gain a large accession of strength, which may not be agreeable to you."

"Gott, yes! Something in that, Sir Thomas. Let us take the other way, then. Where does it branch off?"

"There, your Highness"; and he pointed to the embouchure of a wood road some paces ahead on the right.

Without further speech they turned into it, and rode on beneath the shadow of trees, whose branches, arcading over, hindered sight of the sun. For, though October, these were still in full foliage, the leaves falling late in the Forest of Dean. But green no more; save those of the yew, holly, and frost-defying bramble, with the mistletoe and its pearl-like pellucid berries. All others showed hues and tints varied, and almost as vivid as those of the tropical forests so much extolled by travellers.

A winding path it was, by reason of the steep incline; and as in silence the glittering cohort, forced into single file by its narrowness, slowly followed the sinuosities upward, it might have been likened to a gigantic serpent in crawl towards unsuspecting prey.

This similitude in more ways than one; for at the head of that glancing line there were serpents, though in human shape, making approach to what they intended as victims.

Chapter Fifty Five
Hawking at Home

The peregrines had killed cushat and partridge, the merlin its half-score of buntings and turtle-doves, and the ladies having had a surfeit of sport, were about setting faces homeward. Not that it was late—still wanting two hours of sunset—but the news from Monmouth had disquieted them, and they were feeling anxious about their father's return. He might be back already, and if so, would wonder at their being away from the house.

Van Dorn had called off the dogs, rehooded the hawks, and made all ready for the start home, when game, of a sort that day unseen by them, came unexpectedly in view. A heron on its way across the Forest from the Severn to the Wye, flying low as it passed over the park.

Hapless heron! A temptation no falconer could resist; and at leave, or rather command, from the younger of his mistresses, off went hoods again, leashes were let loose, and once more away flew the noble falcons, mounting spirally upward.

Just at that moment the gates of the park were thrown open to admit Prince Rupert and his retinue. With Lunsford still by his side, the two had already looked through the rails and up the avenue. To see there what gave them satisfaction; the house with windows no longer shuttered, smoke ascending from several of the chimneys, in short every sign of occupation.

"The family here, as anticipated. Your Highness will not be disappointed this time."

"Ah, *wohl*. I was beginning to think the lady of the golden locks an *ignis fatuus*—never to be caught."

"There will be an opportunity of catching her now; and keeping her, if your Highness so desire."

"You would counsel making the *fraüleins* our prisoners then? Is that what you mean, *mein* Colonel?"

"Their father at least should be made so. There's every reason and right for it. He your prisoner, taken back with you to Bristol, 'tis but natural his daughters should accompany him, and share his captivity. If they have the true filial affection they'll be but too willing to do that. Does your Highness comprehend?"

"Quite!" was the laconic response.

The suggestion, cruel and ruffianly, did not jar on Rupert's ears; rather was it in harmony with his wishes, and half-formed designs. He was proceeding to ponder upon it, having ridden through the gate, when a cry, peculiarly intoned, came from a remote corner of the park, quick followed by a shrill whistle.

The air was still, and sounds could be heard from afar; these being clearly distinguishable.

"Ho-ho!" exclaimed the Prince, reining his horse to a stand. "Sport going on here! Somebody out hawking."

The *hooha-ha-ha* was familiar to him.

"Yes," said Lunsford. "That was a falconer's cry — the cast-off."

"Who might it be, Sir Thomas?"

"Impossible to say, Prince. The party must be behind that spinney of Scotch firs. But see! yonder the hawks! Peregrines in chase of a heron."

"By'r Lady, yes! A splendid caste. Trained to perfection. How handsomely they mount up! Over him now! That stoop and rake, superb. A fig for your chances, master lance-beak. Hey! One of them bound! Now the other. Now down, down. *Wunderschön!*"

Absorbed in watching the actual conflict, all eyes directed upward, Rupert and his following for a time neither saw nor thought of anything else. No more did they of the hawking party, who, led by the chase, had pushed on through the spinney of firs to be forward at the kill. Only when the bound bird was writhing to free itself, in its last struggles lowering down to earth, did the two parties catch sight of one another. Not so near yet, a wide stretch of the park being between; but near enough for a mutual making out of what they were.

"Soldiers!" exclaimed they of the hawking party.

"Wenches!" the word that came from the lips of the Cavaliers.

"We're in luck, Prince," said Lunsford. "You see yonder?"

"Two ladies; yes. Are they the birds we're in search of, think you?"

"Sure of it, your Highness."

"Playing with other birds. Ha-ha! Well; suppose we join them at their play?"

"As your Highness commands."

"Do you know them, Sir Thomas—I mean personally?"

"I've never been introduced, Prince; but Captain Trevor—"

"Ah! I remember your saying something about his—Trevor!" he called back to an officer of his suite, "come hither!"

Reginald Trevor it was; who, parting from his place in the line, rode up, respectfully saluting.

"If I'm not mistaken, sir," said the Prince, "you have acquaintance with the ladies we see yonder? Presumably the daughters of Master Ambrose Powell."

"If it be they, your Highness, I once had. But it's been dropped long ago."

"What! A quarrel?"

"No, Prince," answered the young officer, somewhat hesitatingly. "Not exactly that."

"Only a little coolness, then. Well, perhaps I may be the means of restoring, friendly relations. But first I want you to perform the ceremonial of introduction. I hope you haven't so far offended the damsels as to render you ineligible?"

Trevor stammered out a negative, at the same time announcing his readiness to comply with the Prince's wish. He could not help himself, knowing it was more a command than request.

"Come along, then! Let us on to them. You, Colonel, keep the escort at halt here, till I ascertain whether we can have a night's lodging at Hollymead House. That is," he added in a jocular way, "whether we'll be made welcome to it."

Saying which, he gave his Arab a touch of the spur, and started off at a canter over the green sward, direct for the hawking party.

Of course Reginald Trevor went along with him; though with a reluctance which had only yielded to authority not to be gainsaid. Despite her withering words spoken at their last interview, he still loved Vaga Powell himself—hoping against hope—still had respect for her; and to introduce Prince Rupert was like being a party to the accomplishment of her ruin.

"Humph!" grumbled the ex-Lieutenant of the Tower as he looked after them, some little chagrined at being left behind; "High Mightiness thinks he's going to have it his own way with yellow hair. He won't though; unless he do as I've counselled him. But 'twill come to that—must, before we go back to Bristol—and I shall carry thither my share of the sweet spoils."

Chapter Fifty Six
An Introduction in the Saddle

"Who can they be? Not soldiers of the Parliament?"

"No; too much gaud and glitter for that."

"Sir Henry Lingen's!"

"Scarcely either. I heard Richard say Sir Henry's men carry lances. These have none. More probably they're from Monmouth, or rather Raglan. The old Marquis of Worcester's greatly given to display; and his son, Lord Herbert. The shining peacock at their head is likely Herbert himself. They are Royalists, anyhow; that's certain."

The dialogue was between the sisters, commenced as they caught sight of the scarlet-coated horsemen, who had entered within their park. Hurriedly they talked, and in tone telling of agitation. For it was a spectacle to cause them alarm; King's soldiers coming to Hollymead could mean no good, but all the opposite. Just the visitors foreshadowed by Vaga's fears; her presentiment fulfilled after all!

"What can they be wanting, I wonder?" she queried in a half mechanical way. "Nothing with us, hope?"

"Not likely with us; but father. We were wishing him at home. How fortunate he isn't?"

"But he may come at any time?"

"Indeed, yes. What's to be done?" The elder sister seemed perplexed. Only for a short while; then a thought came to her aid; and half turning to the groom who attended them, she said, —

"Rees! Ride back through the firs; gently, and as if looking for something left behind. When on the other side go as fast as ever you can; out through the back gate. First round to Ruardean, to the cadger's cottage. Tell Winny to come up to the house in all haste. Then gallop along the Gloucester road, and, if you meet your master, turn him back. You understand?"

Rees was a quick-witted Welshman, and did understand. Said so; and at once started to execute the order; riding slowly off towards the spinney, in zigzags, with body bent and eyes searching over the ground. Once under cover of the trees, however, he straightened himself in the saddle, and was soon outside the inclosure.

The despatching him had been but the work of a few seconds, and he was gone before any movement had been made by the soldiers, who were still halted at the gate.

"What have they stopped for?" again wondered Vaga. "Surely they intend going on to the house?"

"'Tis we who have stopped them. Their faces are turned this way—they see us?"

"Ah, yes! And two have separated from the rest—are coming towards us! What ought we to do?"

"We may as well await them here; 'twould be impossible to shun them now."

"How should we receive them?"

"Why, civilly of course. We've no alternative but be civil to them. If it be the Lord Herbert we need not fear any special rudeness. Although they are Papists, the Raglan people have never yet—"

"It's not the Lord Herbert?" interrupted Vaga of keener sight; her eye more occupied with the two making approach.

"How know, you it's not?" demanded her sister, in some wonder. "You never saw him did you?"

"No; but I've seen the one we've been taking for him—the shining peacock, as you call him. So have you."

"Who is he, then?"

"Prince Rupert!"

"So it is, indeed! And the other—"

"Reginald Trevor!"

By this the two horsemen were so near, there was no opportunity for the sisters to exchange further speech, save in undertone; Sabrina, as a last word of caution, whispering,—

"We are helpless, and must play a part I've thought of it; will tell you when we're alone. So be more than civil; very polite."

"I will try."

Rupert, a little in the advance, was now up; and suddenly checked his charger to a halt, in such wise as to present the attitude of Mercury just alighted on a "heaven-kissing hill."

"Fair ladies?" he said. "I have not the pleasure of knowing you. But this gentleman, who has, if you object not, will do me the honour of an introduction."

"His Royal Highness, Prince Rupert," announced Trevor, after saluting on his own account, somewhat awkwardly.

The "fair ladies" acknowledged the introduction with a bow; even smilingly, which was more than might have been expected. They said nothing, however, leaving the Prince to direct the course of conversation.

Well pleased with his reception he went on, —

"Apologies are owing for the interruption of your sport. I fear we've done that?"

"No, your Highness," said Sabrina. "We had finished for the day."

"Egad! A good finish too. I myself witnessed the kill, and never saw handsomer. Your peregrines are noble birds, and well trained to their work. Ah! you have a merlin, too. Pretty creature?"

By chance the merlin was perched upon the neck of Vaga's palfrey; and, while speaking, the Prince had drawn close up, as if to get a nearer view of it. But his eyes were on the girl's face instead, and the "pretty creature" seemed an apostrophe to her rather than the bird. For it was spoken with peculiar emphasis, and in a subdued tone, as if he did not desire her sister to hear it. Nor did she, having become engaged in conversation with Captain Trevor, some distance apart.

"She's very clever," rejoined Vaga, referring to the merlin, and without appearing to notice the gaze directed upon her, — "can kill everything she's cast-off at."

"Ah!" sighed the Prince. "Fatal to all the larks and buntings, just as the eyes of her mistress must be to all men."

She looked at him with a puzzled expression. What a strange remark to make about her sister, whom he could never have seen, save that once as they passed him going out of Bristol! But she understood it, on his adding, —

"The little beauty is yours, I take it?"

"No, your Highness," she answered, without making any allusion to the implied compliment, though its *braverie* jarred upon her ear. "The merlin belongs to my sister. The peregrines are mine."

"Happy peregrines!" he exclaimed, pretending to apostrophise the two great falcons, that, now hooded, had been returned to their kedge. "How I should like to be one of you! Ay; would consent to be held in leash for life, could I but hope for caresses, such as you receive from the hands of your beautiful mistress. Ah! that must be sweet?"

There could be no mistaking the character of speech like this, rude even to impertinence. It brought the red into the young girl's cheeks, and she would have angrily resented it, but was restrained by the caution late received from her sister. Still, to let it pass unnoticed was out of the question, and would likely lead to her being yet further insulted. Making an effort to curb her kindling indignation, she rejoined, calmly as she could,—

"Such language may befit the fine Court ladies, with whom your Highness is accustomed to hold conversation. We simple country girls are not used to it."

Regardless of modest manners, even of common decency, as was this German Prince, he felt the rebuke, and quailed under it. For the glance of quiet scorn that went with the words told him he was putting on airs, and paying compliments to no purpose. In that quarter all would be thrown away.

With a light laugh he endeavoured to conceal his discomfiture, saying apologetically,—

"Oh! mistress, you must pardon the free speech of a Cavalier. Our tongues, as our swords, often fly out without reflection. Be assured I meant not to offend—far from it."

Apology was a bitter pill for Prince Rupert to swallow; but he gulped it down with a better grace, confident of having the "bit of saucy sweetness" in his power. If he failed to make conquest of her, there was another way to fall back upon; that to which his low familiar, Lunsford, had been all along counselling him.

The little *désagrément* brought their *tête-à-tête* to an end, the Prince not caring to continue it. It could be resumed at a more favourable opportunity, which he meant to find before leaving Hollymead. Seeming suddenly to recollect himself, he said, in voice loud enough to be heard by the elder sister, as he intended it,—

"But, ladies! I've only half apologised for our intrusion, and trust you will pardon it, when you hear my excuses. I was on the way to visit your worthy father, with whom I have some business. When hearing the *hooha-ha!*—ardent falconer as I am—I couldn't resist coming across to learn the result. Permit me to take leave of you, with thanks for your gracious reception. Unless, indeed, you do me the further honour of letting me escort you to the house. If I dared make so free, I would even ask the favour of being introduced by you to your father, with whom I regret not having personal acquaintance."

"Our father is not at home," said Sabrina, speaking for both.

"Indeed?" he exclaimed, looking half-disappointed, half-pleased. "That's unfortunate. But I suppose you expect him soon?"

"We cannot tell what time he may return, your Highness."

"Ah! he's gone upon a journey, then. May I ask whither? You'll pardon the inquiry, in view of my business with him?"

"To Gloucester," she answered, without hesitation, too glad to have the questioner think that he inquired about was in that safe city.

"His absence is disappointing," said the Prince—half in soliloquy, and half addressing himself to Captain Trevor. "It will necessitate our staying here for the night." This loud enough for the ladies to hear. "I regret that," he pursued, again turning to them, "not on my own account, but because the quartering of my escort at Hollymead cannot be over agreeable to you. However, I can promise best behaviour on their part; and should your servants have any rudeness to complain of it shall be punished with all severity."

This self-invitation to the hospitality of Hollymead House, however vexatious to the daughters of its absent owner, did not at all surprise them. They had been expecting it as the upshot; for, despite his fine phrases of apology—all pretence—the Prince's bearing and manner told them how much he felt himself their master.

Withal, they were not dismayed, Sabrina making calm rejoinder, with some formal words, that Hollymead would be too much honoured by his presence. Then in a whisper to Vaga, as they drew side by side to ride home,—

"Keep up courage, Vag. Above all keep your temper. Everything may depend on that. We're among wolves, that may tear us if angered."

"Go back, Captain!" called the Prince to Trevor. "Give my commands to Colonel Lunsford, and tell him to bring the escort on to the house."

"Lunsford along with them!" ejaculated Sabrina, in undertone to her sister. "That makes my words good. We *are* among wolves."

The evil repute of this man justified her speech. It had been spreading day by day, till his name was now become a synonym of inhumanity—a bogie to stop the crying of the babes in the cradle.

Chapter Fifty Seven
A Crime in Contemplation

Still self-invited, Rupert accompanied the ladies to the house, and assisted them to dismount with great show of courtesy and respect. The little ruffle with Vaga had determined him not to try on that tack again.

He did not go inside with them, having some directions to give to his suite, seen approaching up the avenue. Besides, it was nearing dinner hour, and they must needs repair to their dressing-rooms.

Left by himself, the Prince seemed all impatience for his escort to come up. He had even shown haste when helping the ladies out of their saddles, as if wishing to be disembarrassed of them with the least delay. Some new thought, or scheme, had evidently entered his mind; and recently, or since despatching Trevor with the order to Lunsford, as then he had said nothing about time.

When they were near enough to hear him he called out, making a sign to the officer at their head to hasten them on. This was Lunsford himself, who, perceiving that something was wanted, separated from the cavalcade, spurring his horse to a quick canter. As the haw-haw gate had already been opened, he passed through it without. Stop or interruption, on to the house.

"Come up—nearer!" said the Prince, speaking low, and in a cautious manner as if he feared being overheard. He was standing in the porch, a little elevated above the ground, and as the other drew alongside, seated in the saddle, their heads were close enough for conversing in whispers.

"What is it, your Highness?" asked Lunsford, wondering at the air of mystery.

"I suppose Trevor has told you the *pater* isn't at home?"

"He has, Prince; but I knew it before."

"Indeed! How learnt you? When?"

"Just after your Highness rode away from us. One of Powell's people, a sort of shepherd, or cowboy, chanced to be coming into the park; and with a little cross-questioning I got out of him, both the fact of his master's absence, and the whereabouts."

"He's at Gloucester."

"Yes, Prince. But the affair of Monmouth will draw him home, soon as he receives news of it. He should have had that long ago; so may be expected here at any moment."

"Just so. But if he get word of our being here before him, he may turn back and give us the go-by. So I want half a dozen files detached, and sent off along the Gloucester road, under a trusty officer, in all haste. If they meet him, he's to be made prisoner at once."

"It's already done, your Highness."

"What! Has Powell been taken?"

"No, Prince; pardon me. I meant the detachment has been sent to intercept him. I took the liberty of doing that without your orders. There was not time to communicate with your Highness, unless at the risk of being too late."

"True, Colonel, true."

"And it would have been too late," he went on to explain in justification of his act. "As your Highness started to join the hawking party, perhaps you may not have noticed a man separating from it, and riding back through the trees?"

"*Nein*, Colonel. I did not."

"But I did, Prince. He appeared to be one of their attendants—a groom—though in the distance one couldn't be sure what. But from the way he went off I suspected it had something to do with our being seen. Soon as I learnt the other thing, I was sure of it. Besides, shortly after he had passed out of sight behind the firs, I distinctly heard hoof-strokes, as of a horse in full gallop. Putting that and that together it occurred to me he might have gone off to give the very warning your Highness apprehended."

"If such were his intent, he may still?"

"No, Prince; not likely. He won't be in time. Going out by a back gate he'll have to ride the whole round of the park before he can get upon the Drybrook road, which is that for Gloucester. The detachment started only a few minutes—less than five—after; and on the direct route will easily head him off. They have orders to lay him by the heels, and bring him back here; it's to be hoped the other with him."

"*Gott*, Colonel! you've been clever. A capital stroke of strategy. If it fail, I shan't blame you."

"Your Highness's approval gratifies me. I think we need not fear failure. At all events the messenger, if such he is, will be stopped, and something will be squeezed out of him as to his errand. I gave instructions that a file be sent back with him, soon as taken. So we may expect seeing him ere long. I suppose your Highness designs to quarter here for the night?"

"Any number of nights, Colonel, if one be not enough for accomplishing my purpose."

"Half a one will be enough for that, Prince, if you proceed to accomplishing it in the way I would advise you. No timid measures will avail here; only the bold course, which conquest gives a right to, all over the world."

Without a blush did the ruffian give utterance to his atrocious counsels; for he knew they were congenial to him into whose ears he was pouring them.

"Belike, that will be the best way," rejoined the Prince, well knowing what was hinted at. "I come to be of your mind, Colonel. But now, return to the escort. Give directions for their going into quarters. See that sentries are set round the house, with outlying pickets. We cannot be too careful, though Monmouth is in our hands. When you have everything settled, come to me inside. Then we can talk about further action."

Light of heart, Lunsford proceeded to the execution of the orders thus given. By the Prince's manner—and speech, half admitting—he saw that the latter had received a rebuff, and was in the mood for violence, even to outrage. It would be nothing new to him; nor the first time for the ex-Lieutenant of the Tower to be his aid and companion in such a criminal escapade as that they were now contemplating.

Verily were Ambrose Powell's daughters in danger! And a danger neither had conception or suspicion of.

Chapter Fifty Eight
A Messenger Despatched

The girls had gone upstairs, their maid, Gwenthian, attending upon them to dress for dinner, of which something had been said to the Prince when parting with him at the door.

Once inside the dressing-room, however, Sabrina, instead of proceeding to change her attire, made direct for an *escritoire*, the flap of which she pulled open. Then seating herself before it, she drew a sheet of paper from its drawer, and commenced writing with nervous haste.

A letter it was of no very great length, and in a few seconds finished. But before folding it up she turned to the maid saying, —

"Gwenth! Go down to the back door, and stay about there till you see cadger Jack's sister. I expect her to come up to the house; and if nothing has hindered, she should be here very soon now. When she arrives bring her to me, without losing a moment. Do it all quietly."

Gwenth signified her comprehension of the orders, and was about starting to execute them, when her mistress said, "Stay!" Then, after reflecting a moment, added, —

"Go into the kitchen, and tell the cook dinner is not to be served before Winny goes away—that is, if she come. In any case, it's not to be put on the table till she has further directions about it."

"But must we really dine along with him?" asked Vaga, as the maid passed out of the room. She had commenced making her toilette, and, inattentive to what her sister had been doing, only overheard what she said about the dinner.

"Either that or give offence. I had to speak of dinner—could not help it—and the Prince will expect us to sit at the table."

"I'd rather sit down with Beelzebub. Oh, Sab! you can't conceive what a vile, vulgar man—Prince though he be."

"Yes I can; know it. Richard has told me all about him. But we must bear, and dissemble; do our best to entertain both him and his officers. I think we needn't fear any special rudeness just yet; and if we can keep them to their good behaviour for twelve hours I ask no more."

"Why do you say twelve hours?"

"Read that."

It was the note she had just written; and, soon as the other had run her eyes over it, she added,—

"Now you understand?"

"I do. But how is it to be taken there?"

"By Winny. It's just for that I gave Rees orders to send her up."

"Couldn't Rees have taken it himself? On horseback he would go much faster."

"True, he might, if permitted to start. But he wouldn't be—not the least likelihood of it. If he return to the house—which I hope he won't—they'll not let him leave it again. But Win will do better every way. We can trust her, and for speed she'll get to her journey's end quick as any courier on horseback. She knows all the short cuts and by-ways through the Forest. That will be in her favour to save time—besides safety otherwise. The fear I have is her not being at home. What a pity we didn't know of their coming, when she was with us in the morning!"

"Perhaps not so much," rejoined Vaga, whose subtle ear had caught the sound of footsteps ascending the stairs; two sets of them, as told by the lighter and heavier tread. "That's Win now coming up with Gwenth. I'm almost sure of it."

In a few seconds after both were sure of it, as the opened door discovered their maid outside on the landing with the cadgeress close behind.

"Oh, Win! we're so glad!" exclaimed the sisters in a breath, as she was ushered into the room.

"Glad o' what, my ladies?" asked the woman, with a puzzled look. She did not understand how they could be joyful under the circumstances.

"At your being here," answered Sabrina. "We were afraid you might not be at home, or unable to come to us."

"Well, mistress, I wor at home, an' comed soon's I got your message. But my comin' wor nigh all bein' for nothin'."

"How so?"

"The Cavalière sodgers warn't for lettin' me in o' the house, nor yet through the back gate. They ha' got sentries all roun'. Besides, the yard be full o' them wi' their horses, an' their imperence too."

"They were impudent to you?"

"'Deed, yes, my ladies. Swored at me, an' said I mauna set foot inside the gate."

"You see what courteous guests we've got, sister?" said Vaga. "The attendants of a Prince! I thought it would end so."

"Me tried to get past they," continued the cadgeress, "by tellin' a bit fib. I sayed us wor the washwoman come for the clothes."

"How clever!" exclaimed Vaga, admiringly.

"Not much o' that, mistress. Anyways it warn't no use. Them wouldn't allow me in after all; if't hadn't been for a young officer, who chanced be near, an' ordered they let me pass. He spoke me kindly too, which wor the strangest thing o' all."

"Why strange?" asked Sabrina.

"On account o' who him wor, my lady."

"Who?"

"Captain Trevor, the one's used to come to Hollymead fores the war."

She had no need to particularise which. The sisters knew, and exchanged glances; that of the elder showing a peculiar intelligence.

"Odd o' he bein' civil to me," pursued the woman. "Him must 'a knowed we well enough, an' had remembrance o' what happened on the Cat's Hill two years ago. I tolt you about it, my ladies."

"You did," said Sabrina. "And it does seem a little strange of Captain Trevor not being, spiteful if he recognised you, as he must have done. But," she added, becoming impatient, "*no* matter for that now. Time is pressing, and we want you to do us a service, Win. You will?"

"Why needs thee ask if us will?"

"Because there's some danger in it."

"That be no reason; and don't speak o' the danger. Please to say what's weeshed done, Mistress Sabrina; an' 't shall be did if in the power o' we to do't."

"This then, dear Winny. We want it taken to Gloucester."

She held out what appeared a spill for lighting pipe or candle. It was the note she had just written, folded and doubled-folded till no longer recognisable as a sheet of paper, much less a letter. For all the cadgeress knew it to be such; and not the first of its kind she had received from the same hands, for surreptitious conveyance.

"It shall be tookt theer," she said, in a determined way, "if the Cavalières don't take't from me on the way. Them won't find it without some searchin', though."

Saying which, she made further reduction in the dimensions of the sheet by double knotting it; then thrust it under the coils of her luxuriant hair, and by a dexterous play of fingers so fixed it that, only undoing the plaits, could it be discovered.

The letter bore no address, nor was name signed to it. Neither inquired the cadgeress to whom it was to be delivered. Enough that Mistress Sabrina had given it to her, and it was for Gloucester. She knew there was a man there it must be meant for; she herself, for a special reason, being always well posted up as to the whereabouts of Sir Richard Walwyn and his Foresters.

"Thee weesh me to start immediate I suppose, my lady?"

"At once—soon as you can get off. How long will it take you to get to Gloucester?"

"Well, for usual me an' Jack be's 'bout four hours fra Ruardean. But I once't did the journey myself in a bit less'n three, an' can go t' same again."

"It's now a little after six—only ten minutes," said Sabrina, consulting her three-cornered watch. "Do you think you could get there by nine?"

"Sure o' that; an afores, if us be alive, an' nothin' happen to stop we on the way."

"Oh! I hope there won't, dear Winny. Time is of such importance; so much depending upon it. Ay, it may be lives."

She leant forward, and whispered some words into the woman's ear; either a last pressing injunction, or, it might be, promise of reward for the service to be performed. Whatever it was, on the face of the Forest Amazon there was an expression of ready assent; then a humorous smile, as she made haste to be gone, saying, —

"Now, Gwenthy! gie us the clothes for the wash!"

The maid, as her mistress, looked a little puzzled. But quickly comprehending, all three set to collecting such *lingerie* as they could lay hands on, soon making up a bundle big enough to represent a week's consignment for the laundry.

Which the pretended washerwoman having hoisted on her head, started downstairs with it; Gwenthian, by direction, going along to see her out of doors, assist her in cajoling the sentries, and bring back report whether these had been safely passed.

Chapter Fifty Nine
Brought Home a Prisoner

After the cadgeress had gone out of the room the anxiety of the sisters was, for a while, of the keenest. The first flush of excitement over, they saw danger in what they had done. Should their messenger be stopped outside, and the note found upon her, there was that in it which could not fail to compromise them. Moreover its contents had reference to an important matter, a design that would be all defeated.

Luckily they had not long to endure suspense. A light tread on the stairs told of Gwenthian returning; and as she appeared in the doorway, kept open for her, the joyous expression on her face betokened a successful issue to the affair she had been sent upon.

"Win's got safe away?" was her triumphant announcement, as she tripped lightly into the room.

"Good!" exclaimed both, Sabrina going on to inquire particulars.

"Did they let her pass without any questioning?"

"No, indeed, mistress. The sentries at the back gate—there are two at it—stopped her; and one pulled the bundle off her head. They were going to open and examine it, when Captain Trevor came up, and ordered them to put it back again. Then he passed her through the gate, saying something—like in a friendly way."

"Did you hear what he said?"

"Only to the soldiers; telling them to let the washerwoman alone. But Win gave them a bit of her tongue too, as if she was real angry?"

"You saw her well away?"

"Yes, mistress; beyond where there were any of the people. She took the path to the falconer's lodge, where she's to leave the things."

"Why leave them there?"

"Because she don't intend returning to her own cottage. That, she said, would delay her; besides, some of the soldiers might be straying along the Ruardean road, and stop her again. She's gone the way through the woods."

The ladies felt relieved. Win would manage it if woman could; and should she succeed in reaching Gloucester, they might ere long look for other relief from the dangers that environed them.

But there was something to be done meanwhile; their unwelcome visitors to be entertained. And how to extend hospitality to such was a perplexing problem. Not only their numbers, but their character made it so. The common soldiers could take care of themselves outside; the signs and sounds told they were already doing so; but the Prince himself, and the officers in his suite, would have to be treated in a different way. Dinner had been spoken of—supper as called then—and this was the first thing to be thought about.

"Go down again, Gwenth," commanded Sabrina, acting mistress of the mansion, "tell the cook to set it upon the table as soon as it is ready."

"For how many, my lady?"

"Oh! I can't tell. Let her count for, say a score; and send in all the eatables she can command."

As the maid went kitchenward to deliver the somewhat indefinite directions, her young mistresses turned to making their toilette at length and at last. And, perhaps, never was one made more reluctantly, or less elaborately, for a Prince of the blood Royal. Little cared they how they might look in his eyes, or any other eyes that were to be upon them. For their hearts were full of heaviness; oppressed by keen anxiety about their father—still apprehending his return home. They knew how much he was compromised with the King's party; had been ever since the rebellion began, and before. For, ere blow had been struck, or sword drawn, had he not resisted the loan by Privy Seal? And here again at Hollymead were the two men who had attempted to levy that loan upon him—Colonel Lunsford and Captain Reginald Trevor! They would be satisfied with no money contribution now; but meant making him their prisoner, with some severe punishment for his "delinquency."

So feared his daughters at that hour; and, as a consequence, had little care or thought about anything besides; even of the peril impending over themselves.

"It's strange, Rej Trevor behaving in such a way to Win," remarked Vaga, as she stood before the mirror adjusting her rebellious tresses. "He couldn't help knowing her, as she herself says. Once seen she's not the sort to be easily forgotten. And after that encounter they had on the Cat's Hill! Very strange, isn't it?"

"Yes, indeed," assented Sabrina; "I've been wondering at it myself, and at something besides."

"What besides?"

"His behaviour in every way. He seems altogether changed."

"I've had no opportunity of observing it. What makes you think so?"

"While you were apart with the Prince we had some conversation. He talks quite differently from his old frivolous way. And no more has he the swaggering manner which used to be so offensive."

"Then he's not the conceited Cavalier of twelve months ago?"

"Anything but that. Had I not known him in the past I should set him down for a modest young fellow, of rather melancholy temperament; or more like one who had some sorrow preying upon him."

"What can it be, I wonder?" She had her conjecture as to what, but forbore declaring it. She had not forgotten—how could she?—his confession, made in passionate appeal, at their last interview. She knew his indifference at their parting was the purest affectation, and that the fish he had gone to catch had not been caught.

Recalling that scene, her sister could have answered the question with a near approach to the truth. But she, too, retentive of her real thoughts, but said in careless rejoinder,—

"Oh! I suppose the events of the war, which have had a saddening effect on everybody."

"Not everybody. These self-invited guests of ours are at least an exception. Listen to them!" By this the officers of the Prince's escort had entered the house; and from their loud talk and laughter were evidently making themselves at home and free with everything. They could be heard issuing commands, and calling out orders to the servants, as though the place were a public inn.

"Like as not," continued Vaga, still incredulous about Reginald Trevor's conversion, "like as not your 'modest young fellow of rather melancholy temperament' is laughing among the loudest of them. I fancy I hear his voice."

"No, Vag, I don't think you do. I can't."

"Well, may be not. And it's to be hoped he's sobered, as you say. He needed it. Strange if he is though, in the retinue of Prince Rupert, whose precept and example are more likely to have a reverse tendency. Possibly Master Rej is only humble in the presence of the High Mightiness, his master. When the big dog is by, the little one has to be on its good behaviour."

"I scarce think it's that; and you may be wronging him."

"If I am I shall be glad to know it. But how odd all this?" she added, yielding to a sudden recollection. "Time was when you, Sab, were all the other way about Rej Trevor; used to caution me against him!"

She had faced towards her sister, and stood with hands full of loose hair that fell as a cataract of molten gold over her ivory shoulders.

"True, I did. And with reasons then. Our father was against him more than I; which may have influenced me."

"And now?"

"Now I admit never having believed him so very bad—I mean at heart."

"Oh! nobody ever said he had a very bad heart. His head was more blamed for getting him ill repute."

"His habits rather."

"Say habits, then. But why are you thus defending him?"

"Because of his seeming so friendly to us. All he said to me just now, with his manner, was as one who felt sorry at our being thus intruded on. He knows it's not agreeable to us—cannot be. And his behaviour to Win— that confirms my belief that he has no hostile feelings to us."

"Don't be so confident till we're sure she's safe off. It may be only a trap to catch us. How know we he hasn't followed to bring her back again, and so win favour from his princely patron. I wouldn't wonder if it's something of that kind. For in what other way is his conduct to be accounted for?"

"Heaven help us if it be that! But I won't—can't believe it."

"Well, we shall soon know, now. If Win get away, I'll think better of Rej Trevor than I've ever done."

"If she do, to-morrow's sun may see soldiers here in green uniforms, with red ones as their prisoners, and you and I, sister, will have done something for the good cause—for Liberty!"

In her most tranquil mien Sabrina Powell was an imposing personage; but now, excited to enthusiasm by the word "Liberty" on her lips, and its inspiration in her heart, with her grand eyes aglow, she looked its very Goddess.

She had finished her toilette, and stood at the window, a front one, commanding view of the avenue and entrance gate of the park. But not long was she there before seeing that which brought a black shadow upon her brow, with chill fear into her heart.

"Oh, Vaga?" she called to her sister, still at the mirror, "come hither! See what's down yonder!"

The summons, in tone almost of agony, drew the other instantly to her side, with tresses trailing. To see three horsemen, who had just passed through the gate, and were coming on for the house. They rode abreast; he in the middle being in sombre civilian garb, the two who flanked him wearing the scarlet uniform of the soldiers already around the house.

"'Tis Rees!" exclaimed Sabrina, recognising the groom. "They've taken him prisoner!"

"Indeed, yes; 'tis he. Oh, sister, dear! if father should be coming home now? I hope he's still in Gloucester!"

Vain hope; almost on the instant to know disappointment. For before those already entered were half-way up the long avenue, more red coats were seen riding through the gate, in their midst a man in dark dress—he, too, evidently conducted as a prisoner. "'Tis father!"

Chapter Sixty
Quartered upon the Enemy

Night had descended over Hollymead. A dark night, too, though there was no lack of light inside the house or around it. Nearing November the atmosphere had a frosty feel, and great wood fires were burning in the wide chimney places of the reception rooms. Without, in the centre of the courtyard, a very bonfire had been kindled, which sent its red glare and glow to the most distant corner of the inclosure. Around this were seated or standing, in every variety of attitude, such of the common soldiers of the escort as were not upon duty. Carousing, of course. For the rank and file of the Royalist army, especially that portion of it which acted under Rupert, followed the fashion of their officers; and one of the affectations of Cavalierism was to display a superior capacity for indulgence in drink.

About the house they had found the wherewithal to give them a good supper, with more than drink enough to wash it down. For when Monmouth fell into the hands of the Parliamentarians, the Master of Hollymead, thinking it safe, had done something to restock his pastures, as also replenish larder and cellars! And once more these were in the way of getting speedily depleted; the thirsty troopers around the courtyard fire quaffing at free tap from a cask of ale they had rolled out upon the pavement; while they bandied coarse jests, told indecent stories, or sang songs of like character, roaring in chorus.

Inside there was revelry also. Of a less rude kind; still revelry, and coarse enough, considering that they who indulged in it composed the *entourage* of a Prince. In the dining-hall was it being held, around a table on which stood a varied assortment of bottles and decanters, goblets and glasses. There had been a repast upon it, that same dinner-supper; but the dishes and *débris* of solids had been removed, and only the drinking materials remained. Nearly a score of guests encircled it, all gentlemen; and all in military uniform— being the officers of the escort—not a man in citizen garb seen among them. For the master of the house was not at the head of his own table, as might have been expected. Instead, shut up in one of the rooms adjacent; its door locked, and a sentry stationed outside!

His daughters were upstairs, in their private apartment, from which they had never come down. Through the window they had seen their father brought back under guard, as a felon; saw it with indignation, but also fear. Greater became the last, when told they could not hold speech with him, or have access to the room in which he was confined. Denied interview with their own father, in their own house! Inhumanity that augured ill for what was to come after.

What this might be they could neither tell nor guess. They even feared to reflect upon it; trembling at every footstep on the stairs. Though no key had been turned upon them, nor sentry set at their door, they were as much imprisoned as their father. For the Prince's retinue of servants filled the house, tramping and roaming about everywhere, and bullying the family domestics. It was not safe to go out among them; and the young ladies had locked themselves up, dreading insult, if not absolute outrage. Even Gwenthian dared not trust herself downstairs, and shared their confinement.

What did it all mean? Why such change in the behaviour of the Prince, so late pretending amiability? For his people must have sanction, or they would not be so acting.

The explanation was simple, withal. Shortly after Rupert's arrival at Hollymead, a courier, who had followed him from Monmouth, brought tidings of another Royalist reverse—Chepstow, with its castle, taken or closely beleaguered. Exasperated by the intelligence, he no longer resisted the wicked proposals of Lunsford, but gave willing assent to them. And now, having thrown off the mask, he had determined on taking the whole Powell family back with him to Bristol. As his prisoner there he could do with the "bit of saucy sweetness" as it might please him; as he had done with many other unfortunate women whom the chances of war had brought within his wanton embrace.

It had been all settled, save some details about the departure from Hollymead, the time, and the return route. These were now being discussed between him and the commanding officer of his escort, as they sate at a side table to which they had temporarily withdrawn, to be out of earshot, of the others.

"Should we remain here for the night, *mein* Colonel, or make back to Monmouth? We can get there before midnight."

"That we could, easily enough, your Highness. But why go by Monmouth at all?"

"Why not?"

"There are two reasons against it, Prince. Both good ones."

"Give them, Sir Thomas."

"If it be true that Chepstow's lost to us, there may be a difficulty in our crossing the Wye down there. Or getting over to the Aust passage of the Severn, with such a weak force as attends your Highness."

"*Gott!* yes; I perceive that. But what's your other reason against Monmouth way?"

"A more delicate one. To pass through that town with such a captive train as your Highness will have might give tongue for scandal. The venerable Marquis of Worcester is rather squeamish; besides not being your best friend. You know that, Prince?"

"I do know it, and will some day make him sorry for it, the old Papist hypocrite. But what other route would you have us take?"

"Down through the Forest direct, and across the Severn, either at Newnham or Westbury. There's a ferry at both places, with horse-boats enough to take us all over in a trip or two. We may reach Berkeley Castle before daylight; where, if it be your Highness's pleasure to lie up for the day, you could enter Bristol on the following night without all the world being the wiser as to the sort of prisoners we carried in."

"Egad! your reasons are good. I'm inclined to follow your advice, and return by the route you speak of. Are you well acquainted with it, *mein* Colonel?"

"Reasonably well, your Highness. But Captain Trevor knows it better than I. He was longer with Sir John Wintour, and is familiar with every crook and turn of the Forest roads in that quarter. There can be no danger of our going astray."

"But the night's dark as pitch. So one has just told me."

"True it is now, your Highness. But there'll be a moon this side midnight, and that will be time enough to start. We can make Berkeley before morning—prisoners, crossing the Severn, and all delays notwithstanding. Next night your Highness may sleep in your own bed within the walls of Bristol Castle, with a sweet creature to share it—whom I need not designate by name."

"She *shall* share it!" rejoined the Royal reprobate, in reckless, but determined tone, his wicked passions fired by the wine he had been drinking. "And we go that way, Colonel. So see that all be ready for the route soon as the moon shows her sweet face. Meanwhile, let us back to our comrades and be merry."

Saying which he returned to the chair he had vacated at the head of the table, the other along with him; then, grasping a filled goblet, he called out the Cavalier's orthodox sentiment "The Wenches!" adding, —

"Colonel Lunsford will respond with a song, gentlemen!"

Which the Colonel did; giving that they liked best, with a chorus they could all join in, —

"We'll drink, drink;
And our goblets clink,
Quaffing the blood-red wine.
The wenches we'll toast,
And the Roundheads we'll roast,
The Croppies and all their kind."

The coarse refrain, with the ribald jests that followed it, could be heard all over the house, reaching the ears of its imprisoned owner. Even those of his daughters, more distant, did not escape being offended by them. No wonder at both having in their hearts, if not on their lips, the prayer, — "God speed Win upon her errand!"

Chapter Sixty One
A Courageous Wader

The Severn was in flood, its wide valley a sheet of water, which extended miles from either bank, and far up north towards Worcester. Viewed from an eminence, it looked as if the primeval sea which once washed the foots of the Malvern Hills had rolled back over its ancient bed.

The city of Gloucester seemed standing on an island, some of its houses, that lay low, submerged, and only approachable by boats; while the causeways of the roads leading from it were under water, in places to a depth of several feet.

This it was which had hindered Ambrose Powell arriving at Hollymead House many hours earlier than that on which he was taken to it a prisoner. For, soon as receiving news of the re-capture of Monmouth, instinctively apprehending danger to the dear ones so unwisely left alone, he had hurriedly started homeward; to be delayed by the obstructing flood. Nearing home with heart a prey to anxiety, harassed by the thought of his own imprudence; at length reaching it to find his worst fears realised; himself no longer free.

The waters still prevailing in the Severn Valley and around Gloucester, it seemed impossible to enter that city, save by boat. Yet on that same night a pedestrian could have been seen making towards it from the direction of Mitcheldean; one who meant it as the objective point of her journey—for it was a woman.

The great cathedral clock was just tolling nine p.m. as she descended into the lowlands near Highnam, and came to a stop by the edge of the inundated district. It was dark, the moon still below the horizon; but her precursory rays, reflected from fleecy clouds above it, threw a faint light over the aqueous surface, sufficient to make objects distinguishable at a good hundred yards' distance. Copses that seemed islets, with the tufted heads of pollarded willows rising weirdlike out of the water, were the conspicuous features of the flooded landscape. Rows of the latter marked the boundaries of meadows; but two running parallel, with a narrower list between, indicated the causeway of the road.

The woman had approached this point at a rapid pace; and, though brought to a stand, it was but a momentary pause, without thought of turning back. Her attitude, and the expression upon her features, told of a determination to continue on, and get inside Gloucester if that were possible. In all haste, too; for as the strokes of the great clock-bell came booming over the water, she counted them with evident anxiety, in fear of their tolling ten instead of nine. Even the lesser number seemed scarcely to satisfy her; as if, withal, she might be too late for the business she was bent upon.

She but waited for the final reverberation; then, drawing her skirts knee high, walked boldly into the flood, and onward.

Ankle-deep at the first step, she was soon in water that washed around her garters. Here and there, with a current too, which threatened to sweep her off her feet. But it did not deter her from advancing; and on went she, without stop or show of hesitation; no sign of quailing in her eye.

At knee's depth, as ere long she was, still enough of her showed above the surface to represent the stature of an ordinary woman. For she was not an ordinary woman, in height or otherwise—being Winny, the cadgeress.

On tramped the courageous wader, on plunged, till the water was up to mid thigh. No more then did her face show fear; nor sign of intention to turn back. She would have gone on, had it come to swimming. For swim she could; many the time having bathed her body in both Severn and Wye. That was not needed now, though very near it. Even over the raised ridge of the causeway the flood was feet deep. But, familiar with the route, having the landmarks in her memory—for it was not her first time to travel that road when submerged—she knew all its turns and bearings; how to take them; took them; and at length having passed the deepest depths, saw before her the Severn's bridge, with its elevated *tête-de-pont*; and, beyond, the massive tower of the cathedral, amidst a surrounding of roofs and chimneys.

Her perilous journey was near its end, the toilsome journey nigh over; and she felt happy. For, as through frost some twelve months before, she had approached Bristol with pleasant anticipations, so now was she about to enter Gloucester with the same, and from a similar cause.

Her expectancy was realised sooner than she had hoped for; the result identical to a degree of oddness. For just as upon that night at Bristol, so on this at Gloucester, Rob Wilde chanced to be guard-sergeant of the gate by which she sought admission.

And once again went their great arms around each other; their lips closing in kisses loud and fervent as ever.

"God Almighty, Win!" he exclaimed, still holding her in honest, amorous embrace, "what bet now? Why hast thee comed hither through the flood? Dear girl! ye be's wet up to the—"

"No matter how high, Rob," she said, interrupting, "if 'twor up to the neck, there be good reasons for't."

"What reasons?"

"News I ha' brought frae Ruardean; rayther us ought say Hollymead."

"Bad news be they? I needn't axe; I see't in your face."

"Bad enough; though nothin' more than might ha' been expected after the Cavalières bein' back at Monnerth, an' master's theer. Ye ha' heerd that, I suppose?"

"Oh, certainly! The news got here day afore yesterday, in the night. But fra Hollymead?"

"A troop o' 'em there, numberin' nigh two hundred; horse sodjers in scarlet, wi' all sorts o' grand trappins; the Prince Rupert's they be. Us ha' come wi' a message to Sir Richard. So I needn't tell ye who't be from."

"No, you needn't. I can guess. Then ye maun see him at once?"

"Wi' not a minute's delay. Us ha' got a letter for him; an' she as sent it sayed the deliverin' be a thing o' life an' death. I knows that myself, Rob."

"Come along, love! The colonel be in his quarters, I think. He wor by the gate here only a short whiles ago, and gied me orders for reportin' to him there. Another kiss, Win dear, fore's we get into company."

The favour was conceded soon as asked; and, after another hug, with more, than one osculation, the two great figures moved off side by side through the darkness.

Chapter Sixty Two
Their Dear Ones in Danger

As the sergeant conjectured, Colonel Walwyn was in his quarters; Eustace Trevor, his almost constant companion, along with him. The ever-active Governor of Gloucester was absent on another of his many expeditions, and had left Colonel Broughton in chief command of the garrison, Sir Richard commanding its cavalry force, with a separate jurisdiction.

The duties of the day over, with all guards stationed for the night, he, with his young troop captain, having just completed the "Grand Rounds," had returned to quarters, and taken seat by a brisk wood fire; the night, as already said, being chill.

Hubert was bustling about in attendance upon them; for, though a gaudy trumpeter, he took delight in serving his revered colonel in every possible capacity. There was nothing menial in waiting upon such a master—so thought the faithful henchman.

He had uncorked a bottle of claret, and placed it on the table between them, which they proceeded to discuss as they reviewed the events of the day. The knight was no anchorite, neither the *ci-devant* gentleman-usher; both accustomed to take their wine in a moderate way. And both habitually cheerful, save when some reverse of arms gave reason for their being otherwise.

Such there was now, or lately had been—that of Monmouth still in their minds. Sir Richard regretted not having been himself charged to keep the place he had been chiefly instrumental in capturing. Had it been so, the enemy would not so easily have retaken it. That he might well think or say, without any self-conceit. For in the most blundering manner had Major Throgmorton, left in temporary command, managed its defence; in truth, making no defence at all, but allowing the Royalists to re-enter almost without striking blow.

The affair was truly farcical, however serious for the Parliament. Its County Committee was at the time in session; decreeing fines and sequestrations against the Monmouthshire "malignants"; when all at once confronted by the very men with whose estates and chattels they were playing at confiscation; these armed, and angrily vociferating—"Surrender! you are our prisoners!"

Never were judicial deliberations brought to a more abrupt ending; never transfer of authority more ludicrously sudden. Though it was aught but a jesting matter to the dispossessed ones, who from a comfortable council-chamber were instantly hurried off to the cells of a dismal jail.

Of course the Cavaliers made much fun over the affair; while reversely their adversaries were chagrined and humiliated by it.

Few grieved over the event in a greater degree than Colonel Walwyn and Captain Eustace Trevor; for they had special reasons.

"I only wish I'd known of that danger when we got Massey's order to march hither," observed the former, as they sat sipping their wine.

"What would you have done, Sir Richard?"

"Disobeyed it; and marched our men in opposite direction—to Monmouth."

"Ah, true! A pity you didn't. It might have been the saving of the place."

"No use lamenting the disaster now it's done. Would that the taking of the town were all you and I, Trevor, have concern about! Unfortunately it isn't. What madness leaving the girls at Hollymead—absolute insanity?"

"It was. I thought so at the time, as did Vaga."

"Sabrina too; everybody but Powell himself. He couldn't be convinced there was any danger; and I still hope there may not be. But who knows what the upshot now? I tremble to think of it."

"It's to be regretted, we didn't more press him to come away with us."

"Oh! that would have been of no use. I did urge it on him—far as I could becomingly. But he had one of his obstinate, pig-headed fits upon him that day, and would listen to no reason. It's not pleasant having to speak so of him, whom we both look forward to as our future father-in-law; but when he's in that frame of mind Heaven and earth wouldn't move him. Nor the devil frighten him either. You remember how he braved Lunsford, and that precious cousin of yours, when they came to collect the King's loan. True, he had us, and something besides, at his back. But without that he'd have defied them all the same; ay, had the whole Royalist army been there threatening him with instant death."

"That I fully believe. Yet one cannot help admiring his independence of spirit—so much of manhood in it, and so rare!"

"Ay, true. But in that case too much recklessness. It has begot danger, and may bring disaster upon all of us—if it hasn't already."

The last words, spoken in a grave, almost despondent tone, fell unpleasantly on the ear of Eustace Trevor, already sufficiently apprehensive of the thing hinted at.

"In what way, colonel?" he queried anxiously. "Are you thinking of any special danger?"

"I am, indeed; and to our dear ones."

"But how? From what—whom?"

"Rather ask 'from where?' and I'll answer 'Monmouth.' Now that the Royalists are masters there, almost for certain they'll be raiding up into the Forest; and likely, too likely, a party pay visit to Hollymead. That, as you know, Trevor, were danger enough to those we have fears for?"

"But now that their father has gone to fetch them away? He should be there long before this."

"And long before this may be too late. Just what I'm most anxious about—the time of his arrival at Hollymead; for I know he won't stay there an instant. Poor man! he's sadly repentant of his imprudent act, and will make all haste to bring them back with him. The fear is of the flood having delayed him too long at starting—my fear."

"Good Heavens?" exclaimed the young officer; "let us hope not."

"If Massey were here," continued the other, a thought striking him, "I'd ask leave to go after him. Indeed, I feel half-inclined to take it, without asking."

"And why not, Colonel? We could be at Ruardean and back before morning—riding at a pace."

Sir Richard was silent, seeming to ponder. Only for a few seconds; when, as if resolved, he sprang to his feet, saying,—

"I'll risk it, whatever the result. And we shall start at once, taking our own fellows along with us. Hubert!"

Quick as the call came the trumpeter from aft ante-room, where he had stayed in waiting. To receive the order,—

"To the men's quarters, and sound the 'Assembly'! Lose not a moment!"

And not a moment lost the trumpeter, knowing that when Colonel Walwyn gave an order in such excited strain it meant promptest obedience. Snatching up his trumpet, as he hurried out through the ante-room, he was in the street in an instant hurrying towards the cavalry quarters.

Chapter Sixty Three
An Exciting Epistle

"Trevor!" cried the colonel to his troop captain, now also upon his feet, and sharing his excitement; "send out an orderly to summon Harley and our other officers. Perhaps you had best go yourself. You know where to find them, I suppose?"

"I think I do, colonel."

"Use all despatch. As we've made up our minds to this thing, the sooner we're in the saddle the better."

The counsel to make haste was little called for. Eustace Trevor itched to be in the saddle, as ever disciple of Saint Hubert on the first day of foxhunting. But just as he was about to step over the threshold of the outer door, he saw a party approaching evidently with the design to enter. Two individuals they were, a man and woman, still within the dim light of the overshadowing houses. For all, he had no difficulty in recognising them. Colossal stature as theirs was far from common; the pair being Rob Wilde and Winny.

He saw them with some surprise—at least the woman. For he had not expected seeing her there. There she was, though; and, as quick intuition told him, her presence might have some bearing on that he was about to issue forth, for he awaited their coming up.

Soon they stood at the door, face to face with him; the sergeant saluting soldier fashion, while the woman curtseyed.

"You, Winifred!" exclaimed the young officer. "I was not aware of your being in Gloucester."

"Her han't been in it more'n ten minutes, captain," said the sergeant, speaking for her. "I ha' just lets her in at the gate. Her be wantin' a word wi' the colonel."

"She'll be welcome to that, I'm sure. But first go in yourself and see."

This was in accordance with military etiquette, indeed regulations; no stranger admitted to the presence of a commanding officer without being announced, and permission given. Rob himself came not under the rule, and was about to pass inside; when a thought occurring to Captain Trevor, the latter turned upon his heel and preceded him.

"Well, Wilde, what is it?" asked Sir Richard, as they entered the room. Eagerly, too, seeing that the features of the big sergeant wore a portentous expression. "Any trouble with your gate-guard?"

"No, Colonel; nothin' o' that."

"Some news come in?"

"Just so, Sir Richard; an' not o' the best neyther."

"Indeed! What news? Whence?"

"Fra Ruardean, or, to speak more partickler, fra Hollymead House."

Both colonel and captain were now all ears. No spot on the habitable globe had such interest for them as Hollymead House, and from nowhere was intelligence so eagerly desired.

"Tell it, sergeant!" was the impatient command.

"A party o' the King's soldiers be quartered there—cavalry."

"O God?" exclaimed Eustace Trevor, almost in a groan; the knight also showing grievously affected. "How did you get this news?"

"Win ha' brought it."

"Win?"

"Yes, colonel. Her be outside the door—waitin' permission to speak wi' you. She ha' been trusted wi' a letter from the young ladies."

"Bring her in—instantly!"

"Singular coincidence, Trevor!" said Sir Richard, as the sergeant passed out. "Already at Hollymead! Just what we've been fearing!"

"Indeed, so. And all the more reason for our being there too."

"I wonder who they are. Lingen's, think you?"

"Rob says they're quartered there. That would hardly be Lingen's—so near his own garrison at Goodrich? More like some of Lord Herbert's Horse from Monmouth. And I hope it may be they."

"Ah! true; it might be worse. But we'll soon hear. The cadgeress can tell, no doubt; or it'll be in the letter."

The door, reopening, showed the Forest Amazon outside, Rob conducting her in. They could see that she was wet to the waist, her saturated skirt clinging around limbs of noble outline; while her heaving bosom with the heightened colour of her cheeks, told of a journey but just completed, and made in greatest haste.

"You have a letter for me?" said Sir Richard interrogatively, as she stepped inside the room. "Yes, your honner, fra Hollymead." She spoke with hand raised to her head, as if adjusting one of the plaits of her hair. Instead, she was searching among them for the concealed epistle. Which, soon found, was handed over to him for whom it was intended.

No surprise to Sir Richard at seeing a thing more like curl-paper than letter. It was not the first time for him to receive such, in a similar way; and, straightening it out under the lamplight, he was soon acquainted with its contents.

So far from having the effect of allaying his excitement they but increased it, and he cried out to the sergeant, as he had to the trumpeter,—

"Quick to the men's quarters, Wilde, and help getting all ready for the route! Hubert's there by this time, and will have sounded the 'Assembly.' Read that, Trevor! There's something that concerns you," and he handed the letter to his troop captain.

The sergeant hurried away, leaving Win to be further questioned by the colonel. And while this was going on the young officer perused the epistle, to be affected by it in a similar fashion. It ran thus:—

"Ill tidings, Richard. Prince Rupert here, with his escort—about two hundred. Has just arrived, and intends staying the night; indeed, till father return home, he says. I hope father will not come home, unless you come with him. I'm sure they mean him harm. That horrid man, Lunsford, is in the Prince's suit; Reginald Trevor too. Winny will tell you more; I fear to lose time in writing. *Dear Richard! come if you can.*"

So the body of the epistle, with below a postscript, in a different handwriting, well-known to Eustace Trevor:—"Dearest Eustace! we are in danger, I *do* believe." The words were significant; and no form of appeal for rescue could have been more pressing. Nor was such needed; neither any urging of haste upon the men thus admonished.

Never was squadron of cavalry sooner in the saddle, after getting orders, than was "Walwyn's Horse" on that night. In less than twenty minutes later, they went at a gallop through the north-western gate of Gloucester, opened to give them exit; then on along the flooded causeway, riding rowells deep, plunging and flinging the spray-drops high in air, till every man was dripping wet, from the plume in his hat to the spurs upon his heels.

Chapter Sixty Four
A House on Fire

The moon had risen, but only to be seen at intervals. Heavy cumuli drifting sluggishly athwart the sky, now and then drew curtain-like over her disk, making the earth dark as Erebus. Between these recurrent cloud eclipses, however, her light was of the clearest; for the atmosphere otherwise was without haze or mist.

She was shining in full effulgence, as a body of horsemen commenced breasting the pitch which winds up from Mitcheldean to the Wilderness. Their distinctive standard was sheathed—not needing display in the night; but the green uniforms, and the cocks'-tail feathers pluming their hats, told them to be Walwyn's Horse—the Foresters.

They were still wet with the flood-water through which they had waded after clearing the gates of Gloucester. Their horses too; the coats of these further darkened by sweat, save where the flakes of white froth, tossed back on their necks and counters, gave them a piebald appearance. All betokened a terrible pace, and such had they kept up, scarce slowing for an instant from the flood's edge till they entered the town of Mitcheldean.

Then it was but a momentary halt in the street, and without leaving the saddle; just long enough to inquire whether Master Ambrose Powell had that day passed through the place. He had; late in the afternoon. On horseback, without any attendant, and apparently in great haste.

"Prisoner or not, they have him at Hollymead now," observed Sir Richard to Eustace Trevor, as they trotted on through the town to the foot of the hill where the road runs up to the Wilderness.

To gallop horses already blown against that steep acclivity would have been to kill them. But the leader of the party, familiar with it, did not put them to the test; instead, commanded a walk. And while riding side by side, he and his troop captain held something of a lengthened conversation, up to that time only a few hurried words having been exchanged between them.

"I wish the letter had been a little more explicit as to their numbers," said Sir Richard. "About two hundred may mean three, or only one. A woman's estimate is not the most reliable in such matters."

"What did the cadgeress say of it, Colonel? You questioned her, I suppose?"

"Minutely; but to no purpose. She only came to the house after they had scattered all around it, and, of course, had no definite idea of their number. So we shan't know how many we'll have to cross swords with, till we get upon the ground."

"If we have the chance to cross swords with any. I only wish we were sure of that."

"The deuce! They may be gone away, you think?"

"Rather fear it, Sir Richard. Powell must have reached Hollymead before nightfall; and if they intended making him a prisoner 'twould be done at once; with no object for their staying afterwards."

"Unless they have done a long day's march, and meant to quarter there for the night. If they went thither direct from Bristol, which is like enough, that's just what they'd do; stay the night, and start back for Bristol in the morning."

"I have fears, Colonel, we won't find it so. More likely the Prince was at Monmouth on account of what's happened there; and will return to it—has returned already."

"If so, Trevor, 'twill be a black night for you and me; a bitter disappointment, and something worse. If he's gone from Hollymead, so will they—father, daughters, all. Rupert's not the sort to leave such behind, with an abettor like Tom Lunsford. As for your cousin, remember how you crossed him. It's but natural he should feel spiteful, and show it in that quarter."

"If he do, I'll cross him worse when we come to crossing swords. And I'll find the chance. We've made mutual promise to give no quarter— almost sworn it. If ill befall Vaga Powell through him, I'll keep that promise faithfully as any oath."

"But right you should. And for settling scores you may soon have the opportunity; I trust within the hour."

"Then, Colonel, *you* think they'll still be at Hollymead."

"I hope it rather; grounding my hope on another habit of this German Prince. One he has late been indulging to excess, 'tis said."

"Drink?"

"Just so. In the which Lunsford, with head hard as his heart, will stand by him cup for cup."

"But can that affect their staying at Hollymead?"

"Certainly it can; probably will."

"How, Sir Richard?"

"By their getting inebriated there; or, at all events, enough so to make them careless about moving off before the morning. The more, as they can't be expecting any surprise from this side. You remember there was a fair stock of wine in the cellars when we were there, best sorts too. Let loose at that, they're likely to stay by it as long as the tap runs."

"God grant it may run till morning then?" was the prayer of the young officer, fervently spoken. In his ways of thought and speech two years' campaigning had made much change, deepening the gravity of one naturally of serious turn.

"No matter about morning," rejoined Sir Richard. "If it but hold out for another hour, and we find them there, something else will then be running red as the wine. Ah, Master Lunsford! One more meeting with you, that's what I want now. If I'm lucky enough to have it this night, this night will be the last of your life."

The apostrophe, which was but a mental reflection, had reference to something Sabrina had been telling him, vividly recalled by the words in her latest letter, "that horrid man."

At the same instant, and in similar strain, was Eustace Trevor reflecting about his Cousin Reginald; making mental vow that, if Vaga suffered shame by him, neither would his life be of long endurance.

By this they had surmounted the pitch, and arrived at a spot both had good reason to remember. It was the piece of level turf where once baring blades they had come so near sending one or other out of the world. Their horses remembered it too—they were still riding the same—and with a recollection which had a result quaintly comical. Soon as on the ground, without check of rein or word said, they came to a sudden halt, turned head to head, snorting and angry-like, as if expecting a renewal of the combat!

All the more strange this behaviour on the part of the animals, that, since their hostile encounter, for now over two years they had been together in amiable association!

A circumstance so odd, so ludicrous, could not fail to excite the risibility of their riders; and laugh both did, despite their serious mood at the moment. To their following it but caused surprise; two alone comprehending, so far as to see the fun of it. These Hubert, the trumpeter, and the "light varlit" then so near coming to blows with him, who through thick and thin, had ever since stuck to the ex-gentleman-usher, his master.

No doubt the little interlude would have led to some speech about it, between the chief actors in the more serious encounter it recalled, but for something at that moment seen by them, turning their thoughts into a new channel. Away westward, beyond Drybrook, beyond Ruardean Ridge, the sky showed a clearness that had nought to do with the moon's light; instead was ruddier, and shone brighter, as this became obscured by a thick cloud drifting over her disk. A glowing, gleaming light, unusual in a way; but natural enough regarded as the glare of a conflagration—which in reality it was.

"House on fire over yonder?" cried one of the soldiers.

"May be only a haystack," suggested a second.

"More like a town, judgin' by the big blaze," reasoned a third.

"There's no town in that direction; only Ruardean, where's we be goin'."

"Why maunt it be Ruardean, then?" queried the first speaker; "or the church?"

"An' a good thing if't be the church," put in one of strong Puritan proclivities. "It want burnin' down, as every other, wi' their altars an' images. They be a curse to the country; the parsons too. They've taken sides wi' the stinkin' Cavaliers, agaynst Parliament and people, all along."

"That's true," endorsed another of like iconoclastic sentiments; "an' if it a'nt the church as be givin' up that light, let's luminate it when we get there. I go for that."

A proposal which called forth a chorus of assenting responses.

While this play of words was in progress along the line of rank and file rearwards, the Colonel and Captain Trevor, at its head, were engaged in a dialogue of conjectures about the same—a brief one.

"What think you it is?" asked Sir Richard, as they sat halted in their saddles regarding the garish light. "It looks to be over Ruardean, or near it."

"A fire of some kind, Colonel. No common one either."

"A farmer's rick?"

"I fear not; would we were sure of its being only that!"

"Ha! A house you think?"

"I do, Sir Richard."

"And—?"

"The one we're making for!"

"By Heavens! I believe it is. It bears that way to a point. Ruardean's more to the right. Yes, it must be Hollymead!"

Both talked excitedly, but no more words passed between them there and then. The next heard was the command—"March—double quick!" and down the hill to Drybrook went they at a gallop over the tiny stream, and up the long winding slope round the shoulder of Ruardean Hill—without halt or draw on bridle. There only poising for an instant, as they came within view of the village and saw the conflagration was not in, but wide away from it; the glare and sparks ascending over the spot where Hollymead House should be, but was no more.

As, continuing their gallop, they rode in through the park gates, it was to see a vast blazing pile, like a bonfire built by Titans—the fagots' great beams heaped together confusedly—from which issued a hissing and crackling, with at intervals loud explosions, as from an ordnance magazine on fire.

Chapter Sixty Five
Very Near an Encounter

Mitcheldean lies at the foot of the steep *façade* already spoken of as forming a periphery to the elevated Forest district. The slope ascends direct from the western skirts of the little town; but outlying ridges also inclose it on the north, east, and south, so that even the tall spire of its church is invisible from any great distance. So situated, railways give it a wide berth; and few places better deserve the title "secluded." The only sort of traveller who ever thinks of paying it a visit is the "commercial," or some pedestrian tourist, crossing the Forest from the Severn side to view the more picturesque scenery of the Wye, with intention to make stoppage at the ancient hostelry of the Speech House, midway between.

In the days of the saddle and pack-horse, however, things were different with Mitcheldean. Being on one of the direct routes of travel from the metropolis to South Wales, and a gate of entry, as it were, to the Forest on its eastern side, it was then a place of considerable note; its people accustomed to all sorts of wayfarers passing daily, hourly through it.

Since the breaking out of the Rebellion these had been mostly of the military kind, though not confined to either party in the strife. One would march through to-day, the other to-morrow; so that, hearing the trample of hoofs, rarely could the townsmen tell whether Royalists or Parliamentarians were coming among them, till they saw their standards in the street.

They would rather have received visit from neither; but, compelled to choose, preferred seeing the soldiers of the Parliament. So when Walwyn's Horse came rattling along, their green coats, with the cocks'-tail feathers in their hats, distinguishable in the clear moonlight, the closed window shutters were flung open; and night-capped heads—for most had been abed—appeared in them without fear exchanging speech with the soldiers halted in the street below.

Altogether different their behaviour when, in a matter of ten minutes after, a second party of horsemen came to a halt under their windows; these in scarlet coats, gold laced, with white ostrich feathers in their hats—the Prince of Wales's plume, with its appropriate motto of servility, "*Ich dien.*"

Seeing it, the townsmen drew in their heads, closed the shutters, and were silent. Not going back to their beds, however; but to sit up in fear and trembling, till the renewed hoof-strokes told them of the halt over, and the red-coated Cavaliers ridden off again.

It need scarce be said that these were Rupert and his escort, *en route* for Westbury; and had Walwyn's Horse stopped ten minutes longer in Mitcheldean, the two bodies would have there met face to face; since they were proceeding in opposite directions. A mere accident hindered their encountering; the circumstance, that from the town two roads led up to the Forest, one on each side of the Wilderness, both again uniting in the valley of Drybrook. The northern route had been taken by the Parliamentarian party ascending; while the Royalists descended by the southern one, called the "Plump Hill." Just at such time as to miss one another, though but by a few minutes. For the rearmost files of the former had barely cleared the skirts of the town going out, when the van of the latter entered it at a different point.

The interval, however, was long enough to prevent those who went Forestwards from getting information of what they were leaving so close behind. Could they have had that, quick would have been their return down hill, and the streets of Mitcheldean the arena of a conflict to the cry, "No Quarter!"

As it was, the hostile cohorts passed peacefully through, out, and onwards on their respective routes; though Prince Rupert knew how near he had been to a collision, and could still have brought it on. But that was the last thing in his thoughts; instead, soon as learning what had gone up to the Forest, who they were, and who their leader, his stay in Mitcheldean was of the shortest, and his way out of it not Forestwards but straight on for the Severn.

And in all the haste he could make, cumbered as he was with captives. For he carried with him a captive train; a small one, consisting of but three individuals—scarce necessary to say, Ambrose Powell and his daughters. They were on horseback; the ladies wrapped in cloaks, and so close hooded that their faces were invisible. Even their figures were so draped as to be scarce distinguishable from those of men; all done with a design, not their own; but that of those who had them in charge. In passing through Mitcheldean precautions had been taken to hinder their being recognised; double files of their guards riding in close order on each side of them, so that curious eyes should not come too near. But, when once more out on the country road, the formation "by twos" was resumed; the trio of prisoners, each with a trooper right and left, conducted behind the knot of officers on the Prince's personal staff, he himself with Lunsford leading.

Soon as outside the town the two last, as usual riding together, and some paces in the advance, entered on dialogue of a confidential character. The Prince commenced it, saying, —

"We've had a narrow escape, Sir Thomas."

"Does your Highness refer to our having missed meeting the party of Roundheads?"

"Of course I do—just that."

"Then, I should say, 'tis they who've had the narrow escape."

"*Nein,* Colonel! Not so certain of that, knowing who they are. These Foresters fight like devils; and, from all I could gather, they greatly outnumber us. I shouldn't so much mind the odds, but for how we're hampered. To have fought them, and got the worst of it, would have been ruinous to our reputation—as to the other thing."

"It isn't likely we'd have got the worst of it. Few get the better of your Highness that way."

Lunsford's brave talk was not in keeping with his thoughts. Quite as pleased was he as the Prince at their having escaped an encounter with the party of Parliamentarians. For never man dreaded meeting man more than he Sir Richard Walwyn. Words had of late been conveyed to him—from camp to camp and across neutral lines—warning words, that his old enemy was more than ever incensed against him, and in any future conflict where the two should be engaged meant singling him out, and seeking his life. After what he had done now, was still doing, he knew another encounter with Walwyn would be one of life and death, and dreaded it accordingly.

"Still, Prince," he added, "as you observe, considering our encumbrances, perhaps it's been for the best letting them off."

"Ay, if they let us off. Which they may not yet. Suppose some of the townsmen have followed, and told them of our passing through?"

"No fear of that, Prince. If any one did follow it's not likely they could be overtaken. They were riding as in a race, and won't draw bridle till they see the blaze over Hollymead. Then they'll but gallop the faster—in the wrong direction."

"The right one for us, if they do. But even so they would reach Hollymead in less than an hour; then turn short round to pursue, and in another hour be upon our heels. You forget that we can't say safety, till we're over the Severn."

"I don't forget that, Prince. But they won't turn round to pursue us."

"Why say you that, Sir Thomas? How know you they won't?"

"Because they won't suspect our having come this way; never think of it. Before putting the torch to the old delinquent's house, I took the precaution to have all his domestics locked up in an out-building; that they shouldn't see which way we went off. As they and the Ruardean people knew we came up from Monmouth, they'll naturally conclude that we returned thither. So, your Highness, any pursuit of us will take the direction down Cat's Hill, instead of by Drybrook and down the Plump."

"Egad! I hope so, Colonel. For, to speak truth I don't feel in the spirit for a fight just now."

It was not often Rupert gave way to cowardice, and more seldom confessed it; even in confidence to his familiars, of whom Lunsford was one of the most intimate. But at that hour he felt it to very fear. Perhaps from the wine he had drunk at Hollymead, now cold in him; and it might be his conscience weighted with the crime he was in the act of committing. Whatever the cause, his nervousness became heightened rather than diminished, as they marched on; and anxiously longed he to be on the other side of the Severn.

Not more so than his reprobate companion, whose bravado was all assumed; his words of confidence forced from him to gloss over the mistake he had made, in recommending the route taken. Sorry was he now, as his superior, they had not gone by Monmouth. Within its Castle walls they would at that moment have been safe; instead of hurrying along a road, with the obstruction of a river in front, and the possibility of pursuit behind. Ay, the probability of it, as Lunsford himself knew well, feigning to ignore it.

"In any case, your Highness," he continued, in the same strain of encouragement, "we'll be out of their way in good time. From here it's but a step down to Westbury."

By this they had reached the head of the ravine-like valley in which stands Flaxley Abbey, and were hastening forward fast as the *impedimenta* of captives would permit. The road runs down the valley, which, after several sinuosities, debouches on the Severn's plain. But, long before attaining this, at rounding one of the turns, their eyes were greeted by a sight which sent tremor to their hearts.

"*Mein Gott!*" cried the Prince, suddenly reining up, and speaking in a tone of mingled surprise and alarm, "you see, Sir Thomas?"

Sir Thomas did see—sharing the other's alarm, but without showing it—a sheet of water that shone silvery white under the moonlight overspreading all the plain below. The river aflood, and inundation everywhere!

"We'll not be able to cross at all?" pursued the Prince, in desponding interrogative. "Shall we?"

"Oh yes! your Highness, I think so," was the doubting response. "The water can't be so high as to hinder us; at least not likely. There's a pier-head at Westbury Passage on both sides, and the boats will be there as ever. I don't anticipate any great difficulty in the crossing, only we'll have to wade a bit."

"*Gott!* that will be difficulty enough—danger too."

"What danger, your Highness? Through the meadows there's a raised causeway, and fortunately I'm familiar with every inch of it. While with Sir John Wintour I had often occasion to travel it; more than once under water. Even if we can't make the Westbury Passage, we can that of Framilode, but a mile or two above. I've never heard of it being so flooded as to prevent passing over."

"It may be as you say, Sir Thomas. But the danger I'm thinking of has more to do with time than floods. Wading's slow work; and there's still the possibility of Walwyn and his green-coats coming on after us. Suppose they should, and find us floundering through the water?"

"No need supposing that, Prince. There isn't the slightest likelihood of it. I'd stake high that at this minute they're at the bottom of Cat's Hill, or, it may be, by Goodrich Ferry, seeking to cross over the Wye as we the Severn. And, like as not, Lingen will give them a turn if he gets word of their being about there. Sir Harry has now a strong force in the castle; and owes Dick Walwyn a *revanche*—for that affair on the Hereford Road the morning after Kyrle led them into Monmouth."

"For all, I wish we had gone Monmouth way," rejoined Rupert, as his eyes rested doubtingly on the white sheet of water wide spread over the plain below. "I still fear their pursuing us."

"Even if they should, your Highness, we need have no apprehension. The pursuit can't be immediate; and, please God, in another hour or so, we'll be over the Severn, as likely they on the other side of the Wye, with both rivers between them and us."

"Would that I were sure of that, Colonel," returned the Prince, still desponding, "which I'm not. However, we've no alternative now but to cross here—if we can. You seem to have a doubt of our being able to make the Passage of Westbury?"

"I'm only a little uncertain about it, your Highness."

"But sure about that of Framilode?"

"Quite; though the flood be of the biggest and deepest."

"*Sehr wohl*! with that assurance I'm satisfied. But we must have things secure behind, ere we commence making our wade. And we may as well take the step now. So, Colonel, ride back along the line, detach a rear-guard, and place it under some officer who can be trusted. Lose not a moment! stay at halt here, till you return to me."

The commanding officer of the escort, as much alive to the prudence of this precaution as he who gave the orders for it, hastened to carrying them out. Done by detailing off a few of the rearmost files, with directions to remain as they were, while the main body moved forward. Then instructions given to the officer who was to take charge of them; all occupying less than ten minutes' time.

After which, Lunsford again placed himself by the side of the Prince, and the march was immediately resumed, down the valley of Flaxley, on for the flooded plain.

Chapter Sixty Six
On the Trail

Words cannot depict the feelings of Sir Richard Walwyn and Eustace Trevor as they reined up by the burning house. With both it was anguish of the keenest; for they knew who were the incendiaries, and that incendiarism was not the worst of it. They who ruthlessly kindled the flames had, with like ruth, carried off their betrothed ones. And for what purpose? A question neither colonel nor captain could help asking himself, though its conjectural answer was agony. For now more vividly than ever did Sir Richard recall what had been told him of Lunsford's designs upon Sabrina; while Trevor had also heard of Prince Rupert's partiality for Vaga.

As they sate in their saddles contemplating the ruin, they felt as might an American frontiersman, returned home to find his cabin ablaze, fired by Indian torch, his wife or daughters borne off in the brutal embrace of the savage.

No better fate seemed to have befallen the daughters of Ambrose Powell. White savages, very tigers, had seized upon and dragged them to their lair; it were no worse if red ones had been the captors. Rather would the bereaved lovers have had it so; sooner known their sweethearts buried under that blazing pile than in the arms of the profligate Rupert and Lunsford the "bloody."

Only for an instant did they give way to their anguish, or the anger which accompanied it—rage almost to madness. Both were controlled by the necessity of action, and the first wild burst over, action was taken— pursuit of the ravishers.

Some time, however, before it could be fairly entered upon; inquiry made as to the direction in which they had gone. There were hundreds on the ground who could be interrogated. Half the people of Ruardean were there. Roused from their beds by the cry "Fire?" they had rushed out, and on to the scene of conflagration. But arrived too late to witness the departure of those who had set the torch, and could not tell what way they had gone. Neither could the house-servants, now released from their lock-up; for to hinder them doing so was the chief reason for their having been confined.

As it was known to all that the Royalists had come up from Monmouth, conjecture pointed to their having returned thither. But conjecture was not enough to initiate such a pursuit; and Colonel Walwyn was too practised a campaigner to rely upon it. Certainty of the route taken by the enemy was essential, else he might go on a wild-goose chase.

As that could not be obtained at the burning house, not a moment longer, stayed he by it. Scarce ten minutes in all from the time of their arrival till he gave the command "About?" and about went they, back down the long avenue, and through the park gate.

Soon as outside, he shouted "Halt!" bringing all again to a stand; he himself, however, with Captain Trevor and Sergeant Wilde, advancing along the road in the direction of Cat's Hill. Only a hundred yards or so, when they reined up. Then, by command, the big sergeant threw himself out of his saddle; and, bending down, commenced examination of the ground.

Had Wilde been born in the American backwoods he would have been a noted hunter and tracker of the Leatherstocking type. As it was, his experience as a deer-stealer in the Forest of Dean had been sufficient to make the taking up a horse's trail an easy matter, and easier that of a whole troop. He could do it even in darkness; for it was dark then—the moon under a cloud.

And he did it; in an instant. Scarce was he astoop ere rising erect again, and turning face to Sir Richard, as if all had been ascertained.

"Well, Rob," interrogated the latter, rather surprised at such quick work, "you see their tracks?"

"I do, Colonel."

"Going Cat's Hill way?"

"No, Colonel. The contrary—comin' from. None o' 'em fresh neyther. Must a been made some time i' the afternoon."

"Have you assured yourself of that?"

"I have. But I'll gie 'em another look, if ye weesh it, Colonel."

"Do."

The colossus again bent down and repeated his examination of the tracks, this time making a traverse or two, and going farther along the road. In a few seconds to return with a confirmation of his former report. A troop of cavalry had passed over it, but only in one direction—upward, and some hours before sunset.

"Sure am I o' that, as if I'd been here an' seed 'em," was the tracker's concluding words.

"Enough?" said Sir Richard. "Into your saddle, and follow me."

At which he gave his horse the spur, and trotted back towards the park gate. Not to rejoin his men, still at halt, however. Instead, he continued on along the road for Drybrook; the other two keeping with him.

At a like distance from the halted line he again drew up, and directed the sergeant to make a similar reconnaissance.

Here the reading of the sign occupied the tracker some little longer time; as there was a confusion of hoof marks—some turned one way, some the other. Those that had the toe towards Hollymead gate he knew to have been made by their own horses; but underneath, and nearly obliterated, were hundreds of others almost as fresh.

"That's the trail of the scoundrels," said Sir Richard, soon as the sergeant reported the result of his investigation. "They've gone over to the Gloucester side; by Drybrook and Mitcheldean. How strange our not meeting them!"

"It is—very strange," rejoined Trevor; "but could they have passed through Mitcheldean without our meeting them?"

"Oh yes they could, Captain," put in Wilde, once more mounted; "theer be several by-ways through the Forest as leads there, 'ithout touchin' o' Drybrook. An' I think I know the one them have took. Whens us get to where it branch off their tracks'll tell."

"Right; they will," said Sir Richard, laying aside conjecture, and calling to the officer in charge of the men to bring them on at quick pace.

At quick pace they came; the Colonel, Captain Trevor, and the big sergeant starting off before they were up, and keeping several horse lengths ahead.

The route they were taking was the same they had come by—back for Drybrook. But coming and going their attitude was different. Then erect, with eyes turned upward regarding the glare over Hollymead; now bent down, cheeks to the saddle bow, and glances all given to the ground. For, as Wilde had said, there were several by-ways, any one of which the pursued party might have taken; and to go astray on the pursuit, even to the loss of ten minutes' time, might be fatal to their purpose—the feather's weight turning the scale.

But no danger now; the moon was giving a good light, and the road for long stretches was open, the trees on each side wide apart. So they had no difficulty in seeing what before they had not thought of looking for; the hoof marks of many horses, that had gone towards Drybrook. The tracks of their own, going the other way, had almost obliterated them; still enough of the under ones were visible to show that two bodies of horse had passed in opposite directions, with but a short interval of time between.

As this could be noted without the necessity of stopping or slowing pace, Colonel Walwyn carried his men on in a brisk canter, designing halt only at the branch road of which the sergeant had spoken.

But long before reaching it they got information which made stoppage there unnecessary, as also further call on the ex-deer-stealer's skill as a tracker—for the time. Given by a man mounted on a hotel hack, who, coming on at a clattering gallop, met them in the teeth. His cry "For the Parliament?" without being challenged, proclaimed him a friend. And he was; the innkeeper of Mitcheldean, recognised on the instant by Sir Richard and Rob Wilde.

His coming up caused a halt; for his business was with Colonel Walwyn—an errand quickly told.

"Prince Rupert and two hundred horse, with prisoners, have passed through Mitcheldean!"

Half a dozen questions rapidly put, and promptly answered, elicited all the circumstances—the time, the direction taken, everything the patriotic Boniface could tell. They had come down the Plump Hill, and gone off by Abenhall—for Newnham or Westbury; or they might be making for Lydney.

Down the Plump Hill! That accounted for their not being met. And the time—so near meeting, yet missing them! All the way to Hollymead and back for nothing!

But lamenting the lost hours would not recover them. They must be made good by greater speed; and, without wasting another word, the spur was buried deeper, and faster rode the Foresters. Rode with a will; few of them whose heart was not in the pursuit. They were on the slot of a hated foe, against whom many had private cause of quarrel and vengeance. Prince Rupert, for the past twelve months, had been harrying the Forest district, making their homes desolate; his licentious soldiers abusing their wives, sisters, and daughters—no wonder they wanted to come up with him!

At mad speed they went dashing around Ruardean Hill, down into the vale of Drybrook; then up by the Wilderness, and down again to Mitcheldean; once more startling the townspeople from their slumbers, and filling them with fresh alarm; soon over on seeing it was the green-coats.

Only a glimpse of them was got, as they galloped on through; staying not a moment, never drawing bridle till they came to the forking of the roads by Abenhall—the right for Littledean, Newham, and Lydney; the left to Westbury. Then only for an instant, while Rob Wilde swung his stalwart form out of the saddle, and made inspection of the tracks. For the moon was once more clouded, and he could not make them out, without dismounting.

As before, brief time it took him; but a few seconds till he was back on his horse, saying, as he slung himself up,—

"They're gone Westbury ways, Colonel."

And Westbury ways went the pursuers, reins loose and spurs plied afresh, with no thought of halting again, but a hope there would be no need for it, till at arm's length with the detested enemy.

Even when the turn in Flaxley Valley brought the Severn in sight, with its wide sheet of flood-water, they stayed not to talk of it. To them it was no surprise; but a few hours before they had waded it farther up. No more was it matter of apprehension, as it had been to the party pursued. Instead, something to gratify and cheer them on; for, extending right and left, far as eye could reach, it seemed a very net, set by God's own hand, to catch the criminals they were in chase of!

Chapter Sixty Seven
A Guard Carelessly Kept

Notwithstanding Lunsford's assurances—at best rather dubious—the river could not be crossed at Westbury, without much difficulty and delay. The large horse-boat had received some damage, and it would take time to repair it. So Rupert and his following were constrained to keep on to Framilode Passage, three miles farther up stream.

It would bring them into dangerous proximity with Gloucester; and should any of Massey's men be raiding down the river, they might find an enemy in front, even when over it. Still this was little likely, as Massey was believed to be himself out of Gloucester, operating on the northern side in the direction of Ledbury. Besides, Walwyn must have had information of their being at Hollymead, to have drawn him into the Forest at that time of the night.

Still from behind was the Prince most apprehensive of danger; now greater by the traverse of flooded tracts that must needs be made before they could reach the Passage. His failure to get across at Westbury seemed ominous of evil; and he had grown more nervous than ever. What if he should fail also at Framilode? Then, indeed, would he have to risk encounter with the redoubtable Foresters, outnumbering his escort, as he knew.

Already had they passed across several stretches of inundated ground; at each the rear-guard being left on the dry land till the main body was well-nigh through; and then following on to the next. But now one of longer extent lay before them; more than a mile of road leading on to the ferry being under water. Still the causeway, or rather where it ran, could be told by certain landmarks; and these Lunsford, as others of the escort, was acquainted with. But the flood was high over it, and the fording must be done cautiously, entailing loss of time. Moreover, if caught on the narrow way, with no chance of manoeuvring, scarce width enough for an "about face," any party pursuing would have them at a disadvantage—almost at mercy.

Greater vigilance would be called for on the part of the rear-guard, its strength needing to be doubled. And this was done; the Prince, before taking to the water, himself inspecting it, and giving minute instructions to the officer in command. It was to be kept in ambush behind some trees that grew conveniently by; and, should pursuers appear, they were to be fired at, soon as within range; the firing continued, and the point held at all hazards, till the last moment of retreat practicable. If no pursuit, then the guard to follow as before, at signal of bugle sent back.

Reginald Trevor it was to whom the dangerous duty was assigned; and, as regarded courage and acquaintance with the ground, no officer of the escort was better fitted for it than he. None half so well, had his heart been in the work. Which it was not, but all the other way; for every movement he was making, every act he had been called upon to accomplish since leaving Bristol, was not only involuntary on his part, but sorely against his will. Forced upon him had been the ceremony of introducing Prince Rupert to the woman he himself loved; and now was he further compelled to be one of those conducting her to a prison—as it were to her grave! For, well knew he it would be the grave of her purity, the altar on which her young life's innocence was sure of being sacrificed.

In the past, sinful himself, profligate as most of the Cavalier school, he had of late become a much altered man. That one honest love of his life had purified him, as such often does with natures like his. And now a great sorrow was to seal his purification; the object of his love about to suffer defilement, as it were before his face; and as it were, with himself aiding and abetting it!

His thoughts were black and bitter, his constrained duties repulsive. And as he stood by the flood's edge, looking after the escort that had commenced making way through it, he felt faint and sick at heart.

Nor took he any steps to carry out the commands of the Prince, either by placing the guard in ambush, or making other disposition of it. So the men remained in their saddles, exposed on the high ridge of the road, just as they had come up; receiving but one order from him: that, should pursuers appear, they were not to fire till he gave the word.

After which he separated from them, and walked his horse back along the Westbury road; stopping at some fifty paces' distance, and there staying alone. The soldiers thought it strange, for they had overheard the instructions given him. But as they were acquainted with his courage, and could not doubt his fidelity to the King's cause, they made no remark about his apparent remissness, supposing it some strategic design.

Yet never was officer entrusted with guard less careful of his charge, than he at that moment. Caring, but not for its safety; instead, wishing it attacked, defeated, destroyed, though he himself might be the first to fall.

For still another change had of late come over his sentiments—a political one. Brought about by the behaviour of Prince Rupert and his associate crew; which, for some time past, had been a very career of criminal proceeding. It had inspired Reginald Trevor with a disgust for Cavalierism, as his cousin Eustace two years before. Growing stronger day by day, the last day's and this night's work had decided him. He was Royalist no more, though wearing the King's uniform. But he meant casting it off at the first opportunity; was even now blaming himself for not having sought an opportunity since they passed through Mitcheldean; reflecting whether, and in what way, such might yet be found.

As he sate in his saddle, listening, glad would he have been to hear hoof-strokes in the direction of Westbury; to see horsemen approaching, with the hostile war-cry "For the Parliament?" That might still save Vaga Powell, and nothing else could. In another hour she would be across the Severn, and on for Berkeley Castle, whither he must follow. But with no hope of being able to do anything for the doomed girl. On the one side, as the other, all powerless to protect her, even with the sacrifice of his own life. And at that moment he would have laid it down for her; so much had generosity, love's offspring, mastered the selfishness of his nature.

An interval of profound silence followed; the only sounds heard being the screams of wild fowl flying low over the flooded meadows, the occasional stamp of a restive steed among those of the guard, and the plunging of nigh two hundred others far off in the water, gradually becoming less distinct as they waded farther. But, ere long, something else broke upon the night's stillness, as it reached the ear of Reginald Trevor, causing him to start in his saddle. There sate he, listening and vigilant; the sparkle of his eyes proclaiming it no sound that alarmed him, but one welcome and joy-giving.

A dull pattering as of horses' hoofs—hundreds—making way over soft ground, or along a muddy road. And so it was, the road from Westbury, the horses ridden by men in military formation, as the practised ear of the young soldier told him. But no other noise, save the trample; no voice of man, nor note of bugle.

Soldiers were they notwithstanding; and pursuing soldiers, led by one who knew how to carry pursuit to a successful issue. For it was Walwyn's Horse.

Still at a gallop, their hoof-strokes were quickly nearer, sounding clearer. For there was no taking up of trail to delay them now. Away over the white water they saw a long dark line, serried, by a turn in the route which brought Rupert's following quarter-flank towards them; saw, and knew it to be that they were after.

At the same time seen themselves by Reginald Trevor, who rode back upon his guard. But not to inspire it to resistance, nor place it in a position of defence. Instead, he seemed irresolute, uncertain whether to make stand or retreat. His men, heavy Dragoons, had unslung their dragon-muzzled muskets, and awaited the word "Fire!" But no such word was spoken, no order given. Even when the approaching horsemen were charging up to them, shouting "For God and Parliament!" even then, no command from their officer to meet or withstand the charge.

Nor did they then wish it; they saw the assailants were ten to their one; it was too late, even for retreat. Should he call "Quarter!" they were ready to chorus it. And just that called he, the instant after, to a man among the foremost of the charging party—his cousin! Their swords came together with a clash, Eustace the first to speak.

"At last!" he exclaimed. "At last we've met to keep our promise made. 'No Quarter!' I cry it!"

"And I cry 'Quarter'—beg it."

Never dropped blade quicker down from threatening thrust than that of Eustace Trevor; never was combatant more surprised by the behaviour of an adversary.

"What do you mean?" he asked, in utter astonishment.

"That I fight no more for Prince, or King. Henceforth, if they'll have it, my sword's at the service of the Parliament."

"God bless me, Rej; how glad I am to hear you say that! And so near making mince-meat of one another!"

"Not of one another, Eust. You might have done that with me—may still, if you feel spiteful."

"Good Heavens! cousin; what has come over you? But I won't question now; there's no time."

"There isn't. See yonder. Rupert and Lunsford, with the Powells as their prisoners."

"We know all that. But where are the ruffians taking them?"

"Berkeley first; then Bristol. They're making to cross at Framilode Passage. It's but a short way beyond."

"They shall never cross it—can't before we come up with them. You'll be with us now, Rej?"

"I will."

The strange episode, and dialogue, took up but a few seconds' time; during which Rob Wilde, with a half-score files of Foresters, had disarmed the unresisting rear-guard. It was now under guard itself, and all ready for continuing the pursuit.

And continued it was instantaneously; Sir Richard, at the head of his green-coats, spurring straight into the flood, and on after the red ones, without further precaution either of silence or concealment. For he knew they would be seen now.

Chapter Sixty Eight
A Fight in a Flood

Still but half-way across the inundated tract, and up to their saddle-girths in water, Rupert and his escort were floundering on. As already said, they marched "by twos"—this necessitated by the narrowness of the causeway—and so were lengthened in line. Two hundred horse in file formation take up a long stretch of road, however close the order.

They had not yet sighted the enemy behind, nor had any intimation that one was there. For the snapping up of the guard had been done with little noise, the few shouts uttered being inaudible to them amid the continuous splashing and plunging of their own horses.

It was only after the pursuing party was well out into the flood, clear of the tree-shadowed shore, that some of the hindmost, chancing to look back, saw what they took to be their rear-guard in the water and riding after them. Saw it with surprise, as the signal for its advance had not been given; no note of bugle sounded. Neither could it be in retreat, driven in. There had been no firing, not a shot; and, by the Prince's orders, there should have been a prolonged fusilade Guard of his, rear or van, retiring from its post without execution of his commands, had better have stayed and delivered itself up to the enemy.

Well knowing this, they who first sighted the pursuers, thinking them of their own, were enough astonished to give way to ejaculations. Which ran along the line quick as lightning.

"What is it?" demanded he at the head, on hearing them.

"The rear-guard, your Highness," answered one away at the back. "They're coming on after us."

"Halt!" shouted the Prince, in a voice of thunder, half-wheeling his horse, spurring out to the utmost edge of firm footing, and, with craned neck, looking back land-ward.

For a time to see nothing much beyond the tail end of his escort. Only the grey glimmer of water, with here and there the top of a pollard willow. For the capricious clouds had once more muffled the moon.

But he heard something; the sound of the wading horses, that made by his own now ceased from their being at a stand.

And soon he saw the moving ones; the clouds, by like caprice, having quickly drawn off their screen, letting full moonlight down upon the water. Saw them with alarm; for a dark mass was that in motion, too dark and too large for the score or so of files that had been detached as a guard.

"*Gott*, Colonel!" he exclaimed, "there are more men there than we left with Trevor. And why should he be coming on contrary to orders? It cannot be he?"

"Very strange if it be, Prince," rejoined Lunsford, the colonel spoken to; "and stranger still if not."

"Could a party have slipped past without the guard seeing them?"

"Hardly possible, your Highness; unless by some swimming, and a long roundabout way. These seem to come direct from it."

The two talked hurriedly, and with dismay upon their faces. For the dark mysterious thing, still drawing nigher and nearer, seemed some unearthly monster—a hydra approaching to destroy them.

There was no time for further conjecturing. Friend or enemy, it must be met face to face; and Rupert, commanding the "about," put spur to his horse and started towards the rear of the line.

Time elapsed ere he could reach it. The deep water, with the men wheeling in file, impeded him; and, before he was half-way rearward, there were shots, shouts, and the clashing of steel—all the sounds of a conflict. The monster had closed up, and declared its character, as could be told by the hostile war words "King?" and "Parliament?" fiercely commingling.

Never shone moon on a stranger affair in the way of fight. Two long strings of horsemen confronting one another on a narrow causeway, where less than half a score of each could come to blows; no engaging in line, no turning, or flank attack, possible. And all up to the saddle flaps in water; up to the horses' hips where the fighting was hand to hand.

Nor for long did it last. Little more than a minute after coming to close quarters the Royalists found themselves overmatched, and began to give way. File after file went down before their impetuous assailants, sabred, or shot out of their saddles, till at length they doubled back on their line in retreat towards its former front. Some, in panic, forsook the causeway altogether, plunging into the flood on either side, in the hope to escape by swimming afar off.

Sword in hand, with curses on his lips, Rupert met the rout, bursting his way through the broken ranks, slashing right and left in an endeavour to stem the retreat. More than one of his own men fell before his desperate fury. But on reaching the rear, he had to cross blades with a man who was his master at sword-play, and all the skill appertaining. Which he knew, soon as coming to the "engage," and in his antagonist recognising Sir Richard Walwyn.

It was quick work between them; at the very first lunge from guard, the Prince's sword getting whipped out of his hand, and sent whirling off into the water! The old trick by which Sir Richard had disarmed the ex-gentleman-usher.

With a fierce oath Rupert drew a pistol from his holster, and was about to fire at his adroit adversary, when another face presented itself before him, that of a man he had better reason to shoot down.

"Dog! Traitor! Turncoat!" he shouted, in tone of vengeful anger. "'Tis to you we owe this! I give you death in payment!" And the shot sped, tumbling Reginald Trevor out of the saddle.

But there was still a Trevor on horseback to confront the Prince, with sword already fleshed and blade dripping blood. A touch of his spur brought him face to face with Rupert, and alone. For, just as the latter, Sir Richard had caught sight of another man he more wished to have dealings with—Lunsford—and dashed straight towards him.

But not to attain close quarters. In the cowardly ex-lieutenant of the Tower there was neither fight nor stand. The sight of Colonel Walwyn was of itself enough to palsy his hands; alone the bridle one obeying him. And with it, wrenching his horse round, he made ignominious retreat.

No more did the other pair get engaged. Rupert had but his second pistol, which, being discharged at Eustace Trevor, fortunately without effect, left him weaponless; and, seeing all his escort in retreat, he turned tail too, soon disappearing amid the ruck.

The route now complete, with the scarlet coats it was *sauve qui peut*; with the green ones only a question of cutting down the panic-stricken fugitives, or making prisoner those who cried "Quarter!" And most cried that—shouted it to the utmost strength of their lungs.

On went the victorious Foresters along the flooded way, alternately sabreing and capturing—the big sergeant and Hubert doing their full share of both—on till they came to a party of captives they had not taken. Nor guarded these; their late guards having been too glad to get away, leaving them to themselves.

"Sabrina!" "Richard?"—"Vaga!" "Eustace?"

Four names, pronounced in joyous exclamation amid the din, and by four distinct voices; all with the epithet "dear" conjoined.

Not another word then, not another moment there; for the pursuit must be continued. The capture of Prince Rupert would be a thing of consequence, independent of all private feelings; and Sir Richard longed to settle scores with Lunsford. So on went he, and his, in chase of the now scattered escort.

But not again to come up with the pair of profligates. The stoppage, short as it was, had given them time to make Framilode Ferry; where, leaping from their horses, and into a light boat, they were out of sword's reach, and range of bullet, before the pursuers could close upon them.

Still within earshot of angry speech, however, hurled after them by the triumphant Foresters, with many a taunt, many the vile epithet bestowed.

A degradation deserved; and other men than they would have felt its sting and shame. But not this scion of Royalty, toast, type, and model of Cavalierism. Happy at having escaped with a whole skin, he but laughed back, rejoicing in the life still left him for future crimes to be committed.

And many the one was he afterwards guilty of; though short from that time was his rule in the city of Bristol. Once again, and soon, was it enfiladed by an armed force, not for siege or leaguer, but instant assault. For the man who commanded was he who, later on, gave laws to all England, gave her the only glimpse of real liberty she has ever enjoyed—the only gleam of true glory. When Cromwell stood before Bristol's gates, and said "Surrender!" it was in no tone of doubting requisition, but stern demand. The son of Elector Palatinate, hearing it hastened to comply, but too glad to get terms for his life.

Which he got, with his liberty, and more—far too much being conceded by his generous conqueror—permitted to march out, bag and baggage, with a long retinue of bullies, sycophants, and strumpets, leaving behind a longer list of victims, among them the ill-starred Clarisse Lalande. As he passed away from the place he had made a "place of bawdry," it was amid jeers and bitter curses.

A scene pleasanter to describe—one more congenial to honest pen—occurred shortly after in the sister city of Gloucester, within its ancient Cathedral, at whose altar simultaneously stood four couples in the act of being made man and wife.

Wedded they were, and their names entered in the big book of marriage registry; from which the writer does not deem it necessary to copy them *verbatim.* Enough to give them as already known to the reader; the brides being Sabrina and Vaga Powell, Winifred, and Gwenthian; their respective bridegrooms Colonel Sir Richard Walwyn, Captain Eustace Trevor, Sergeant Wilde, and Trumpeter Hubert.

While being made happy, amid the many joyous faces around, one alone wore a cast of sadness, yet with resignation—that of Reginald Trevor, still living. For the shot which struck him out of his saddle on the flooded causeway of Framilode had but wounded him, and he was well again. In body, not spirit; for within his heart was a wound that might never be well. He had suffered bitterly, was still suffering; but with soul now purified and subdued was better able to bear it, and bore it manfully. Generously too; for just as, when meeting his cousin outside Hollymead gate he had offered him his sword to avenge defeat, now honoured he him by his presence at a ceremony which was as the sacrifice of himself.

Still another incident calls for record: of date some six years later, and some months preceding that event which again brought England's liberty to its lowest ebb, her glory to greatest shame—the so-called Restoration. Before this curse of curses came, Ambrose Powell, predicting it—foreseeing evil to him and his—gathered up his household gods, and took ship with them to the colonies across the Atlantic, accompanied by all the personages who had appeared at that marriage ceremony in the cathedral of Gloucester, and by many more—Cadger Jack among them.

Reginald Trevor, too, was of the colonising band; long become accustomed to bearing the broken heart, which "brokenly lives on," with but little pain, growing ever less. For he could now look upon Vaga Powell as his cousin's wife; to himself as a kind sister—almost without thought of the unhappy past.

Well was it for all of them they went away, to become part of that people, the freest, most powerful, and most prosperous on earth. Had they stayed, it would have been to suffer persecution; the fate of all who then fought for England's freedom, save the false ones and cravens, who cried "Quarter!"—on their knees, basely begged it from that loathsome monster of iniquity—the "Merry Monarch."

And Rupert, Prince of Cavaliers, what became of him? He too returned with the Restoration—another of its curses—fresh from a long career of piracy in the West Indian seas, to be made Lord High Admiral of England, with no end of other honours and emoluments heaped upon him! To live for years after a life of luxurious ease, die "in the purple," and be buried with all pomp and ceremony. For though a pirate, he was still a Prince of the Blood Royal!